Welcome
Distractions

WELCOME DISTRACTIONS

Michael Wilde

Mill City Press, Minneapolis

Mill City Press, Inc.
322 First Avenue N, 5th floor
Minneapolis, MN 55401
612.455.2293
www.millcitypublishing.com

ISBN-13: 978-1-62652-502-3
LCCN: 2013919170

Cover Design by Sophie Chi and Saul Dixon
Typeset by Mary Kristin Ross

Printed in the United States of America

WELCOME DISTRACTIONS:

Included are these stories and others.

"Aporia," reveals buried amongst the mounds of trash and hoarded items, in the home of Elda Patras, a discovery without explanation.

"Drones," is the story of a decorated sniper and the drone operator desperate for his friendship.

"Elmhurst," offers a glimpse into the life of Iris, an elderly widow living on her own, trying to maintain her household. When Iris's grandson appears at her doorstep, needing a place to stay, Iris welcomes him but soon reconsiders her decision.

In "The Power of the Warrior," to protect his son Burl Jenkins makes his last stand with shotgun in hand.

"Pray," begins with a young man suffering a horrific attack while on vacation. Then returning home realizes his nightmare has just begun.

In "Ghost are Bullshit," a pragmatic media mogul is offered a chance to partake in an exclusive séance.

"In Bloom," A young woman meets a charming older man at the bar. The attraction is mutual but their connection carries an ominous warning.

TABLE OF CONTENTS

Aporia 1

Communion 13

Drones 29

Elmhurst 101

The Power of the Warrior 127

Deceiever 137

Witness 153

Pray 157

Ghosts are Bullshit 229

Stoned Wheat Thins 255

In Bloom 265

APORIA

Matthew 5:5 *BLESSED ARE THE MEEK: FOR THEY SHALL INHERIT THE EARTH.*

No, Matt. They'll just be dead and out of the way.

Hello. You don't know me.

I work for a business. That's all there is. The government, the private sector, the street -- its all business. Constant competition, most necessary.

Our mandate: Obtain and secure.

Intelligence is my field of acquisition. Acquire information and control it. Dig through mountains of bullshit until you find the truth or the closest acceptable version.

Destroy the competition. Remove the opposition. Everything works for us. Just the facts, as always.

Here's one that's unavoidable: Death. Trust me, I've looked into it. While I'm still sucking air I'd like to talk about the Immaculate Conception.

I was coughing up blood that morning. I'm washing it from the sink when I get the call. An hour later I'm in the air.

The house was on North Christiana Avenue, Chicago, Illinois. A minute's walk from Belmont subway station. The house is nondescript. You'd walk right past it without giving it a moment's notice. It has white plastic facing and green trim. At the front of the house is a small bay window concealed by a hedge. The hedge is planted on a patch of grass that constitutes the front lawn. The backyard is dirt and gravel enclosed by a four-foot high mesh fence. Outside of the fence are two parking spaces facing the back alley.

The humidity's oppressive. The heat index is in the high 90s. A storm warning is in effect. The initial call is placed to 911 at 4:27 am. Ray Wirth requests an ambulance with police presence to the address on North Christiana.

Officers Russell Hamsun and Cheryl Pressfield are patrolling the area and are first to arrive on the scene. Ray Wirth is on the front lawn administering chest compressions to his aunt, seventy-eight-year-old Elda Patras, while the neighbors watch on. Paramedics Glen Hoss and Juan Medero arrive a minute later. They immediately place Elda in the ambulance and rush to the hospital.

The police question Ray:

"Did the suspect try to harm you?"

"No."

"Is the suspect still in the house?"

"Look under the fold-out couch."

"Under the fold-out couch?"

"Yeah, in the living room."

"Do you know the suspect?"

"No."

"Was the suspect carrying any weapons?"

"I don't know."

"Can you describe the suspect?"

"Yes."

"Describe the suspect."

"It's my aunt Elda."

Confused? Everyone else was.

"This is all kinds of wrong" are the words Officer Hamsun used while describing the scene to dispatch.

Another team of paramedics, Jane Klassen and Arvin Besara, are sent to North Christiana. They cannot detect a pulse, yet the pupils contract when light is directed at the eyes.

Discretion is key. Assess the situation. Act accordingly.

It's a residential area in a densely populated city. Keep it quiet. Act swiftly. Secure and detain. Lock it down. If anyone resists, quickly silence. Infiltrate and control. Isolate. Quarantine.

By the time my plane touched down, we'd secured the location.

Mrs. Patras lived on the ground floor of her two-story house. Along with the roaches and mice, Elda shared the house with her tenants on the top floor and a tenant in the basement.

On the top floor lived Jennifer Merchant and Hector Gonzales. They were married, both on disability, both addicted to prescription meds. Elda met them at church.

Living in the basement was Alex Hindle. Alex was a fast-order cook. He also worked part time as a security guard, evening shift. He kept a degu, also known as a brush-tailed rat, as a pet.

Each dwelling had a separate entrance, accessed from the stairwell, with its own entrance at the back of the house. Elda lived with her dog, a Lhasa Apso named Lilly, on the main floor. Her husband, Nico Patras, a contract carpenter who built the house, had died fifteen years prior from stomach cancer. Elda was ready to nominate him for sainthood after his death, despite the fact that, by all accounts Mr. Patras was an abusive adulterer.

Elda suffered from osteoporosis and hypertension. She was in poor physical condition and could not maintain her home. The fact that Mrs. Patra was a hoarder did not help her cause. Everything was an antique or potential collectible. She kept it all. Broken electronics, decrepit furniture, yellowed newspapers, sun-bleached magazines, expired medications, ancient receipts, used scratch tickets, elapsed coupons, every flyer, every pamphlet -- all of it garbage.

Elda claimed value where there was none. It's a safe bet this condition manifested from her impoverished upbringing. She lived in abject poverty with three brothers and four sisters. Her mother died from meningitis when Elda was ten. Her father raised the family with his paltry earnings, working as a farm hand. Whatever the case, whatever the cause, Elda was slowly burying herself in a trash heap.

There were dead flies on the windowsill. Black mold was spreading over water-damaged dry wall. The kitchen was stuffed to the rafters with garbage bags full of discarded pop cans, the sink and counter lost under mounds of filthy dishes. The fridge was filled with items undergoing various degrees of decomposition and a massive collection of condiment packets.

Elda slept on a foldout couch in the living room because her bedroom was rammed full of discarded boxes of moth-eaten clothes covered in dust. From the foldout couch, her island in the middle of the mess was a narrow path of open carpet leading to the bathroom.

A bathroom fit for a crack den. The tub floor was black with dirt, its walls streaked with rust and mildew. The shower curtain was covered in an algae bloom. The floor tiles surrounding the toilet had been busted out, exposing rotten underflooring. Stuffed behind the toilet were foul smelling wet towels, put there to absorb a leak. The toilet had a cracked foam seat, a perfect breeding ground for bacteria. Floating inside the toilet, clinging to the sides of the bowl, was what looked to be the tattered remains of a shit-hued jellyfish.

The path that led from the couch to the bathroom diverged to a corner of the living room, where the open floor was covered in a papier mâché of piss-soaked newspapers. This was Lilly's corner, where Elda's little dog defecated. The carpet underneath the newspaper was corroded from all the urine that had soaked through. The place was a festering mess, a true cesspool, begging for the bulldozer.

I'd seen the photos. I'd seen the video. I'm sweating before I put on the hazmat suit. Once I'm inside I make my way to the foldout couch and crouch down for a look.

And there it is. Undeniable. Nasty- looking thing. This naked old husk, withered skin hanging off jagged bones. Brittle and twisted. A sack of decay with a hooked nose jutting out between ice blue eyes

I've had my fill of blood and gore but it made my skin crawl like nothing else. This awful manifestation, an abomination. A promise from purgatory. Staring out from the darkness. Its eyes locked into place. I gave orders to remove it. The house, the entire neighborhood, would remain under quarantine.

My next order of business was speaking with Ray Wirth. We had him locked in a padded room. He needed to be sedated. He didn't agree with forced confinement; they rarely do. Ray was still in a stupor when I informed him his aunt had passed away, due to cardiac arrest. I gave him two hours to absorb the news and clear the cobwebs.

The interrogation lasted three hours.

Ray was twenty-nine, unemployed, and transient. He'd been fired from his dry walling job after telling the boss to fuck off. Which meant he couldn't pay rent on the apartment he was renting in Toronto. He needed a loan and after several rejections, he called his aunt Elda whom he hadn't spoken to in years. She offered Ray $500 from her savings, along with room and board. This was on the condition Ray clean, and performs some maintenance on, the house.

Mr. Wirth was out of options and imagined a change of scenery might do some good. Elda paid for his bus ticket to Chicago. He hadn't seen her since he was sixteen.

Ray arrives in Chicago late evening. He's shocked by the abhorrent state of his aunt's living conditions. The place is fermenting under stagnant heat. He is choking on the stench. Cleaning the place will be a massive undertaking. To stave off a panic attack Ray insists on starting right away. Elda won't allow it. It's late. She wants to sit down and talk awhile before bed. He can start in the morning.

Ray forces his way through several hours of conversation centering on the subjects of illness and moral certitude. Finally Elda announces she needs rest. She digs out an old air mattress for Ray, making him clear space for it on a filthy patch of carpet by her bedside. Ray's stress levels are spiking through the roof but he's resigned to his fate. It will be his mission to free Elda from this mess.

The morning is a lifetime away. Ray cannot sleep. He must purchase earplugs if he's going to last another night. Elda snores, wheezes, and smacks her lips, sounding as though she's dying of thirst. At one point Ray wakes her up, offering a glass of water. Elda brushes him away like he's the crazy one.

Ray is exhausted. Between the noise and the smell, it's going to be a battle. The depressing state of his surroundings is crushing. The night will be spent fighting off tidal waves of anxiety. Ray goes to take a piss, then rummages through the medicine cabinet, hoping to find something, anything, to make the night bearable. He finds it. Xanax. Mercy is granted. Ray pops two of 'em, giving himself a fighting chance.

Prodded back from oblivion, Ray rolls onto his back. The confusion of light is dizzying. He looks up from his spot on the floor at Elda, who's flickering the bedside lamp. She stops, leaving the light on. She asks aloud for the Lord's forgiveness, repeatedly making the sign of the cross. It appears she's conversing with the ceiling. Ray asks her what's wrong. Elda proclaims that his father, her baby brother, visited in a dream with a message from the Lord.

It had been thirteen years since Ray's father, Lukas Wirth, passed away from cancer.

During their last family gathering, despite an ever-present nausea, Lukas paid for a feast catered by his favorite restaurant. It was a massive roast beef dinner with all the fixings. Lukas was not religious. The rest of the family was. Ray's grandfather was a pastor in Germany before he moved the family to Canada. Lukas did not abide by his father's teachings. He had no patience for the church. There was no prayer offering before dinner that night. Elda knew it was wrong but respected that it was her brother's house. And this is why, she explained, Lukas appeared in her dream. He needed to confess. He needed to apologize. He'd seen the error in his ways. She was right; he was wrong. They should have given thanks to their Lord and Savior. Lukas understood this now.

Ray didn't doubt the veracity of Elda's dream but placed no investment in it. He would not engage the subject. Elda ranted about the dream's significance while Ray muttered the occasional acknowledgment. At one point during the sermon Ray rolled back onto his side, this time facing the foldout couch. That was the moment he saw what lived underneath.

Eye to eye. Staring him down. Piercing through. Seizing hold. The recoil is fierce. Ray scrambles backwards, boxed in by the hoard. His mind reeling, going into shock. The room is spinning. The edges are closing in. It's all too much. The body initiates shutdown. Seeing stars, ready to puke, Ray forces himself to breath. He slows it down. He fights for control.

His reaction terrifies Elda. She thinks her nephew has gone insane. Elda pleads for him to tell her what's wrong, what's happening. Still, it stares out. It's not going away. Ray tells her they have to leave. They have to leave the house. They have to leave the house now.

Elda, her hands trembling, grabs the phone by her bedside, announcing she's calling the cops. She's shaking so badly she drops the phone between the couch and bedside table. She can't reach it. Elda comes undone and breaks into heaving sobs.

Ray walks to the other side of the bed. He peeks underneath and sees the aberrations crooked spine. There is no movement. His heart racing, Ray assures Elda everything's fine as he helps her out of bed, fearing any moment the impostor is going to wake up and tear the place apart.

Ray directs them towards the door. They are five feet away from it when Elda whimpers she need to use the washroom. Ray pleads with her to wait. Elda screams. She needs to use the washroom. She needs her teeth! She's not going anywhere without her teeth! Her dentures sit in a glass on the bathroom sink.

Ray knows they're seconds away from a full meltdown. He hoists Elda up, drapes her over his shoulder, and walks them outside.

Outside and hopefully out of range. Elda cries to be put down. Ray gently places her on the front lawn. She is terribly shaken. She needs her teeth. She needs her medicine. She needs them. She feels sick. Lies down. Her face twists and contorts. As she clutches her chest, the eyes roll back in her head. Ray makes a mad rush to the neighbors, banging on the door for help.

We take over shortly thereafter.

And how does Ray's story end? For the sake of expedience I will keep it brief. He's out there, alive, stumbling around in heavy fog. Eventually the fog will lift if he stays within the parameters we've set for him.

It works like this: You wake up in a hospital many miles from home. There was an accident. Serious head trauma. No recollection of a previous life. The road to recovery is a long one. One piece at time, we pick up the pieces. The headaches will go away. Acceptance is key. Claim this new life. Don't fight it or those blinding headaches will come rushing back.

Following standard protocol Ray would have been eliminated. The dead don't talk back and it's far cheaper then keeping them under the influence. So why let him live? Pity. It's no excuse but that's my reason. Ray went through hell and we left him there. I just gave him the chance to climb out. I was taken to task for my decision but deftly shut down my dissenters, while knowing full well they were right.

Enough of Ray Wirth. Back to the freak show. The world's most formidable minds, our assault team of scientists, gave Elda's catatonic doppelganger the highly imaginative nametag of Elda 2. Past naming it, what astute observations do they make? What knowledge do they ascertain? What brilliant deductions do they arrive at? What can they tell us about Elda 2?

Well... (The scientist pauses dramatically for effect.) It's not human.

Thank you, scientist.

Off the cuff, here's a quick fact list on Elda 2:

- It has no pulse. If you're alive you have a pulse. Unless you run on a VAD (ventricular assist device).

- An adult human blinks an average of four to twelve times per minute. Elda 2 didn't have a blinking average because it didn't blink. Ever. Never. It had eyelids but didn't use them.

- It doesn't generate any digestive waste. This saved us a great deal on adult diapers.

- Human blood is red. Its blood (if that's applicable) has a deep blue hue.

- Its exterior form, its cover, its costume, its shell, its whatever, was made in the exact image of Elda Patras. Every liver spot was accounted for. A perfect genetic match right down to the last wrinkle. The eyeballs, the skin, the scalp, the hair, the gums, the rotten teeth, all rooted in the sponge. How does the sponge interface with the exterior form? Still working on it.

- The sponge? Yes, the miraculous, all-in-one sponge. In place of any other vital organs. It's all you need! We peeled back the exterior to reveal that its insides are entirely composed of this white sponge substance, varying in density and form, steeped in the blue liquid. The pocket chambers contract and release at seemingly random intervals, flushing blue throughout its system.

It's all observation. We haven't yet begun to decipher its biological mechanisms.

When? Where? What? How? Why? Why? Why? No idea. We sink vast, untold sums of money and resources into finding answers to these questions and what do we get? A pile of unsubstantiated theories. A bunch of guesswork. Nothing that couldn't be dreamt up in a half hour by teenagers hotboxing in their parents' minivan.

How and why did this alien organism replicate the exterior of an invalid old lady living in squalor in Chicago? What's its biological imperative? Where did it come from? It's in our possession but until we figure it out, we can't own it, not in the truest sense. And that pisses me off. It's unacceptable. We understand. We control. We own. That's what we do.

An aside: I watch them stick Elda 2 with a syringe, sucking out 10 cc of deep blue, then injecting it into a monkey. When freed from its restraints, the monkey staggers to a corner of the cell where it collapses. It lies there, sprawled out, eyes open, completely still for eight minutes. Then it curls into the fetal position, closes its eyes, and dies. Respiratory failure.

The next step is clinical testing on a human. I push it through. I'm desperate. We smuggle in a couple of dregs from the penal system as our guinea pigs. When they inject our first human subject I kneel down beside him, this feeble, broken man, now catatonic, eyes pried open, locked in. I ask him what he sees. No response. Tell me. There's no reply. I smack him hard across the face. Nothing. I grip his ear and twist, threatening to rip it off. No reaction. There's no reaching him. I start laying the boots to his stomach before I'm stopped by a hacking cough. Drowning in it. While I'm struggling to breathe our subject curls up and dies. I spit on the floor and walk away.

Whether it's bird, rat, pig, dog, monkey, or human, when deep blue is injected, the effects are always the same: disorientation, collapse, transfixion, death.

In my terminal delusion I had actually convinced myself that Elda 2 was an offering, a reprieve from my death sentence. As if the two were somehow connected. The ultimate arrogance. I believed it brought the cure. If not the cure, an answer. It offered nothing.

I've got a bullet in the chamber and I'm sick with the high science. I've got immediate access to the best treatment modern medicine has to offer. The elite healers at my beck and call ready to inflict more pain for a cure. The best and brightest. That's their answer. More pain. I'm done with it. This disease feeds on me. I die. It dies. Leave it to rot with the mess I've left behind.

The safe is locked and they've changed the combination. My instability has made me a liability. My first and final demotion. By my design, ultimate exclusion is inevitable.

One cannot access the safe without the presence of four of the six chiefs. You have nothing but words. My apologies. Call bullshit. It won't hurt my feelings. I promise.

You have some names and an address. Look into it. See what you find. Just remember, history is written by the winners. I used to find great comfort in that. Then it opened its eyes. That's why it had to burn. I was sick of living under its gaze. The blaze was set but they stopped me, dousing the flames.

The charred husk of Elda 2 remains on a cold slab, forever glaring at us.

I will never be at peace.

Just the facts, as always.

Communion

THE DESK IN THE CORNER OF THE BACHELOR UNIT IS COVERED IN STACKS of unpaid bills. The tenant, a gaunt man, late thirties, with a beard down to his chest and hair past his shoulders, stands in ragged boxers, gazing out the window through a crack in the curtains. He has a black eye and a split lip crusted in blood. He watches the letter carrier trudge through the snow towards the apartment complex. He waits for the letter carrier to exit the building, then throws on his housecoat and rushes downstairs.

Back in his apartment, sitting at his desk, the tenant flips through his mail, adding more unpaid bills to the stack, before finding what he's looking for -- the sky-blue envelope.

He opens the envelope and pulls out a single piece of yellow loose-leaf. Handwritten, the letter reads, "I haven't eaten for eight days. My memory is failing. Still I wait."

The tenant files the letter in the bottom drawer with the others, then writes his reply on his own pad of yellow paper. "What it you wait for? Why aren't you eating? Are you under financial strain? If so you are not alone. Yesterday I had to steal toilet paper from the library washroom."

The tenant seals and stamps his letter in a bronze envelope. The address is written in gold, with the opaque lacquer finish created by an Edding 753 Calligraphy Paint Marker Pen.

Standing inside the lobby in housecoat and slippers, the tenant braces himself before rushing outside into winter. The second he opens the door he's hit with a vicious gust of wind. Halfway to the mailbox, the tenant slips on a patch of ice, his legs swiped out from under him, his slippers launched through the air before he crashes onto his posterior. Miraculously the tenant manages to keep to one arm raised, the envelope held high, never touching the ground. The tenant returns to his feet, limping over to the mailbox. He deposits the letter and collects his slippers from the road.

So goes the exchange:

Blue: I walked. I walked the beach beside the ocean, to the river, following it through the woods, up into the mountains, then down again, riding an avalanche of shale. I crossed many roads as I trudged through the streets. I walked until my legs seized. Then I took the bus back and slept for two days.

Bronze: There's nothing like a good walk to clear the mind. Did it help? Sounds like you had a good rest. How did you feel afterwards? I received my final unemployment check this week and decided to get my haircut. I wish I hadn't. I wanted a clean presentation for potential employers. The style high and tight, as I requested, something you'd expect from a man in uniform. But it turns out I'm not ready to part with my beard. The conservative nature of my haircut does not match the feral state of my facial hair, my physical appearance now manifesting my internal conflict. I am out of balance, in a state of flux.

Blue: Surprise, surprise, they've manufactured another atrocity to inflict upon us. I left seeking dolorifuge only to discover I've walked in a circle. With no end in sight it appears I shall be forced back into battle.

Bronze: What is this atrocity you speak of? This battle? I too am under siege. My eye is swollen shut, my left eye this time. There was an altercation, the second one in as many months. As I was crossing the street a vehicle waiting to turn right honked its horn for me to hurry across. Annoyed by this man's impatience, his rudeness, I stopped in front of his truck and pointed to the traffic light, indicating I had six seconds left. The man stuck his head out the window and screamed at me to "Get the fuck out of the way!" I slammed my hands down on the hood of his truck and spat on his windshield. At which point he left his truck, proceeding to assault me, apparently landing a lucky punch. When I regained consciousness, I looked up from the sidewalk to see a circle of strangers staring down at me. My attacker had fled. A painful lesson. Now I carry my staghorn switchblade with me at all times, a valued purchase I made in grade four. I received the knife from my classmate Remy Brill in exchange for a video copy of "New Wave Hookers," which I made from my father's pornography collection.

Blue: They wish to wound me with flagitious allegations but I am protected by the armor of empirical evidence. These petty fools operate with such mendacity. If one does not submit to their infernal indoctrinations he will be subjected to ruthless character assassination, resulting in the destruction of his social network and ability to work. His safety net is destroyed and, if still one resists, he can expect imprisonment, torture, or death.

Bronze: Who are these evil perpetrators? What is it they seek? How does one defend against them? I've been on edge of late, a state of high alert. Today, walking through the park, I saw an old friend holding hands with his girlfriend. I hid behind a red oak tree until they were gone.

Blue: Behold the promises of technological fundamentalism! Therein lies the answer. Technology will be your savior! The blessed miracles of infinite growth, a testament to man's ingenuity. The manifestation of his will. All hail the grand design! Your mortal frustrations shall be a thing of the past as technology rushes us towards the singularity. And what happens when these miracle machines have consumed all the raw materials necessary for their function? Fear not! Necessity breed's innovation. We will simply lasso passing asteroids for their precious minerals! But wait... What's this? A glimpse into the future.... I see a sallow magician with a hat and no rabbit.

Bronze: I understand your frustration. I'd also like to argue "what good is technology if you can't afford it?"! The bank and my creditors are conspiring to ruin me. I have been threatened with eviction. My bank account has gone into overdraft. Prospects are bleak. On the transit back from the job bank, defeated and tired, I saw a woman on the bus, a splendid vision. I complimented her, proclaiming her beauty, which I felt to my core. My tribute was not appreciated. The woman gave me a curt "thanks," avoiding eye contact, getting out at the next stop.

Blue: How long must we be forced to listen to this vile screed of nepotism, rejoicing in pyrrhic victory? Lazy despots, dastards, we suffer from the hubris of cowards. How dare they flaunt such opulence while the rest live in squalor? Let them experience the shame and hardship they've inflicted upon others. May they be crushed under the weight.

Bronze: Your words inspire, carrying such truth, such conviction. I need to know more. I don't mean to pry but when will you tell me your name? Can you tell me about the previous tenant and your relation to him? Perhaps that's asking too much. If you could simply confirm you're receiving my letters it would mean a great deal.

Blue: I've told so many lies I cease to exist. My spirit is broken. I've been banished from this realm. I betrayed my creed. Now I am a listless ghost stumbling through purgatory.

Bronze: Although we have yet to meet, I know you are a good person. Abandon such negative thoughts about yourself. We're all guilty of fabrication from time to time. I too battle with severe bouts of self-loathing. It is counter-productive. You have a gift. Your words offer strength. They give in a world that takes. They establish a dialogue in a society that has no time to engage in an honest exchange of thoughts. For example, today I visited a walk-in clinic. I told the doctor I work for a major multi-national. I explained that the pressures of the job, along with its travel requirements, put me under considerable duress. In order to continue performing my work at an optimum level I require a multitude of sedatives and stimulants, crucial for me to maintain a balanced equilibrium. When the doctor refused my prescription request I stressed that my livelihood depended on it. He told me to get another job. I told him to start doing his. He asked me to leave or he would call the cops.

Blue: I wake from one nightmare into the next.

Bronze: Indeed, these are trying times, my friend. Reality is teeming with destructive vibrations. Walking towards the bus stop today I saw the bus approaching. I was twenty feet from the stop and the bus was twenty feet behind me. I waved at the bus driver as I ran towards the stop. He looked directly at me yet deliberately drove right past without stopping. Leaving me to wait another thirty minutes in the cold for another bus. Had I been able to chase that bus down I would have rammed the driver's head through the side window, then smashed his face against the steering wheel until I'd pulverized it into a bloody pulp. They could throw me in jail. It would be worth it.

Blue: I am seething. I cannot tolerate these so-called "curators of culture" who glom to anything with the faintest whiff of marketability. Why must we be subjected to their endless sales pitch, forever assaulted by those who insult our intelligence? It's an affront to common decency. Such disrespect warrants a public lynching. At the very least they should be placed in a pillory to receive lashes, while having rotten produce lobbed at their heads.
Bronze: This brutal climate and my depleted faculties have led to a com-

promised immune system leaving me susceptible to illness. As a result I am now suffering from a racking chest cold, fatigue, muscle ache, fever, sinus congestion, watery eyes, and sore throat. Given these symptoms the diagnosis is apparent -- I have acute bronchitis. I am wary of it developing into pneumonia.

Blue: Evanescence is inevitable. Relinquish control magnanimously.

Bronze: What does this mean? Can you clarify? I feel this instruction is somehow key to my condition. Although it pains me to admit, it's become increasingly apparent with age that I've inherited my parents' ugliest traits. No room was left for the good ones. I am a miserable composite.

Blue: While they rush to silence my intransigency with their edict, I take notes.

Bronze: Again I must ask, who are "they" who seek to silence you? What interest do they have in your persecution? Yesterday I stepped outside for the first time in weeks. I needed to go to the market for tea, honey, and chicken broth. The cold gnawed at my bones while the ghastly wind howled. Mounds of dirty ice and snow congested the street and covered the sidewalks. It's a treacherous landscape to navigate. Walking through the park I discovered a yellowed cow tongue wrapped in colorful beads nailed to a black maple tree. Clearly some form of voodoo.

Blue: It's nauseating the way these parasites feed on sentiment, regurgitating bathos for the lemmings to feed on.

Bronze: I too am sickened by the state of society. Today the building manager called me a cockroach. I write this late at night. I cannot sleep. Through earplugs I can still hear the elderly Asian couple next to me fornicating. The old man is a vile creature. I've seen him hork his mucus onto the floor of our building's hallways more then once. When I challenge him over it he sneers and waves me away like I'm a gnat. When I reported him to the same building manager his response was, "Well, I've never seen it Mr. Fung spit on the floor and at least the Fungs pay their rent."

Blue: Oh what now! They wish to speak of debt? Moral obligation? Ha! They sick their army of creditors on us, enforcing commandments etched in stone, laws that suddenly become malleable when applied against their profit margins. The audacity of these so-called "Lords of Finance" to condemn us while they practice convenient capitalism! They are frauds, hucksters, guilty of treason. We have to earn our money while they simply print theirs, to loan back to us with interest.

Bronze: I apologize for my delayed response. I was temporarily incarcerated. Your last letter spoke directly to my current situation, highlighting the injustice, the hypocrisy of our financial system. After reading it I marched into my bank and pissed on the floor. I was arrested shortly after and did not go quietly.

Blue: Damn this daylight, passing judgment, trying to shame me. I long for hibernation, a contagion that lulls us into ceaseless sleep. Why must we wake to this? Can't we just drift off?

Bronze: It's uncanny how our thoughts align. I too have reached the point where I wish it would just go away. My cupboards are bare, my stomach is empty, and my eviction is imminent. How do I escape? I hold my hands to the air and say, "Benevolent Creator take me back! It's more then I can bear!" Only to be greeted with silence.

Blue: We must abolish their dispensations and generate our own code. Destroy their system and its malicious design. Man has been subjugated to its cruel intent for far too long. We cannot accept their sanctimonious tyranny.

Bronze: You are the one whom must lead the charge. Your message carries the promise of revolution. I will spread your gospel and promise to fight valiantly by your side. All I ask in return, as petty as it may sound, is that you formally acknowledge my existence. Cast aside my doubt; let me know once and for all that you receive my reply. Time is of the essence; I will be forced from my dwelling soon.

Blue: Forgive this elegiac lament. With great consternation I must relinquish current operations under the auspice of self-preservation.

Bronze: What does this mean, pray tell? Recently I tried to feed myself by scavenging through grocery dumpsters but the competition was fierce. I was forced out. Now I must accept the generosity of others with visits to the food bank and soup kitchen. The line-ups are long and the mood is heavy. My official eviction has been set for next week. I need a miracle to retain my place of residence.

Blue: There is a vast chasm between objectives. Everything in between shall be classified as collateral damage.

Bronze: What are the objectives? Is the situation critical? I have so many questions and this may be our last exchange for some time. Police will evict me sometime tomorrow. Please withhold your reply until I secure a new address. We must not surrender. Godspeed.

The new tenant collects his mail. There are several bills and a sky-blue envelope. Back inside the apartment he presents the envelope to his girlfriend.
     "What do you think?"

"What is it?"

"I don't know. There's no name on the outgoing, or return, address."

"So who's it belong to?"

"Whoever lives at this address, I guess."

"Should I open it?"

Girlfriend reads the letter.

"Okay then…"

"What's it say?"

The girlfriend reads the letter aloud. "Slander, Slavery, Starvation, these bugaboos have lost sway over me. I've attained a state of equanimity."

"That's it?"

"That's it."

"What the fuck?"

"I don't know."

"What's a bugaboo?"

Bronze: Greetings my friend, I apologize for the wait. The new address is secure. I am officially homeless and have no fixed address but my job councilor has agreed to let me use his until I have a permanent place of residence. It's been a struggle. This has been the cruelest of winters but our communion carries me through it. It gives me hope; lets me know there's a little magic left in this world. I pray this finds you well. I await your response with great anticipation.

New Tenant discovers another sky-blue envelope in his mailbox.

New Tenant and Girlfriend crack open another bottle of wine.

"I've got a gift for you."

"What's the occasion?"

"Just for being awesome."

"Bullshit."

"Just close your eyes."

She closes her eyes.

"Okay, open them."

He holds out the sky-blue envelope for her.

"Another one!"

"Yep."

Girlfriend tears open the envelope and reads out its contents. "We have genuflected the practice of unfettered consumption. On the horizon a black horse, its rider holding a pair of scales in his hand."

"That's it?"

"Yep."

"I'm disappointed."

"You wanted more?"

"More crazy. That one didn't do much for me. Seemed kind of obvious."

"Yeah, there was a touch of doomsday prophesy but mostly just sounded like sour grapes."

Bronze: I sent a prior letter but have not heard back from you. I fear my letter or your response has been lost in the system. I just want to reiterate that my new address is completely secure. Aside from trying to re-establish our correspondence it's been a daily battle scrounging up food and shelter. One day blurs into the next but today was different. I gave blood to earn money for the specialty envelopes I send my letters in. When they were done drawing blood I stood up and my legs gave out. I woke up to a glass of orange juice and the nurse blotting my forehead with a cold compress. I don't mean to martyr myself. Our exchange is well worth my blood payment. It's free after all. God bless. Bring the dawn to all.

New Tenant returns to his apartment. Girlfriend is cooking diner. He removes the fridge magnet and sits at the table with the sky-blue envelope.

"You ready?"

"I've been waiting all day for this."

"Okay, let's see what we've got."

New Tenant reads out the letter. "After the acquisition I'd made incredible progress. There was a dramatic momentum shift in our favor. Now it grinds to a screeching halt. I believe I've been poisoned. Impeccable timing."

"That's a keeper."

"It just got real. We could be dealing with foul play now."

"What do you think the acquisition was?"

"Another part of the puzzle. Let's just hope he survives so we get a chance to piece it together."

"You assume it's a 'he'. It might be a 'she'."

"Valid point."

Bronze: I'm deeply worried. I have yet to hear from you. I harbor great concern for your welfare. I know you have enemies, wicked oppressors seeking to silence you. I fear they've exacted their nefarious intent. I considered contacting the authorities but whom can I trust? Please give word, post-haste.

Girlfriend is watching TV. New Tenant strides into his apartment, hand held high, holding another sky-blue envelope.

"He's alive!"

"Yay!"

He hands the letter to Girlfriend to read. She rips open the envelope. "After another failed attempt on my life, I return from the cusp of death with renewed vigor, being granted divine vision of the life I once knew, a reminder of what we fight to protect. By decree I shall stipulate a new ordinance. Strident measures must be taken to ensure their capitulation."

"Holy shit, he means business now! They fucked with the wrong guy."

"'Strident measures must be taken.'"

"Quick question. What's the 'new ordinance'?"

"Well, he hasn't explained that part yet but when he does, it will be 'by decree'."

"Perfect, that's really the one way to do it."

Later that night New Tenant and Girlfriend are wakened from their sleep by the sound of the apartment buzzer.

"What the fuck?"

"What time is it?"

"It's three in the fucking morning."

"Are you going to answer?"

"Well it doesn't sound like they're going away."

New Tenant answers the intercom.

New Tenant: Hello?

Old Tenant: I'm so sorry to bother you at this early hour but it's an emergency.

New Tenant: What's going on?

Old Tenant: I'm the previous tenant of your apartment. I think you may have some mail for me.

New Tenant: Are you fucking kidding me? You wake me up in the middle of the night for some mail?

Old Tenant: This mail is highly classified. People's lives may be in danger.

New Tenant: Look pal, your mail is redirected to your new address.

Old Tenant: A blue envelope. Did you find a blue envelope in your mailbox?

New Tenant: A blue envelope… no, I didn't see a blue envelope. Now I'm going to bed. I have to work in the morning. You need to speak with someone, talk to building management. It's got nothing to do with me.

New Tenant hangs up and gets back in bed with Girlfriend.

"That was the old tenant, some fucking weirdo trying to collect his mail. He asked about the blue envelopes."

"What did you say?"

"I said I never got one. What am I suppose to say? We fucking opened them."

"That's crazy."

"I know."

"That's creepy."

"No shit."

"You need to talk to building management."

"That's what I told him."

"I'm serious."

"I know."

After breakfast New Tenant leaves for work. He waits in that hallway for the elevator.

"I want my mail."

New Tenant turns around to see Old Tenant standing in the hallway. Emaciated, he is a picture of poor health. His salt-stained, mud-covered winter jacket hangs off his wasted frame. His pale face is raw with razor burn and shaving nicks.

"I don't have your mail."

Old Tenant pops his switchblade.

"You're lying."

Old Tenant walks towards New Tenant with the knife held out.

"Please. I don't want your mail. I promise I'm not keeping anything that's not addressed to me."

The doors of the empty elevator open.

"Don't you fucking move. Stand right there."

The elevator doors close.

"My letters came in a blue envelope."

"I don't have them."

Old Tenant holds the knife up to New Tenant's neck.

"I'll slash a wide smile across your throat if you don't give them to me."

"Why would I lie to you? I'm not risking my life over the mail."

The neighbor's door open. The old man steps out.

Old Tenant points his knife at him.

"Get the fuck back inside."

The old man scowls, spits on the floor, and creeps back into his apartment. Old Tenant cringes. "Disgusting. Disgraceful. You see? That's acceptable but they go and change the locks on me."

New Tenant is frozen in place.

"Okay, we're going to search your apartment. If I find my letters I'm going to gut you. I'm gonna stick this knife in your navel and rrrriiiipppp… all the way to your Adam's apple. Now let's go. Open the fucking door."

"Please."

"What?"

"I apologize. I have your letters. They weren't addressed to anyone. It's no excuse but I opened them."

"You are a liar."

"I'm sorry but you had a knife. I was scared about what you'd do if you found out. I'm still scared."

"Go. Move. Open the door."

"I'll give you back your letters. I'll call my girlfriend and she'll slide them under the door for us."

"Open the fuckin'door and get me my letters now!"

"I'm not risking her life."

"You want to be a hero? I will stick you like a fucking pig, take your keys, and make your girlfriend give me my letters, then I'll step over your body as you bleed out in the hallway."

"Why do you need to go into the apartment? Why can't she just grab your letters and slip them out to you?"

Old Tenant presses the edge of his blade against New Tenant's throat, drawing blood.

"Because you've lost my trust."

"I understand. I'm sorry. No disrespect. We'll grab your letters. I'll get your letters and you can go, just, please..."

"Open the goddamn door."

New Tenant opens the door to the apartment. Girlfriend is in the shower. He grabs the letters from the desk drawer and hands them over to Old Tenant.

"That's all of them, I promise."

"If you receive any more of these, you forward them to this address."

Old Tenant hands New Tenant a slip of paper.

"I will."

"I caught you in a lie and I let you live. Don't forget that."

"I won't."

"If you receive another blue envelope, what do you do?"

New Tenant holds up the slip of paper. "I send it to this address."

Then hear police sirens growing louder.

"Don't let me down."

"I promise."

"I am not a bad person."

"I know."

Old Tenant leaves the apartment. New Tenant locks the door.

DRONES

His name is Bill Barney. Friends and family call him Barney. Like the purple dinosaur, he waddles around with purple cheeks, a rotund belly, and a smile on his face. Anyone who knows Barney will tell you he's "good people." Barney always has a kind word for friends and stranger alike. He's constantly committing himself to a good cause. He volunteers as a dog walker at the animal shelter. (It helps keep the weight off.) He works the local soup kitchen. Barney organizes food drives. He donates blood to the Red Cross. He hosts karaoke and bingo nights at his church, both fundraisers for disaster relief. To encourage a sense of community Barney runs the church's potluck dinners. (A great way to meet your neighbor.)

A secret project Barney's been working on is a click-through donation site, where people can play a crossword puzzle, a word search, or complete a maze and win whatever donated prize is associated with it. The true value is that each game is attached to a charity, and with every click a small corporate donation is made. Of course he'd also sell banner space and that would go to charity too.

Barney doesn't drink, do drugs, or use profanities but he'd be the first to admit he isn't vice free. In fact he jokes about it in his own self-deprecating way. Barney will tell you he has a tendency to ignore cardinal sin number two. Yep, gluttony tends to get the best of him; Bill Barney loves his food. Guilty as charged.

Barney's best friend, former Navy SEAL Kyle Prince, is a "hero," as he's proud to tell anyone within earshot. Three Silver Stars and Six Bronze Stars

With Valor. After leaving the military Kyle wrote a best-selling book entitled *Head Shot: The Autobiography of America's Most Deadly Sniper.* In the book Kyle writes that the U.S military credits him with killing 170 people but in all likelihood the number is much higher: "In the heat of battle you don't have time to check off every kill."

Despite Kyle's legendary status he retains his humility. Barney watches the stoic warrior play it off like he's a simple country boy. Kyle may be a country boy, but he's not simple. Barney has seen him carry the burden, that resigned look of disappointment in his eye, as he takes a slow sip from his beer and with an easy drawl confesses, "I only wish I killed more. The world is a better place without these savages around taking American lives."

It's not about boasting. The kill count doesn't matter to Kyle. The publisher used it to sell books. Kyle knows he couldn't have done it without his fellow soldiers: "People talk about legacy. Mine wouldn't exist without those brave heroes fighting by my side."

Barney knows the war weighs heavily on Kyle's conscience: "I never killed an innocent." Barney is aware of the sacrifice. Insurgents placed a bounty on Kyle's head because he'd inflicted so much damage to their ranks. Kyle had been shot four times. Two of his close friends were killed. But the casualties don't end on the battlefield. The war ended his marriage. The distance, the time apart. Leaving the front, his brothers-in-arms, was the hardest thing he ever had to do but his children needed their father.

That doesn't mean his war against the enemy ends. He no longer places the savages in the crosshair of his bolt-action .300 Winchester Magnum sniper but he's still part of the fight. Kyle now runs a security and weapons training company out of West Virginia, where he trains other brave defenders. Barney was an initial investor in the operation. He leapt at the chance when Kyle offered it: "I'm presenting you with an opportunity to invest in our country's national defense while making some money in return." Although Barney has yet to see the aforementioned "return" he's certain he will. Kyle is a man of his word, the model of integrity. And right now he's focused on building the business, as it should be.

One of Barney's fondest memories is the day Kyle took him out pheasant hunting. He'd never been hunting before. To be perfectly honest he'd never had the desire. Like most, he bought his food at the grocery store.

Out in the woods Barney felt like an impostor, dressed in camo, sweating into his Elmer Fud hunting hat, stopping to use his inhaler. He was soft, weak, pathetic. He felt like dead weight. But Kyle was so patient with him, putting Barney at ease. When they spotted a pheasant, Kyle calmly showed him how to aim, how to breathe, how to fire, and just like that Barney got his first kill! Of course he couldn't have done it without Kyle as his teacher.

The sun was setting during the drive back. Kyle drove, looking straight ahead with a stern look of concentration. "You know these people, these goddamn hypocrites. They're calling me a murderer, saying I'm a sadistic killer, while I'm out there defending their lives. These goddamn insurgents, fuckin' Taliban, imprison their woman and rape little boys. You want to talk about cruelty. These savages invented torture. They use it on their own people. They hate freedom. They really do. This ain't no propaganda. Those evil sodomites, goddamn goat fuckers, want everyone suffering under their tyranny. They hate everything. They really do. Under their rule, personal liberty disappears. There's no movies, there's no music, there's no barbecues, no ballgames, all you can do is pray to their miserable god. And I'm not going to let that happen, not on my watch. I am justified in my actions."

The intensity, the passion with which this man spoke ... Barney felt himself welling up with emotion. "Kyle on behalf of myself and this country, I want to thank you for your courage. Those thankless traitors do not speak for us."

Two weeks later Kyle invited Barney over for dinner. All that was required was his presence and a bottle of red wine to go with the pheasant. For the first time in his life Barney would eat something he killed.

To be friends with Kyle was an on-going education. You were always learning. Barney listened intently as Kyle described the preparation process, how he lets the birds hang for a week, kept cool in his shed, all to tenderize the meat before he plucks and skins them. Then the process of drawing the meat, how he removes the innards, trying to keep the intestinal sack intact, removing the head and neck. How he strips out the gullet, crop, and windpipe by inserting a finger and rotating it gently to loosen and break all attachments, freeing the organs, particularly the lungs. Then how, with a sharp knife, he cuts through the skin around the vent until it comes loose. Inserting his fingers into the body cavity he draws out the innards. Then he washes out the body cavity and salts it. Finally the meat is ready to roast, but first he covers the breast with a sheet of pork fat and ties it on, which helps retain moisture. With that done, he roasts it at 400 degrees Fahrenheit, twelve to fifteen minutes per pound. Kyle likes his meat rare, and that's how game birds are traditionally served: rare, with the breast pink and juicy. Often he'll use the legs, which can be rather chewy, for stewing.

As expected the food was delectable. It was such an honor for Barney to experience this meal with Kyle and his three children: Curtis, Conner, and Kyla. Was it any surprise that at the ages of ten, eight, and six, they were courteous and well mannered, always saying "please" and "thank you"? At Kyle's request, it was the youngest, Kyla, who led them in a dinner prayer:

> God is great, God is good, Let us thank him
> For food in a world where many walk in hunger;
> For faith in a world where many walk in fear;
> For friends in a world where many walk alone;
> We give you thanks, O Lord. Amen.

An angel, speaking with such sincerity, such innocence. From the head of the table Kyle spoke. "This is why we fight Barney. To protect this. Our children. Our values. Our way of life. There are those who wish to drag our good names through the mud for their own selfish agendas. These cowards who question our cause, a right they wouldn't have if it wasn't for our protection." His words always echoed true.

"I couldn't agree more, Kyle." Barney's admiration for this man, this valiant warrior, grew every day.

Towards the end of the meal Barney raised his glass. "Kyle, I would like to thank you for so much. I don't know where to begin but let's start with this blessed mouth-watering meal I have so thoroughly enjoyed. Kirk, Curtis, Kyla, I'm sure you know this, but it warrants repeating -- your father is an extraordinary man. His bravery, his skill, his conviction, his valor. He is a man of principle. In a world so quick to destroy itself for personal gain he gives hope, he shines the light, showing the way with great humility. We are thankful. May his honor guide us."

Kyle is moved by Barney's words but in typical fashion, deflects the spotlight. "Children, this man right here, Bill Barney, is a good, kind, generous man. He cares for his neighbors, fostering the community with his charity work. And using his intellect, his mastery of technology, he defends this great nation, raining fire down upon our enemies with the click of a button. He might work out of an office but don't let that fool you. Bill Barney is one of the brave heroes, keeping us safe, protecting what makes this country great."

Overcome with emotion Barney could barely get the words out. "Coming from you, sir, that is high praise indeed."

After dinner, once the table is cleared, Kyle heated up some apple crumble. He confessed that the crumble was store-bought but with a scoop of vanilla ice cream melting over it, it should make a fine dessert.

It's then, with everyone sitting in the living room, enjoying their crumble, football playing in the background, that young Curtis asked his question. "Mr. Barney?"

"Call me Bill or Barney, which ever you prefer, just leave out the mister."

"Okay. Bill. How did you get your job? Dad said it's like playing video games but you use real weapons."

"Your dad is right. It's just like playing video games, except these ones are a little more complicated. They take some time to learn. You've got to go through many years of training before they'll let you play."

"I play all the war games -- Medal of Honor, Call of Duty, Gears of War, Metal Gear Solid. Would that help with your job?"

"Sure it would. But you know what you really need to do my job?"

"What?"

"Good marks in school. Especially math and science."

"You hear that, Curtis? Like your dad says, you don't do well in school, you might not get that job you want later."

"I know."

"Then why are you bringing home such lousy marks?"

Barney sensed a change in the familial tone and interjected. "You know, Curtis, if you're having problems with any subjects, I'd be happy to help you. I'm sure with a bit of tutoring we could have you at the top of your class in no time."

"You should take him up on that offer, Curtis. Mister Barney's a brilliant man."

Barney blushed, waving off the compliment. "Well, brilliant is a grand exaggeration but I can help with your schooling, if you want me to."

"Okay, maybe. But, um, Bill? Can I ask you something?"

"By all means, go ahead."

"Dad says you fight the same bad guys but you get to stay home and fight them like video games. But it's real people so, um... how does that work?"

"Good question Curtis. Like so many modern-day conveniences, it's technological innovation that allows me to do my job. But in order to make these amazing machines work you need to understand the language of numbers. Remember what I said about getting good marks in math?"

Curtis nodded his head.

"Well, to make these weapons work, you need to input numbers they can understand. These numbers, also called code, tells them what they're supposed to be doing. Coordinates is a word your dad and I use all the time at work. It's a mathematical term where any set of two or more numbers is used to determine the position of point. Now when your dad and I have a target, a bad guy we're after, we need the coordinates to find them. Satellites in the sky help find them for us. Now once your dad has his coordinates, he uses them to find the bad guy, then uses his gun to get the bad guy. Unfortunately I'm not in good shape like your dad, so I couldn't do that. I'd have a heart attack before I found the bad guy."

Kirk who had been listening to the conversation with an icy glare chimed in.

"Why don't you lose some weight then?"

Kyle reaches over the recliner and smacks Kirk across the back of the head. Barney quickly interjected. "No, Kyle, please. It's fine. The boy's right. I should... I really should. I just like food too much and exercise too little."

"You need to learn some manners, boy, or one day you're going to learn the hard way."

"Kyle, it's okay. Really. It's fine."

"No it is not."

Kirk wilted under his father's scornful look.

"So, umm, Curtis... as I was saying. When your dad's in the desert, he uses coordinates to find the bad guy and get them with his gun. But I enter the coordinates into a guidance system for a UAV. That stands for Unmanned Aerial Vehicle. It's an automated airplane. There's no one in it. It's run by remote control, like your racecar. Only the remote control I use to fly it is actually a giant computer system that's stationed at our headquarters here in Old Dominion."

"The plane drops bombs."

"They can do that. They can fire missiles too."

"To blow up bad guys. But they can't get you because you're here."

"That's exactly right."

"If we can do that then why does Dad have to go over there?"

Kyle chimed in "Because we need people on the ground, son."

"Your dad's right. Computers can do a lot but certainly not everything. It's very important that there's brave people such as your dad over there to understand what's happening. They gather intelligence and make sense of things. They understand the true nature of battle. A machine can only perform a function. It can't make an important judgment call like your dad does."

Kirk came back from washing his plate in the sink. "Who's killed more bad guys? You or Dad?"

"Well, I can't kill anybody. Look at me. I can barely buckle my pants. It's the drones I fly that do that."

"And Dad uses a gun."

"Mr. Barney can kill twice as many savages in an afternoon as I could in a lifetime."

"Yeah, but dad's never killed an innocent by accident. Have you?"

"Let me field this one, Barney. Son, as you well know, there's civilian casualties in war. Most of the time it's because the evil ones have forced our hand. They use their own people for shields. Us good guys try as hard as we can to avoid hurting innocents but sometimes it's an unfortunate yet necessary sacrifice for the greater good. That's why you have to believe in the cause. There's many difficult choices to be made along the way. Any time an innocent dies it's a tragedy but you need to understand that, without our help, their lives would be far, far worse."

"What's worse then being dead?"

"These are lesson you learn as you grow older, son."

"Why?"

"Life has a way of teaching you."

"How?"

"By showing us that in order to keep our friends and loved ones safe there is nothing we wouldn't do. That's what being a hero is all about."

Barney welled up again, witnessing this poignant moment between father and son. Seeing how young lives could be shaped, a shining example of how we must educate and offer guidance to each new generation.

It was a lovely gathering, a confirmation of all we should hold dear: friends, family, and faith. Barney basked in the afterglow. During the drive he felt a strong sense of gratitude and goodwill. Then he returned home to an empty apartment and he had to concede that an element of sadness had crept into his perfect evening.

There was no one to greet him at the door. No one keeping the bed warm. No one he could share his day with. Any kind of company would do. He'd welcome a pet but his allergies wouldn't allow it. Barney fell into a funk. Would he ever start a family of his own? And what about the family he did have? Both his mother and father were alive. They lived in Fairfax, not so far away. He'd often make the trip to visit them. Yet when he stopped by they seemed so apathetic, completely disinterested. They'd sit in the living room with their dinner trays, watching their programs, as he prattled on in the background until he grew tired of listening to himself talk and joined them watching TV in silence.

What was it? His job paid well. It was an integral part of the nation's defense strategy. Why weren't they more excited for him? He'd never asked them for anything. He paid his own way in life, doing what he could (although you can always do more) to help others. It was a selfish desire but he wished his parents could show a little more pride in him. How had he disappointed them? Did his appearance embarrass them? His weight? Was it the fact that at the age of thirty-five he'd still not started a family? What could he do? It wasn't his fault. He'd be happy to, but there were no takers. That wasn't completely true. Gladys at work liked him, telling him as much with a perfume-scented letter she slipped him during an employee luncheon. Make no mistake, she was a wonderful lady, but as she tipped the scale at 200 plus pounds, and, sadly, was flat chested, Barney couldn't muster any semblance of physical attraction towards her. He realized, given his woeful state, how hypocritical it was but the rules of attraction simply weren't fair.

The only woman Barney knew to whom he was attracted and might even remotely consider him, was Helen from his church group. She'd always been kind to him, encouraging his ideas for fundraisers. Occasionally she'd rub his arm while saying hello, inquiring about his well-being. Barney knew Helen was in her fifty's, far too old to consider having children with. Still, if the love was there, maybe she'd be willing to consider adoption. Barney cursed himself. What a fool he was for wasting time on such far-fetched daydreams! It was more likely he was reading it wrong. Misinterpreting the situation. It wouldn't be the first time.

Barney felt great shame after these sporadic bouts of self-pity. He knew how privileged he was. He had great friends, a roof over his head, plenty of food in the fridge, his general health, and a job he was proud of. With so much to be grateful for there was nothing to be morose about. What a silly goose he could be sometimes.

At first Barney attributed the frequent urination and increased thirst to the copious amounts of coffee and energy drinks he consumed. The increased hunger was simply the end result of his ever-expanding stomach. When the vomiting started, he considered it punishment for his excess, the cost of over-eating, gorging on high sugar, high fat foods that needed to be eaten in moderation. He assumed the rashes were eczema-related and the blurred vision was a combination of his naturally poor eyesight, countless hours spent in front of a computer, and his recent lack of sleep. He chalked up his fainting spell at the church potluck to exhaustion as well. He'd crashed through the food table covered in baked beans, pulled pork, coleslaw, mac and cheese, and potato salad. It was Helen who called the ambulance, hold-ing a cold compress to Barney's forehead while they waited.

After his blood work was completed at the hospital, Bill Barney, at the age of thirty-five, was diagnosed with type 2 diabetes.

The doctor prescribed oral medications but eventually Barney was required to take insulin injections in conjunction with the Metformin. His doctor stressed how integral diet and exercise were to managing diabetes but it was a real struggle for Barney. Outside of weekly dog walks, he loathed all forms of exercise. He was terribly clumsy and previous attempts at organized sport resulted in supreme embarrassment. The suggestion that he sign up for a gym membership was an unreasonable request. The mere concept pained him. He viewed it as an invasive procedure. Having to dress up in plus-sized gym gear and expose his deplorable physical state to the world, under glaring lights and judging eyes, was a grim prospect. The idea of a personal trainer, some young specimen of health and boundless optimism, clapping his hands in contrived encouragement as Barney gasped for air? It was nauseating. If he must exercise he would do it in the privacy of his own home. Which is how he ended up with a stationary bike as a clothing rack.

Indulging a modicum of exercise was necessary but changing his diet was crucial. This seemed an insurmountable task. Binge eating was unbridled comfort. It filled the void. It brought him a satisfaction that nothing else could provide. It was his refuge. A shelter from the storm. When in doubt, eat. Fast food was his fix, washed back with a steady intake of soda pop. A direct link to his serotonin receptors, triggering a dopamine rush that fizzled fast but was fun while it lasted. Instant gratification.

Eat less fat, use less salt, avoid carbohydrates, abandon concentrated sugars. Eat small portions. Get excited about fruits and vegetables. Make the switch to quinoa and brown rice. Enjoy the cardboard grit of whole grain pastas. Replace the warm hug of coffee with the bitter embrace of green tea. Trade the sweet, sweet carbonated magic of pop for joyless water. Completely abandon your reward system.

With the exception of a wine pairing with dinner, Barney did not drink or do drugs. Why now should he be restricted by what he could eat? It was punishment and for what? For protecting his nation? For donating his time and money to charity? For never indulging in amoral behavior? The only thing he could find fault with was pornography and he'd given up that vice many years ago. How much more should he have to surrender?

2 Corinthians 4:16-18 Therefore we do not lose heart. Though outwardly we are wasting away, yet inwardly we are being renewed day by day. For our light and momentary troubles are achieving for us an eternal glory that far outweighs them all. So we fix our eyes not on what is seen, but on what is unseen. For what is seen is temporary, but what is unseen is eternal.

As always in times of hardship Barney turned to the Bible. What a fool he'd been, fixating on such trivial cravings, the needless self-pity. To obsess over a restricted menu when there were so many blessings on his plate was sacrilege. His body was his temple. Practicing patience and discipline he'd transform himself into the picture of health. He would make the adjustment.

Barney respectfully asked his personal trainer, Daemon, not to post his before and after photos on the web site. Although he took great pride in his weight loss, he felt showcasing his new appearance to be boastful, an act of vanity. He feared the karmic repercussions in doing so. To which Daemon replied, "Bullshit. I call bullshit. You are an inspiration to anyone who thought it wasn't possible. These pictures represent hope. They tell a story of personal empowerment and positive self-transformation. You are an example of all that is possible when someone commits to self-improvement. Now, we're not done yet, not by a long shot. But there's some poor soul who thinks they're trapped in an unhealthy body they're miserable with, these pictures allow us to reach back, to take his hand and say, "Hey, follow me. Let us show you the way. If you can dream it, we can make it happen." Don't ever be ashamed to embrace what you've earned through hard work and perseverance. To do so means depriving those in need of the visual proof in what they can accomplish. It's your duty to showcase the returns on your investment, your investment in your health and spirit. Yes, it's about living a healthy lifestyle and if that yields a desirable physique, a body that looks good in a bathing suit, then flaunt it. By showing them what you're capable of, you show them what they're capable of. Inspiration, we all need it."

Barney not only allowed Daemon to use his before and after photos but also committed to redoubling his efforts at the gym. It was a reinvention. Barney threw out his entire wardrobe. He had to; the old clothes didn't fit anymore. Daemon gave Barney the number of his trusted stylist, Natalia. "You've got the body you've always wanted. Why stop there?"

Barney contacted Natalia, agreeing to her price at Daemon's insistence, then Natalia took care of the rest. She gave him a fresh new wardrobe, complete with tailored suits and designer casual, that brought out his best features, then she sent him to her personal hair stylist, Jeremy. Jeremy told Barney that because his hair was thinning, honesty was the best policy. By keeping his hair long and combing it over he was merely drawing attention to his receding hairline. Barney was extremely apprehensive about shaving his head but with gentle coaxing he surrendered. The cropping was a catharsis. The great frustration gone. Standing over his shoulder, staring at Barney's reflection, Jeremy decreed, "That looks so much better." And for once Barney knew it to be true.

He'd made the changes. Now it was time to reap the rewards. Barney hadn't taken a vacation since he'd travelled with his parents to Tampa ten years ago. His confidence was at an all-time high. Everyone at work, at church, at the soup kitchen, they were all congratulating him for his transformation. Now was the time to venture out, meet new people, experience new things. The question was, where? He knew he wanted fun in the sun but wasn't leaving the United States, not with the current state of the world. After weighing out his options, Hawaii seemed like the perfect spot but Daemon insisted Barney book his vacation to Miami instead.

"Hawaii's great for a honeymoon or if you're retired, but South Beach is where it's at. That's where the party is. Make those numbers work for you.

Beautiful babes everywhere. Hit the clubs at night with your game face on. Girls will be swarming. Keep it simple. They're there for a good time. Find one you like, offer to buy her a drink. She accepts, you play it right, play it cool, you'll be banging by the end of the night."

Daemon also decreed the importance of having a quality wingman when it came to "getting digits."

"It's something you should really think about. A friend can highlight your social skills. They can play you up so it doesn't look like you're bragging or just full of shit. If there's an awkward silence they'll fill it with a joke, or another great story about you. Keeping that party atmosphere going. Let's say the girl you're into has some ugly jealous friend, a nasty pig who's cock-blocking you, trying to hog all the attention for herself. An expert wingman will see that and take action. He'll jump on that grenade for you. He'll spear the whale, slay the dragon. This way no one's feeling left out, everyone's happy, and you can hook up with your girl."

Unfortunately Daemon denied Barney's request to be his wingman. "Sorry man, it's a teacher-student thing. I can't blur the lines." Contradicting the story he recently shared with Barney about doing a house call to "service" one of his clients, "a rich bitch soccer mom with a brand new boob job, married to some limp dick executive," was how he phrased it.

Under duress, with his vacation fast approaching, still in desperate need of a wingman, Barney paced his living room. His palms were soaked, drenched. He sweated profusely when he got nervous. He'd hoped he'd vanquished the condition along with the extra pounds but it continued. Barney wiped his brow with the towel draped on his spin bike, took a deep breath, exhaled, picked up the phone and dialed the number.

"Kyle Prince speaking."

"Hi Kyle. It's Bill Barney."

"Barney, how are you? You keeping in good health?"

"Yes, I am. Thank you for asking."

"Well, your health comes first."

"Absolutely. Absolutely it does. But how 'bout you? How are the kids? How's business?"

"Busy. Very busy."

"That's great. So things are going well?"

"We've secured some major contracts."

"Fantastic! They want to learn from the best."

"Experience has taught me some valuable lessons I'm willing to impart on those that listen."

"Of course, yeah, you've been there, you've seen it."

"Some of it I wish I could un-see but that's the reality of war."

"Absolutely."

"We fight not because we want to, but because we have to."

"Of course."

"These savages would rather watch the world burn then allow freedom to reign free."

"You're true ... I mean, it's true."

"They can't stand our success. They hate us for it. "

"You're right."

"We must protect what is sacred. That's our charge in this life."

"To do so is a great honor."

"Amen, brother."

Hearing Kyle refer to him as a brother sent chills up Barney's spine. Now was the time to ask.

"Kyle, have you ever thought...? Well, I guess what I'm saying is...it's difficult for me to step away from the fight but I realize in order to perform at my optimum ability, I need a moment to recharge. Maybe it's necessary on occasion to step back and if only to confirm... Sorry, not to confirm -- it doesn't needs confirmation -- but to appreciate how privileged we are."

"Like a vacation."

"I was thinking about it, yes."

"I'm sure you've earned one Barney."

"And so have you, and that's why I'm calling. I've booked a flight to Miami, hopefully a little fun in the sun, and I wanted to extend the invitation for you to join me. There's beautiful beachfront, we can go snorkeling, jet skiing, maybe charter a boat, go deep-sea fishing. I'd love to check out the Everglades. There's so many options. It could be really, really fun, really great."

"My schedule is chockfull, Barney. Besides Miami's got a little too much flavor for my taste. A little too colorful."

"I understand. Of course. I didn't think...you know...I knew ... I know how busy you are...but... so you've been to Miami?"

"No, but I know all I need to."

"Oh really... I... should I be worried?"

"Well, there's certain elements you might want to watch out for."

"Wow...Okay."

"Look, you'll be fine. Just be smart about it. This is our country. These are our borders. We have the right to enjoy what is ours."

A wave of anxiety crashed down on Barney. He had serious reservations about Miami. Kyle's warning echoed in his head. He called Daemon hoping for reassurance. He got the answering machine. "Hey, this is Daemon Bexson. Personal trainer and life coach. Please leave your name and number. As always, keep it real. Peace."

"Hi, Daemon. This is Bill Barney. Sorry to bother you. I'm... so I've booked my flight, my hotel, to Miami. Excited. I just have a couple questions for you. Some safety concerns were brought to my attention. Hoping to run them past you, maybe get your thoughts. Anyway, I'll being see you tomorrow, so maybe we can talk so, yeah... we can just talk then. Anyway thank you and see you tomorrow."

The focus was on core strength that morning. Seated on the exercise ball, Barney burned his last set of woodchoppers with the medicine ball. While

Barney caught his breath Daemon set him straight on Miami. "Dude, you can find trouble anywhere but the cocaine cowboy days are long gone. It's safe. You're going on vacation. This ain't Scarface. Stop stressing. You're going to love it. The amount of eye candy you'll see ... I'm jealous. Good times, man, good times. Kick back and chillax."

The taxi fare is a flat rate of $32 from Miami International but Barney, being thrifty, finds the super shuttle kiosk at the lower level of the terminal. The shuttle brings him to the Palms Hotel and Spa for $20. Expensive but still far cheaper than a taxi.

Barney believes in the old adage "a penny saved is a penny earned." Of course, you have to loosen the purse strings now and then or you'd never go on vacation. Keeping in mind there are simple compromises you can make along the way, to ease the financial burden. Barney earned a respectable living but he knew that didn't grant him the right to be frivolous.

For example, when looking for rooms online, Barney saw there were two rates to choose from for five days' accommodation. The first rate was for the oceanfront view with one king-sized bed, the grand total being $2,093.21. The second option was city-view with double beds. This cost $1,795.46 all included. If he went for the city-view he saved $297.75, plus he got an extra bed. Needless to say, he chose city-view. It was an easy choice. The room was simply his sleeping quarters. The rest of the time he'd be out exploring or relaxing at the beach.

As soon as Barney arrives he unpacks his bags and hits the gym, as he'd promised himself. It was important to set the right tone, establishing a healthy routine. Being on vacation wasn't an excuse to abandon his commitment to physical fitness.

As always Barney works on his core conditioning, then focuses on legs and shoulders. After finishing his weight workout he runs the treadmill for twenty minutes. There are several attractive women using the fitness center. He makes eye contact with one briefly through the mirror. He feels great!

The exercise seems to shake off the jet leg. After his workout, Barney skips his shower. Instead he puts on his swim trunks and goes for a swim. He's by the ocean after all.

Paradise. That's what it is. Barney splashes around in the emerald water with the exuberance of a child. Floating on his back, staring up at the sky, he says a silent prayer of thanks, before a wave crashes over his head, getting water up his nose. Barney coughs and chokes up seawater. Thankfully no one seemed to notice. Barney laughs at how silly he must have looked.

Back on his beach towel, Barney can scarcely wipe the smile off his face, watching so many splendid young women walk past him on the beach. He can't wait to tell Daemon how right he was. Barney sips water from his Nalgene bottle, understanding the importance of hydration in such a climate. Less then twenty feet away, he watches a fetching, brown-skinned, full-figured woman pull her bikini bottom out of her butt crack with absolute confidence.

Splashing around in the surf most of the afternoon, Barney has worked up quite the appetite. After watching the most stunning of sunsets Barney returns to his hotel room to dress for dinner.

He's famished by the time he sits down at Essencia, the restaurant of the Palms. He is quite impressed by the menu. Every item sounds delicious. It's impossible to decide. Barney wants to indulge in all of them but he has to be mindful of staying away from the breads and pastas.

His three-course meal starts with a cup of roasted cauliflower and leek cream-less "Bisque" with shaved truffle and lump crabmeat. For an appetizer, seared diver scallops. For the main course, pancetta-wrapped yellowtail snapper with heirloom tomato confit, rutabaga and wild mushroom gratin, fava bean, and wilted lemon-essence spinach.

No dessert is necessary. Barney is satisfied. The meal was a dazzling array of flavors. Incredible. An expensive meal but money well spent. He can't be too frugal.

After allowing his food to digest Barney heads back to the gym for a brisk twenty minutes on the treadmill. Barney likes to listen to music while he runs. He needs to. It inspires him. At first he'd had problems with his ear buds slipping out, which was incredibly frustrating. So he did some research and purchased a pair of Shure earphones, which allowed for custom molds. He had them made and from that point on his earphones stayed lodged in his ear. An expensive purchase but he was very pleased with their effectiveness. It greatly improved his jogging experience. What he used to dread, he now looked forward to. Each time he created a new playlist to jog with, there was a tangible sense of excitement. When he hit his stride to the right song with the endorphins pumping, all concerns melted away. He was engaged. He was alive.

After his run Barney showers up and dresses in one of the outfits Natalia had hand-selected before leaving on his trip. It's labeled as evening attire, an ensemble of brown chinos, grey canvas sneakers, and a white (looser-fitting) dress shirt. It's hot and humid. Barney figures it will be safe to leave the navy blazer behind. Making sure he has his wallet, phone, and room key, Barney puts on one last application of antiperspirant and is ready to embrace the night.

He walks up and down Ocean Drive but can't choose a starting point. There's so much doubt, so much pressure. He desperately wants to get it right, to end the perfect day with the perfect night. There's beautiful woman everywhere but he knows it's useless. It's impossible. He can't meet them on his own. He needs someone to lead the way, to make introductions. He can't go this alone. He needs a wingman. With great reservation Barney reaches into his pocket and pulls out his cell phone. One more shot. When Kyle answers Barney has to yell over the din of traffic, inebriated pedestrians, music blaring out from the clubs.

"I know, I know but Kyle, please, just hear me out. It's beautiful here. It is. The weather's perfect. Everyone's really nice. I haven't been offered drugs, or felt threatened, not once. ... I know you can defend yourself. I know that ... I know you would. I didn't mean it like that. It was more about my fear, but what I really wanted to tell you was there's woman everywhere and they're ... I mean they're really wonderful... I know you don't need help with that, of course not... it's more for me. I need help ... but if you could... just hear me out for one second. I have a room with two beds at the Palms Hotel. You wouldn't have to pay a cent. Accommodation is taken care of. I'll take care of all our food and drinks, if you want."

He's embarrassed. Ashamed. What else did he expect? Kyle is an important person running an integral operation with serious obligations. He can't just cast them aside to whimsy. Kyle shouldn't have to explain this to him.

"Barney. It's not the cost. I can afford to travel wherever I want. But I have responsibilities at work, to my employees, to my clients, to my family. I can't just up and leave without notice, without making proper arrangements. That's part of being a boss."

He prays Kyle won't think less of him. Such a disgusting display. He came off completely needy and desperate. Why was he so weak? Why couldn't he stand up on his own? People respect a man with independent vision. Why was he always clinging to other people? All his cloying ... It must be so transparent. He was a loser to the core. Having the coolest job and all the ab crunches in the world wouldn't change that.

And what now? There's no way he can force himself to interact with strangers at some bar. What an idiot. He was an idiot to think he could. Barney hangs his head, cursing himself, his nature, as he walks back the hotel, making a stop at Johnny Rockets to gorge on a smokehouse double cheeseburger, french fries, and a milkshake.

Back at the hotel Barney feels sick from the glucose spike and gives him self an insulin injection. He feels a crushing anxiety, a fierce self-loathing. He'd lost the weight, he had the job, he made the money, he gave to charity. Where was the reward? Why did he always have to extend his hand first? He kept the world safe but may as well be invisible. What would it take to be recognized?

Barney smacks his forehead. How dare he think such thoughts? What a selfish fool. Protecting America was reward enough. What did he expect? A Purple Heart? He wasn't out there risking his life like Kyle. How could he be so selfish? No wonder the world conspired against him. He yells into the empty room, "Darn it, Barney, you just stop that right now!" Then his phone rings. Barney checks the call display. It's Kyle. Barney fumbles the phone, dropping it before picking up to answer.

"Hello, Bill Barney speaking."

"You ready to have some fun?"

"Kyle?"

"Are you ready to have some fun?"

"Sure. Yeah okay, I'm ready. Sounds great. How?"

"Linda's watching kids. Luger's taking care of things at the office. I'm booking a flight to Miami leaving tomorrow morning. We'll be sipping pina coladas by sun set."

Someone was listening. Hope and faith restored.

Barney wants to greet Kyle at the airport but is told not to. "I need wheels. Renting a car. I'm not paying for cabs all weekend. I'll see you at the Palms."

The next morning Barney works hard at the gym, trying to burn off his surplus of nervous energy. He is buzzing with excitement over Kyle's arrival. He can't believe his good fortune. It's actually happening! That night they'll be sharing the same sunset.

When Barney receives the text that Kyle has landed, he checks himself in the mirror one last time before rushing downstairs to wait. Sitting on the white sofa in the lobby, Barney watches Kyle, a vision of quiet confidence, stride into the hotel like he owns the place. Wearing a tank top, camo board shorts, and flip flops, with army issue duffle bag slung over his shoulder, Kyle is the epitome of cool. Slowly removing his Oakley's, Kyle squints, scanning the lobby. Barney tries to play it casual but practically leaps out of his chair, speed walking towards him with a ready salute. Kyle laughs.

"At ease, solider. We're on vacation."

Lounging poolside Barney goes over the nuances, explaining various drafts of the travel itinerary he meticulously constructed for them. Kyle stretches his arms out, soaking in the sun.

"Barn, relax. Enjoy that virgin piña colada. You don't need to schedule every minute of the day. You gotta let it find you sometimes. Keep it simple. I say we have a few more drinks, grab some dinner, let our food digest, maybe take a nap, then head out for the night."

"Great, that sounds great, and I have a list of bars and nightclubs for us to choose from. They were recommended to me, and I've checked them online and saw they had very positive reviews."

"Easy, Barney, I've just come off a long day of travel. I don't know if I feel like chasing the club scene tonight. I'm thinking we keep it simple, low key, and kick back at the strip clubs, work up an appetite. Then tomorrow I put my game face on."

"Okay, that works. That sounds fun. But before that maybe if I could, for your first night, suggest one thing."

"What's up?"

"Well, we really shouldn't miss the sunset. I mean it's spectacular. Truly beautiful. We should be on the beach for that. I think we should walk to the beach for that."

"Should we be holding hands too?"

"What? No? What? No, I don't mean like - "

"...I'm just fucking with you."

"Yeah, no, I know. That's funny. I just think it's kind of cool, the light and everything."

"I'm sure it is."

Kyle shakes his head and laughs.

"God bless you, Bill Barney."

They make the walk to the beach. The golden orb sets in a hot pink sky, brilliant streaks of orange and blue. Kyle passes the lighter so Barney can light his cigar as they watch the sun sink behind the ocean.

"Speaking of golden orbs, they come in pairs on this beach."

Barney nods, trying to mimic Kyle's movement, rotating the cigar in his mouth while puffing his lips. The cigar starts burning and Barney inhales the smoke, triggering a spastic cough. Kyle chuckles, patting Barney on the back.

"Smooth, Barney. Real smooth."

The world is thrown off axis. Barney feels nauseous. Everything's spinning. He can't hold his weight. Staggering forward, unable to lift his arms out in front of him, he folds, face first into the sand. Kyle rushes to his side, trying to pull him up.

"Breathe man. Just breathe. You'll be fine. You can't be inhaling this shit, that's all."

"I feel sick. Gonna puke, gonna puke..."

Some beach patrons rush over, unsure of the situation. Kyle assures them everything's fine, demanding some space. Barney pukes up a vile blend of stomach acid and ice cream drinks. The spinning stops, equilibrium restored. Barney is humiliated, exposing Kyle to such a scene.

"Kyle, I'm sorry. I'm so sorry to embarrass you like that."

"Fuck off. It's nothing. It's a strong smoke. You got the spins. No big deal. That was one hell of a face plant though."

"I'm sorry I ruined your sunset."

"There'll be another one and I'm not here for the sunsets."

They'd just been removed from the Goldrush strip club after Kyle insulted one of the dancers, calling her, "A lazy cunt con artist with a miserable attitude." When the bouncers told him he had to leave, Kyle informed them he was Special Forces, and if they so much as laid a hand on him there would be hell to pay. A warning they ignored.

Standing outside the club, head titled back, pinching a broken nose gushing blood, furious over the assault that had just take place, Kyle screams over the injustice. "You just assaulted a decorated war veteran, you cheap shot, chicken shit motherfuckers. I've served in Iraq, Afghanistan, places you don't even know about. I've got three silver, and six bronze, stars with valor, motherfucker. You're going to take the word of some cheap hooker raft rat that washed up on the shores of this great nation over a certified war hero? It's a goddamn travesty. A national tragedy. You should be ashamed!"

Barney wants to cry but needs to get them in a cab. The police are on their way.

The cab drives them back to the hotel. The cabbie didn't want to take them with all the blood and yelling but Barney slipped him an extra fifty to let them in. Kyle is still foaming at the mouth.

"I'm not afraid of the fucking cops. I'll tell them exactly what happened. The malicious assault of a decorated war veteran, that's what the fuck happened!"

"I know, Kyle, but you threw a beer bottle at them. They were going to press charges."

"Charges? For what? I was defending myself! You sure as shit didn't have my back."

"Kyle, I'm sorry. I tried. It happened so fast. That one bouncer twisted my arm so hard behind my back I thought he was going to break it."

Kyle shakes his head, glaring out the window. "I'm going to sue those cock suckers and burn that place down. Heads will roll. Mark my words. Heads will fuckin' roll."

At the hotel Kyle has Barney take pictures of his broken nose and swollen eye, evidence for the pending lawsuit. Barney pleads that they go to the hospital so Kyle can have his nose looked at. Kyle, who is busy pouring himself a drink from the minibar, denies his request. "Fuck the hospital. I said I was buying you a lap dance. We have a mission to complete."

The final stop on their tour of Miami strip clubs is Club Madonna, the only strip club on South Beach. During the cab ride, Kyle quotes General Patton. "I do not measure a man's success by how high he climbs but how high he bounces when he hits the bottom."

Barney insists they should be back at the hotel, applying ice, a cold compress, to Kyle's broken nose. Kyle dismisses his concerns. "Unless it's in a drink, I don't need any fuckin' ice."

Kyle can't believe it. He can't fucking believe it. "How the fuck does a strip club not serve alcohol?" Miami beach regulations prevented Club Madonna from serving alcohol.

While sipping on a six dollar glass of carbonated water and coke syrup, a peroxide-blond stripper named Svitlana approaches Kyle with a thick Eastern European accident, asking what happened to his nose.

"Don't fuckin' worry about it. And mind your manners."

Svitlana apologizes and suggests Kyle let her make it up to him in the champagne room (at a cost of $250). Kyle scoffs, "What the fuck for? They can't serve champagne."

Svitlana compromises, offering a table dance instead. Kyle waves her off. "I'm in no mood for games. I'm drinking fucking fountain pop. You find me a real drink and we'll talk."

Defeated, distressed, Svitlana flops down on the chair beside Barney. She complains about being stuck in Miami with no visa, simply trying to earn enough money to return to her family in the Ukraine.

"Don't listen to her bullshit, Barney. This ain't no Cinderella story. She's got money. Someone had to pay for those fake-ass titties."

"Excuse me?"

"You heard me Natasha, Natalia, whatever the fuck your name is."

"What the fuck's your problem?"

Kyle points an accusatory finger at Svitlana. "Listen up honey. You're just another treacherous cunt from the Eastern bloc. As far as I'm concerned the cold war's still going. If you and your people hate my country so much, then why do so many fucking Cossacks end up here, trying to copy our style?"

"I see why you got your nose broken."

"Don't change the subject. America doesn't want your fucking rubles, so take that toxic pussy back to Chernobyl. "

"I'm Ukrainian, you ignorant pig!"

"Same fucking shit. You're all a bunch of pinko bastards."

The tension is too much. The anxiety overwhelms him. Barney throws up, trying to catch it in his hands. It splashes off the table onto Svitlana. She screams. Kyle laughs. The bouncers are on their way.

The next morning, after returning from the gym, Barney apologizes to Kyle for his behavior the previous evening.

"Kyle, I am so sorry about last night. But that bouncer really did twist my arm and I thought he was going to break it. Then at Club Madonna I just fell apart, and they tossed me into the street so fast and I've never been in a fight and they wouldn't let me back in and I didn't know what to do. Kyle, please ... Please, I'm sorry."

Kyle, lying in bed with a bag of ice over his face, says nothing.

"Kyle, please? I want this to work. We can salvage this. We still have three more days of vacation. We've got Swamp Tromp booked for tomorrow and that could be a lot of fun. And today we can out snorkeling, shopping, sightseeing, whatever you want."

Kyle offers no response, a slow death for Barney.

"Kyle, tell me what to do. I'm sorry I barfed. I'm sorry I didn't have your back. I'm sorry I'm such a terrible wingman. I'll do better. I promise. I'll do better. Just tell me what to do."

Kyle grumbles from under the bag of ice. "They punched me in the fuckin' nose again. They punched my fuckin' nose again. Motherfuckers need to die."

"Kyle...I don't... I don't..."

Kyle springs up and whips the bag of ice against the wall. "I need a fucking drink is what I need and don't say another word until I've had it."

Kyle demands beer with breakfast so they drive to 11th Street Diner, a 24-hour diner in an art deco dining car that Barney wanted to check out.

The blood has dried on Kyle's split lip. Both eyes are black. His nose is swollen so badly the ridge sticks out past his forehead. It's only after his second Budweiser, mid-way through steak and eggs, that Kyle finally addresses Barney. "I've decided to accept your apology. I'm going to take the high road and forget last night ever happened. I will have my revenge on the cocksuckers that assaulted me, mark my words, but I won't let it ruin my vacation. As for you, Barney, you need to sack up and grow a pair for the rest of this trip. If we're in battle you need to unleash the beast. None of this 'Waahhh!!!! He twisted my arm behind my back. I'm a big fucking baby.' In hand to hand combat, you've got to be willing to rip someone's throat out with your teeth if that's what it takes. That's survival. That's war."

"I know. I'll be ready. I won't surrender."

"And when we go out tonight, when we're talking to the ladies, I can't have you freezing up, stuttering and stammering like you got special needs and this is the Big Brother program. Fuck polite. You need to own your shit. You need to hype me up. There's plenty of material to work with. If you don't help me, how can I help you?"

"I know. I'll make sure this time. I'll make sure they know."

"I'm the most lethal sniper in American history. That's a pussy magnet for both of us. But I can't say it, doesn't work that way. You need to tell them."

"Yes sir, I will."

"It's to your benefit. You'll be there sweeping up what's left over. Understand?"

"Understood."

"Good. How's your omelet?"

"Delicious, thanks."

"After breakfast we go back to the hotel so I can take a shit. After that we head to the beach. I can kick back, catch some rays, and crash out for a couple. Restore my energy for tonight."

"Sounds great, but you're sure you don't want to get your nose looked at?"

"Do not ask me again, Barney. I'm serious. I don't need your pity. That goddamn grease ball juice monkey bouncer is lucky I didn't connect with my spinning roundhouse kick 'cause it would have broke his fuckin' jaw. They'd have to wire that shit shut. He'd be wearing a collar because of the whiplash."

"I'm glad it missed. You might have killed him, then they'd charge you with manslaughter, not understanding it was in self defense."

Kyle takes a slow slip of his beer. "True, but I can't be worrying about that when I'm under attack."

Barney frolics around in the ocean while Kyle snoozes on his beach chair. They'd managed to put the ugliness of the previous night behind them. All is right in the world. They were back on vacation. Facing the beach, in water just past his waist, Barney waits for the wave to arrive, then jumps back into it. He loves the sensation of crashing through and dropping down over.

Waiting for the next big wave Barney notices a group of young men, college frat boys, making their way down the beach tossing a football. They're loud, obnoxious, obviously intoxicated, hurling comments at any girl that glances in their direction.

Their passes are getting reckless, errant, the distance increasing with each throw. The group continues down the beach, drawing closer to Kyle passed out in his camo board shorts, mouth hanging open, with drool running down his chin. Barney sees it coming -- it's inevitable -- but from his vantage point he's a helpless observer. There are forces at play that can not be stopped, Barney's fear confirmed as he watches the football sail through the air, crashing into Kyle's broken nose.

Kyle falls off his chair, screaming in pain, his nose a running faucet of blood. The group of nervous frat boys huddles around him, checking to see if he's all right, offering their automatic apologies. As soon as Kyle registers what's happened, the rage is immediate, unrelenting. "What the fuck... what the fuck...what fuck was that?! You fucking idiots! You fucking morons! I can't relax on the beach … for two fucking seconds without getting beaned in the face by a football? Fucking shitheads!

The frats boys continue spitting out apologies but Kyle is not accepting them. He shoves the biggest guy in the group away from him, the one who missed the Hail Mary pass. The young man holds his hands up in defense, still trying to apologize. Kyle gives him several more hard shots square to the chest before the young man pushes back, telling Kyle to back off.

Kyle throws the first punch, missing, and gets lit up by a flurry of punches and heavy knees. Barney, running full tilt across the beach, breaks through the crowd of gawkers, launches himself through the air, and lands on the assailant's back, wrapping his arms and legs around him. Frantic, Barney chokes down on the frat boy's neck while his friends start drilling Barney with punches and kicks to his ribs, trying to get him to let go. This only makes it worse, and Barney clenches down harder, latched onto the frat boy, stumbling around in the sand trying to toss Barney off him. But Barney will not release his grip. Eventually Frat Boy goes down, and his frat boy friends start kicking Barney in the back full force, only elevating his level of panic, tightening the clench.

Kyle tries to pull them back but gets hit in the nose by an elbow and drops instantly. The veins in Frat Boy's face start popping out as it turns from red to purple. The stomping continues. Barney's neck flexes as he releases a high-pitched squeal that gives everyone pause. Kyle, with blood on his hands, looks up from the sand through rows of legs, and Frat Boy goes under, his body limp, choked unconscious, while the kicks continue to rein down on Barney.

The sound of the four-wheeler racing towards them announces the arrival of Beach Patrol. They break through the circle and scream at Barney to let go. Still squealing, he can't hear them. He's locked on.

Kyle springs to his feet, taking charge. "Let him go, Barney! At ease, solider! Stand down!"

Barney releases the clench. Shaking, he gasps for air.

It takes several moments before the frat boy regains consciousness. Beach Patrol takes statements from both sides of the conflict and eyewitnesses. Both sides threaten to press charges. At a stalemate they agree to drop it and both parties are escorted from the beach. Kyle tells Barney, still shaking, to hold his head up high. They defended themselves proudly.

Back at the hotel, sitting by the water bar, Kyle raises a Bud Light. "Cheers to you, Bill Barney. Heart of a lion. A true warrior. I knew you had it. I knew. The way you slapped the rear naked choke on that piece of shit. He didn't stand a chance. Lights out. Nighty- night. Bedtime."

Barney's back and sides ache. They are covered in welts. If he turns at the wrong angle, a sharp pain shoots through him. He is sure he's fractured a rib. But then and there, with Kyle heaping on the praise, pride in his eyes, it doesn't matter. The adrenaline is still pumping and Barney is beaming ear to ear. He defended his friend in the heat of battle, with the odds stacked against them. It was an act of courage he never believed he was capable of.

"I'll tell you what, Barn. It was an honor to fight by your side."

"I wish I could frame those words, Kyle. I can't tell you how much they mean to me."

Several hours later Barney can hardly walk. It hurts to sit, it hurts to stand, it hurts to breathe. His back has tightened to the point he can't turn his waist or neck without a stabbing pain in his side. Kyle tosses him a bottle of Percocets. "I save 'em for special occasions. Wash back a couple of these with another cold one. You'll be right as rain. Fight through it. Tonight we're taking over South Beach."

The percs are a saving grace. The pain is still there but Barney feels fine, almost euphoric. Nothing worries him. There's a lightness of being. It's time to start their evening. It's decided they'll drive to Joe's Stone Crabs, another spot Daemon recommended. "If you dig sea-food, Joe's Stone Crabs is the place. Get the crab claws and half-shell oysters. Can't go wrong. Well worth it."

Kyle plays it cool for the first fifteen minutes, waiting in line for a table, before the aggravation sets it.

"I don't do lines Barney. I got no time for them. This is ridiculous."

"It's probably a good sign there's a lineup, right? People aren't going to line up if the food isn't good. But we can leave if you want."

"I know you're all excited about this place so I'll give it another ten minutes, but if we're not seated by then I'm gone."

Five minutes later they're seated at their table. Kyle's good mood has completely soured.

"Why the fuck is it so cold in here?"

"Yeah, it's a little chilly."

"Chilly? This place is fucking freezing."

Kyle shakes his head. "This better be worth it."

Barney prays it will be. He feels responsible for making Kyle wait so long.

At the end of their meal Kyle wipes his face with his napkin. "What a fucking rip-off. The crabs are tasty enough, I guess, but there's not enough, not for that price. I'm still fucking hungry."

"I'm sorry, Kyle. We wanted seafood, this place was recommended to me, I'd read good things about it --"

"You don't need to apologize. This place is a tourist trap. I knew that the second we walked through the door. Fuck it. Let's head back to the hotel for a nap. Those shit heads and their football ruined my last one. I need to be rested and on point for tonight."

Back at the hotel Barney pretends to be asleep, still napping, but it's impossible to ignore the phone conversation. Kyle needs to be heard.

"Now listen... Susie ... No, you listen; you've had your chance to talk, now let me speak. I deeply resent you insinuating this is somehow my fault. May I remind you that you are his mother? Parenting is a shared responsibility, if you can somehow grasp that ... it doesn't matter where I am ... No ...

no, that's not true ... shut your mouth. You shut your mouth... Oh really, is that so... Neglect? Neglect? You want to throw that word around? You really want to go there? You selfish bitch ... Your goddamn rights? ... I will. Take a hard look in the mirror and you'll understand what I was dealing with ... Yeah, yeah, it's my fault, of course it is ... maybe if you took a little pride in your appearance ... No, you don't. No, you do not ...You have no idea the sacrifices I make ... That won't happen. That will never happen.... 'Cause I fuckin' said so ... I swear to God, Susie, you better not be recording this conversation. I'm done playing games."

Kyle paces the room like a caged animal, stopping briefly to sit down at the edge of the bed, put his leg up on the chair, and slap his hand against the wall.

"I don't give a good God-damned what they tell you. Kirk is a good boy. He's a hell of lot stronger then his mother. Yeah, sure ... sure ...Keep talking 'cause that's all you do. You goddamn wind bag. His behavior's to be expected, it's a cry for help, against a mother who is so selfish she puts her needs above her own children ... I know. I know what it's like, dealing with your sickness. That's why I had to leave. I wasn't letting you take me down and I'm not letting you ruin my children, then pile the blame on me. No way."

Kyle stands at the edge of Barney's bed. Barney curls up in the fetal position, continuing to feign sleep.

"You think I give a flying fuck what the trash man thinks of me? No! Shut your mouth! Shut your fucking trap. That garbage dispenser of yours, no wonder you moved in with a trash collector ... Yeah ... yeah, that's right. That's right, I did. You gave me no choice. Look at ya. It's embarrassing. I was just supposed to sit back and do nothing, watch you stuff your face like a pig? ... Of course. No surprise there. I'm sure he does and he tells you that 'cause he's a loser. You two are perfect for each other ... Listen to yourself. No wonder Kirk's acting out. He's ashamed, shamed of his slob of a mother and her trash-picking boyfriend. No! No you do not! The goddamn garbage man does not have a say in how my child is raised. That filthy degenerate needs to cut his disgusting hair and mind his stinking business before I destroy him."

Kyle whips the TV remote at the wall, shattering it.

"Yeah... Yeah, I am...You got that right. 'Cause when my children's welfare is at risk I will do whatever it takes. So let me tell you how it's going to be. You're going to calm the fuck down and do as I say. When I get back I will deal with this ... Why? Why? You want to go over my credentials for you? Leaders of this country, the elite of the elite, have recognized me for my bravery in the face of evil and you're a lazy piece of trash that lives with the garbage man ... Oh, please ... give me a break ... Will you listen to yourself? Always with the hysterics ... He's ten years old! No one's pressing charges, you moron!"

Kyle stares at the phone with disdain.

"She hung up on me. The bitch hung up on me. Typical. She sees she's losing the argument and hangs up on me."

Barney sits up in bed, pretending to rub the sleep from his eyes. "Is everything alright?"

"Oh, just that my bitch ex-wife can't leave me be. Her life sucks so she has to make sure I'm miserable as well. She's jealous. Jealousy, that's all it is."

"Why was she calling you?"

"Just to be a miserable cunt. Trying to use my own children against me. She tells me Kirk got caught trying to burn his school down, like it's somehow my fault. She's making accusatory accusations about my choices as an individual, when she shacked up with a pot-reeking, dirty, hippy garbage man. Forcing that degenerate lifestyle on my kids. And I won't stand for it. I won't."

"I'm sorry to hear that. I'm sorry you have to deal with that. It's got to be tough on you, really really tough. You'd think -- I mean, you'd hope - Susie would have more appreciation for the sacrifices you've made for your family, for this country."

"I know, Barn. I know"

Kyle sits at the edge of his bed with a deep sigh. "You've got to stay positive. That's all you can do. I can't let her negative energy bring me down."

"Glad to hear it. That's the right attitude. Kirk will be fine. Boys like to play with fire, it's what they do. She's making a mountain out of a molehill."

"She acts like Kirk's going to turn into a goddamn serial killer or something. So he's a bit of firebug? So what? I loved starting fires when I was young, playing with fireworks and such, I still do."

"And it worked out for you. You're a decorated war veteran, a national hero, chief executive officer of a business you built from the ground up, providing jobs in a down economy, training future generations to defend this great nation. No, I'm not worried about Kirk. He's a good kid with the greatest of role models for a father. You'll be proud of him one day, like I know he's proud of you."

"You're right, Barn, but a concerned father can't help but worry."

"That's your nature and that why Kirk's going to turn out just fine."

"I know it. I know."

Barney says nothing, letting the moment breathe.

"Well, so much for my nap. Bitch had to ruin that but I won't let her ruin this night."

Kyle holds up his hand for a high-five which Barney fumbles, only connecting with half his hand. Kyle leaves it held up.

"Weak. You're going to have do better than that, Barn."

Barney connects on the second try.

"Attaboy."

Barney steps out of the washroom wearing gray slacks and a pale blue dress shirt. Kyle goes past him, stepping back into the washroom. "You need to change that shirt. We can't be wearing the same shit." Kyle is also wearing a pale blue dress shirt, albeit it with vertical strips.

"Oh, sorry. I guess you're right. Yeah ... Sorry, Kyle."

Kyle shapes his hair in front of the mirror, using hair paste. "I don't care. Just wear another one."

Barney remove his shirt and takes another one off the hanger. "How 'bout this one?"

"Barney, that shirt's pink."

"Yeah, Natalia picked it our for me. She thought it looked good. She said the color worked for tropical climates."

"Who's Natalia?"

"Oh, she's someone ... a friend."

"You want to wear pink. Fine. I truly don't give a shit. Are you wearing a matching G-string?"

"No, no. Yeah, no ... that's funny. No, nothing like that."

"I could rock a pink shirt, no problem. I can pull it off. Others, it might look a little silly, like they're trying too hard. You just need to be honest with yourself."

"You might be right. Probably better to err on the side of caution. I've got a white shirt I could wear?"

"Yeah, let's go with that."

Before leaving they check their pockets, making sure they have their wallets, cell phones, key cards. Everything is accounted for. They head for the door about to step out.

"What's that smell?"

"I'm not sure."

Kyle leans in, sniffing Barney. "Are you wearing my cologne?"

"Yeah, I put some on. Is that ... is that bad? I'm sorry. I liked how it smelled but I should have asked. I'm sorry."

"I don't care if you ask. It's a spray of cologne --who gives a fuck? -- But we can't be going out smelling the same. People are gonna think we're rolling around together. You've got to wash it off. You gotta change that shirt."

Their first destination is LIV. Daemon was adamant that it was an essential Miami experience. "Dude, it's Mecca. It sets a standard no club can compare to. I saw the 'Fuck me, I'm famous' show. The music ...wow ... you could feel the bass in your balls. The show effects were out of this world. If the place didn't have a ceiling, you could see the light show from outer space. The aliens would have come down to party with us. I mean there were babes everywhere. I'm talking solid tens, and they're hanging from the rafters on these sex swings or riding these giant silk scarves. I've never seen so much talent. It's prime and primed at that place. Hold on to your eyeballs 'cause they're going to be popping out of your head."

They don't bother stopping. They drive right past LIV, per Kyle's orders. The mass of people waiting outside LIV, hoping to get in, it will be a two-hour minimum.

"Are you fucking kidding me? You'd need a gun to get through that mob and you'd still have to pay a $20 cover." Their cab driver informed them it was $40, depending on the event it could be $70, and a guy wasn't getting in without an attractive girl on his arm or an inside connection.

"Well, LIV can lick my ass. I'm a goddamn war veteran, not some fucking sheep following the herd. I've served tours in Iraq and Afghanistan. I'm not waiting in their fucking lineup, or paying their bullshit cover."

The cab driver suggests Mango's Tropical Cafe.

"That's not a fuckin' gay bar, is it?"

The cab driver assures Kyle it's not. "Plenty of females, boss, and they make a damn good mojito. And you know the expression - one mojito, two mojito, three mojito, floor."

The expression makes Kyle laugh. "Sounds like a real panty-dropper."

Mango's has showgirls on staff, dressed in animal print bikinis, jumping up on the bar, dancing to the music. Kyle yells into Barney's ear over the music. "I don't really like this salsa shit but the cabbie was right about the babes."

Kyle surveys the terrain, eventually targeting two women he deems worthy. Leaning against the bar, he notifies Barney. "Look over my right shoulder. Be discreet about it. You clock those two honeys, the blond and brunette. They're not local. Watch how their eyes dart around. Hear the nervous laughter? They're new here, tourists, out of their element. We need to make them feel comfortable, show 'em a good time, bring them back to the hotel. I'm going to go make introductions. You get a round of drinks going. Four mojitos. They ask about my nose, which they will, it happened cage-fighting, an accident during training for an upcoming MMA tournament. Understood?"

Barney hates lying, but the truth seems far worse. "Cage-fighting. Copy that."

"Another thing, we are here celebrating the fact that my book, my life story, just got optioned for a movie."

"Kyle, I knew it! I knew it! I said that! I told people! I said *Head Shot* needs to be a movie. Kyle's book needs to be a movie. This is great! What a surprise! How long have you known? I knew there was something. I knew it. I knew there was a reason. So who's going to play you?"

"Barney..."

"Yes?"

"I don't know. The producers want me to give them a list, my top five, then go from there."

"Who are they? Who're your top five?"

"Let's save this conversation for the ladies."

"Roger that. Four mojitos coming up."

"After you bring the drinks over, we do quick introductions, then you propose a toast to my movie deal."

"I got it, Kyle. I won't get nervous. I know exactly what to say."

Barney is elated. Now the whole world will see Kyle's story up on the big screen. He loves the book but it's meant for the movies. No doubt Kyle will become an international celebrity. Carrying the drinks over on a tray Barney sees that Kyle's in the middle of a story, so he stops himself, not wanting to interrupt. He stands off to the side waiting for Kyle to finish.

"It's practice, but you're training for a fight, you have to fight. So I had him dazed, he's on the ground, and big mistake, I let my guard down to check on him and he tags me right on the nose with this wild swing. He'd had his bell rung, he was in survival mode and just started flailing, so I had to put him in a guillotine and tap him out. But my nose was broken and I couldn't compete in the tournament. He felt awful about it afterwards. Unfortunately injuries are a reality of the sport and I didn't protect myself, a lesson for next time."

Kyle sees Barney standing there and waves him in. "Barney, this is Lisa and Mary. They're from Canada."

"Oh wow, Canada, eh?" jokes Barney "What province?"

"I'm impressed. You know we have provinces."

"And you have a prime minister. We're not all ignorant Americans."

"We're from Manitoba."

"Winnipeg?"

"That's right. That's the capital."

"How do you know so much about Canadian geography?"

"I think it's important. You're our neighbors to the north."

Kyle raises his mojito. "Well, we're all here now. I would like to propose a toast to good times and a great night in beautiful Miami."

Everyone raises a glass. Kyle gives Barney a kick under the table. Barney takes the cue.

"If I could make an addendum to that. I would like to commend my dear friend, Kyle Prince. Kyle's autobiography and best selling book "Headshot" was recently optioned by a major studio to be turned into a movie. It could not happen to a more worthy individual. As his friend I can say his character is beyond reproach. He is a true American hero. A national treasure -- "

"All right, you're laying it on a bit thick there, Barney. Our arms are getting tired. I was just doing my job."

"And we're all safer for it. Cheers, everybody."

Lisa nudges Kyle's shoulder.

"Wow, you're some kind of a star. Who is this guy?"

Kyle shrugs it off, playing bashful.

"Kyle is one of America's most decorated soldiers. He has the highest kill count of any sniper in recent memory."

"Are you serious? Is he being serious?"

"The US military credits him with 160 kills in Iraq alone."

"This isn't about bragging rights. I do what needs to be done to defend this country. I protect the innocent, fighting to liberate the oppressed from evil. Honestly, I couldn't care less if Hollywood is interested in me in or not."

"So you're a cage-fighting super sniper?"

"MMA is a recent undertaking now that I'm no longer in active duty. I'm not sure how far I'll take it. It's a massive commitment. Running my security and weapons training company takes up most of time. But MMA is a discipline I respect greatly."

"Wow, you're hardcore. And what do you do, Barney?

"National defense. Nothing exciting. I work a desk job."

"Sure you do. So we've got a super sniper and super spy. That's what you tell all the girls right?"

"No, goodness no, nothing like that. I'm very safe at my job. Certainly no one's asking to make a movie about me. Kyle's the one risking his life in battle."

"How long have you two known each other?"

"Several years now. Funny story, actually. Well, not really funny, but its just another example of how -- "

Kyle cuts of Barney " -We met at a mutual friends barbeque. How long are you two in Miami for?"

"Two more days."

"How 'bout that? We've got two more days in Miami as well."

"Yeah ... enjoy them."

"Oh, I think so. It's been great so far. Tomorrow we're going on the swamp tromp." says Barney.

"Ladies, if I may be so bold, what do you do for a living?" interjects Kyle.

"I'm a flight attendant." Says Mary

"I'm a cop." Say Lisa

"You're a stewardess, and she's a cop."

"Yep."

"Don't worry, I won't make any mile-high jokes."

"How nice of you."

"Being a flight attendant, that's really neat, but I Imagine the travel can be exhausting," adds Barney.

Kyle shakes his head in frustration. "'That's really neat'? What are you, twelve?"

"Sorry, it's just ... yeah, I guess ... it's somewhat ambiguous, I suppose. I should have selected a stronger word."

Mary comes to Barney's defense "Why are you sorry? Don't be sorry."

Lisa backs them up "There's nothing wrong with 'neat'. I like 'neat'. Neat and tidy."

Kyle takes a slow sip of his mojito, scanning Lisa from head to toe. "So, being a cop, do you travel with handcuffs in your suitcase?"

Lisa cringes. "Wow, really? That's what you're going with?"

Barney squirms under the awkwardness of the moment and excuses himself to use the washroom, his fourth trip to urinate since arriving at Mango's. When he returns to the table he sees Lisa and Mary whispering to each other with Kyle glowering at them. From there it's a steady and swift decline. The more Lisa and Mary try to distance themselves, the more aggressive and belligerent Kyle becomes. Completely parched Barney crushes and swallows the ice from his mojito while Kyle directs his attention to Mary.

"You gotta a boyfriend?"

"I do."

"So what's he do?"

"He's a firefighter."

"A firefighter, wow. Brave man. Those firefighters, I'll tell ya. How do they find time to rescue cats from trees with all that calendar modeling?"

"Yeah, I guess it's not as heroic as killing 'rag heads' for oil."

Barney tries to intervene "Please, Kyle. Please don't. They can't understand."

Kyle is simmering, shooting daggers at Mary. Barney wants to crawl under a table. "I've got friends that are firemen. Good Americans, true patriots like myself. I was telling a joke, sweetheart. I guess you don't get a sense of humor growing up in an igloo." Kyle informs Mary.

"You're right. You're hilarious. You really are."

"Sure, I guess I am. Obviously it's all a big joke to you. You want to talk about oil?"

"Not really."

"Too bad you're the one that brought it up, so listen up. There's a resource crunch coming the likes of which we've never seen. The battle lines are drawn and I will fight to the death to protect my nation's interest."

"You need to relax." Says Lisa.

"Relax? You tell me to relax? Easy for you to say, eating your fucking doughnuts in some parking lot while you're on 'patrol'. I guess you'd rather live in a society run by goat fuckers throwing acid in their wives' faces. Would you prefer that? Have us surrender? Let the savages take over so they can rape or stone you to death for looking at them the wrong way?"

"You need to calm down."

"Fuckin' hypocrites. You're all bleeding hearts liberals because you've never been face to face with the enemy. You don't know how real it gets. So I suggest you keep your fucking mouth shut and let us do our job, which is keeping your spoiled ass safe."

Lisa grabs Mary by her arm. "Let's go. It's not worth it."

"Go. Run. Run from your problems. I fight for what I believe in. No wonder all the draft dodgers ran to Canada. Go bury your heads in the sand."

Lisa stops and does a slow turn around. "What's with all the anger? You're obviously overcompensating for something."

"Honey, you couldn't handle what I got."

"It would never get that far."

"It would if you weren't such a fucking dyke."

"No, because you're disgusting and desperate with your G.I Joe bullshit. Walking around, chest puffed out, while your little friend jerks you off to keep your ego intact."

Barney desperate to intervene, tries interjecting, but his words come out in a jangled slur. "Nowsholdsonisecondscusesme weresjustistryingtooss."

Lisa and Mary have already turned their backs, walking away.

"Better then handing out traffic tickets! Go back to your shitty country, you fucking carpet munchers!"

Both woman stick up their middle finger as they disappear into the crowd. Barney feels queasy, his body depleted, running on fumes. His body aching from the beach assault. It gnaws at his back, a pain previously tempered with the elation of victory, booze, and Percocets. Now, with their sudden fall from grace, the pains returned with a vengeance. He's no longer able to suppress it. Barney is beaten and exhausted. But his physical wellbeing is an afterthought compared to his concern over Kyle's. He can feel the anger spilling off of Kyle in waves. Barney wants to comfort him but knows if he says the wrong thing it could trigger a horrible tantrum but he has to say something, bring it back from the brink. The dream is in jeopardy.

"Kyle yousisserr...sosmuchbettersthenthosetwos."

Kyle fires back a look of bemused annoyance. "What, are you wasted already? That's your fuckin' third drink. Go get a drink of water."

Kyle dismisses Barney, sipping his mojito through clenched teeth.

"I hate this city. I hate it. Bunch of skanks and scumbags. Trashy. Zero class. Full of ignorant tourists and fucking immigrants. What the fuck am I doing here? A goddamn waste of money. Those bitches ... those spoiled fucking bitches need to learn a lesson."

Barney feels the blood drain from his face. Swaying on his feet, hands shaking, sweat pooling out his pores, the knees go weak, he stumbles, staggering forward, trying to apologize, to say he's sorry, but the words never leave his mouth.

Barney wakes in the ambulance halfway to the hospital, wearing an oxygen mask, attached to an IV drip, with Kyle hovering over him. "You blacked out, buddy. You crashed hard. Smacked your head. Going to hospital for precautionary measures. You're going to be fine. Can you give me a thumbs-up?"

Barney holds up his thumb. "Atta boy. Get this, I saw those two lesbos from Canada, standing there, acting all shocked, pretending to be concerned while you're twitching on the ground, pissing your pants. I let 'em have it. I said, 'You see. You see what you fucking started?' They didn't have much to say after that."

After they stabilize his blood-glucose levels, the doctor sends Barney for X-rays. Hearing about the earlier assault, the doctor is looking for possible signs of pulmonary contusion. He's also concerned about trauma to the spleen and liver.

X-rays reveals nothing has been broken but there's significant inflammation and bruising around the area. The doctor diagnoses bruised ribs. "Still incredibly painfully." Because of the suspected concussion he requests Barney stay overnight for observation, for Barney an impossible request. He and Kyle are scheduled for the swamp tromp that morning, at 6 a.m. Barney isn't missing it. He's been looking forward to the everglade expedition since booking the vacation. He was sure it would be the highlight of the trip and now more then ever, he needed something to cling on to.

He knew of Kyle's reverence for nature and was convinced he'd appreciate America's wetlands, seeing the southern half of the watershed for the first time, encountering its splendiferous beauty and majestical wonder, witnessing the unique wildlife. Herons, grackles, turtles, snakes, it was an endless array of fauna and flora. The biological diversity was astounding. They'd stop by the alligator hole and watch the prehistoric reptile in its natural habitat. They'd gaze upon the purple gallinule, voted the most colorful bird in Florida. And by a miracle they might catch a glimpse of the endangered Everglade Kite. No, this could not be missed.

Against his doctor's wishes Barney signs the release forms for his discharge from the hospital. Without being asked Kyle gives the doctor his assurance. "Don't worry, doctor. I know how serious head injuries can be. I'm watching over him. And when things have calmed down a bit I'm going to have a serious sit-down with Mr.Barney about assuming greater responsibility for his diabetes."

It's 3 a.m. when they leave the hospital. It's another solemn cab ride back to the hotel when Kyle announces, "We need to call an audible, change our strategy. We need to let the party come to us. The night's not over yet, my friend."

"Yeah but remember? We've got swamp tromp at 6 a.m. We can't miss that."

"Plenty of time. We only need an hour."

The pictures are impressive. Barney is shocked by how attractive the woman are. They look like playboy playmates and they're available on Kyle's laptop - just a phone call away. Still he has great reservations. It seems like a bad idea. It feels wrong.

"Barney, look at this. Look at those big titties, those thick lips. She's got that onion butt, just ready for a pounding."

"Kyle, what are we talking about here? This is prostitution, right? That's illegal."

"Barney, no one gives a shit. These girls make a good living providing a needed service. They aren't some crack whores off the street. These girls follow protocol. They're well trained. It's a simple business transaction."

No matter how Kyle spins it, he can't appease Barney's anxiety bordering on dread. "Kyle, we're meeting in the lobby for swamp tromp in less then three hours. We cannot be calling escorts up to our hotel room."

Kyle ignores Barney's objections, focusing on the agency's photo gallery. "This is it. I found her. This is the one. Alexis. Look at this little rocket. Damn! Look at the fucking body! Nice tight heart-shaped ass. Look at that belly. This girl's in shape, she likes to train. Well, she can train my dick into her ass." Kyle sips his vodka Red Bull, supplied by the mini-bar. "Fuck, I hope she's available. You know what girl you want, Barney? I'm placing the call."

Barney paces the room, with one hand planted on his injured ribs. "No. No, I don't know. I don't think we should be doing this. We're contributing to the sex trade. We're funding human trafficking."

"Take it easy. Where do you think those girls at the strip club came from? Now what are you into? Blond, brunette, thick, thin? What makes your dick move?"

"Kyle, what if it's a set-up? What if they rob or blackmail us somehow? What if some guy with a gun kicks down the door?"

"Some guy with a gun? What are you talking about?"

"Like their driver or something."

"Okay, now you're starting to piss me off. Stop being hysterical and name a girl or I'm picking one for you."

"I'm sorry Kyle, I just ... I'll take Amber."

"Nice choice. A classic kind of beauty. Her tits look real. So lend me your credit card and I'll place the order."

"My credit card? No. No way."

"Barney, this is standard procedure."

"Why do you they need my credit card?"

"To hire the girls."

"We shouldn't even be doing this. I don't think we should."

"Barney I'd use my credit card no problem, but I'm going through a divorce. I can't leave a paper trail. I will pay you back in cash tomorrow. The service is legitimate. Your credit card invoice isn't going to say 'hooker rental.' It will appear as a legitimate business name, like 'RNP consulting.' That's how they do it. Trust me. They make their money providing an essential service, and they want repeat business."

"Why can't we use your card?"

"You're going to make me repeat myself? I'm a national hero and because of that I have my enemies. There's people trying to dig up dirt on me. Trying to bring me down. The target on my back never goes away. That's a price I pay, part of the sacrifice."

"I know and that's what I'm saying. This whole thing's just a bad idea. And we have to meet in the front lobby for swamp tromp at six. That doesn't even give us three hours of sleep."

"If we let this opportunity pass us by, forget swamp tromp -- I will not be in the mood -- but if you want to be a baby, suck your thumb and go to bed, not even try to salvage this night, then go right ahead."

With his head hung in shame, Barney hands over his credit card.

After placing the order Kyle offers Barney some Viagra. "I don't normally need this shit. It's just an insurance policy. We're spending money on this, I need to be rock hard, the way they like it."

Barney declines. He'd heard Viagra elevated blood pressure and could put you at risk of a heart attack, he warns Kyle, but it falls on deaf ears. "That only happens to decrepit old fucks who have no business boning in the first place."

His stomach in knots Barney sits on the toilet, waiting, praying, asking for forgiveness. Whatever money is spent on escorts, he'll double and donate to a woman's shelter. How has he strayed so far from the path?

At 5 a.m. the phone rings. Barney, still sequestered in the bathroom, feels a surge of panic as Kyle answers.

"Hello? Yes, it is. Room number 306. Perfect. I'll see you shortly."

Kyle pounds on the bathroom door. "You all right, buddy? The girls are on their way up."

"Okay. I'll just be a moment."

"You warming up in there or what? Trying to get the blood flowing?"

"No, it's ... my stomach's a little upset."

"Bad timing, get it together, man. I've got some Imodium and Pepto-Bismol in my bag on the sink."

"Okay, thanks."

"Don't bitch out because of a tummy ache."

There's a knock at the door. The nerves, the dread, the adrenaline, Barney's stomach is in turmoil.

"Ladies, come on in. Thanks for arriving so promptly. Help yourself to a drink from the mini-bar if you'd like one."

Barney tries quietly pushing out the bad energy, but it's as loud as a cannon shot, his flatulence rattling the porcelain. He hears the girls laughing outside.

"O.M.G. Seriously?"

"That's nasty."

"Ladies, please, that's my associate. It's just some indigestion. Be nice. He's had a rough night. He's a good man, more importantly a paying customer, so let's show a little respect."

"Whatever. I hope he's got some matches in there."

There are no matches. He'll have to wait it out. The smell needs to be contained. He can't risk it wafting out, humiliating himself and Kyle in the process. Barney stays locked in the bathroom for another ten minutes until Kyle bangs on the door.

"Barney. Let's go. We're on the clock here. I'm not waiting."

"Okay, I'll be right there."

Barney brushes his teeth and washes his hands, killing another five minutes, with the fan on. When he finally steps out of the washroom, he sees Amber sitting on the edge of his bed, dressed in high heels, bouncing one leg over the other, looking annoyed.

In the opposite corner of the room Kyle is standing with his pants around his ankles, trying to wrap his mouth around Alexis' exposed breast, while she fondles his penis.

Barney freezes, transfixed, watching from the doorway.

Kyle gives his order to Alexis. "On your knees. I'm gonna fuck that sexy mouth of yours."

Alexis goes to her knees. "Yeah, baby, that's it. Now open up."

"Pass me my purse."

"Why?"

"I need to grab a condom."

"Not to blow me."

"I won't do it without one."

"I'm clean. Don't worry about it."

"I won't. No condom. No blow job."

"That's brutal."

"That's business."

"You've got such a beautiful mouth. Let me feel it."

"With a condom."

"Baby, that's awful. You don't want to be sucking on latex. Can't we negotiate?"

"How much?"

"Fifty dollars added to the hour."

"400."

"Bullshit. 100."

"200, final offer."

"Fine."

Amber put her skills to use. Entranced, Barney watches as Kyle's head tilts back in ecstasy.

"That's it baby, slobber on that dick. Yes ... fuck, yes. Fuckin' suck it!"

Amber snaps her fingers, trying to break the spell and get Barney's attention. "You know it's an hourly rate right? Time's ticking. You pay for the hour whether we do something or not."

"Yes ... Okay ... Sure ... Yes, of course."

"I don't want any confusion."

"No, of course not."

"And I'm not going down on you, not with the noises you were making in there."

"I understand. I wouldn't expect that ..."

Barney tries to focus on Amber but he's distracted by Kyle's performance.

"Fuck, yes, yes ... Stop, stop ... Get up ... Get on that bed, get on that bed ... ass in the air."

It's a riveting display. Barney's in awe of Kyle's bedroom acumen. Possessing absolute confidence, he knows exactly what he's doing. Amber follows his every command.

"That pussy's nice and wet. Oh fuck, yeah. It needs this cock."

Kyle rips open the condom packet, slides the condom on, and pushes in.

Alexis moans. Kyle groans.

"Fuck, yeah. That's a tight pussy. Just wrapped around this cock, clamping down on it."

Barney is mesmerized. Although Kyle's penis was not the weighted pendulum he expected, average by his estimation, Kyle was still clearly the master of technique. It was a virtuoso performance. Such focus, the perfect balance of sensitivity and aggression. Amber seemed completely subservient. When Kyle gave her an order, she acquiesced, simply repeating back what she had been told.

"I'm going to fill that hole."

"Yeah, fill that hole, baby."

"You need that dick."

"I need it. I need that dick"

Kyle still thrusting, turns his head to Barney. "You going to fuck this girl or what?" Kyle gives Alexis a quick spank across her ass. "I'm fucking loving this!"

He looks back to Barney. "If you don't, I will. Common man, get your dick wet."

Amber waves him off. "Don't worry about us. Finish what you're doing."

"We're paying for your time and if he won't take advantage of, I will. We can make this a threesome."

"You want me to work with her -- you want both of us -- that's an extra 500 each."

"Fine. You wanna be like that, take your clothes off, wait there, and I'll be with you in a second."

Alexis pushes Kyle off her. "Get the fuck off of me."

"Baby, what?"

"You don't disrespect me like that."

"Baby, no ... Baby, relax, you've got it wrong. I was just explaining to your friend -- "

"Let's get the fuck out of here, Amber. I'm done with this shit."

Alexis starts pulling on her clothes.

"Are you kidding me? This is a joke, right?"

"You see me laughing?"

"You can't leave me like this. That's not how you treat a client if you want repeat business."

The girls laugh in unison.

"Fuck your repeat business."

"Oh really? I don't think your supervisors are going to be too happy when they hear about this."

Alexis grabs her purse and gets up to leave. Kyle grabs her arm. "Baby, please. I apologize. I apologize. Your friend can leave and we'll finish what we started."

Amber reaches into her purse.

"Get your fucking hands off her or I'm spraying this can of mace between your eyes."

Kyle loosens his grip on Alexis who rips her arm away "Did this bitch just threaten me?"

"The hour's not up yet. This is a breach of contract!" proclaims Kyle.

Amber scoffs "Get your boyfriend to blow you. Your credit card's already been charged for the hour. You gotta problem with that, take it up with Visa."

Kyle moves forward. Barney steps in, grabbing Kyle's arm, holding him back. "Please go. Please just go, just leave. I'll accept the charges," pleads Barney with the girls.

Alexis keeps the mace aimed at Kyle. "Let's go shithead. See how tough you really are."

Kyle clenches his jaw, flaring out his nostrils. "Barney, get these skanks out of here while they're still breathing."

Barney yells at the girls, his voice cracking. "Go on! It's over! Get the heck out of here! Stop provoking him."

The girls break out in a fit of laughter. Tossing their hair back, they glide out the door.

Barney can hear them mocking his words, his voice, as they continue down the hallway.

Kyle smacks away Barney's hand. "Get your fucking hands off me."

Still standing too close, Kyle gives Barney a hard shove, putting him on his backside, pain shooting up his spine.

The moment is frozen in time. Kyle stands there naked, with half an erection. Barney looks up from the floor, hurt, betrayed, water welling up in his eyes.

"Barney. I'm sorry man. Stand up. I didn't mean that."

Barney's lip quivers as he tries to collect himself.

"Common. Stand up. Don't be so dramatic."

Kyle offers his hand, pulling Barney up onto the edge of his bed. Barney wipes his runny nose on the sleeve of his shirt.

Barney's voice trembles "I wanted this vacation to be special. I wanted it to work. Something for us to remember, and it's all gone wrong."

"C'mon ... No, it hasn't."

"Yes, it has, and now we're missing the one thing I looked forward to the most."

"What? The fucking swamp tromp?"

"Yes, the f-ing swamp tromp."

"When was that?"

"We're supposed to meet in the lobby in fifteen minutes."

"You want to do the swamp tromp? We'll do the swamp tromp. We can still make it."

"No, we can't."

"Bullshit. Yes, we can. You pack what we need. I'll jump in the shower, rub one out, get dressed. Hopefully we can stop for coffee along the way."

Hope renewed, Barney goes about filling water bottles and packing towels, insect repellent, camera, binoculars, an extra set of clothes, sunscreen with an spf-30 rating. When Kyle slips on his flip-flops, ready to go, Barney reminds him the expedition requires closed-toe shoes.

As they glide through the grass, across the water channels, on the airboat, Barney feels the glory of God's creation. The morning sky is on fire, streaked with vibrant colors, breathtaking. The pain is gone. He feels completely lucid. It's indisputable -- raw, infinite splendor surrounds them. He turns to share the moment with Kyle only to find him slumped over sleeping. As Kyle's friend he can't let the moment pass him by. With the noise of the fan, and the protective earmuffs, Barney gives Kyle's leg a shake to wake him. Kyle, disoriented, confused, almost falls off his seat. Barney smiles ear to ear, arms held high, as if to say, "Look at this! Isn't it amazing!"

Kyle give Barney the thumbs-up. The moment Barney turns around, Kyle goes back to sleep. Oblivious to Kyle's annoyance, Barney wakes him to look through his binoculars whenever there's another wildlife sighting. Not wanting to spoil Barney's moment Kyle begrudgingly obliges.

When the tour visits Clyde Butcher's Swamp Gallery Barney is so impressed by the black and white photographs of the Everglades that he purchases two copies of Mr. Butcher's "Visions of Florida" calendar, one for him and one for Kyle.

For lunch the tour stopped at Pit Bar-B-Que. Barney and Kyle take a seat under one of the thatched huts. Kyle orders a pitcher of Budweiser, while Barney asks for a root beer. For appetizers they have gator bites, frog legs, and conch fritters. Barney is interested in the catfish fillet but they decide to split a full rack of baby back ribs with a side of coleslaw and potato salad. Barney asks for Kyle's assessment when they were done. "Not the best I've ever had but decent."

By the time the tour gets back to the hotel, Barney is struggling to keep his eyes open. All the aches and pains inflicted upon him have returned. He's in desperate need of rest. Back in their room Barney closes the blinds and lies down on his bed.

Kyle sets the alarm on his phone. "We sleep for six hours, recharge, then plan our mission for tonight. It's our last night. We've got to make it count."

It's still an hour until the alarm, both men are submerged in a deep sleep when Kyle's phone rings. A rude awakening. Kyle checks the call display "You've gotta be kidding me." Closing his eyes he begrudgingly answers.

"What? ...Okay, yeah ... So what? You're seriously wasting my time with this...? This is fucking ridiculous ... Kirk may be lighting fires but he would've socked that kid in his ugly face for pulling a stunt like that ... Curtis needs to man up. He can't go crying to Mommy every time ... I don't care if he's eight, I'm not having my son grow into some limp-wristed whiner ... And I wonder where he gets that from...? Yeah, yeah, exactly, that's exactly what you're teaching him. You're turning him into a real diva, crying when things don't go his way ... That's not gonna be my boy. That's not gonna be my son ... As I say... As I say, the best lightening rod is your own spine. Curtis needs to learn that -- no one gives a shit about his feelings ... Oh, here we go again with the hysterics ... Go ahead. Go ahead and embarrass yourself. Call the parents but it won't change a goddamn thing, probably make it worse...

"That's it, Susie. That's it. That's what you do. Turn it into an attack on me ... Yeah, okay... don't you worry, I'll be back tomorrow to clean up the mess as usual... Okay, now you're just running in circles. Text me if there's a medical emergency, otherwise don't call me 'cause I'm not answering any more of your nonsense."

Kyle hangs up the phone.

"Barney. Wake up." Unable to go back to sleep, Kyle insists they start forming their game plan for the night. "We need to find our crowd, our music, our kind of fun."

They find it online. Kyle knows when he sees it. "This is it. This is the place for us."

"The Roundup" describes itself as South Florida's premier Country Western Night Club. The wallpaper on the homepage is plastered with sexy women wearing cowboy hats, with bikini tops and Daisy Dukes. They are advertising 'ladies night' that evening: "Ladies drink for free from 8 p.m. to close." Unfortunately the 'bikini/sexiest tan line competition' takes place after Kyle and Barney leave Miami. Still, if everything went as advertised, there was plenty to be excited about tonight.

"Barney, we need to wrangle up some drunk cowgirls and line dance them back to our hotel room."

It's a forty-five minute drive from the Palms. They stop at Walgreens to purchase a Styrofoam cooler, then drive to the liquor store and fill it with ice, beer, and vodka coolers. "Something sweet for the ladies." Although they're going to the bar Kyle insists on the cooler purchase. "Always be prepared. Never know where the night's gonna go. Might turn into a tailgater."

Having stocked their provisions, they jump on the I-95 to the Ronald Reagan turnpike, then take a couple of lefts, a couple of rights, and pull into the parking lot of

The Round Up.

It doesn't take long to get acquainted with the patrons. Within twenty minutes of walking through the doors, a fellow marine, introducing himself as Staff Sergeant Warren Dugget, salutes Kyle. "I saw you on the O'Reilly Factor. I wish I had your book here to sign. I know you've taken some heat over it, but for me and the men in my company, you're a living legend."

"It's an honor to hear that, Sergeant, but I wrote that book not for me but to recount the heroism of the men I fought beside, those brave warriors. Their story needed to be told."

"Amen. I'll raise a glass to that. Rounds of shots. I'm buying."

Warren Dugget is on leave from his second deployment in Afghanistan. He's at the bar with his sister, Katie Dugget, and a group of her friends. Katie wears white cowboy boots, a cowboy hat, a ripped denim miniskirt, and a piped cowboy shirt with embroidered roses on the shoulders. The top of it is unbuttoned enough to show off substantial cleavage busting through, holstered by a hot pink bra, the bottom of the shirt tied up in a bow to expose her bronzed midriff. Katie had a bright smile, perfect teeth, sparkling white, gleaming out in contrast to her dark tan. Her body is in great shape but it's her breasts that steal the show. Given their dimensions Barney suspects implants. Whatever the case, it isn't long before Kyle is removing shots of Jagermeister from between them, with his mouth.

The party is in full force. Kyle piggybacks Katie around the bar. "Barney, get a picture of this!"

Barney snaps a picture with his phone as Katie pours beer down Kyle's throat. Seeing Kyle so happy, Barney can't wipe the smile off his face. Finally they'd found a place that lived up to Kyle's rightful expectations, where he can cut loose and have some well-deserved fun.

Katie is the ringmaster. Barney is astounded by her ability to control her environment. At one point she orders he and Kyle to do body shots, though Barney has no idea what that entails. Katie convinces two new girlfriends, Becky and Britney, to lie down on a table in front of them, then instructs Kyle and Barney to lick the girls' stomachs below their navels. Barney guesses the girls are in their twenties. One of them has a belly button piercing, the other has a tattooed pistol handle peeking out from her panty-waist. Per Katie's instructions, they lick Becky and Britney's stomachs, then sprinkle salt on them. Katie sticks lemon wedges in the girls' mouths and hands out the shots of tequila.

"Drink, lick it, suck it," shouts Katie, raising a shot for herself.

Kyle and Barney clink glasses, shoot back the tequila, lick the salt off their girls' bellies, and remove the lemon wedge with their mouths. It's exhilarating! Barney is thrilled he managed to keep the tequila down and not make a fool of himself. Kyle clasps Barney's hand, pulling him towards him, patting him on the back. "We made it, solider. We made it."

Barney is sipping a club soda with Britney on his lap. Across the table Staff Sergeant Dugget has Becky draped over him as he orders another round of drinks.

"So Barney, you bad ass, Kyle tells me you fly fighter drones."

"I do. Yes. Surveillance, as well, but yes, that is correct."

"Tell me about it. That's where it's going right? You guys are in India, Pakistan, Africa. You're all over The Middle East. Fuck, you're everywhere now."

"Well, I mean … I mean, this applies to gathering intel as well, but, uh … obviously, as you know, in combat you implant tactics and strategy to inflict as much damage on the enemy as possible, while keeping personnel safe by limiting exposure. That's what drones allow."

"So you were Air Force before you started working with Central Intelligence?"

"Exactly, yes, exactly."

"Dropping hellfire missiles on the bad guys halfway across the world."

"Partly, yes, but the drones possess numerous capabilities."

"What's it like flying those things?"

"You work from ground control station. There's the pilots and sensor operators, We're going off a primary satellite link. But the operation of it ... really, it honestly can be kind of tricky, like flying an airplane looking through a straw. It depends, it varies, and with advancements from the Predator, to the Reaper, to the Avenger, it, um... there's a big push. Technology marches forward."

"Interesting. Now what's the cost on one of those units?"

"Significant, to say the least. For example, the Hawk drone that crashed in the marsh by Bloodworth Island near Dorchester County? An accountability report had it priced at 176 million. Now that's one of the largest, most advanced drones in the military but none of them come cheap."

"No shit."

"Yeah, the Hawk that's a special machine. It can fly for thirty hours without refueling at altitudes as high as eleven miles, and is forty-four feet long with a 116-foot wingspan."

"Technology man, you can't fuck with it."

"Technological innovation combined with the service of our brave military personnel -- that's how we keep America safe from those who seek to destroy it."

"We rule like nobody else can. We run this shit."

"Well, in essence, I agree."

"God bless America, boys!"

Barney and Warren spin around to see Kyle double fisting two beers while Katie makes out with a buxom blond girl directly in front of him.

"Your sister sure knows how to recruit 'em, Sergeant Dugget!" yells Kyle.

The night is playing out better then Barney could ever dare imagined. He feels a real connection with Britney. They're really hitting off. He tells her about his love of crossword puzzles and math games, revealing his idea for the donation site.

In the middle of explaining pay-system options Britney excuses herself to make a phone call.

Barney doesn't want to leave his seat but after waiting thirty minutes for Britney he desperately has to pee. On the walk to the washroom he spots Britney at another table, doing shots with a group of well-built guys. They have a brief moment of eye contact. Barney waves, Britney quickly looks away. Barney keeps walking.

Leaving the washroom, slouched over, defeated, Barney's gets his ass grabbed by a full figured woman with long brown hair extensions and a deep tan. She reminds him of how Katie might look in twenty years. Her novelty-sized breasts are boulders stretched between cracked leather, hanging over what appears to be a weight-lifting belt. Her lips look swollen and lumpy. She's surely had collagen injections. Those lips stretch over giant wet teeth as she flashes Barney a salacious smile. "Hey, hot stuff. I think you should buy me a drink."

Barney hands the bartender his money, then passes the woman her vodka tonic. She smells like hairspray and coconut.

"What's your name, sweetie?"

"Barney. Bill Barney."

"Nice to meet you, Bill Barney. I'm Drusilla."

As they sit for a drink, Barney watches Drusilla moisturize her hands, neck, and arms at least three times. Drusilla tells him she is s a realtor but makes her real money in front of a web cam, taking her clothes off for strangers in private chat rooms. Drusilla described herself as the dream MILF. In fact, she says Barney might be a bit too old for her. That doesn't stop her from quickly flashing him her glow-in-the-dark nipple ring. After asking him his favorite position, she announces hers before he can answer. "Mine's cowgirl, and it's the best view in town."

When the lights come on at bar close, the bouncers starts clearing everybody out. Kyle is groping Katie in one corner while her brother makes out with Becky in another. Meanwhile Barney sits alone, dejected, sipping his water, waiting patiently for them to realize it's time to leave.

Because he'd stopped drinking so early in the night, Barney claims the role of designated driver to everyone's applause. The group consists of Barney, Kyle, Katie, Warren, Becky, and Stacy (the naturally buxom blond with whom Katie had been making out earlier). It's decided they need some grease to sop up the alcohol. Barney's first directive is to locate the "golden arches". They aren't hard to find. Within minutes the gang are placing their orders at the drive-through: Two Big Mac combos, one quarter-pounder combo, forty McNuggets with sweet and sour sauce, as well as barbeque sauce, an extra order of large fries, and extra McChicken sauce.

They eat on the drive back to the hotel, stopping once for gas and a pack of Captain Blacks for Kyle. When they arrive at The Palms, Kyle grabs the cooler from the back and Barney hands the keys to the valet.

Walking across the beach, Kyle carries the cooler like it's a trophy fish. Finally he settles on a patch of sand and puts the cooler down. Kyle passes out beer to Sergeant Dugget and Barney. He offers Smirnov Ice to the girls but they ask for beer instead. Once everyone has a bottle in their hands, Kyle fires up a Captain Black, offering one to Warren, who accepts, then Barney, who declines.

Kyle raises his bottle in the air, "I'll keep it simple. Here's to making new friends and the good times that follow."

Once again Barney is impressed by how Kyle could make the simplest statement, so profound, so true. He encapsulated the sentiment perfectly in such a succinct manner.

Kyle sits with Katie by his side and, like an omniscient king, as he shares his wisdom the waves lap against the shore. "People say I'm some kind of an action hero but that bullshit doesn't exist. How can you fight with honor when the enemy has none? My first kill was an eight-year-old who approached our patrol with a soccer ball under his arm and a grenade behind his back. I've killed women too. No choice, they're ready to fire on me. Us against them since the dawn of time."

Kyle takes a slow draw from his beer.

"The accumulation of rapidly dwindling natural resources -- that's what these wars are about. Everything else is a distraction. There's not enough gold left in the earth to pay the world's debt. The Federal Reserve is a giant counterfeiting operation for the bankers that own it. Our money's not worth the paper it's printed on. The entire financial system is built on a house of cards and they know it. That's why there's such a massive land grab right now. That's where the real value is. It's a race to the finish line. You take what you can get and make sure you're on the side that gets it. Everyone's hiding behind a cause, pretending they're part of the solution when they're the fuckin' problem. This world is so full of hypocrites it's sickening. You can't disguise the fact -- all this chaos and bloodshed is for nothing more then material gain - but you know what? That's good enough for me. That's the only excuse I need to kill for my country. 'Cause in the end it comes down to one thing --survival."

Barney sees the way Katie looks up at Kyle, entranced. She knows she's looking at a real man, something most woman have probably never experienced. Then her brother clears his throat to speak.

"Kyle's right. One hundred per cent. These ignorant entitled assholes who shit on us and our actions, they need to realize major portions of the world are nothing more than industrial dumping grounds. If it weren't for us, they'd be living in that toxic mess. You can't stop progress and you don't shit where you eat, so pick a side. They're crying about the military industrial complex, the evil empire, up on their soap box, preaching equality and inter-connectedness, these fuckin' whiners would change their tune real fucking fast, if their kids were forced to claw through trash piles. They don't fuckin' get it, we get our hands dirty to keep theirs clean. 'Cause its all one love till you start getting fucked with."

Kyle reaches into the cooler for another beer. "Bravo, Staff Sergeant. Fuckin' bravo. You speak the truth, brother."

Barney concurs, "Those quickest to condemn are often the least informed."

Kyle cracks his beer. "A bunch of sheltered panty waists, fuckin' traitors, is what they are."

Katie springs up, her boobs bouncing with her. "No more angry talk. Right now we're here to have fun." She dusts the sand off her bottom, removes her top. Stripping down to her pink push-up bra and G-string. "Let's go swimming!"

Kyle smirks. "At this hour? I don't think so. You never seen the start of Jaws?"

Katie grabs Kyle by his wrist, trying to pull him up with her. "C'mon big tough army man. There's no sharks. Let's go."

"Girl, does it look like I'm wearing swim shorts?"

"Who cares? Go in your boxers. Go nude!"

Kyle plants his feet in the sand. "Go on, girl. You have your fun."

"Please? I'll make it worth your while."

"You can do that back in the hotel room. I'm not stepping in that water."

The new recruit, Stacy, whips off her shirt and shorts, revealing white bra and panties. "I'll go with you, Katie!"

Becky follows, shedding her dress, ready to hit the water in a baby blue bikini.

Katie bounces up and down in excitement, her breast threatening to spill out of her bra. "Yay! Girls rule, boys drool! Have fun being all grumpy and serious!"

The girls scamper and squeal their way into the water.

"I gotta ask, Warren. Katie -- obviously I'm sweet on the girl, but damn, as her brother, you ... shit, I mean ... I mean, don't take this wrong, but she's got a certain way about her."

"Katie's a little slut. She fucked all my friends in high school. She wanted breast implants for her graduation gift. She's a freak but so what? I don't give a shit. She's nice to me, always introduces me to her horny friends so I don't complain. So long as she's having fun and being safe about it."

"Does it get confusing when she starts making out with your girl-friend?"

"I roll my eyes and wait till she's done."

The girls' scream and splash around in the water, just being frisky at first, but when their breasts start rubbing together and the kissing starts, it proves to be too much for Kyle.

"Fuck sharks, Barney, we're going in. Warren's got Becky, you grab Stacy."

"Yeah, Stacy and I we haven't really ... formally met. It would be kind of presumptive of me."

"Barney, what have I been telling you? Take charge. Own the situation. Those milky white globes are waiting for you to motorboat them."

Kyle and Staff Sergeant Dugget charge into the water. Barney nervously wades in. Stacy laughs, splashing him with water. "Don't be scared. It warms up fast." She walks towards him, placing his hands on her waist, then running her hands over his chest. "You've got a nice body. How often do you work out?"

"I have to admit I've been somewhat lax during this vacation but normally I work out every day in one variation or another. Really though, diet is half the battle. I start the day with a nutritional shake in the morning that includes kale, pears, ginger, celery, and cucumber. For lunch and dinner, I have a lean meat protein, such as chicken, turkey, or grass-fed beef with a vegetable side. The key to healthy diet is to remove all added sugars. Pop is a big no-no. You want to cut back on refined grains as well. I substitute white rice with brown and pasta with quinoa. I love quinoa. For one dish, I'll pour marinara sauce over it with some ground turkey and."

"Is this how you normally receive a compliment?"

"My apologies. Yes, enough of that. I have a tendency to ramble when I'm, uh, I guess 'nervous' is the word."

"You're adorable."

Stacy leans in and locks lips with Barney. It was happening. This was real and he wasn't paying for it. Stacy slides his hand up her waist to her breasts. Barney feels the blood flowing to his nether regions. Then, because his mind insists on sabotaging the moment, he recalls Stacy's ex-boyfriend. On the drive to the hotel he overheard her complaining to Katie about what an inconsiderate asshole this boyfriend was. She also mentioned in passing that he played football for the Miami Hurricanes. She never said if he was black but, given their percentages among college athletes, it was more than likely. This realization leads to a surge of panic. Barney backs away as Stacy tries sliding her hands down his shorts.

"Whoa, whoa, whoa, perhaps we're getting a little carried away? It is, well ... It's a rather public setting."

"No one's watching. Don't be shy."

Barney needed to recalibrate. It was common knowledge, almost irrefutable, that, out of all ethnicities, black men had the largest penises. Pornography and National Geographic had proven as much. It was documented in scientific journals! Barney imagined it took Stacy two hands to wield her boyfriend's lengthy girth; for himself, one would more than suffice. How could he lessen Stacy's disappointment when he revealed himself to her? Should he warn her? A pre-emptive strike to lower expectation? But surely she must know the same standards do not apply. What did she expect from him? It must be torture for any black man not measuring up to at least eight inches.

His anxiety only makes matters worse. His attributes, already under question, are rapidly diminishing. Still Stacy keeps pushing forward. Another rejection on his behalf, at this initial stage, risks undoing their fragile union.

Forever his hero, Kyle interrupts the awkward moment "Everybody listen up! We need to bring this party back to the hotel room before we get arrested for public indecency!"

Standing in front of the Palms, Warren and Becky say their good-byes to the group, Kyle snaps into performed sobriety.

"Staff Sergeant, it was an honor. I'm a good judge of character and although we've just met, I can tell you're one of the good ones."

"The honor is all mine, sir. You lead by example and that's all one can ask."

They exchange a salute.

"Barney, it was nice to meet you. When the drones take over I'll know who to blame."

"Ha! Yes, well, my apologies in advance. But to be serious, it was great to make your acquaintance."

"Keep it real, Bill Barney."

Staff Sergeant and Becky get in their cab.

Stepping out of the elevator with Katie slung over his shoulder, squealing with laughter, Kyle jogs down the hallway with Barney and Stacy trailing behind them. Kyle bursts into the hotel room, flopping Katie down onto his bed.

"Take that wet bra off, girl. Let me see those beauties."

Katie laughs, unclasping her bra. "They cost me enough. No point hiding them."

Stacy ogles Katie's breasts. "You've got great tits."

"No, you've got great tits."

"Not like that, I don't."

"But yours are natural."

Kyle pounces on Katie. "Baby, it doesn't matter how they got there. So long as they look good and feel right. I can assure you these ones do." Kyle starts licking and nibbling her nipples. Katie's giggles turn into quiet moans.

Barney had hoped for a return to conversation but Stacy takes off her wet clothes and hops on Barney's bed, curling her finger at him in a "come hither" motion.

Barney cautiously lies down on the bed beside her.

"Your shorts are soaking wet. You going to take them off?"

"Yes, of course. Yes, sorry about that. Give me one second."

Barney grabs a pair of boxer shorts and disappears into the washroom to change. When he steps out, Stacy appears confused.

"I didn't really care that your shorts were wet."

"Oh, okay."

"I meant you should take them off, not get changed."

"Oh, okay." The moment of truth. "Excuse me one second."

Barney retreats to the bathroom. He knows he can't compare to the ex-boyfriend but he has to try. He has to take the chance. He's never been presented with such an opportunity. He hopes that, with an open mind, Stacy can lower her standards and accept his offering. He's ready to risk embarrassment, prepared for the rejection. In desperation he masturbates to correct his flaccid state but nothing works. He can't shake the imagined look of disappointment and disgust. No. It's impossible. Not with Kyle and Katie in the room to witness his humiliation. Barney relents, resigned to his flaccid fate. There he will hide, hoping to be forgotten. Sitting on the edge of the bathtub he closes his eyes, trying to disappear, but hears the gentle knock on the door. There is no escape.

"Are you all right?"

The question reveals the answer.

"No, unfortunately not. I'm very sorry. My stomach's turned on me. The fast food and alcohol -- I'm not used to it. I imagine I'll have to suffer through this until I empty out. Sorry to be so crude."

"Um, that's okay. I just ... I'm sorry you're not feeling well."

"Thank you. I appreciate your concern. Unfortunately I think I may be relegated to the bathroom for the rest of the evening. My stomach's really churning."

"Okay. Well, I don't want to seem rude but I think I might leave."

"No, no, please do. My sincere apologies. It's a regrettable turn of events. I was truly enjoying myself."

"Yeah, it's too bad."

Kyle pounds on the door. "Barney, what the fuck's going in there?"

"I'm having stomach issues."

"This poor girl's standing out here, waiting, feeling foolish, while you're in there shitting yourself again."

"Sadly, yes."

Stacy's nervous laughter can't conceal her discomfort. "No, it's all right. Really. He's not feeling well. I'm going to go."

"Don't let this ruin your night. There's room in our bed. You're welcome to join us," offers Kyle.

"No. Thank you. I should leave."

"Well, that's too bad. I'm sorry you have to leave here disappointed. It doesn't need to be that way."

"No, it's fine. I'm fine. It was nice to meet you, though. Bye, Katie."

"Bye, Stacy! Call me this week about the basketball tickets!"

Kyle slaps the bathroom door. "Hear that, Barney? She's leaving. I tried."

"Thanks, Kyle. I appreciate it."

Stacy confirms this "Bye, Barney. It was nice to meet you."

"Likewise Stacy. It was a real pleasure making your acquaintance. Again, my sincerest apologies."

Barney hears the door close as Stacy exits.

"You blew it, Barney. That chick was into you and you let her walk."

"I know. I'm sorry."

"Don't apologize to me. It's your loss."

"Okay..."

Barney doesn't leave the bathroom for another twenty minutes. Before leaving, he places his ear to the door, not wanting to interrupt anything. If Kyle and Katie are engaged in coitus, it's inaudible. He assumes it's safe for him to step out.

Sixty-nine. That's what they call it. Barney has an unimpeded view of Kyle's anus, with his legs spread wide, while Katie strokes his phallus.

"Excuse me, guys. Sorry..."

Kyle removes his nose from Katie's ass cheeks and glares at Barney, while Katie smiles and waves.

"Sorry to interrupt."

"Exactly. You're interrupting."

"I know. I'm sorry. Can I turn off the lights? Offer you a bit more privacy?"

"I've got the best view in town and you want to ruin it?"

"No, not at all. Of course not. It's just ... we kind of have an early flight tomorrow."

"While I've got this beautiful box in my face, the lights stay on."

Katie gently slaps Kyle's leg. "If he wants to sleep, let him turn the lights off."

"Let him put a pillow over his head. He's not going to ruin our good time because he let his walk out the door."

"No, Katie, he's right. Sorry for the intrusion. Really. I have an eye mask and ear plugs I can use."

"Then why the fuck are you bothering us?"

"I don't know. No excuse. I forgot. I apologize."

Ashamed by his transgression, his lack of consideration, Barney avoids eye contact while setting his alarm. Barney puts in his earplugs, pulls on his eye mask, and lies back in his bed. A sour note to the end of his night, the end of his vacation.

He awakens in darkness, his bladder full, unsure how long he's been asleep. One hour? Two? Three? Four? He stays still, not wanting to risk another disturbance until the alarm goes off. Ready to burst, he holds on for as long as he can until the pain is too much. Peeling off the eye mask, bracing for light, greeted by night. Everyone's sleeping, the lights are off. Barney tiptoes to the washroom.

There's a used condom floating in the toilet. Barney stares down at it while urinating, contemplating its existence. Was it a message from Kyle or did he simply forget to flush?

Ambient light from the windows highlights the contours of their naked bodies, Katie's head resting on Kyle's chest, a leg draped over his waist.

"God bless them," whispers Barney as he gets back to bed. Leaving his ear plugs and eye mask on the dresser, he falls asleep to the soothing sound of Kyle's stertor.

The ocean is black. The beach is covered in trash. Concrete rubble is scattered between giant cubes of rotting flesh. Kyle, ready for war, is dressed in full combat fatigues, yelling into a pink walkie-talkie, a children's toy.

Barney looks up, marveling at the cube, noticing the extensive marbling. "Who made these?"

Kyle does not hear him or chooses to ignore the question, continuing his communication over the walkie-talkie. "We have confirmation. Roger that. On our way."

Kyle sprints over the ruins. Barney runs after him, desperately trying to keep up.

In the midst of the debris, they reach a clearing of sand. Staff Sergeant Dugget is there waiting. When he sees them, he springs to his feet and charges towards Barney. Kyle holds him back.

Staff Sergeant Dugget points his finger in accusation "This motherfucker almost ruined it! This fuckin' chicken shit coward! He's lucky I found one!"

Kyle stays focused on the mission. "Where is it?"

"Stashed it around the corner." Staff Sergeant Dugget drags a woman's body -- naked with its head blown off -- across the sand. Kyle seizes control, shedding his backpack, kicking off his boots, then dropping his pants and underwear. He takes the body, hooking his arms under its legs, holding it up by the hips. Squatting over it so he can enter it vaginally, Kyle plunges downwards "This position places considerable strain on their necks."

Staff Sergeant screams in Barney's face. "You see! You see how we fuck these girls?"

With intense focus Kyle works the body like a jackhammer.

Barney panics. "Show me. Show me how. Show me how it works!"

White acrylic walls, a soothing steam, the shower set at the perfect temperature. Kyle stands naked under the showerhead, holding a bar of soap, looking at Barney. His eyes communicate love and understanding, his smile hints at play. "Let's get you cleaned up. Make you presentable."

Kyle begins washing Barney's privates. The sensation is incredible. Gentle at first as the warmth washes over him. He feels it rise, pressure mounting. Kyle smiles, scrubbing harder, working up a strong lather. It starts to pulse and surge.

"Kyle...Kyle... I can't... I can't... Oh God, oh my God, oh my God..."

On the cusp of release Kyle stops. "Okay, time to rinse off."

"No, please. Please. Don't stop. Not yet."

The moment begins to blur and fragment and blur...

Barney wakes in full tumescence. He hears them before he sees them. Katie and Kyle cast in the morning light, their bodies sliding over each other, the boorish showmanship removed from the act, leaving something pure and primal. Naked lust.

Barney turns to check the clock. As always he's wakened thirty minutes before the alarm. Rolling over, he faces the wall, his steadfast erection refusing to give way. He tries to ignore it, tries to ignore the grunting, the low lusty moans. Why could he not procure the pleasure of the flesh? Must he always be forced to the periphery? They'd found their rhythm. He could hear them slapping up against each other, wet expulsions of air from Katie's vagina. He contemplated putting his earplugs back in but the temptation to keep listening was too much.

Barney rolls back over. Peeking out from his bed sheets, he can see it from the perfect vantage point. Kyle lies behind Katie, holding one of her legs up in the air as he drives into her. Hypnotic. Mesmerizing. Barney strokes himself, keeping time with Kyle thrusting. Hard cock and pussy lips ...

"Oh my God, oh my God, oh my God!!!!"

"Fuck... fuck ... oh baby ... Oh fuck ... Fuck ...Yes!"

The trigger, the rush ... Everything quakes until the cycle explodes into a toe-curling gush of ecstasy, Barney climaxing with his dearest friend.

"Unnnhhhuuughhhhhnnnnn!"

Barney wipes off the semen onto his bed sheets.

Katie is in the shower when the alarm goes off. Kyle remains in bed, Barney watches him playing with his penis, staring at the wall like he's trying to remember something.

"Barney wake up."

Barney quickly closes his eyes then feigns grogginess, pretending to wake from deep sleep.

"Jesus, you're a heavy sleeper. You sink like a stone, don't ya?"

"Maybe ...Yeah. I think the sleep deprivation finally caught up with me."

Katie steps out of the bathroom, dressed, toweling her hair off. She smiles at Barney. "Morning, Barney."

"Morning, Katie."

"Thanks for being cool about everything."

"Certainly. No problem."

Kyle scoffs. Katie throws her towel at him. "Cover up, cowboy. Put some pants on."

"You couldn't wait to get them off last night."

"Playtime's over. You two have a plane to catch and haven't packed your bags yet."

"You hear that, Barney? She's got what she wanted and wants to send me packing. How 'bout I buy an extra ticket and take you home with me?"

"Nope, but you can visit any time." Katie grabs her purse. "Have a safe trip back, gentlemen."

With the wink of an eye and a shake of the ass, Katie walks out the door.

"Damn, that girl knew how to ride. Top five easy. What a night."

"So, you're glad you made the trip?"

"Hell, yeah."

The approval he's been waiting for, music to his ears. Barney smiles and nods back. "Well, it wouldn't have been the same without you."

On the drive to the airport, Kyle's phone rings. Barney suggests he take the call on speakerphone while driving to be safe. Kyle ignores him.

"This better be a medical emergency ... When did that start...? And you took her temperature? Was it something she ate? What'd you feed her last night? Don't you fuckin' start ... I'm not ... Look, I'm trying to rule things out. It's called the process of elimination ... You're unbelievable. Our little girl's sick and you're attacking me. You need a serious adjustment ... Listen. Stop talking and listen. I'm on my way to the airport right now. It's a three-hour flight. I will call for a status report as soon as we hit the tarmac. Make sure you keep her hydrated. If her temperature spikes, if she keeps throwing up, you take her to the hospital ... No. ... No, I think I do. I do have to tell you that -- "

Kyle holds the phone out in front of his face. "That fucking bitch. Fucking hung up on me again. Our daughter's sick and she's playing games."

"Is it serious?"

"She's throwing up. Probably picked up the stomach flu at school."

"Food poisoning, maybe?"

"No, she ate with her brothers and they're fine."

"Then it's probably a stomach bug. I'm sure she'll be fine."

"I think so. Kids get sick. I've been through this before."

After a bumpy start the turbulence levels off and it's a smooth flight the rest of the way. Barney had given Kyle his window seat and he's glad he did. He likes watching Kyle look out the window. As the plane commences it's landing, Kyle is lost in contemplation. "You know, there's just no way to guarantee your children's safety. It's tough."

"It's to bad there aren't more fathers like you, Kyle. The world would be a better place."

"It's a tremendous responsibility but if you can't commit to your children, provide for them and their future, what good are you?"

"That's a good question."

"You imagine you'll have kids one day?"

"If I meet the right person, the right woman. I also have a number in mind, a financial marker I need to meet, before I'd consider it."

"Word of advice, Barney. You're not getting any younger. You find that special someone, don't wait. You've got a high-paying job that's not going anywhere. You're safe. Start a family."

"You're probably right."

"Sure I am. You know people often ask me, what it means, what it takes, to be a leader of men. You know what I tell them?"

Barney waits with bated breath.

"Sacrifice. It's about sacrifice. Pure and simple."

ELMHURST

IRIS SPENDS THE MORNING IN THE GARDEN PULLING WEEDS, PRUNING, planting, and watering. Around noon she goes inside for lunch. Having an appetite was a good thing at her age. After lunch she'll mow the lawn and skim the Koi pond with no Koi.

During lunch Iris is startled by a deafening screech followed by a series of high-pitched beeps. They sound mechanical, alien. Iris puts down her BLT and grabs the deer rifle from the kitchen closet. She creeps down the hallway toward her bedroom, the volume increasing as she approaches the source. Iris stops at the doorway. Safety off, finger on the trigger, she peeks around the corner into the bedroom.

Nothing. The room is empty, everything in its place. The noise has stopped. Iris steps inside, inching towards the closet when another screech spins her around, nearly tipping her over. Steadying herself Iris notices the door to the bedroom bathroom is open, then another jarring beep, confirming to her that it is in her bathroom.

Colors ablaze, a dazzling display of green, yellow, and orange, each one fading seamlessly into the next. It sits perched on the shower curtain rod, its striking plumage popping out against the stark white tiling.

The bird's beauty strikes Iris. It must have flown in through the open bedroom window. The question is where did it come from. Obviously it was someone's pet. There were no parrots indigenous to Winnipeg.

Possessing a myriad of vocal gestures, it beeped, squeaked, screeched, squawked, clicked, and clacked.

The small parrot captivates Iris as it flutters around her bathroom, hopping from the windowsill to the towel rack and back to the shower curtain. And it seems equally inquisitive about her, staring back, its tiny head bobbing, swiveling back and forth.

Iris closes the open window and goes around the house closing all the blinds to ensure the bird will not fly into the windows. When she comes back to the bathroom the bird leaps from the curtain onto Iris's shoulder. It happens in an instant, before Iris can react. Slowly, with caution, Iris turns her head briefly, making eye contact, and then the parrot goes back to scanning its surroundings. The parrot stays on its new perch as Iris walks into the living room. Iris takes this as a compliment.

Animal control sends a toad of a man with a giant beer belly, large hairless calves, and a ponytail. The parrot is patrolling the couch when he arrives. The man throws a sack over the bird, wrapping his hands around it, and then empties the bird into a cage in the back of his truck. Iris asks him if he knows the breed of the parrot. The man shrugs his shoulders. "Some kind of a parakeet." He closes the back door of the panel and drives away.

Days pass. Iris keeps thinking about the bird. She visits a pet store. None of the birds match her parrot. Iris describes it to a worker that grabs a book on parrots. They leaf through it together until Iris spots the page with her parrot. It was a Sun Conure.

Iris hoped she'd hear a response from the owners once they recovered their parrot, a confirmation of its well-being, a thank-you perhaps, but surely they would have claimed it by now. She wonders if animal control would call to let her know if someone has collected the parrot.

Two weeks pass with still no word. Iris calls animal control, inquiring about the parrot. The woman who answers gives an exasperated sigh, brusquely informing Iris in a most patronizing manner that the parrot has a home and is being looked after.

Summer draws to a close. Iris calls her friend Mabel. They discuss one last trip to the perennial garden before fall and partnerings for bridge that week. They discuss whether or not they're attending their church's potluck dinner, and what they might bring if they do go. Mabel envisions scalloped potatoes. Iris decides she'll bring a dessert, make a pie with the crab apples she's collected from the backyard. They talk for close to an hour, exchanging idle gossip and opinions on the week's news. Eventually the conversation wanes and they agree to end it. Iris flips through TV channels for several minutes before deciding it's time to turn in.

She reads in bed, absorbed by a book about the doomed Franklin expedition, until her eyes grow heavy. Ready for sleep, she remembers to take her heart medication. Standing at the kitchen sink, washing her pills back with a glass of water, a light flashes on outside the kitchen window. Iris realizes it's coming from the basement, the laundry room, which is directly under the kitchen. It fills her with immediate panic. There's someone in the house.

Did she forget to lock the garage door? How'd they get in? What do they want? Iris grabs the fridge handle, the imminent threat provoking a rush of fear so strong it weakens her knees. What if they come upstairs? They will. Very soon, she'll hear their footsteps. Paralyzed, she forces herself into action, creeping into the living room where she last left the phone, desperate not to make any noise that will alert the intruders.

Iris apologizes profusely to the police for wasting their time. The officers insist she has nothing for which to apologize. It's always better to err on the side of caution. She had good reason to call them. A loose lighting fixture looked to be the culprit. A light tap on the bulb could turn it on or off.

Iris is ashamed. She overreacted, like a helpless old fool, coming unglued so easily, jumping to the worst possible conclusion and completely unraveling at the thought of it. Age and an overactive imagination are no excuse. To abandon her faculties so easily is an embarrassment.

The leaves change color, heralding the fall. There's a chill in the air. Iris aches from her arthritis, which has started acting up. She wonders how many more seasons she'll last in her home on Elmhurst. The maintenance on the house is getting more expensive each year, the cracks in the foundation spreading. Friends and family suggest moving into an assisted living center. There are many options for her to consider with price, service, and location being the key factors. Right now that doesn't matter. She needs to get preparations underway for another winter.

Iris puts on her boots and jacket, ready to go out and get some yard work done, when the phone rings.

"Hello?"

"Hi."

"Hi ...Oh, hi! How are you? It's been so long. You sound different."

"Sorry. I'm losing my voice."

"Are you sick?"

"A little run down, no big deal."

"Well, you're taking care of yourself, I hope?"

"I'm fine. How are you?"

"Well, there's not a lot to tell. I'm amazed this old house hasn't collapsed on my head yet," says Iris.

"Why, it's falling apart?"

"There's a long, expensive, list of repairs. The biggest problem is a shifting foundation."

"What do you about that?"

"Sell the house if anyone's desperate enough to buy it."

"Nah. That house is solid."

"Tell that to the cracks in my ceiling."

"What else is going on?"

"Nothing. My life is boring. I had surgery for my cataracts in May. I'm still working in the garden, volunteering at the church, playing bridge on Wednesdays."

"That's good. You're staying active, keeping sharp."

"Oh please, I'm walking around in a fog half the time. One day blurs into the next."

"Come on, now."

"Listen, I go to more funerals then birthdays at this point. If I want to see a friend I just look in the obituaries."

"Now you're just being morbid."

"It's true! They're all dropping off. My friends are dying. I could be next." Iris laughs. It was too cruel not to joke about.

"I know. There's a lot of fight in you yet."

"Oh, you think so, do you?"

"I know so."

"Well, I'll tell you, I can hardly be bothered to get out of bed some mornings but we'll see. How have you been? Where are you these days?"

There's a pause. Iris can hear the gears turning.

"You know, I wanted to ask. I was hoping to stay with you for awhile, just a couple of weeks."

"Of course. You're always welcome here."

"It's appreciated. I'll probably be there sometime next week. I'll give you a heads-up when I'm close."

"You're driving?"

"Yeah."

"Where are you now?"

"On the road."

"Where?"

"Between here and there. Sorry, I'm using somebody else's phone. I should let you go. I'll call you when I'm close."

Iris wakes up cold. She'd need to turn the furnace on soon. A week has passed since Clyde's phone call. The weather channel issued frost warnings for that week. Iris puts on her housecoat and brushes her teeth. She leaves the radio off while making breakfast; sick of hearing the same recycled stories.

Peeling a hardboiled egg, Iris stares out the window at dreary grey skies, the wind howling, blowing the last leaves from the branches. "What a miserable day," she mentions to no an empty house.

The phone rings.

"Hello?"

"Hi."

"I was wondering when I was going to hear from you."

"Yeah, sorry. I was held up for awhile, but I'm close now. I'll be crossing into Manitoba this evening."

"Will you be here for supper?"

"Probably not."

"I'll have something waiting for you. What do you want? I'm going to the grocery store this afternoon. Is there anything I should get for you?"

"I don't know, whatever you're having."

"I could make the chicken-stir fry. I know you like that and it's easy to heat up."

"Perfect. I'll see you this evening."

"Okay, I'll have your room ready."

He arrives in the freezing rain. The light is fading fast. Parked in the driveway, Clyde grabs a canvas duffle bag from the back seat of his truck. It's been five years since Iris last saw Clyde. But his face has aged at least ten years, it's lined and cracked, showing stress fractures beyond his years. Bright eyes now dull carry dark bags under them. Iris is shocked to see Clyde so bloated, a gut protruding over his waist. He's packed on at least sixty extra pounds. Iris knows clothes don't make the man but in this case, with Clyde wearing that filthy grey sweater and torn blue jeans, they certainly don't help. She can feel her anxiety levels rising.

She watches Clyde cover the chicken stir-fry in rooster sauce and devour it as if he hasn't eaten in days. When he's finished eating they move into the living room. Iris rests in the lounge chair. Clyde sits opposite her on the couch in front of the window. Outside, streetlights illuminate icy globules of rain as they streak past.

"So, what have you been up to?"

"Not much. Working when I have to."

"Where?"

"Wherever it's available. Last job was working on a seismic line crew around Alberta."

"How was that?"

"Entry level, low pay, long hours. You'd be out of town thirty days at a time."

"My goodness. That's a stretch, and what kind of work are you doing?"

"First I worked as a packer carrying supplies, clearing debris from the lines. Then they had me working as a jug hound, helping the observers, installing and retrieving their equipment, hauling cable, geo-phones, all their recording gear. Eventually they offered to make me a line boss. At my age I probably should have accepted, kept working, climbing the ranks, the pay scale."

"Why'd you stop?"

"I don't know... My ego got in the way. I wanted to create and develop my own business."

"What kind of business?"

"Never figured that out."

"So when did you stop doing the seismic work?"

"Over a year ago."

"Okay."

"How's Ingrid doing?"

"It was tough losing Bernie, but she's doing well otherwise. Apparently cousin Peter received a lucrative promotion from his firm."

"Great."

"He just bought a vacation home in Florida. He's flying Ingrid out there this Christmas."

"Nice."

"It's beautiful, right by the ocean with its own boat launch."

"Wow."

"Yeah. He got it cheap during the housing crash."

"Deals to be had if you've got the money."

"There sure is."

"How's Henry? He still with Angie?"

"Oh yes, they just moved from Swift Current and bought a home together in Saskatoon."

"He made the commitment."

"They've been together awhile now. It makes sense."

'Henry works in Potash, right?" asks Clyde

"Yes."

"What's he do again?"

"Maintenance supervisor."

"He must be raking it in."

"I don't know. Last time we spoke he'd bought a new snowmobile."

"Did he sell his old sled?"

"Oh, I don't know."

"Sounds like he's doing well."

"I think so. He seems happy."

"Good."

Clyde yawns.

"You must be tired."

"A lot of driving today."

"You get all the rest you need while you're here. Your bed is made. There's clean towels hanging on the rack if you need a shower."

"Perfect. Thanks."

"My pleasure. I'm just so happy to see you."

"Yeah ... You want to hear a joke?"

"That depends on the joke."

"A clown is walking hand in hand with a child into the woods. The child looks up at the clown and says, 'It's getting dark out! I'm scared! Let's go back!' The clown shakes his head and they keep walking. The child cries, begging the clown, 'Mister, please! It's dark. I'm scared. I want to go back.' The clown stops, turns to the kid, and says, 'How do you think I feel? I have to walk out of here alone.'"

"I don't get it?"

"You don't?"

"No."

"They walk into the woods together and the clown leaves by himself."

"I don't understand."

"The implication being that the clown kills the kid."

"Oh, that is awful. Clyde, that's not funny. How is that funny?"

"Because it's so awful, I guess."

"Well, that's really terrible. You've got to be some kind of sicko to think that is funny."

"I guess so."

"I mean, really, that's really evil."

Clyde can't keep a straight face.

"What? I'm serious. You think that's funny?"

Clyde cracks up laughing.

"Well, that's just awful."

"I know. I know it is. I'm sorry."

"Honestly, you should have your head examined if you think that's funny!"

The laughter becomes contagious, Iris joining in despite herself.

During her prayers that night Iris gives thanks for her grandson arriving safely. She welcomes his company and hopes it will be a visit she'll remember fondly.

In the middle of the night Iris wakens with a dry throat. The glass of water by her bedside is almost empty. She walks to kitchen to refill it. As she turns the corner into the kitchen, the basement light flashes on again.

Iris tries to remain calm, resist the panic, be rational. It's merely a broken light fixture or faulty wiring. She knows this, but she can't shake the feeling of dread. Trying to ignore it, Iris pours herself a glass of water, working up the courage to go into the basement and unplug the bulb.

Iris grabs the flashlight from the closet when she's startled by Clyde opening his bedroom door. She manages to contain her yelp, realizing its him. Clyde crosses the hallway into the bathroom. Iris waits. When he's finished in the bathroom she calls his name.

"Clyde, while you're still up, would you mind going to the basement and removing a light bulb for me? It keeps flicking on and off. I might have to change the fixture but just take the bulb out for now."

Clyde nods, half asleep. Iris hands him the flashlight and he goes downstairs. She watches the light go off. Clyde returns, handing her the bulb.

"Thank you."

"No problem," Clyde mumbles, going back to bed.

Iris stashes the bulb in a bag of spares in the broom closet.

She has breakfast by herself the next morning. It's past noon and Clyde has still not risen from a slumber that's going on for fourteen hours. She'll leave him be. He must be exhausted from his travels. He can sleep all day if he needs to. On that thought, she hears his door open, then the bathroom door close. The shower turns on. The day has begun.

Iris makes Clyde breakfast: eggs (over easy) and bacon, with a side of toast (marble rye), orange juice, and a cup of coffee. During breakfast Clyde mentions he'd like to change rooms. Currently he's in his uncle's old room, two doors down the hallway from Iris's bedroom, which is where he used to stay when visiting. He wants to move to the guest room in the basement. Iris understands. It's a bigger room with more privacy and its own bathroom. It's agreed he'll move into the basement.

While Clyde loads the dishwasher, Iris asks if he has any specific plans during his stay.

"Not really. Take some time to figure things out. Strategize. Come up with a game plan. Help you out with any chores that need to get done."

During his first few weeks back Clyde raked the lawn, burned the leaves, cleaned out the eavestroughs, washed the windows, pulled back the awnings, chopped down some trees, stacked firewood. He helped Iris with the groceries, driving to the store and carrying the bags. Iris paid for everything but with his help around the house she considered it a fair trade. He was family after all.

It was a fine arrangement during those last weeks of fall, and then winter arrived. At which point Iris rarely saw Clyde. He withdrew, only leaving the basement for food and to shovel the driveway if needed. As the days grew darker so did the silence. Clyde rarely spoke a word during their meals, which were the only times she'd see him. He evaded every question with short, stilted responses.

Something was wrong. One night, during dinner, she asked him outright what it was. He said, "Nothing," and kept eating.

The next day Clyde came up from the basement and announced he was going for a walk to get some fresh air. Iris was happy to hear it. With the exception of some obligatory snow shoveling Clyde hadn't left the house in over two weeks. To her great surprise Clyde returned that day cleanly shaven with a haircut.

Things were improving. Clyde stopped sleeping past noon. He checked the classified section for work. He was back on the job hunt. Iris didn't have a computer so Clyde would drive to the library in the afternoon to go online and search for job postings. He'd take her car to get there. His insurance had lapsed. He'd renew it as soon as he started earning again. Iris was just relieved to have him talking again. There was a spark in his eyes again, the foreboding specter of depression lifting. Iris found the two of them engaged in actual conversation. Clyde expressed his desire to travel to Asia, Europe, and South America. Despite having never been to these places, he had a gift for describing what made each location unique. He spoke of their people, their culture. He was interested in the "character and circumstance" that formed a society.

This positive charge carried on through December. The holiday season was imbued with story and laughter. Clyde was curious about his ancestors on Iris's side of the family. She informed him as best she could, enjoying the process of reflection. Iris was grateful to share the holidays with her grandson. He helped her hang lights outside. He helped her bring back a tree from the church's Christmas tree sale, and they decorated it that same night. Iris couldn't recall the last time she had set up a tree for Christmas, but they'd picked the right one, the branches were full, and it was the perfect height for the living room. Iris was so proud of their tree, she took a picture of Clyde standing in front of it, giving the thumbs-up.

Clyde's job search continues in the New Year. Clyde heads to the library each afternoon. Iris suggests he might want to consider going back to school, furthering his education. She'd continue providing room and board if he could acquire student loans to pay for his tuition. Clyde agrees it's worth considering once he finds a career path he can commit to, one with a future, but he doesn't feel there's any point in pursuing a diploma if it doesn't translate into work. He can't be left unemployed when school is over, carrying a massive student debt. Iris sees his point but warns him not to drag his heels. He'd need to start applying for the fall semester soon, if he decides to go. She recommends looking into travel tourism.

The next day, after returning from an early doctor's appointment, Iris sits at the kitchen table to write out a grocery list for the afternoon. When she hears Clyde making his way upstairs, she looks up. Clyde is standing with one towel wrapped around his waist, another towel pressed into his face, soaked in blood.

"I need a Band-Aid or something."

"What happened? Clyde, what happened? Let me see."

Iris pulls away the bloody towel from Clyde's face. Blood is seeping out of two gashes, one down his forehead, the other across the bridge of his nose.

"What happened?"

"I stepped out of the shower, slipped and crashed into the mirror."

"You need stitches. We need to take you to the hospital."

"No. No, I'm not going there. That's not happening. I just need to clean it up and get a few Band-Aids on it, use some Crazy Glue in there. I'll be fine."

Blood leaks down his nose into his eyes. It drips onto the kitchen floor.

"Forget Crazy Glue. You need to sit down."

Clyde takes a seat at the table, keeping the towel pressed to his face. Iris grabs the first aid kit. They cuts are deep and jagged. She cleans and disinfects before pinching the skin close with butterfly bandages, and then wrapping the forehead in gauze.

"You need stitches."

"It's fine."

"That's not going to close up properly."

"Sure it will."

"It's going to leave a scar."

"Chicks dig scars. I'm not going to the hospital. It'll congeal. I'll be fine."

"I don't like this. You should be going to the hospital. How the heck did you manage to hit the mirror like that?"

"I'll clean up all the broken glass as soon as the bleeding slows down."

"You think I care about that? It's you I'm worried about."

"Looks worse, then it is."

For the next three hours Iris hounds Clyde about going to the hospital but he refuses to go.

"Is that because you're stubborn or scared?"

"Both, but most importantly, I don't feel the need to waste anyone's time on this. It'll heal on its own."

While cleaning up the mess of glass and blood in the basement Iris has to wonder how Clyde managed to fall face first into the mirror. It doesn't make sense with the angles of the washroom. There was no room for it. You couldn't just stumble into the mirror. You'd have to be smashed against it.

After the bloodletting things return to a version of normal. Conversation was stilted somewhat, but at least Clyde was still being proactive about finding work. The important thing was forward progress.

They had lamb chops for dinner on the night he asked her about the burn ward. Clyde hadn't spoken a word during dinner before bringing it up.

"When you were a nurse you worked the burn unit right?"

"I did. Why?"

"I remember seeing some hospital drama, probably ER, a patient was brought in ... I think it was a firefighter, maybe an electrician. Anyway, he has third-degree burns covering his body. It looks horrific. He's conscious the whole time, screaming in agony. They pump him full of morphine and bring in his family to say their final good-byes because he's not going to survive the night. In his condition his body won't be able to fight off bacterial infections, is that true?"

"Deep or widespread burns can increase your risk of sepsis infection, which can kill you."

"It's just brutal."

"I did not like working the burn unit. I hated its existence. The smell, the sound, it was awful. With serious life-threatening burns you're witnessing the worst suffering imaginable. It's a nightmare. It breaks your heart."

"How did you deal it?"

"You do your best to treat the patient and comfort their family. Save your tears for later."

"That would ruin me. I couldn't do it."

"You could, you would, if that was your training, if it was your job."

In the following weeks productivity grinds to a halt. Clyde secludes himself in the basement again. He stops going to the library, stops searching for work, stops helping. From January to February it seemed to Iris that the only time she saw Clyde was during the meals he didn't sleep through. It was unacceptable. Finally, one day during lunch -- or, in Clyde's case, breakfast -- Iris gives an ultimatum.

"Clyde, you're thirty-six years old, living in your grandmother's basement. I don't mind covering your expenses, if you're making an effort. It's either back to school or back on the job hunt. You don't get to stay in bed all day, then make an appearance when you're hungry. That's not how it works."

Clyde places his dishes in the dishwasher. He says, "I'll start setting my alarm again," and heads back downstairs.

The following morning, after a fretful sleep, Iris sits down in front of the TV with her coffee and toast. She turns to the Weather Channel. It's -30°C outside and dropping. Iris switches channels to the morning news.

From the corner of her eye she catches Clyde standing in the doorway between the kitchen and living room. He's ghastly pale, dressed in a baggy white T-shirt and grey jogging pants. The noise rises in his throat, a low creaking enunciation.

"Wwwrrronnggggg..."

His eyes roll back with his tongue. Legs buckling, Clyde's head smacks against the side of the doorframe as he crashes to the ground. Iris rushes to the phone, ready to call an ambulance.

"What are you doing?"

Iris, holding the receiver, looks down at Clyde, who's groggy but conscious.

"Calling an ambulance," answers Iris.

Clyde snaps into focus. "Don't do that."

"You fainted."

"I'll be fine. Leave it. Don't call an ambulance"

"I'm calling an ambulance."

Clyde sits up. "Do not call an ambulance."

"Then I'm bringing you to the hospital."

"No, you're not."

Clyde stands and staggers over to the couch. Iris hangs up the phone, following him. She checks his pulse. It's low, 48 beats pets minute. His skin is cold and clammy. Again, she insists they go to the hospital. Clyde refuses.

"Let me sleep, get some rest. That's what I need."

Iris watches Clyde while he sleeps. His breathing is so shallow that several times she has to check to see that he hasn't stopped breathing.

When Clyde wakes in the late afternoon, Iris brings him freshly squeezed orange juice. He guzzles it back, thanks her, then descends back into the basement.

The sun has set. It's well past dinner. Clyde had yet to surface. Iris is worried. She goes downstairs. She turns on the lights to see her way to his room at the back of the basement, past the pool table.

The door is locked. Through the crack beneath the door she can see the lights are off. Her fear is palpable, the flight instinct screaming to turn around, go back upstairs. But her stubborn rational and concern for her grandson keeps her in place.

Iris gently knocks on the door. "Clyde?"

She knocks again, louder this time. "Clyde. I'm going to start making diner."

Her hearts thuds inside her chest. "Are you hungry?"

No response.

"Clyde?" Something is wrong. "How are you feeling?"

Then a voice from the darkness. "What happened?"

"To what? Can you open the door?"

She hears him humming. The hum mutates into a menacing vibrato that shift into a broken croak.

"Clyde?"

Clyde slams against the door, pounding against it. Iris stumbles back, bumping into the pool table. Reaching her limit, scared beyond comprehension. Iris breaks away, praying it doesn't follow. Clutching the railing, she climbs the stairs. As she reaches the top, the noise stops, and the house falls quiet.

On the verge of tears Iris wants to call the police. But what will she tell them? She doesn't want to get Clyde in trouble. He hasn't broken any laws. But what if it escalates? Is this how it started with his mother? Should she intervene now?

Iris calls her son Henry.

"How's he scaring you?"

"He's acting very strange."

"How?"

"This morning I'm watching the morning news when Clyde appears in the doorway looking white as a ghost, uttering something unintelligible, like a croak, before passing out, crashing to the ground, hitting his head on the door frame."

"He fainted?"

"I was ready to call an ambulance. I had the phone in my hand ready to dial 9-1-1 right when he regained consciousness. He was adamant that I not call them, insisting he was fine. I should've. I should've called them right then and there."

"So how is he now?"

"I don't know. That's the problem. He'd been in the basement all day. When he missed dinnertime I went to check on him and his door's locked. I knock, he doesn't answer. When I ask him to open the door, he starts humming, making this awful rattle with his throat, this horrible croak."

"Was he having a seizure?"

"Maybe. Maybe, I don't know. Because then he started slamming against the door."

"What? What's happening now?"

"I left. I went upstairs."

"So he's downstairs, you're upstairs."

"Yes. Don't ask me to go back down there."

"No, don't. You should call the cops."

"I don't want to get him in trouble, but it's not normal, he's not right."

"They're just going to make sure you're both safe."

"What do I tell them?"

"Tell them your grandson is acting strange, mention he fainted earlier, hit his head. Say you're concerned for his safety as well as yours."

Clyde is not responding to the police officers request to open the door. Iris finds the key and opens it. The police officer flips on the light. Clyde appears to be asleep. The officer shakes him by his shoulder.

"Clyde, wake up. You need to wake up, buddy."

Clyde can barely keep his eyes open, as though someone shot him with a tranquilizer.

"Clyde, your grandmother's concerned about you."

"Why are the cops here?"

Clyde is barely audible. The officer holds up his hand, signaling Iris to stand down, he'll handle the question, giving her a nod of assurance.

"She's worried about you, Clyde. I understand you fainted earlier?"

Clyde's eyes droop, then close.

"Clyde, I need you to stay awake. Did you take something, Clyde? Are you on any drugs or medications? You're not in any trouble. We just need to know."

"No." His eyes remain closed.

"I understand you fainted earlier."

"Yeah."

"Any idea why you fainted? Do you have any medical conditions?"

No answer.

"Clyde, can you sit up for us? We'd like to ask you some questions."

With some struggle, Clyde props himself up against the headboard.

"Why do you think you're so tired, Clyde?"

"Winter doldrums. Lack of vitamin D. I don't know."

"Think you're coming down with something?"

"Maybe."

"How long have been staying with your grandma?"

"Since late September."

"Where were you before you arrived at your grandma's?"

"Nackawic."

"Where?"

"Nackawic, New Brunswick."

"What were you doing there?"

"Guarding the world's largest ax. Am I being charged?"

"With what, Clyde?"

"You tell me."

"We're just asking standard questions. Do you have a problem with that?"

"If you want to do a background, my wallet's on the dresser."

"Should we?"

"If that's where this is going."

"How long do you plan on staying at your grandmother's for?"

"Why?"

"It's a simple question."

Iris doesn't like the direction of the conversation and interjects.

"He's a good person, a good grandson, and he's done nothing wrong. My concern was more for him, and he seems better now. In my old age I lean towards hysteria. Officers, I thank you for stopping by and I apologize for wasting your time."

The police officers pull Iris aside to confirm her wishes. She insists her concerns have been alleviated, persuading them to leave. Iris sees them to the door, promising to call if there's any reoccurrence.

The moment their car leaves the driveway Iris hears Clyde walking up the stairs. She feels the neurons firing, her sympathetic nervous system taking over. Bracing for retaliation, Iris keeps one hand on the door, ready to walk, ready to scream. The footsteps stop at the top of the stairs. She waits.

"Clyde?"

She heard footsteps. She heard them. What is he doing?

"Answer me. I've got the phone in my hand. I'll call the police right back."

Her threat is greeted with silence. Was her mind is playing tricks on her? Were the footsteps some kind of auditory hallucination? The argument plays out in Iris's mind as she stands there, clutching the door handle. The stress is more then she can bear. She contemplates putting on her snow boots, going to her neighbors'.

She must choose. Stay or leave. She can't stand by the door all night.

Iris takes deep breaths to steady her heart rate. She walks into the kitchen and peeks around the corner to the basement staircase. The landing is empty. Iris takes the deer rifle from the closet, brings it to her room, locks the door, stashes it under the bed, and calls Henry.

"So he's sleeping now?"

"I guess. He could barely keep his eyes open. I thought he'd start drooling at one point, he was so out of it."

"And you're sure he's not taking anything?"

"I don't know. I don't know anything."

"Don't hesitate to call the cops again."

"I don't want him here, not anymore, not like this. He needs help. But he's got nothing. He's broke. Where's he going to go, who is going to take him, if I kick him out into the cold? So what do I do? Send him to the psych ward, for all the good that did his mother?"

"I'll fly down. You want me to fly down?"

"Could you? Can you? I mean will work let you?"

"It is what it is. I'll explain there's a family situation. There shouldn't be any problems. I'll book the earliest flight, probably going to be something for tomorrow morning."

"I really appreciate it, and I'll pay for your plane fare."

"Don't worry about that. Just stay calm. Things get weird, you call the cops."

With the bedside light on, Iris stares at the ceiling. She's exhausted, hoping to make it through the night unscathed. Unable to quit her thoughts, the gears kept grinding. Clyde's crazy. He's slowly going crazy. He's weak like his mother. They suffer the same condition. They can't handle it. When the world doesn't meet their expectations they crumble. He's in his late thirties, unemployed, with no savings, no prospects, living in his grandma's basement. He's starting to crack. That's their coping mechanism, his and his mother's, succumbing to delusion, embracing madness while everyone else scrambles to save them. They can't get past their flaws, their suffering, and the system eats them alive.

Alive. That's the trigger. She reflected back to when she was nurse matron at Norman Wells, the small town and outpost for Imperial Oil on the north side of Mackenzie River. That night they were attending to an expectant mother in labor. Nada was her name. The young Dene woman and her family lived in a small community along the river eight hours away by dog sled. Her father ran trap lines in the area. Arrangements were made for Nada to arrive at the hospital nearing her due date and stay until the baby was born.

After twelve hours of labor, Nada gives birth to a girl. It's not breathing. There's no cord issues or meconium staining. With its blood pressure dropping they administer oxygen and infant CPR, but the baby's vitals signs continue to crash. Everything stops. There's no corneal reflex. They cannot detect a heartbeat. There's no chest excursions, no sounds of breathing, no air movement at the mouth. With a heavy heart Doctor Drummond must pronounce the child's death.

Nada and her family are solemn, without hysterics, but they wish to leave that night despite Iris asking them to wait until morning. It's blustering outside with frigid winter temperatures. Nada shouldn't travel in these conditions. She needs rest. But, with Nada's agreement, the family insists on leaving. Despite her reservations Iris respects their wishes and completes the paperwork while another nurse shrouds the infant's body.

Everyone on staff feels the loss. It's a subdued atmosphere for the rest of the night. Everyone keeps to themselves. Doctor Drummond remains in his office, refilling his tumbler glass with whiskey several times, while Iris runs the nightly operation of the hospital.

To everyone's surprise Nada and her family return at dawn. Nada's father, covered in snow, walks into the hospital carrying the shrouded baby, handing her to Iris. He utters the only two words of English she's ever heard him speak: "Alive. Breathing."

There's no way. Iris brings her ear to the baby's mouth. She can hear it, just barely, the faintest of sounds. Breathing. Distressed breathing -- but breathing. Iris, at a complete loss for words, looks up the grandfather. She's completely rattled. The grandfather gives Iris a quiet nod, bringing things into focus. Iris sends a nurse to get Doctor Drummond, while she rushes to get oxygen for the baby.

When Doctor Drummond arrives to confirm the miracle, he's red in the face, whiskey burning off his breath. He sees the baby alive, struggling for air, clinging to life, and his hands start shaking. Another nurse sits him down.

Iris works well into the next shift, monitoring the baby, attending to the family. She sends Doctor Drummond home. He's a liability at this point. Iris begins to believe there's a lesson at work, a revelation in waiting, a higher power.

By mid-afternoon the breathing stops, for certain this time. Efforts to resuscitate fail. The child has passed on. The deceased infant is returned to its mother. The family thanks the hospital staff and leaves. For Iris it's a night that echoes back, forever imprinted on her mind, simultaneously confirming, yet denying, her faith.

The phone rings jolt her awake. The bedside light is still on. It's daybreak outside her window. She's survived the night, but this early-unexpected phone call is disconcerting. Spinning from the rude interruption of sleep, Iris takes a moment to center herself before answering.

"Hello?"

"Hi, Mom."

"Hi."

"Sorry, I know it's early. Did I wake you?"

"No, no, I just woke up."

"I'm at the airport. My flight's delayed. They said it was for de-icing but it's been over an hour now. I don't what's happening. Anyway my arrival times changing but I'm just checking to make sure everything's all right over there."

"Thankfully, there weren't any more disturbances."

"He's still sleeping?"

"I'd imagine so."

"Have you spoken to him since the cops showed up?"

Iris steps out of bed and pulls back the drapes as Clyde walks past outside the window.

"He just walked past. He just walked past."

"Past what?"

"He's outside. In the backyard. In the snow. Walking in the snow. In his boxers. He's got no shoes on."

Iris opens the window, cracking the seal of ice.

"Clyde! What are you doing? Get back inside!"

Oblivious he keeps walking.

"Where are you going? Where are your clothes?"

Clyde stops in the middle of the yard, scanning the skyline.

"Mom. What's going on? What's he doing?"

"He's standing in the backyard, staring at the sky in nothing but his boxer shorts."

"Call the cops."

"He's just standing there. I've got to get him inside. He's got to get inside."

"Mom, wait, don't go out there. You need to call the cops. Just call the police."

With the police on their way, Iris fears an altercation, her disturbed grandson getting shot down in the snow. She pulls on her parka and winter boots.

Trudging through knee-deep snow she approaches Clyde who's shaking, his feet planted in the snow, lips turning blue, eyes on the horizon. "Clyde listen to me. I don't know what this is, but you get back inside right now."

Iris clenches her arms together, trying to shield herself from the wind. Clyde's mouth hangs open, slack-jawed. "Clyde!"

Iris is struck by the power in her voice. Clyde slowly turns his head towards her with a blank expression.

"Did I tell you about the wolf?"

"Let's go inside. Tell me about it there. You're hypothermic. We need to get you warmed up."

Clyde turns away, looking over the tree line.

"When I was a baggage handler at the Yellowknife airport, this wolf walked onto the tarmac."

"Clyde, let's get back in the house. You can't be out here."

"It lays down on the tarmac. They fire a warning shot to clear it from the runway."

"You're standing in the snow in bare feet! You want them to fall off? Please, it's freezing. Let's go back inside."

"The wolf runs off but comes right back, laying down on the tarmac again."

"Tell me this inside. I want to hear your story but not here."

"So they fire another warning shot but this time, it's not moving. It stays right there, panting, you can see its breath. It's staring at us, waiting."

A train echoes past in the distance.

"Henry's on the phone. He wants to speak with you. Let's go inside. Let's talk to him."

"After a third warning shot it's still not going away. So they shoot it."

"Clyde, you're shaking. Your lips are turning blue. I'm begging you, let's get back inside the house."

"They shoot the wolf and load it into the back of the truck. Its fur's matted in blood. Jim turns it over and the wolf's entire underbelly is covered in abscesses, these knotted tumors. I swear to God, that's why ... it wanted us to kill it."

"Clyde, it was a sick animal that was taken out of its misery and put to rest. You've told your story, now let's go the heck back inside."

Clyde holds his gaze, locked into the distance. Iris sees she's not getting through and takes his hand. It's gone cold.

"I can't make you follow me, but the cops are on their way. I'm not letting you freeze to death. "Iris squeezes her grandson's hand before letting go.

The Power of the Warrior

I know there ain't much time. You're coming after us and we don't plan on surrendering. I'm making this recording so you know just what the hell you're looking at when it's over.

I'm sixty-eight years old. I been here my entire life. Before I retired I worked as a locksmith and a roofer. Been married once, but it didn't take. I got no kids but consider Hail to be my own. That's about the sum of it.

I found Hail, whom I named after my grandfather, in the marshland behind my house. That's where his spaceship crashed. It woke me up in the middle of the night. I felt the impact in my chest.

I only got the three neighbors and we're all set at a significant distance apart with nothing around us. There's Hattie Coleman and her daughter Daphne, Charles and Betty Polk, and of course Dove McGowan with his brood. Of the people I just mentioned I was the only to investigate the disturbance. I know Dove would have been sticking his nose in it but thankfully they were away on vacation. Charles and Betty never mentioned it, both in their 80's wearing hearing aids. I think they slept right through it. As for Hattie and her daughter, they're just nervous people. Both so awkward they wouldn't call the cops 'cause it meant having to talk to them.

After I was woken by the crash. I checked out the window and could see a fire glowing down by the marsh. I marched down with a flashlight in one hand and my shotgun in the other, my dog Gideon chasing beside me. As we got closer to the marsh I could see the steam coming off it. The spaceship, this sphere, had buried itself 'bout twenty feet in the mud bank. Now I'm guessing this ship was shot out a worm hole --some kind of inter-dimensional portal must've opened up lower to the ground -- 'cause who-ever's on sky watch should have seen that, and nothing was reported the next day about it.

Anyway, I'm staring down this crater, waters flooding into it, and the outside of the ship is on fire. That's when the top of the orb -- its hatch -- cracks open. Inside you've got two pilots in armored black flight suits. They're both slouched over. Only one of them is moving. They're wearing full gas masks attached to the ship's control panel, which is also on fire. With my heart a-racing, I slide down the mud and climb into the ship.

I'm looking for a way to remove the mask on the pilot that's moving and get us out of there, but I can't find the locking mechanism. Gideon's pacing around the edge of the crater, barking, looking down at me with con-cern. I'm still searching for the release when the pilot slides his long fingers into these groves on the side of the mask. The grooves glow for a second, then, just like that, the front of the gas mask disengages, exposing its face.

And there it is, with pale green skin. It has the strangest facial struc-ture, like a cartoon character that got its face stretched out in a vacuum. Its mouth splits under its nose with flaps that go back to holes on the sides of its head that I assume are ears. It has these luminous blue eyes. I watch the pilot scan our surroundings, locking eyes with me for an instant before gazing up at the sky during its final moments, before the blue goes black.

When you search the house you'll see for yourself: the two pilots are in the basement freezers. Their ships are still sitting in the crater, half underwa-ter. But let's get back to the moment. The pilot's just died, the fires are still burning, water's pouring in. I should be climbing the hell outta there, and I'm about to, when I hear the crying start. It's coming from inside this glass dome sticking out of the raised floor, ten feet behind me, at the back of the ship. I go over, shine my flashlight through it, and that's when I see Hail.

The poor little guy's strapped down, all these IV tubes sticking into his arms and legs. I don't want to smash glass over him but I've got to get him out of there. I bring my Mag light down hard, but it bounces right off the dome. I'm madly searching but I can't find a way to access this thing. So I leave it, rush back to the house, return with a fire extinguisher, and put out the flames. Then I go back for tools.

It took me six hours using an acetylene torch, an eight-inch metal-cutting saw, and a crow bar. I was worried I was going to get electrocuted the entire time but eventually I got through the floor and under the enclosure. Finally gaining access to him, I pulled out all the IVs, removed the restraining straps, and carried him out of there.

Hail was shaking when I brought him inside. I was cold too. I wrapped him in a blanket, got the fireplace going, then sat there rocking him till he fell asleep, right about the time the sun started coming up.

Hail slept through the day, waking up round dinnertime. He just crawled out of bed and walked into the kitchen while I was heating up some venison stew. There he was, this strange creature, staring up at me -- my little space gorilla.

He was essentially a much smaller version of what he is now, with the smooth alabaster skin, same bone structure, just less pronounced, long arms, barrel chest, thick skull, bulging forehead, strong brow. He's got that same ridge on the nose with the wide nostrils. His muzzle covering those giant canines has gotten longer. Also those iridescent horns running from his forehead, down the middle of his back, had just started coming in. But those amazing eyes of his haven't changed, still with the crazy colors pulsating and swirling around. That's how he communicates, by shifting the colors. By watching his eyes and body language I can get a pretty clear read on how he's feeling.

When I first found him he was standing about two feet, weighed fifty pounds. He's filled out quite a bit since. Now he's five-foot ten, fifty inches across the shoulders. I don't have a scale I can weigh him on, but it's a safe bet he's over 400 pounds, all muscle, not an ounce of fat. Anyway you'll see soon enough.

So there's little Hail standing in the kitchen, tilting his head at me with those crazy colors slowly swirling around. I say, "Good morning. You hungry?" and he walks up and hugs my leg.

He loved that venison stew, still does. He loves any kind of protein actually. There's no end to his appetite. It doesn't need to be cooked either. I realized that in our first week. I had a raw T-bone steak on the counter. I went to grab some salt and when I turned back around it was gone. He ate it bone and all. He did the same with the chicken I had defrosting on the counter. Both times I sent him to his room. He quickly learned to wait.

Hail was a good boy, a receptive learner. Just like any other kid you praise them when they do right and scold 'em when they do wrong. I had him potty trained in a week. By the end of our first year he had learned to brush his teeth, bathe himself, get dressed, do the dishes, clean his room, make his bed, vacuum, wash his clothes, and feed and brush Gideon. He could quickly mimic anything I showed him.

The language barrier was a bit of a problem though, an impediment to his ongoing education. He couldn't speak a word -- still can't -- just grunted, growled, and made a kind of chuffing. I tried my best to teach him to talk, reading to him every night, which he seemed to enjoy. He certainly loved flipping through the pages of his picture books. I tried teaching him the alphabet, so we could start spelling words, but he just couldn't grasp it. He can read emotion; he just can't read. I tried teaching him basic math but that wouldn't take either.

Those skills may be beyond him but he can chop wood all day. And that's not me making him. I've got to make him stop 'cause he'll just keep going. He likes working outside: mowing the lawn, watering the garden. Fortunately, until today, he's been safe outside as long as he's stayed on our property, which is a fair distance from the road and sheltered by the trees from anyone's curious eyes.

Still I had to be careful he didn't go chasing after the wildlife. One time, he was helping me paint the exterior of the house when something caught his eye. He dropped the roller and sprang off into the woods. When I finally caught up to him he was standing over the carcass of a large buck. He'd snapped its neck. We dragged it back to the property, and he watched me field dress it. I handed him the heart. He ate it while the blood was still warm.

Hail's favorite thing outside of eating is watching wrestling. I don't have cable -- can't waste the money on that -- but I have a VHS player and boxes of old wrestling tapes, recordings of the weekly show and various wrestle manias. I watched them with my nephew Clive when he was a boy. He really loved it -- all the colorful characters -- Clive's favorite being Jake the Snake Roberts. I remember him screaming "DDT!" when Jake was set up for his finishing move. Clive would jump up and act it out. He actually convinced his mama to buy him a ball python and named it Damien.

That python's still alive, living at my sister's. She took Damien in after Clive's death -- a drug overdose. It hurt to lose him. My heart still aches over the loss. Clive was a kind soul. He wanted to be friends with everybody, possessed by a genuine wonder about life, the natural order of things. He was always searching, inquisitive about the greater mysteries, but sometimes that can lead down the wrong path.

It's a shame he never got to meet his cousin. He'd have gotten a real kick out of watching wrestling with Hail, especially when Warrior is on. That's Hail's favorite character by far. His ears perked up the second he heard his theme music. The first time Hail watched Warrior rush the ring, shake the ropes, then start clobbering people with clothes lines, he was transfixed, glued to the screen. That first time, and every time afterwards, I 'd see the colors of his eyes exploding. By the end of the match he'd be chuffing, on his feet, pacing the room, pounding his chest.

He'd get so amped up watching it; I'd have to take him outside to throw his tractor tires around to burn off the energy. He'd press a tire over his head, spin around with it, just like Warrior, then launch it fifteen feet into the air. I mean this is a full-sized tractor tire. He'd sling it around with one arm, smashing it into the ground. I'd let him carry on with that for an hour or so -- let him get it out of his system -- before calling him back inside.

I remember on his birthday I went out and bought some face paint and some colorful fabrics to cut up for arm tassels. Then I painted him up like Warrior and tied the tassels around his arms. When I let him look in the mirror, Hail nodded his head in agreement, bobbing with excitement. You should have seen it. I couldn't stop laughing, watching him posing, flexing like Warrior in front of the mirror. I let him wrestle his tires for the rest of the evening.

Despite the fun we had, I was always aware of the danger. It was a precarious situation. I had to keep him safe from others and others safe from him. It was a fine balance between security and imprisonment. I just did what was necessary. Whenever I went out to grab groceries or whatever other supplies were needed I'd have to lock Hail up in a heavily fortified cage that I'd built in the basement. I hated having do that to him, but I couldn't call a babysitter. I tried to make the cage as comfortable as possible. I installed a toilet. There was a couch. I made sure he had entertainment: a shelf full of picture books, another TV and a VHS player set up to watch movies on.

I never left for very long, and before leaving I'd put on a nature documentary or a Disney cartoon, which he seemed to like. I wouldn't play the wrestling 'cause it got him too riled up. Whenever I got back from errands he'd still be sitting there with his blanket, watching the TV or looking through his books. I knew it couldn't last forever though. That's what kept me up at night. If I got hurt or sick ... I shuddered to think what might happen to him. If he wasn't discovered and killed, he'd be taken from home and locked away by strangers so they could run experiments on him. No, I can't have that. I won't abandon him.

I'm forever thankful that Hail was brought into my life. He's added an exciting new chapter to it that I'd never expected. I was resigned to living out my days in the same old doldrums, going about the daily maintenance, until my body broke down and I ceased to exist. He gave my life some meaning. I've been his guardian. I've tried to provide for and protect him to the best of my abilities. Having said that, for the record, let me explain the incidents that brought you here.

This morning I went into town to grab groceries. I saw Dove McGowan and his boys, Roddy and Ronnie, in the parking lot. Now Dove and I got some history. It goes back as far as high school. He was a sniveling turncoat back then and nothing's changed since. Slippery bastard only cares about himself. Recently we've had quarrels over our property lines and water rights. This started when I rejected his offer to buy my property, which I'm sure ended up kyboshing some kind of land deal he was plotting with developers.

Anyhow, there we are in the parking lot. Dave's leaning against his truck, smirking at me with his boys, acting tough in all his bloated glory, an old bullfrog sucking on a cigarette, watching while I load my groceries into the back of the pickup. Finally he pipes up and says, "Burl, you and I got business we need to discuss." I tell him straight to his face, there's no business I need to discuss with him, and drive off with my middle finger raised.

In my rear-view mirror, I can see Dove and his boys sniggering, like I'm some kind of joke. I circle back, stopping ten feet away, and get out of the truck.

Dove steps forward. "Whatchya gonna do, Burl?" He's acting brave with his boys beside him.

So I reach into a grocery bag, grab a giant russet potato, and whip it at his head, hitting him in the face. You could hear the smack. I'd put my arm into it, knocking him right over. His boys rush to his side. Dove's squealing on the ground with his face covered, kicking his feet. I just get back in the truck and drive off.

Back home Hail helps me unpack the groceries. I'm nervous, waiting for a response. Sure enough Gideon starts barking. I see the McGowan's truck driving towards the house with the cops trailing behind them. I can't believe what I'm seeing. How do they get their own police escort? I rush Hail downstairs to put him in his cage. He's confused, panicked by all the commotion. I get him in his cage, am about to close it, when there's a loud hostile-sounding knock on the front door.

It was utter chaos from there. It happened so fast. Hail blows past me up the stairs. I rush after him, but it's too late. He's exploded through the front door, taking it right off its frame, knocking unconscious the officer standing behind it. His partner, who stood to the side avoiding the door, fires his gun at Hail, who catches the bullet in the corner of his eye. It barely phases him, unable to penetrate his skull plate. Hail springs at the officer, raining down hammer fists until the man's a broken mess. I'm screaming at Hail to stop but he's gone berserk.

The McGowans are in their truck, spinning their wheels, trying to drive away. Hail leaps off the back deck, then hurls himself through the air at them, driving his feet into the hood of their truck, destroying it. He dismounts with a back flip. They scramble to lock their doors, but Hail drives his fist through the driver side window. Roddy and Ronnie escape out the other side. Hail chases after them. Running full speed, arms raised, he clobbers them with an ultimate Warrior-style clothesline, carrying so much force I'm surprised it didn't take their heads clean off.

Gideon's going crazy with the barking, and there I am trembling on the front porch, paralyzed by the savagery of what I'm witnessing. Hail stands over Roddy's and Ronnie's bodies while they twitch on the ground. He looks back at Dove, who's trying to crawl away from the truck.

That's when I snap out of it and rush for the shotgun. When I come back Hail's flaring his teeth with one hand wrapped around Dove's neck, holding him four feet off the ground. I fire the shotgun into the air several times, then scream for Hail to put the man down. He mulls it over for a second, drops Dove, and returns to me. I'm shaking my head, asking, "Hail, what have we done?"

I go over to check Roddy and Ronnie. They're both dead, necks snapped from the whiplash. That's when I hear the cop start to move, the cop that got knocked out by the door. He stands up, still in a daze. Hail looks ready to pounce. I fire another shot into the air, and Hail stands down.

I yell to the cop, "Do not reach for your pistol. You take Dove, get back in your car, and drive on out of here."

He follows my orders, helping Dove to his feet and leading him to his car. Poor Dove's a slobbering mess, screaming for his boys. I tell him they're dead, and he'll have to come back for them later.

I feel truly awful. Despite our differences I would not have wished that upon him. As they drive away I know the retaliation will be fierce.

None of it was done in malice; Hail was just protecting his territory. I bring him inside and put on his arm tassels and war paint. I know this will be our last stand. Maybe he's just reflecting my solemn demeanor, but he seems to know it too. After I apply the paint I give him a big hug, look him in those wondrous eyes, and tell him I love him. We'll meet again in the next life.

Now we wait, ready for battle.

DECEIVER

MARK PASSED THE BOTTLE AROUND WITH THE DREGS AT THE PARK. THE SUN was shining through the trees. He told Liza to wipe her mouth before he handed over the vodka. She was already in a stupor, her chin covered in drool. Her cousin Rankin was sprawled out in the grass snoring, his soiled T-shirt pulled back over his bloated sunburned belly.

Abdi, with his yellow eyes, sat bent over, legs crossed, twisting a lock of hair, muttering madness. Akimaq "The Machine Gun" Manitok was shadow boxing, five feet away. He stumbled back, staggered by an invisible opponent. "Bitch and Moan" Bernie, a.k.a "The Sultan of Sneer," watching with a permanent scowl.

Hank Elksblood, the prodigy from The Pas, pulled a half-smoked cigarette from his shirt pocket and fired it up. In his youth, Hank had a stint in the WHL with the Regina Pats but missed one too many practices, so they cut him from their roster. Telling his coach to "fuck off" didn't help the cause.

Rounding out this day's group is "Hand to God" Heather, a.k.a "Badlands," and her servile paramours, the duelling suitors of "Slack-jawed" Stu and Douglas "Dumbfounded," a pair of malnourished lapdogs, if there ever was.

Heather was furious about having to throw out a mattress because Stu burnt a smoldering crater into it when he fell asleep with a lit cigarette in his hands. "Could-a killed us! Stupid bastard woke up when his leg caught fire!"

Douglas starts laughing; Heather smacks him hard across the back, bringing the full force of her arm down. "Think that's fucking funny, do ya? A real joke is it? How 'bout my couch you pissed and puked on? When you going to replace that?"

Browbeaten, smile removed, Douglas hangs his head in shame. Heather demands a cigarette, which he immediately hands over. She sparks it and crosses her arms. "Yeah, not so funny is it? No, I guess not. Honestly, I don't know why I put up with it. I'm trying to help you two fuckups and that's the thanks I get. That's the fuckin' thanks I get. I'm getting real sick of it. Things are gonna change, I'll tell ya that much."

It was all background noise to Mark since he'd destroyed his back in a "work place accident." A friend he hadn't seen for years was in town the night before. Their drinking increased exponentially as the night progressed, inevitably resulting in a toxic hangover. Mark wanted to call in sick but it was just his second week on the job. He couldn't, he hadn't earned it. Nauseous with a blinding headache, he pulled on dirty work clothes, grabbed his tools, and forced himself into his car. The tank was near empty. On the way he pulled into the gas station for a fill-up and purchased a Gatorade he chugged back, trying to replenish lost electrolytes. It was a long painful drive through traffic to the work site. There were several moments he considered turning around, so sick and useless, he'd only make things worse. But they needed him and he needed the work. It's how he got the job; they were overworked and short-staffed.

Mark kept going, eventually forced off the highway to puke in a big box center parking lot. An instant improvement. He felt much better. With that out of the way he had a chance of making it through the day's work unscathed. It wouldn't be easy, but if he paced himself, stayed hydrated, and took a fifteen-minute nap at lunch, he might last till five.

When he reached the job site Mark cursed himself for forgetting his sunglasses. The week's worth of rain had lifted, blue skies now. The sun's harsh glare bounced off the siding. Squinting through the day wouldn't help his headache.

The ground was mud, puddles everywhere. After strapping on the tool belt, his first order of business was getting the extension ladder in position. Mark placed waterlogged wood planks across the trenching surrounding the house, so the ladder had even ground to stand on. Mark put the ladder on the planks and his weight on the ladder. It felt solid, sturdy, ready to climb.

The morning trudged along. Mark was exhausted, and lunch couldn't come soon enough. The ladder work was the hardest part. Up and down forty feet, readjusting the angle, resetting the planks. That's what slowed him down.

Climbing the ladder to install the last light before lunch, Mark realized he was too far from the fixture. It was a dangerous lean-in. Already exhausted, moving the ladder even two feet was an arduous task he wanted no part of. In a stretch he could reach the fixture but given his current state, he decided to err on the side of caution. He climbed down the rails and reset the ladder.

It took him five minutes before he began his ascent. Now he was under the fixture. The problem was the overhang. He'd have to reach too far back. There was nowhere to put the ladder. He couldn't lean it against the overhang because the ladder would crush the eavestrough.

His journeyman Denis told him once, "You fall off a ladder, you're fired before you hit the ground." There was no time for safety; they were always cutting corners, with management breathing down their necks to make impossible deadlines. So what now? Climb down the ladder and try again.

All this bullshit aggravation. Mark checked his watch. Still thirty minutes till lunch, too early to shut down. With a defeated sigh, he refocused on the task at hand. If he built the base up, shoveling some dirt underneath, adjusting the angle, he might be able to reach it.

He remembered falling, the world dropping out from under him, the speed of descent, bracing for impact. Then he hit, striking solid ground from forty feet, blunt force trauma, crushing the air out of his lungs. Sickening.

Flip the breaker.

The doctors warned there were a number of medical complications he needed to be aware of, including pressure sores (decubitus), thrombosis, and pneumonia. Vigilant self-observation was required in conjunction with physiotherapy to prevent future complications and mitigate existing ones. The key factor was to gain as much functionality back as possible. He must focus on strength, range of motion/stretching, and transfer skills. Mark needed to learn his ADL'S (activities of daily living), which at first can prove quite challenging for those with a SCI (Spinal Cord Injury). However with the aid of his physiotherapists and occupational therapists, the doctor was confident he could learn new skills and adapt previous ones to maximize independence.

In time Mark would learn to feed, groom, dress, and bathe himself. He'd be able to manage bladder and bowel care and wheelchair transfer on his own. Driving was still a possibility using vehicles adapted with special hand controls.

Outside of injury diagnosis and treatment, there was accident assessment - litigation. The contracting company, wanted to protect themselves, and the workers' compensation board, had their own report to file.

The WCB ruled there were a number of potential and apparent contributing factors:

"The baseboards had water rot and were cracked through. The uneven terrain they were placed on was unstable. The dirt had given way under the weight."

"There was evidence of improper use of the extension ladder: The flipper on the fly locks were damaged, which would suggest flipper-lock. This occurs when the swinging gate member of the fly lock rests on the ladder rung, a very unstable form of false-locking occurring due to friction between the gate and the rung."

"It should also be noted that the ladder angle might have exceeded the 1:4 ratio to ensure a stable working platform."

Of course none of this mattered to Mark.

He'd lost the use of his legs, his dick was dead, he pissed in a bag and could shit himself at any moment without warning. But these were secondary concerns compared to the chronic nerve pain that took residence in his crippled back.

The physicians called it "phantom pain," a misnomer if there ever was one. The pain was real, excruciating, and severely hindered attempts at rehabilitation. It was impossible to manage, and refractory to treatment with traditional drugs. As is often the case with phantom pain, it proved extremely difficult to treat. Benzodiazepines, opioids, barbiturates, calcitonin, neuroleptics, and sodium channel blockers were tried with varying results.

Upon his release from hospital Mark's mom, Jennifer, moved in with him. Their financial situation demanded it. Neither of their apartments was feasible from a practical standpoint, both being third-story walk-ups. In her search for new accommodations Jennifer found a bungalow to rent and was given permission to make the necessary modifications for wheelchair accessibility. It was there Mark implemented his own pain management strategy. He found the drugs, especially the opioids, worked best with an alcohol kicker. It accelerated and amplified the effects; smoking marijuana sustained them.

Shortly after they moved into the area he found the park. It was simply a place to drink, away from his mother's scorn. During their last confrontation, Jennifer broke down in tears after another futile protest. Mark, beaten down, exhausted, voice hoarse from yelling, surrendered.

"My life is over. Fuck off. Let me get drunk."

Jennifer, kneeling at her son's feet, took his hand, while he turned his face away, staring at the ground. "I can't let you give up. Things will get better. I promise. Fight for it. Battle through this. I know you can. I know it's there -- a life you can take pride in, find joy with. One day at a time, you'll get there, you'll find your way."

Mark tried to face her but couldn't. "Mom... I'm done. I love you, but I'm done. "

Short of locking Mark in his room, there was nothing Jennifer could do or say. Mark had been warned many times by his doctor about the dangers of consuming alcohol in conjunction with his medications, how it significantly heightened the risk of an overdose and continued abuse would result in liver and kidney damage. He didn't care. Whatever it took to alleviate the pain.

During their last visit Doctor Sykara mentioned a recent study on phantom pain:

"Researchers have reported the first evidence that phantom pain following spinal cord injury is the result of hypersensitive neurons in the thalamic region of the brain that can be suppressed with specially designed molecular agents. The study showed that, in rats with spinal cord injury, third-order neurons within the thalamus spontaneously and abnormally fire signals in the absence of any incoming signals from the first-order neurons. And these rogue neurons contain abnormally high levels of a particular type of sodium channel, called Nav1.3."

Doctor Sykara continued unaware the Mark's eyes had already glazed over.

"Understand that sodium channels serve as batteries during the conduction of nerve signals. Abnormal presence of Nav1.3 in these neurons are linked to changes in their physiological temperament. They are hypersensitive and spontaneously fire signals at higher-than-normal rates, even in the absence of a painful stimulus! This is the key to the understanding of phantom pain."

Mark couldn't help but stare at the hair growing out the tip of Doctor Sykara's nose.

"Armed with this information the researchers designed targeted molecular agents against Nav1.3 and injected them into the spinal fluid of the injured rats. This produced a significant reduction in the presence of Nav1.3 in second- and third-order neurons, accompanied by a reduction in the signals they produced! Suppressing the activity of Nav1.3 in these neurons can mitigate pain!"

Doctor Sykara tempered his excitement, not wanting to create false expectations. He warned that he studies had to be validated in higher-order animals before testing in humans. Still there was reason for hope.

"With all due respect, Doctor, I don't need the reason, I need the resolution."

Removed from obligation. No need to participate. Pain was his intermediary. Nothing could seek his council without its consolation. It ruled him. Cruel discomfort. Drink, smoke, crush, snort, pop. Whatever it took.

Mark knew he could only implement his particular brand of pain suppression for so long. He expected a system crash soon enough. Till then he'd observe with detached amusement whatever other pratfalls life might bestow upon him. He'd grind it out till it ground him down.

He tried to adhere to this but there were flare-ups, acting-outs. He was shackled by his physical state, the maintenance, the tedium, the routine. For example, the time-consuming process of removing waste from his mangled being. He could laugh at the indignity, but how much should be stolen from him?

Everyday, without fail, Mark had to empty and clean his catheter bag. Each evening, switch from a day bag to the larger night bag. Above all he could not forget the importance of bowel maintenance, to avoid fecal impacting. Mark's daily bowel routine lasted as long as an hour on bad days. There were many contributing factors: diet, fluid intake, medications, emotional stress, the weather. And there were various means and methods of extraction: positioning (the Valsalva maneuver), external massage, digital stimulation, suppository, mini-enema. He was encouraged to experiment, take notes, to find what worked best for him, the most basic of biological acts now a laborious chore.

Mark knew he was slowly being snuffed out. He was simply accelerating the process towards it inevitable conclusion, a heedless spectator, killing time till the credits rolled. He'd pass the bottle but that was the extent of his participation. He'd atrophy into delirium, withering under the predictable death spiral of systematic organ failure, his prayers for a thunderous reckoning unanswered.

Wilting under the oppressive heat. Sunburns all around. Cooked in concrete with a mouth on the tailpipe. Seek shade you fool. Earlier that week Mark watched two dregs, Kendra "The Husk" and "Manatee" Mike get carted away by paramedics for sun-stroke/heat exhaustion. They'd been warned on the perils of consuming alcohol in extreme heat. You want to stay drunk, keep hydrated. Mark brought a two-liter bottle of water, for that very reason, so he could keep drinking.

Booze, water, booze. It seemed every hour he'd have to empty his catheter bag into the bush. His kidneys were working overtime. It was so hot, that old man Poseidon asked Mark for a sip of his water. It was so hot the cops couldn't be bothered to leave their air-conditioned patrol cars to hassle them about open alcohol and public intoxication.

Today the dregs are quiet for the most part, sitting still, still sweating. They hear him before they see him, singing the gospel, preaching his commands. Then it turns the corner, hell on wheels.

No one recognizes this man. Long ginger hair held up in a bun matched with a feral copper beard. Wild eyes, mad brows jutting out above smudged spectacles, resting on the razor's edge of a long angled nose, sharpened to a point.

He is shirtless, this scrawny man with broad freckled shoulders, all knees and elbows. A tattered hiking bag, half his size, strapped to his back, bursting at the seams. Sleeping bag and floor mat fastened on the outside. Pots and pans rattle off the side, clasped on with carabineers. Baggy cargo shorts tied around a scrawny waist with yellow nylon rope. The toes and heels of glued sneakers peeling apart.

Crooked teeth, soaked in a coke-can brown, he carries the message with that broken smile.

They've been spotted. He's found his flock. Riding towards them. A gentle breeze cracks the stagnant heat. Getting ready for the show Mark washes back another oxy with a swig of warm water and waits for it. He can count the ways this man is crazy before the words leave his mouth.

"My friends. I greet you with revelation!"

Hank pays no mind, horking on the ground five feet away. Heather puts a cigarette in her mouth. Stu and Douglas scramble, searching their pockets for a lighter. Stu wins, finding his first, sparking Heather's cigarette. Heather takes a deep drag, squinting at the stranger.

"Yeah, kay... so, what's your story?" she asks, blowing smoke at him.

"In a dream a demon spoke to me. I am the new Messiah."

On cue, Bernie sneers, snagging the bottle from Abdi.

Heather chimes back, "A demon told you that? Shouldn't it be an angel?"

"The messenger matters not. It is the message."

Mark speaks from the sideline. "You think it's wise to trust a demon?"

Bernie scoffs in disgust, thinking Mark has taken the bait.

"The demon simply stated a fact. He recognized me for what I am."

Heather rolls her eyes; smoke streams from her nose. Machine Gun, a wrecking ball of pent-up hostility teetering on the edge, snatches the bottle from Bernie.

"The word of God coursed through me! This was simply a confirmation of what I knew to be true."

"Being the Messiah, what are your job duties?" Mark inquires, while breaking up the weed in his lap with a pair of scissors.

"To show the way of God. To find those lost souls and lead them back to the light. To bestow His divine mercy and end their suffering."

Hank pulls the vodka bottle away from Machine Gun, who's sinking further into angry stupor, firing threatening glances. Hank tips the vodka down his throat. They watch air bubbles rip through the bottle. Eyes water but Hank doesn't so much as flinch, bringing the bottle down, handing it to Mark. "So you think you're gonna save us, do ya?" Hank cracks his knuckles. Holding his hands out, he combs over the scars, like he's checking an old map.

"I can only save those who heed His teachings, the lessons of our Father, the Almighty. Praise be."

"You cracked out or just cracked?"

The stranger sighs. "This rampant cynicism will be our undoing. I understand your apprehension. And we must reject false prophets but rest assured I am the one. Follow me to our Lord and Savior. Together we shall restore His kingdom on earth."

Mark sparks his joint. "So do you have special powers? Water-to-wine type shit?"

"The power is in the word, and the word is God."

"Words can't be trusted. Any silver-tongued devil can string together a sermon."

"Those who appropriate His name for their own material gain shall incur His wrath."

"Shouldn't He have given you some of that God magic to prove it?"

"I do not require trickery to fill the ranks. For it is those with faith that find salvation."

"I'll tell you what, man, you want my vote, you've got to prove yourself. Use your connection; get me out of this chair. I want to walk, heal my pain. Do that and I'll follow you every step of the way, converting non-believers."

"My friend, it simply does not work that way. God need not prove himself. He is the Creator. It is us who have lost his favor, his trust. We must earn it. We must fight our way back into the light."

"Sounds like excuses to me. Come on, man, show us a miracle."

Mark passes the joint to Hank. The stranger buries his arm in his backpack, riffling through until he retrieves a crinkled paperback dictionary, with its cover hanging off. He opens to a page bookmarked with a scrap of yellow caution tape.

"Let us reacquaint ourselves with the concept of faith by examining its very definition."

The stranger holds the dictionary aloft, open to the page, displaying it for all to see. The stranger clears his throat. "Faith: 'The confident belief in the truth, value, or trustworthiness of a person, idea, or thing. Belief that does not rest on logical proof or material evidence. The theological virtue defined as secure belief in God and a trusting acceptance of God's will.' So take heed. A secure belief in God that doth not rest on material evidence."

The stranger shakes the tattered dictionary in his hand. "Brothers and sisters, the onus is on you! God need not prove himself to us. We must prove ourselves to him! To ask otherwise is sacrilege, an affront to His divine power from which all life springs forth!"

Mark begins to feel queasy. The oxy is not mixing right. Mark feels the toxic flush. The conflict. He's about to get sick on display.

Heather notices Mark's deteriorating condition. Deathly pale, beads of sweat, slack-jawed, eyes drooping, slumping over in his wheelchair.

"Honey? Sweetie? Are you all right?"

Stomach twists. Noxious knots. Words slurred through the crash.

"Layysssmeedown."

Hank knows. He understands the inevitable return to earth. He hooks his arms under Mark's, propping him up for the moment. "It's all good, buddy. We're gonna lay you down on the grass here, nice and cool down there."

Hank lifts Mark from his wheelchair and gently lowers him to the ground.

It churns and chokes. Mark can hardly breath. It won't let go.

The stranger reaches in. "Let the Lord layeth his hand upon you."

Hank knocks his hand away and with a hard shove plants the stranger on his backside, then casually kneels back down beside Mark.

The stranger springs to his feet. Manitok locks on, clasping the stranger's arms behind his head in a full nelson. The stranger screams to the heavens. "Father!!! Why have you forsaken us?"

His eyes roll back as he lapses into tongues. Manitok, confused, shakes him like a rag doll. Hank demands the stranger to "cut that shit out" before standing up and cuffing him across the face. The stranger drops, going limp, slipping through Manitok's arms. When he hits the ground the convulsions start.

His body in turmoil, Mark moans for mercy.

Hank stands over the stranger, smacking him. "You gonna fuckin' knock it off? Quit flopping around like a fish."

The stranger falls still, playing dead.

Suffocating agony, brought to the brink, then it breaks. A chill washes over him. His skin tingles, pins and needles, electric. Mark can feel the breeze; he can hear the birds, the bugs, the traffic, the rustling of leaves under all of it. He thinks, "Let me die here. I'm ready to leave."

This fleeting moment, tranquility, wiped out by the final surge. A torrent of sewage rushes forth.

His pants are filled with shit but the pain is gone. Drenched in a cold sweat on solid ground. Exhausted. Mark imagines sinking through the grass, being absorbed by the soil.

Yet he remains. Stubborn, this reality. Nowhere to hide, he must deal with it. Get home, get cleaned, and sleep like it's not an option.

Mark, eyes still closed, asks for a lift back into the chair. Hank lifts him up, sits him down, and props him up.

The stranger stirs, making strange gurgling noises. Mark watches the resurrection. The stranger's arms twitching out in Christ pose, his head rolls with open eyes flittering. His chest heaves, he jolts up. Sitting upright, leaning back on his hands. Breathing heavily, panting, hyperventilating. "HuhuhhuhwhereamIwhereamIwhereamI?"

No one answers.

The stranger leans forward, resting on his knees. Clutching his face in the palms of his hands, overwrought with emotion, he rocks back and forth. Then he stops, bringing his hands together in prayer. With dramatic pause he breaks the prayer, slowly places his hands back down by his sides. The stranger scans his surroundings, seeing the world anew. His eyes ablaze, a smile slowly creeps back across his face.

"My friends. I saw it. I saw the kingdom. I saw it... yes I did." He arcs his neck towards the sky. "Such divine creation. There is a place for us. Heaven awaits those that heed His calling."

Tears stream down the stranger's cheeks. He throws his arms to the sky. "Thank you, father. Thank you."

Oblivious, Abdi sitting on the bench rummages through his collection, a zip-lock bag of discarded cigarette butts.

Mark notices "Machine Gun" Manitok teetering closer to the stranger, senses trouble. Manitok plants his foot into the stranger's back, between the blades, driving him into the dirt, ugly and unwarranted.

Mark projects his voice into the fray. "Manitok, leave it! Leave him alone!"

Abdi covers his ears, humming through clenched teeth, frantically rocking back and forth.

Hank jumps between Akimaq and the stranger. He glares at Akimaq, who averts his gaze, falling back in line.

The stranger drags himself across the grass, reaching out in desperation towards an invisible presence. "Father forgive them. Forgive them. They know not what they've done."

The stranger crawls past Bernie who stands up, stepping back in disgust. "Oh, please. Pathetic. Embarrassing. Ya see what ya started? Would you stop already?"

And the stranger crawls forward. "Forgive them. Forgive them. Please. I beseech you. Show them mercy."

Soaking in shit stew, Mark looks on in disbelief, watching a performance for the ages - "What a fuckin' spectacle." Heather chokes, wheezing through another round of hacking coughs before she catches her breath long enough to ask, "Who's got a smoke for me?"

On cue Stu and Douglas race to the cigarette packs. When the blip of police sirens announces the arrival of law enforcement as the cops drive over the sidewalk into the park. The stranger, still on his hands and knee, looks back. The spell is broken.

"Afternoon officers," coughs Heather when they step out of the car. The stranger is sprinting full tilt across the park. The cops, not interested in a foot chase, call over their radios for back up. Mark registers how young they look, babies, new recruits from the academy, posing hard with expensive haircuts to match their expensive sunglasses. Back in their car, they blast their sirens, peeling out in hot pursuit.

Heather looks at Hank. "Whatchya think that's about?"

Hank shrugs. "Who the fuck knows?"

Mark, lacking the energy to discuss and review such lunacy, spins around and wheels it back home, where he can wash the shit off and go to sleep.

Mark breaths a sigh of relief when he returns to an empty home, his mom not yet back from work. After showering he pulls on a fresh pair of boxers, then carefully drops his soiled pants, underwear, and socks into a garbage bag, wheeling it down the ramp to the garbage bin outside.

The sun is still out, but Mark couldn't care less. The sleep of angels waits. Extreme fatigue blunts the pain. No joints. No beer. No pills. He's run out of anger. He shakes his head. It's so obvious, so rudimentary, the link between body and mind. Pent up, blocked up, the agitator and the excrement, a most necessary expulsion.

Summoning his last ounce of energy, Mark lifts himself from his chair to the bed. Floating, weightless, his thoughts drift over the day's events. Before he recedes into sleep, Mark speaks into an empty room, repeating the words of the deceiver. "Forgive them, please, I beseech you." A smile crosses his face. "Fucking hilarious."

WITNESS

WE CURSE IN FRONT OF CHILDREN.

We ruin the game for those who paid hard-earned money to be there.

We are drunk but this does not excuse our behavior. It never does.

Afterwards at the bar we are accused of not paying our bill.

They block the door to prevent us from leaving. They put their hands on me. I rip their hands off me in righteous indignation and in my drunken state almost fall over.

I demand answers.

The waitress rolls her eyes and says we stiffed her five dollars on the bill.

I open my wallet and hand her a dirty five in the form of a scroll that I'd had up my nose an hour earlier.

We take a cab back to the Holiday Inn.

My friend has been drinking all night on a forkful of Greek salad.

He complains of the spins. Shortly after he is puking with a vengeance, trying to expel some horrible demon but the claws are sunk in deep. My friend has the bathroom sink tap opened full flow and leaves it running. He must hope the sound of running water will ground him. Over the course of the night he wastes enough water to sustain a small African village for a year.

I am not yet ready for sleep.

I look out the window of our hotel room while my friend moans, retches, and sloshes around in the bathtub.

It is winter and the smoke hangs in the air. The brittle and twisted tree branches reach out for nothing from the park below. The streets are empty, which is rare at any hour in the city. I am at peace for the moment despite the exorcism going on in the bathroom.

My quiet moment is ruined when I look across the street to the only apartment in the condominium with its lights on. At the window is a naked man pulling his dick while looking directly at me. I quickly duck out of view and turn off the lights.

After several minutes I take another look outside. The lights in the apartment across the street are off.

I return to watching the frozen city.

My friend staggers out of the bathroom, mumbling something about ginger ale. Light spills into the hotel room from the bathroom. Like a moth to a flame the light across the street flicks on again. The naked man returns to the window and starts tugging his dick, while staring in our direction.

I laugh and tell my friend to take a look out the window at Buffalo Bill.

My friend stands in a pair of ragged boxer briefs. His skin is blotched red, and his eyes are bloodshot.

He doesn't understand my request,

So I say, "There's some naked dude pulling his dick in front of a window across the street."

My friend squints his eyes and peers out the window.

He mumbles, "Wha ... what ... Fuckin' weird..."

He doesn't trust what he has just seen as though he's had some oxygen-deprived hallucination. My friend has more pressing concerns then the sideshow across the street and collapses onto the bed. He moans and begs for relief from some unsympathetic god. He just wants it to stop.

I can't deny that the inherent and intrusive creepiness of our neighbor's strange proclivities pisses me off.

I don't close the curtains on the fuckin' weirdo because I feel in a strange way it might give him satisfaction, but I've had my share of full frontal male nudity for the night.

I go to the bathroom to brush my teeth. The bathroom stinks of someone's damaged insides. There is puke in the sink, in the toilet, and in the garbage bin. There are wet towels on the floor, on the sink, and in the bathtub.

I finish brushing my teeth and pull out the couch to sleep.

My friend lurches out of bed, returning for battle to his mess in the bathroom.

I crack open the four-dollar complimentary bottle of water and drink down half of it.

I lie down on the pullout bed. I'm pleasantly surprised by how comfortable it is.

What a world.

I look forward to breakfast in the morning, but I don't think my friend will be joining me.

Pray

THE FIRE ALARM IS DEAFENING. HOTEL SECURITY DIRECTS EVERYONE TOWARD the nearest exits. Steve and Jason stagger down the hallway, beers in hand. The other guests file past them.

Steve has the spare key card to Greg's room. Greg had given it to him earlier in the day so Steve could get in to borrow a pair of sunglasses. They smell smoke from the room. Despite Steve's level of intoxication, he remembers to check the temperature of the door by pressing the back of his hand against it. The door does not feel abnormally warm. He looks to Jason, whose chin is wagging, eyes as wide as saucers. Jason wipes his nose and twitches out a nod.

Steve opens the door to the room. The smoky haze stings their eyes. It emanates from the bathroom. Steve calls Greg's name. No response. Jason steps inside the bathroom, immediately slipping on the blood.

Greg was based in Toronto but plied his trade throughout Ontario and occasionally in other provinces. When Greg wasn't working as a welder, he usually got stoned in front of the TV, where he played video games, watched movies, and followed sports. Outside of couch-surfing Greg played hockey in a downtown men's rec league. Greg was a grinder with a decent wrist shot. Most of his goals were garbage rebounds but on the rarest of occasions he'd show a flash of his potential and go top shelf. There was no better feeling. A local sports bar sponsored Greg's team where they gathered for beers after each game, which was half the reason they played.

All was well in Greg's life but for one crucial aspect -- he needed to get laid and didn't want to pay for it. He had no moral quandary with prostitution. He'd paid for sex before. During a booze-soaked vacation in Rio de Janeiro Greg met a beautiful local girl with an incredible ass at one of the many discotecas stumbled upon by he and his friends. The young woman accompanied Greg from the club back to his hotel room. He couldn't believe his good fortune until the woman flopped onto his bed and quoted him a price of $40 American.

That was two years ago and Greg hadn't removed a pair of panties since. The women weren't interested, and he refused to go through the rest of his life paying for it. The dry spell was starting to play with his head. Greg would stare at himself in the mirror, trying to figure out what wasn't working. At thirty-two years old it was obvious his hair was thinning. But he kept it short and had a decent shape to his skull. His teeth were a little crooked. But he wasn't a snaggletooth. He noticed his high cheekbones were looking somewhat sunken with age. And his nose had gotten bigger. But overall he still possessed good facial structure. He wouldn't be posing for the cover of *Men's Health* any time soon but his body still had definition. He didn't have a six-pack but he kept his gut in check. What was it? What was missing?

A drought had fallen over the land, and for the life of him, Greg couldn't figure out why. He knew 'handsome' was not the first word associated with him but he was a far cry from ugly. There were selling points: He could carry a conversation, had a well paying job, and a sense of humor. A woman could do worse. His lecherous friend, Johnny Lucas, explained that women could smell desperation and it repelled them. Nothing made them dry up faster. Johnny insisted Greg get drunk and slay a dragon to break the curse. "Fuck the first thing that moves. Sometimes spearing a whale is all it takes to restore a man's confidence."

Greg had stopped worrying about quality some time ago and still wasn't having any luck. During this time of anguish, Greg received a call from Jason and Steve, two of his rowdiest friends. Jason and Steve were a couple of roughnecks who had been living in Alberta for several years working the oil sands. They had a two-week turnaround coming up and wanted to spend it drinking beers with slutty drunk chicks on a beach in Mexico. They demanded that Greg join them. He'd probably need a new liver by the end of it, but Greg understood he was being presented with an opportunity to end the dry spell. Maybe, just maybe, with trusted wingmen by his side, he could convince a drunken señorita to take a leap of faith onto his lap.

It's their first night in Mexico. The cocaine is heavily stepped on. Whatever it's cut with makes Greg feel like shit. He has no shot with the girls; he's too sketched out. He's become self-conscious of how badly his jaw is twitching and can't stop gnawing the inside of his cheek. He has to piss every five minutes and has broken out in a cold sweat. Conversation is going in circles. The party is over. He needs to get back to his hotel room. Trouble is brewing in his stomach.

"What the fuck was in that shit?" Greg wonders aloud, while tenderly wiping his ass. Whatever it was burnt like hellfire. He'd been making mad dashes to the bathroom all night. He contemplates taking an Imodium but decides it best to suffer through it and flush the poison out of his system.

Greg is back in bed but nowhere near sleep, his jagged nerves are shot. He loathes being so strung-out. He gets out of bed and grabs his toothbrush to gnaw on, hoping to relieve the nervous tension in his jaw and maybe stop the grinding.

Greg struggles to keep his mind blank as he fights back the introspective nightmares of the cocaine comedown. Frustrated, Greg tosses the mangled toothbrush to the corner of the darkened room and starts taking deep measured breaths through his mouth to calm himself. It's impossible to breathe through his clogged nose. Greg's heart is still racing. He can feel it pounding inside his chest. He grabs a warm bottle of water from the nightstand and drinks from it, trying to soothe his raw throat. The stale water tastes awful. He spits it out onto the carpet and tosses the bottle aside. He's in purgatory. His body is completely exhausted but his brain will not turn off. He takes a soak in the bathtub hoping it might help him relax.

It's been an arduous battle, but finally his mind is ready to relinquish itself to sleep. Shutdown mode has been initiated. Back in his bed, Greg is drifting out of consciousness when it slams into his face. The force of impact breaks his nose. Hooked appendages dig deep into his skin, Greg swipes it off, its clawed legs rip open his face. He can hear the hostile buzz hovering three feet over his head. Greg's eyes regain their focus. For a half second he sees it silhouetted against the darkness before it thrashes out again for his face.

It plunges its stinger into Greg's cheek. Searing pain shoots through his body. Greg screams and with both hands tears it from his face. The spines on its hard shell pierce Greg's skin as it sinks its mandibles into the meat of Greg's thumb. Greg tries whipping it off but it's firmly entrenched in his hand. He feels the blood seeping down his face and arm. He smashes his hand against the wall several times with no result. The mass is inflicting more damage and not letting go. Greg grabs his lighter from the nightstand and runs to the bathroom as the attack continues.

He lights on fire a roll of toilet paper and holds it at the creature. The light from the flames illuminates the huge insect, a horrid hybrid of beetle, mantis, and wasp. Its compound eyes are blood red and large enough that Greg can see the flames reflected in them. Its exoskeleton, it's armor, is black and white. There's a distorted skull pattern on its head plate. The finest poker-straight black hairs cover parts of its shell.

Greg watches the insect's mandibles slowly open and close. It seems mesmerized by the flame. He notices a glistening layer of pink foam under its raised wings.

Greg holds the flaming ball of toilet paper up to the insect, feeling the burning heat on his arm. The insect's grasping front legs instinctively rear back from the fire, then slowly creep back towards it. Touching the flames, its appendages begin to burn and smoke, causing it to reel back from the fire. It pauses before detaching itself from Greg's mangled hand, then lunges at the fire, attacking in full force.

Greg throws the flaming ball of toilet paper and the insect into the bathtub. The insect's exoskeleton blackens in the flames. Forgetting his own dire state, Greg watches in a horrified trance as the insect burns.

The smoke stings his eyes. With his blood dripping onto the bathroom tile, staring down at the burned remains of the insect, Greg hears the hotel fire alarms sound. The insect's charred exoskeleton remains mostly intact. Greg picks up a plastic garbage bin and slams it down onto the burnt insect, crushing its remains. Just to be sure.

With the insect nothing more then a pile of ash, Greg examines the extent of damage to his hand. It looks like he plunged it into a bucket of broken glass. He feels lightheaded, and his vision began to blur. Greg grips the bathroom counter to hold himself up. The room is spinning. An intense pressure near his right eye is forcing it shut.

Greg lifts his head and catches his reflection in the mirror. His face is covered in blood. There are gaping slashes cris-crossing his face, with flays of skin hanging off them, revealing muscle fibers and frayed white tendons. On his cheek, where the insect had sunk its stinger, is a crater-sized abscess leaking pink foam. That entire side of his face and neck are swelling to noxious proportions. His eyes water, his throat burns. The air feels thin while he feels heavy. The trauma is impossible to digest. Greg collapses under the weight of it all.

When he regained consciousness, Greg was in a darkened hospital room. The dividing curtains between him and the other patients were drawn. He heard labored breathing and the beeping of machines. The bright fluorescent lights in the corridors lit the doorway. His window was cast in an orange light shining up from the parking lot lights below. Simply remaining conscious was exhausting. He was alive. That was enough. Greg closed his eyes.

When he awoke, Greg's bed sheets were covered in blood. He had accidentally ripped out his IV in the middle of the night. The sheets were replaced, and his IV had been reinserted.

During his first communication with the nurses, they explained that he'd been in a coma for seven days. His friends Jason and Steve had visited several times. Greg's major concern was whether his medical expense would be covered by his travel insurance. The nurses said not to worry, but to rest.

The doctor spoke in broken but comprehensive English. Greg had been rushed in under cardiac arrest due to blood loss. Defibrillation and blood transfusion had kept him alive. Now that his vital signs had stabilized and he'd awakened from the coma, he would be visited by a plastic surgeon.

The surgeon arrived later that afternoon. A nurse removed the stained bandages, and the surgeon examined Greg's wounds with a look of intense focus, breathing heavily through his nose.

The lacerations and puncture wounds on his hand and face were extensive. Greg had suffered significant nerve damage. The surgeon had performed initial restorative surgery during the time Greg had been in a coma, but much more was required. Due to the extent of damage, it was unlikely motor function could ever be fully restored to Greg's right hand. And his face? There was a visible downturn of the mouth and an eyebrow droop while at rest, both prognosticators of peripheral facial paralysis. The good news was that any damage to oral competence seemed limited. Greg expressed relief that his skills in cunnilingus had not been compromised. The surgeon continued with his medical dissertation, either failing to understand Greg's joke or choosing to ignore it.

Time had no currency in the hospital. Everything blurred together. Greg was semi-conscious when the detective entered the room and respectfully called out his name.

"Mr. Adler?"

Greg opened his eyes to see a large, heavy-set man with a bushy handlebar moustache standing in front of him.

"Yeah."

"I'm Police Detective Eduardo Flores. I represent the Agencia del Ministerio Público."

"Hello," muttered Greg, trying to gain his bearings. He focused on the detective's hound-dog face. It possessed a look of innate kindness. His skin tone was ashen, his eyes were emerald green with dark bags under them. The man looked like he hadn't slept in years.

"Mr. Adler, I realize you're in recovery, and I apologize for having to disturb you, but I need to ask some questions about the circumstances that brought you here."

"Okay." Greg waited.

"Mr. Adler, what do you remember from that day?"

"Everything until I blacked-out," replied Greg without hesitation

"At what point was that?" asked Detective Flores.

"I saw my reflection in the mirror, everything started spinning, and the lights went out."

"The lights went out?"

"The lights went out. I passed out. ... I fainted."

"Okay. And what do you remember up until that point?"

"I remember the insect," said Greg.

"The insect?"

"Yes an insect."

"An insect, like a bug, a cockroach?"

Greg offered no response.

The detective repeated himself. "An insect did this to you?"

Greg inhaled through his nose, filling his lungs, then releasing it with a prolonged exhalation. "Its ashes were in the bathtub."

"The bathtub," confirmed Detective Flores.

Greg spoke slowly and deliberately. "I burned the insect with a roll of toilet paper that I set on fire. That's how I got it off my hand. The insect climbed onto the fire. Then I threw it and the burning roll of toilet paper into the bathtub."

Detective Flores looked Greg in the eyes while nodding thoughtfully, as if he were trying to absorb what he was hearing. He took a moment to formulate his next question but, in fact, returned to the first one. "So you believe the damages you acquired to your face and hand were sustained by the attack of an insect?"

Greg closed his eyes. He didn't blame the detective for his confusion. He could hardly digest what had happened to him. He opened his eyes. "I'm not crazy. This isn't the drugs talking. I know what happened to me."

The detective shifted in his seat. "Sir, we have to ask questions to ensure that your memory of the events is intact."

"It is." Greg fired back.

"Okay, so ... how big was this insect?"

"Big enough to cover my fist."

The detective appeared completely unfazed by Greg's description. He skipped along with the questioning. "What were you doing that evening, before the attack?"

"I was having some drinks with my friends in their hotel room."

"Which friends?"

"Friends I traveled with from Canada and some girls we met at the resort. I don't remember the girls' names."

"How many people do you remember in the hotel room?"

"Five: myself, Jason, Steve, and the two girls from Vancouver."

"When did you leave their hotel room?"

"Like three, three or three-thirty a.m."

"Why did you leave?"

"I was tired."

"Where did you go?"

"My hotel room."

"You went back by yourself?"

"Yes. I brushed my teeth, went to sleep, and woke up when the insect attacked my face." For Greg the absurdity of the discussion was becoming more apparent with every answer given.

"What kind of insect?

"I have no fucking idea. The kind that shouldn't exist."

"You don't know?"

"I don't know."

"Describe it."

Greg cringed, recalling the insect. "I don't know. It was like this twisted mix of wasp and praying mantis and beetle ... with a hard shell -- what do you call it? --An exoskeleton, with black and white markings. Honestly this fucking thing, it had these huge black eyes. There was this glistening pink foam under its wings. And this monster was armed! It had these nasty black pincers with a shitload of crazy arms and claws, fuckin' covered in spikes, and this massive disgusting abdomen with a mean-looking stinger that it plunged into my fucking face. The pain was ... the pain is ... What is pain? What the fuck is pain? ... Go past that ... then ... I don't know, it fucking hurt."

Greg stopped, catching a look of confused bemusement on Detective Flores' face. "You think I'm loco. Fucked in the head right?"

"No, please, I'm listening. Please continue," Detective Flores encouraged.

"You think this is bullshit."

"Sir. I am listening," the detective assured him.

Greg went on the offensive. "You tell me what kind of fuckin' bug that was, cause there's nothing like that in my country."

Detective Flores decided to steer the conversation away from insects. "The doctors think your wounds were inflicted by a knife."

"Well, they're wrong," replied Greg without hesitation.

"This is what they think." Detective Flores shrugged.

Greg held his bandaged hand. "Yeah, that's what they think. And this is what I know."

Detective Flores leaned in, asserting eye contact. "They know you were viciously attacked. That is what they know. This is what we know."

Greg felt threatened. "You think I'm protecting someone? If some fucking asshole with a knife did this to me, I would be the first to tell you. I'm an honest, hardworking Canadian who came down here to sip Coronas and splash around under the sun."

"No one disputes this sir," answered Detective Flores passively.

"I don't know what fuckin' fruit basket that thing rode in on cause I swear to God, man ... How can that thing exist and you have no idea what the fuck I am talking about?" Greg asked, his nerves shot.

Detective Flores replied calmly, "This is why we ask questions, so we can understand ... so we can understand what happened."

"I told you what happened."

Detective Flores stood up abruptly. "Mr. Adler, I thank you for your time."

"You're leaving?"

"I am."

"So where's this go? What now?"

"Now ... now you rest."

Greg demanded that the nurse remove his catheter. She would not. Greg demanded to know why. The nurse asked him to calm down. As she was walking away, Greg screamed after her, "A plastic tube is stuck inside my dick and I want it out now!"

At that moment, Jason and Steve appeared at his door. Steve asked, in perfect dead pan, "So, how you enjoying the vacation so far?"

Greg was happy to have friends by his side. It reminded him of a life where you weren't at risk of being shredded by hostile insects. Jason and Steve were a couple of hooligans, but they could be counted on when the shit hit the fan, even if it was usually a direct result of their own actions.

Steve had a stocky frame and walked like a brawler. He never dodged a fight, but didn't go out of his way looking for one. Steve's eyes were always puffy and red, with dark circles under them like he didn't get enough sleep, which he didn't. Steve's ingrained sense of personal responsibility often conflicted with his hard-living lifestyle; in many ways they came from the same place. Steve believed in good times and had the right sense of humor to keep them rolling.

Jason was Steve's physical opposite. He was tall and wiry, even attractive, except for his yellowed teeth, resulting from a steady diet of coffee and cigarettes. Jay was a high-strung individual with a proclivity for drugs and gambling. He had screwed himself over more times then he cared to imagine but tried his damnedest never to fuck over a friend.

Greg had hoped their vacation would be filled with laughter, recounting old stories while gaining new material for the next one. Now Greg was looking up at his friends from his hospital bed.

"Shouldn't you guys be back in Fort Mac destroying the environment?" asked Greg.

Steve checked his watch. "Nah we're too busy playing beach volleyball with some babes we met at the hotel."

"Perfect tens and they love to drink," chimed in Jason.

"Do these gentlemen have names?" asked Greg without missing a beat. Laughter broke the ice, followed by an awkward pause, before Jason got right to the point. "What the fuck happened to you?"

"You know, comparing medical systems. Just being a tourist," joked Greg.

But the question was too big to ignore and Jason pressed on. "For real, Greg. We're the ones who found you."

Greg nodded his head solemnly at the news. Steve continued, "The fire alarm went off. We stumbled over to your room."

"We smelled the smoke from your room and started banging on your door," Jason added.

"I had that spare key card you gave me," said Steve.

Jason was fidgeting. "Man, I've never seen that much blood. You were sprawled out on the bathroom floor like someone took a hatchet to you."

"I bolted to the lobby, yelling for an ambulance, while Jay stood there shitting himself," quipped Steve.

"Fuck that. Steve was just searching your pockets for more blow."

It was good to see that, despite the trauma and bloodshed, everyone's sense of humor was keenly intact. "You guys saved my life. You did. You saved my life. When they loaded me into the ambulance, I went into cardiac arrest. They gave me the shock paddles and a blood transfusion."

An awkward silence hovered between the men. Steve ended it. "The federales thought we were the ones who did this to you."

"They were trying to steer us into it. They kept pressing us about drugs, asking how business was going," stressed Jason.

"One cop would leave the room and a new cop would come in, asking the same fucking questions in a different order. They wouldn't give us a phone call or let us speak to a lawyer. I started demanding names and badge numbers and they'd slap me in the back of the head, laughing in my fucking face," said Steve, clearly full of disdain for his former captors.

"How did you get out?" asked Greg, shocked by his friends' experience.

"We stopped talking and eventually got to see our lawyers who talked to some Canadian diplomats who put the heat on them to let us go," Steve explained. "They had to. There was no weapon, no motive. Remember those girls from Vancouver?"

Greg nodded.

Jason jumped in. "They gave a statement that we were with them when the fire alarm went off. And we found you minutes after."

"They had to let us go," said Steve.

"Thank God, they didn't plant some fuckin shit on us," added Jason.

"What a fucking nightmare. I'm sorry, guys."

"You were in a coma. What the fuck were you going to do?" said Steve.

"You're alive, that's all that matters. Forget the other bullshit," said Jason.

Greg fought back a sudden flood of emotion. He was not going to cry. Not here. No way. Jason and Steve gave him a moment to gather himself.

When Greg looked composed, Steve asked, "Greg?"

"Yeah?"

"What the fuck happened to you?"

Greg knew the question could not be ignored this time. "When you found me, did you look in the bathtub?"

"There was a garbage bin and a pile of ashes," said Steve, confirming what Greg knew to be true.

"No word of a lie -- my face, my hand, what you saw, the blood, the smoke, all of it was the aftermath of me getting attacked by a vicious insect the size of my forearm."

"Is there a hidden camera here somewhere?" joked Steve.

Greg reinforced his claim. "On my mother's grave, it was a giant wretched fucking wasp-mantis-thing that carved me up like this."

The conversation stopped. Greg spoke with conviction but he could see Jason and Steve were unable to process what he was telling them.

Jason spoke first. "You were unconscious in a pool of blood when we found you. That kind of trauma has got to fuck with your head. I'm surprised you remember anything. But if that's what you believe, then some wires got crossed or something."

"They put you on morphine and you know that shit will spin you around. When they gave Johnny morphine after he wrecked his bike, he saw his dead grandpa shitting in the corner of his hospital room," said Steve, supporting Jason's point.

Greg had heard their friend Johnny Lucas recount his story on more than one occasion. It made no difference. "I know what happened to me."

Jason's mounting frustration was starting to show. "You got fucked up, man! This is your brain's defense mechanism against what really happened. Or maybe you just got strung out on your meds, because this bug bullshit is crazy talk. "

"Defense mechanism? You think my subconscious decided to lighten the blow to my fragile psyche by swapping out the memory of actual events with the memory of being attacked by a carnivorous insect straight from Dante's inferno?"

"Personally, I think that ... no, I *know* that what happened was an inside job. Some dirty fuckin' spic whose sister's a cleaning lady was let into your room to steal shit."

"Easy, Jay. Show some respect for my roommates behind the curtain here. This is not the place." Greg could see how distraught Jason was and he didn't want him to create a disturbance in the hospital. Jason was next to impossible to rein in when he got fired up.

"No! Fuck that! This place is one con after another. They think ripping off gringos is their God-given right. Some greasy Mexican was rifling through your hotel room when you walked in and busted him, and the motherfucker went at you with a knife!"

"For what, Jay? They know we have safes for valuables. They break into my room for what? My T-shirts? A pair of underwear? Steel my fuckin' toothbrush?" said Greg.

Jason was having none of it. "They're desperate, man. They'll grab anything. They fuckin' hate us! Whitey owns their beaches, we own their business, we own their land. We own their resorts and pay them pennies to keep 'em clean and serve us. The only thing we buy from them is their shitty fuckin' drugs. They'll scam a dollar any chance they get. They greet you with a smile, but half these fuckers would love to put a knife in our backs!"

"Jay, ease off, man. Enough dude," said Steve, stepping into the fray.

"Fuck off, Steve! Look at Greg's face, man! They spray down the room for bugs every week. You'd be lucky to spot a single fucking cockroach! Where the fuck was this demon bug hiding? Was it sipping drinks down by the wet bar and we never noticed?"

Greg winced at the volume in Jason's voice. "Jay, please! Seriously, fuckin' relax, man! Keep the volume down. They're going to kick your ass out of here. We don't need anyone getting arrested again."

Clearly Jason wanted to start breaking things.

"Jason just stop ... just stop. It's alright," begged Greg.

Jason could hear the desperation in his plea and fought hard to choke down his rage. "I'm sorry, man. It's just ... those sick motherfuckers ...what they did to you..."

Greg decided to try to diffuse the situation by changing the topic. "I'm on the mend. It's cool. We're good. Just relax. Talk to me. Tell me what's going on. What's happening? What's happening with you guys, now? When you flying back?"

"When you're ready to fly back with us," said Steve.

"No man left behind," said Jason, looking shaken but composed.

Greg didn't know when he could return home. He knew Jason and Steve needed to return to work. The damage had been done, and there was a good chance they would be fired if they missed another turn around. They'd already been put on warning.

A nurse arrived to redress Greg's bandages. Greg asked Jason and Steve to leave while she did so. Steve followed Jason outside for a cigarette. Greg asked the nurse if there was any progress on getting his catheter removed. The nurse looked confused. Greg waved it off in frustration and let the nurse do her work.

When Jason and Steve returned, Greg made his request. He wanted them to fly back to Canada without him. He didn't want anyone waiting for him. It was a hard-fought battle that took some serious convincing, but eventually Jason and Steve begrudgingly agreed to respect Greg's wish.

After the two men left, Greg was emotionally drained. He felt queasy from exhaustion and knew sleep would be a reprieve, but had trouble drifting off with the catheter still in place.

Greg awoke in the night and it could not be denied. He was paralyzed with fear. The slightest movement would trigger the onslaught. Greg was not a man of faith but he prayed. In the grips of terror he prayed to make it go away, just make it go away.

There it sat on the windowsill, holding its grasping front legs to its face. It's crimson eyes revealed nothing. Was it resting, listening, watching, waiting?

Greg heard footsteps in the hallway. A nurse was making her rounds. He couldn't speak but his mind screamed for her to go away. The nurse entered the room and the insect flared its wings.

Greg's scream carried him into consciousness. It cut through the drug-induced slumber of his roommates and sent their weakened hearts racing. A nurse rushed in to the room. She found Greg curled in the fetal position, clutching the arm of his damaged hand. The nurse wanted to know what happened. Greg appeared catatonic and was drenched in sweat, his soaked sheets cling to his skin. The nurse was worried about infection. She needed to change his bed sheets.

Greg had been in the Hospital Americano for a total of six weeks but it felt like a year. Jason and Steve had returned home at Greg's insistence. Now, thanks to the help of the doctors and nurses, that time had arrived for Greg. All medical documents would be transferred to his doctor back home. Greg had been inquiring about his personal possessions. He was ready to book his flight home and was concerned about his missing passport. Phone calls were made.

Greg was attempting to sketch a Tyrannosaurus rex with his left hand. Greg was a decent illustrator but drawing with his weak hand made it look like he'd drawn the T-rex on an Etch-a-sketch. It was a struggle, but he'd have to get used to it, as restoring the motor function in his mangled right hand was an unlikely prospect.

Greg was working on the T-rex's teeth when he heard a knock and looked up to see Detective Flores. The detective was standing in the doorway, holding Greg's missing suitcase. "They tell me you're ready fly home. You might need this."

Greg had wondered if he'd see the detective again. Detective Flores brought the suitcase to Greg's bedside. "You should check and make sure nothing's missing."

Greg rose from the bed to take his suitcase. He put it on the bed, opened it, and looked inside. On top of his folded clothes were his sneakers, flip-flops, and bathroom kit.

"Your wallet, sunglasses, iPod, and passport are in the inside pocket."

Greg zipped open the inner lining of his suitcase and saw that all items were accounted for. "I appreciate you bringing it by. *Gracias.*"

"*De nada,*" said Detective Flores. "We haven't given up. We're going to find who did this to you," said the detective with such conviction that Greg's heart went out to the man.

"The question is not who, it's what. My attacker was cremated in the bathtub before you arrived on the scene. If you have the ashes, get them analyzed. I don't know what else to say," was all Greg could offer.

"Mr. Adler to be blunt, your story is.... is not possible. The most dangerous bugs in Mexico are scorpions and black widows, there isn't an insect on the planet that could shred a persons flesh like this. "

Greg closed his suitcase. "If you think I'm withholding information and want to arrest me for it, then go ahead. I have nothing left to say. So with all due respect, I am done talking to you. I appreciate your efforts and thank you again for bringing me my suitcase."

Greg hugged and thanked the nurses who had cared for him during his stay, then caught a crowded elevator to the hospital's ground level. A lineup of taxis waited outside the entrance. He walked to the nearest one. The driver wanted to put Greg's suitcase in the trunk, but Greg brought it into the back seat with him. He asked the driver for a price to the airport, knowing from the nurses that it should cost no more than 300 pesos. The driver asked for 500 pesos. Greg responded with a suggestion of 350, and the driver countered with 450. Greg gave 350 pesos as his final offer.

"No, *señoor*," replied the driver.

Greg got out of the taxi.

The driver relented. "Okay, okay, 350."

Greg paused. "You take me to the airport for 350 pesos?"

"*Sí, sí.* Yeah, okay."

"Alright, then." Greg stepped back into the taxi. Even though his face was bandaged like the invisible man, he still had to haggle over a taxi fare.

In the past, Greg had experienced a creeping dread while waiting in airport terminals. When they called out row numbers to commence boarding, he had to fight off a full-blown panic attack. Flying was a hellish experience. If they encountered the slightest degree of turbulence, his hands immediately turned clammy and his body odor kicked into overdrive. He'd become a twisted, knotted ball of tension and frayed nerves. It was a grueling endurance test. He would sit up straight, with his hands locked together, in tight-lipped silence. At no point during a flight would he ever recline his chair, fearing the slightest hint of relaxation might anger the gods, as though the plane was being kept aloft by his humility alone.

If the 'fasten seat belt' sign came on, and the people wandering the cabin, including the flight staff, did not take an immediate seat, Greg had to bite his tongue not to scream at them for risking the safety of others by offending the gods with their arrogance. This twisted logic was part of the reason Greg did not sedate himself for air travel. For him it was a penance to be served. If he denied it, there would be severe consequences. He realized this was pure superstition but could not ignore it. Even if he could have, Greg was convinced there wasn't a drug on earth that could quell his fear.

When he was young, there was no fear attached to flying. He'd stare out the window, daydreaming. If the plane hit an air pocket, he'd feel a tickle in his stomach. As an adult, air turbulence produced a fear so intense it felt like poison in his veins. Greg's heart would pound in his chest, the stale cabin air a blanket smothering him. If the turbulence did not relent, he'd start hyperventilating. Only by a sheer willpower would Greg keep from collapsing in on himself.

A flight from Toronto to Vancouver when Greg was twelve had planted the seed of fear. He was traveling with his mother to visit his uncle in Campbell River. The first hour and a half of the flight, there was moderate turbulence but nothing to cause alarm. At some point over the mountains, the plane experienced an unexpected drop in altitude, so severe that flight attendants walking the cabin, and several passengers with their seatbelts off were slammed into the ceiling.

Greg felt what it was like to fall from the sky. It did not tickle his stomach. He kept his ass clenched trying not to shit himself.

The screaming continued, while the wings rattled and the cabin shook. The moment the plane stabilized, there was another sickening plummet. Greg's mom squeezed his hand, digging her fingernails into his skin. She leaned over and spoke to him, but Greg heard nothing. He was numb. This was his reality. It could not be denied. He was twelve years old and his life was about to end.

He turned to his mother. Her lips were pursed, her jaw clenched. She was staring straight ahead with a look of intense focus. He knew she was still fighting to protect him. His mother didn't deserve this. Greg wanted to tell her how sorry he was, how much he loved her, how he understood her sacrifice.

When the plane landed safely on the tarmac, the cabin erupted in applause. Greg's mother looked down at him. He was wide-eyed and ghostly pale, soaked through with sweat, his hair stuck to his forehead. Greg looked up at her, shaking his head in disbelief. With a forced smile and a nervous laugh, she patted his knee. "Well, we made it."

Greg waited, seated at his departure gate in the Cancun International Airport. He was feeling a strong buzz from the Percocets and beer. A mother, sitting across from him, reprimanded her little boy for staring at the bandaged man. Anyone who looked at his mummy-wrapped face had to wonder. Greg amused himself with the idea of wearing a T-shirt with the words, 'Whatever you think happened is wrong'.

The return flight to Toronto was scheduled to board in twenty minutes. The dread normally associated with flying was gone. Greg didn't have the emotional reserve. After his encounter with the insect, flying was an afterthought. If the plane went down, God bless … what's a guy to do? Barely survive a carnivorous insect destroying your face, just to get eviscerated in a plane crash? Fuck it. He'd had enough. He owed nothing.

The flight over the ocean was a bumpy ride. In the past, Greg would have focused on a screw in the seat in front of him, to the exclusion of everything else, try to go zen in order to maintain sanity. If the flight was six hours, that's how long he'd stare at the screw. Now the persistent turbulence had little effect. He could sleep through it. What bothered Greg was the kid screeching in the seat behind him and the old man beside him eating a hardboiled egg that he'd pulled from his pocket wrapped in tin foil, a stink bomb that should have never made it past security. Flying first class had never occurred to him before. It made no sense paying for a better seat in hell. Now, he thought, the extra legroom might be nice.

There was snow on the tarmac at Pearson International. Greg's flight had arrived twenty-minutes behind schedule and had been waiting another twenty minutes for an available unloading bridge. The passengers were anxious to disembark after the five-hour flight. Greg was content watching the snowfall outside his window. He would have to dig out his sweater from his suitcase. His toque and winter jacket were waiting in his truck at the Park 'N Fly.

After a thirty-minute wait and many intercom apologies from the flight staff, an open-air bridge revealed itself. Greg waited for every other passenger to exit the plane before leaving his seat. At arrivals he stood ten feet behind the fence of people surrounding the carousel, waiting for their luggage.

The snow was coming down in heavy wet flakes. Greg hunched his shoulders, holding his arms close to his chest, protecting his core from the piercing wind while he waited for the Park 'N Fly shuttle bus. Greg picked up his luggage; ready to go back inside the terminal when he saw the shuttle turn the corner towards him.

It felt good to sit inside his truck. He threw on his jacket and cranked the heat. Greg plugged his iPod into its radio adapter and scrolled through music while the truck warmed up. He decided on Charlie Byrd Parker for the drive home. It was 3 a.m., the 401 as quiet as it could get.

Winter was firmly entrenched in the landscape. Flurries of snow rolled across the highway like broken ghosts.

Greg opened the door to his apartment, dropped his luggage inside the door, and walked to the kitchen. There was a frozen pizza in the freezer. He put it in the oven and cracked open the six-pack of beer he had placed in the fridge in anticipation of his return. The first sip was ice-cold perfection.

He flopped down on the couch to watch hockey highlights. Greg nodded his encouragement as the Leafs beat up on the Senators. Some things never got old. It felt good to be back where hockey took precedence over soccer.

That week, a new set of doctors took turns assessing how to improve the patchwork of Greg's face. He received workers' compensation while undergoing what seemed like an endless battery of reconstructive surgeries, including tendon transfers, as well as skin and nerve grafting. His face still looked like it had gone through a windshield. It was a chaotic mix of scarring: elevated, linear, hypertrophy, webbed. There was a lazy droop on one side of his face and sporadic facial twitches when he was tired. The insect had left him looking like a Dick Tracy villain. The scarring on his hand matched the patchwork of his face and required an ongoing rehabilitation of motor skills to simply learn how to hold a pencil again.

Greg emailed the Toronto Entomologist Association, to notify them he'd encountered a new species of carnivorous insect, not in the jungles of the Amazon, but in his hotel room at a 3-star resort in Mexico.

In his initial e-mail Greg did not describe the vicious nature of the encounter. If the group assumed he was crazy, it could hinder his chances of a reply, which he subsequently received from TEA member, Stanley Cho.

Stanley could not identify the insect based on Greg's description. The only insects that came anywhere close in size were *Titanus giganteus, Megasoma acteon, Megasoma elephas,* and *Phobaeticus serratipes* (three scarab beetles and a stick insect). None of them matched the description of the mantis-wasp hybrid Greg had encountered, but Stanley sent photos of them anyway.

Stanley had the utmost confidence in his expertise, but, to be certain, he consulted an entomologist in Latin America, the region of discovery, and she couldn't identify the insect Greg described either. Stanley informed Greg that his mystery insect would have to remain a mystery for now. Greg thanked Stanley for his interest and promptly sent a $100 donation to TEA.

Every day Greg scoured the news but there was nothing. It was beyond comprehension that he was the only person to ever encounter the insect. It had to come from somewhere. There was nothing to do but wait for another sighting. He would not question his sanity. If it was some strange suppression of a traumatic memory, why would his mind manifest such an abhorrent replacement? No, it was as real as the scars on his face.

Although he had the capacity, Greg had no desire to return to work. He would take workers' comp until it ran out. The lack of any subsequent proof to legitimize the story of his attack threw him into the grips of depression. He bought himself a water bong, an ounce of weed, and the newest PlayStation. He had a supply of painkillers and a fridge full of beer. He had no aspirations beyond -- and these were in no particular order -- sleeping, getting stoned, playing video games, watching TV, and jerking off to Internet porn. If he got hungry, he'd order in. That was the recovery plan.

Greg removed his bathroom mirror. There were nights he'd sleep with the light on. He grew more lethargic as the days passed. He could no longer be bothered to leave the couch for a piss and instead went in near-by Slurpee cup.

His hair had grown past his shoulders. It was not a good look for a man with a thinning hairline. Greg stopped shaving. His beard was feral and grew in around his scars. Greg refused all invitations from his friends before deciding to turn his phone off. Then Johnny Lucas came knocking with a twelve of Blue.

Johnny had just returned from an epic bender on the west coast with Jason and Steve. They'd spent it in a state of suspended intoxication, floating down the Shuswap in a rented houseboat. They had tried to convince Greg to join them, but he'd lied, saying he had another skin graft scheduled, when in fact he had canceled all subsequent surgeries.

Greg heard Johnny pounding on his door. He would not be denied. This was a rescue mission. "Greger! Open this fuckin' door or I'm kicking it down! You'll leave me no choice. For all I know, you've choked on a god-damn pizza crust and you're rotting away in your own filth. I can't allow that!"

Greg opened the door. He knew Johnny would make good on his threat. Greg saw Johnny's look, alarmed at first by the severity and extent of his scarring, but his buddy adeptly covered up his shock with his own unique brand of bluster and bravado.

"Holy shit! Wonders never cease! Howard Hughes is gonna bless us with his presence."

Johnny waltzed inside, needing no invitation. He marched straight to the fridge with the twelve bottles of Blue and opened the door. " Christ almighty, when's the last time you were in here? Time to change the baking soda, buddy."

Johnny put the beer in the fridge, then grabbed two for him and Greg. They cracked them open, then clinked their bottles together. Greg led Johnny into the living room. Empty boxes of take-out covered the coffee table. In the middle of them was the plastic Slurpee cup filled with piss. Greg tossed his blanket and some clothes off the couch to make room for them to sit. Johnny sparked a cigarette. On TV, a young Jeff Goldblum was is in the middle of an arm-wrestling match, then snapped his opponent's carpal bone so badly it pierced through the skin.

"Jesus Christ, man. That's fucking vicious." Johnny blew smoke into the air and flicked ash into the Slurpee cup.

At Johnny's instance, Greg not only dumped the dirty bong water but rinsed the bong itself. When he brought the cleansed bong back to the living room, Johnny packed a bowl and they filled their lungs with smoke. On TV, Jeff Goldblum had started pulling his fingernails off. Johnny demanded they switch to the ballgame. "I'm not into this horror shit."

"It's a cautionary tale."

"What, don't drink and teleport? You'd have to be drunk to step into one of those fuckin' things."

"Yo know it was filmed in Toronto. David Cronenberg, a Canadian, directed it."

"Yeah, yeah. I know who the fuck David Cronenberg is. I also know he's a sick fuck, and so are you, if you enjoy watching poor Jeff Goldblum's face rot off while he turns into a shit-eating fly."

Greg was glad to see Johnny. It was a welcome distraction from his despondency. Johnny was crude, crass, stubborn, ignorant, and at times exasperating, but always entertaining. Johnny was genuine. His moustache-mullet combo didn't contain a trace of irony.

Greg paused the movie and switched to a Jays game. The Yankees were crushing them. They had the bases loaded. Johnny couldn't take it any more.

"Fuck the Yankees! If those motherfuckers win another World Series, I'm going to throw up."

"What do you want to watch?"

"Nothing. Fuck TV. Let's go to a bar."

"I'm not into it."

"Bullshit. Let's find some music. It's Monday night. Let's go to the Dakota, hear some music. Remember the last time when that sultry little copperhead was up on stage with that country band, making love to her violin. That body with those fiery locks? You're gonna pass that up?"

"I need to chill tonight."

"Just chill out and grow your beard some more. Fuck that. Let's go to Filmores then. I'll buy you a lap dance."

"Honestly, I'm not feeling well. I want to keep things low-key."

"You know what will help you feel better? Some fresh air. How great does that sound? So go take a shit, shower, shave that road kill off your face."

"I'm not into it."

"What? Are you on your period?"

"Johnny, leave it alone. I'm not going out."

"So what? You're gonna make me beg? You're gonna make a friend beg? That's what you're gonna do? You're gonna make me beg."

"Fuck you ... Okay, we go some place close. No bullshit, no confrontation, no rowdiness."

"Can we go someplace with women or do you want to be the only pussy in the room?"

"Hey, Johnny?"

"Yes, boss?"

"Go fuck yourself. You're buying the first round."

Greg re-hung the bathroom mirror that he'd stored in his bedroom closet. He used paper scissors to shear down his beard before he could use the razor. Running the razor over his cheeks took patience. It was next to impossible to shave over the web of scars without cutting himself. There were some hairs poking through condensed areas of scar tissue that he had to pluck out with tweezers. Driblets of blood ran down his face as he wiped the hair from his sink with wads of toilet paper.

He offered Percocets to Johnny before they went to the bar. Johnny wanted to crush and snort them. Greg had tried this method of ingestion but one crushed pill created a mountain of powder that you needed to a snowplow to get through. The burn wasn't bad but it caked the nose like you were snorting flour and there was little improvement in the desired effect. It was much easier to wash the pills down with beer. So it was decided. They popped two percs each, chugged back their beer, and left for the bar.

He awoke with a gasp, wrenched back from oblivion. The inside of his mouth was desiccated; there wasn't a particle of moisture left. His lips were split and caked in blood. A hardened white film covered his cracked tongue. Greg pushed himself off the bathroom floor and staggered to the kitchen. He cranked the cold water, leaned over the dirty dishes, and stuck his head under the tap. His mouth was dust and cotton. It took several seconds before he could feel any semblance of moisture on his tongue. The world spun around him as he sucked in water.

He tried to lie back down in bed but nausea overwhelmed him. Greg burped and was repulsed by toxic fumes of whiskey. He rushed to the bathroom. His poisoned stomach, triggered by the sudden inflow of water, rejected all its contents.

When he awoke later that afternoon he was still drunk. The pressure behind his eyes threatened to split open his skull. There was a stabbing pain in his sides. Greg was hit by another heavy wave of nausea and lurched towards the washroom. His stomach felt empty but was not done purging itself.

Greg stopped at the sink to rinse the puke out of his mouth. When he caught his reflection in the mirror, his knees buckled. Parts of his face and neck had swollen to monstrous proportions, as if someone had inflated giant pockets of saline underneath his skin. The obscene swellings were numb to his touch. He felt faint and took a deep breath to calm himself. His mouth instantly ran dry and tasted of all things expired.

Greg went to the kitchen and filled a Viking-sized beer mug with water. Cold water ran down the sides of his chin. His eyes were being forced shut by the swelling. His vision blurred with patches of gold and a million microdots of color rushing past him. His legs gave way. Everything melted.

Cold sweat, water, blood, and broken glass ... Greg regained consciousness on the kitchen floor. He touched his face. The swelling had gone down, sensation had returned. He'd survived whatever reaction he'd been having. Greg was left alone to suffer his hangover.

A dull ache in Greg's side persisted over the following weeks. It was an internal pressure that was increasing in discomfort. He had to pee every twenty minutes and was constantly thirsty. Greg stopped drinking alcohol and stuck to water. His body couldn't get enough of the H2O. He worried that he had done damage to his kidneys and liver with all the mixing of booze and prescription painkillers that he'd done in recent months. When Greg did a Google search on "persistent thirst and urination," possible symptoms included hyperglycemia, kidney damage, diabetes, liver disease, intestinal bleeding, stress, and incontinence. He didn't like his options.

Health was now Greg's number one concern. No drugs, no booze, healthy eating, exercise, scheduled sleep. It was time to take control and face the world again. He'd commit to clean living, hoping it would cure whatever was ailing him. With his health restored, he'd make some phone calls and get back to work. He'd wallowed in his sorrows long enough. It was time to take charge and face the world. Greg filled a glass of water and raised it to his recently cleaned kitchen. "To new beginnings."

Greg left his apartment for the first time in weeks. He got a haircut, purchased a new pair of running shoes, then went to a natural health store and purchased $200 worth of vitamins. Then he went for groceries at Fiesta Farms, where he bought cranberry juice, green tea, yogurt, fruits, vegetables (lots of dark greens), multi-grain breads, lean ground beef, chicken, and wild salmon.

He starting going to bed early and rose with the dawn to go jogging. He ate right and took his vitamins, never wavering from his new health regimen, yet his condition was deteriorating. His thirst became dysfunctional.

One afternoon when the temperature was hovering around 27°C (80.6°F), Greg went for a jog through Cedar Vail, a nearby park. It was busy with people out enjoying the day. Greg felt the heat of the sun bearing down on him. The camel pack of water he now needed when jogging was empty. There were white pasties in the corners of his cracked lips. He smacked his mouth together, desperate for water. Finally Greg reached a water fountain beside a collection of busy tennis courts.

He was hooked on the first sip. The euphoric rush was overwhelming. It was cold and clean. He was not drinking water --he was drinking the life source known as water. It was the only way to cleanse the poison from his body. He closed his eyes and absorbed.

The rational part of him knew to stop. It understood there was a queue of people forming behind him but he was tapped into the mainline and could not let go. The cold water tied him to something ancient, something true. Drink, was the message. Drink while it flows.

He heard the noise in the background growing but he would not listen. *This is why we thirst. So we can drink. Connect to the flow, to the truth.* They were yelling at him. *Do not let go. Cold and clean. This is why. Do not let go. Drink.*

A hush fell over the collection of people waiting at the fountain. There was something wrong with this man. They backed off but could not turn away.

There was no more room. It started to rise from his stomach. Greg fell to the ground as he puked torrents of water. The crowd gasped in horror. When he stopped regurgitating water, Greg heard someone ask from a safe distance, with a tremble in his voice, whether he was all right.

Greg forced himself up off the ground and started the walk back. When he returned home, he filled a plastic juice jug with water and brought it to the living room. He sat on the couch with the jug of water shaking in his hand. Something was very wrong. He had lost control. For the first time since his mother died, Greg completely broke down.

It was utter turmoil. There were nights he fell asleep on the toilet due to the constant threat of sudden, violent evacuation. Everything was being rejected. With each passing hour the contents being dumped into the toilet became more and more suspect.

Greg felt his stomach churning with another gastric surge. He broke out in chills as his knotted insides twisted tighter. His discomfort was so severe that he had to breathe through clenched teeth just to keep himself on the toilet. He grunted and moaned in absolute torture. He was ready to keel over when he was finally shown mercy and the noxious torrent ripped through his bowels.

When Greg woke up on the bathroom tiles with his pants around his ankles, he had no idea how long he'd been there. He pushed himself up to wipe his ass. He looked back into the toilet. There was blood in the water. The murky waste consisted mostly of what appeared to be thousands of tiny black branches. Greg made sure to flush.

Greg scraped the white film off the top of his tongue with a butter knife, then wiped the knife on a hanging towel. Underneath the white film was a half-inch thick, scabrous gray shell with the texture of bark. Greg pulled it off in flakes until he reached the final layer. This last layer had planted roots in his tongue. Greg ripped off a piece and wailed from the shock of pain. He cursed aloud and could taste blood. Tears ran down his cheeks.

Greg inspected the chunk of grey scab. Pink flesh hung in tatters from underneath it. Greg spit a mouthful of blood into the sink, then stuck his tongue out at the mirror. The pulled scab left a crater in the top of his tongue that instantly filled with blood.

Dried meat embedded in the walls. The walls formed in wax. The carcass grows. Gnarled, twisted, bones, teeth, tusks, claws, hooves, fingernails. Alive, now dead, always dead. Stacked and stored. The husk is home. Feed, drink, build, breathe.

Greg awoke, gasping for air, sucking wind through a pinched straw, his chin resting on the monstrous goiter that had bloomed in his neck. He scraped more yellow crud from his mouth with his fingernails and wiped it off on the couch. He chugged back the jug of water and his mouth went instantly dry.

Greg was oblivious to the wafts of urine rising from his piss-soaked floor. He had found shelter in a daydream of summer days spent by the lake where she took him camping. That's where he could breathe, before the open sky was replaced with drywall. She was gone, but the lake remained. *Find the lake. Freedom to breathe. Freedom to drink.*

Cathy Russell had just driven across town to drop off a missing hockey glove for her boy, William, at his dad's house. Now she was stuck in traffic on Eglinton, trying to turn onto Allen Road to access the 401 highway. She was exhausted and just wanted to get home. It was 10:30 p.m. "Why the fuck am I still stuck in traffic?" she screamed. Cathy shook her head and fell quiet after her outburst, then, as she inevitably did in such moments, began stressing over money. This is what she did while stuck in traffic. This is what she did while waiting for the light to turn green.

It had been a particularly bad week. Cathy's insurance company raised her car's monthly premium by $100 because of three ticket infractions in four years. She had been nailed with the third infraction by, as she put it to a friend, "some patronizing, asshole cop who just learned to shave." The police officer had been parked around a corner, picking off drivers who were trying to escape rush hour gridlock by turning off the congested main street into a residential zone during off-hours.

Cathy was hoping her insurance premium would go down that year. She could barely keep her car on the road as it was. It didn't help that the city seemed to add a new vehicle tax every year.

Cathy's mood went from bad to worse as she stewed in traffic. Always, always stuck in traffic. Half her life seemed to be spent in it. The population outsized the infrastructure but they kept packing them in like sardines. Expenses went up across the board while wages stayed the same and hours got scaled back. The money the government wasted on bullshit committees and think tanks made her sick. The city complained about their empty coffers but was too chickenshit to go after the real money, giving major property developers every concession they wanted. Tax the assholes making millions, building glass towers to the sky as homes for the next influx of wealthy immigrants. Don't go after the single mom barely scraping by enough hours at Home Depot to pay rent. Fuck them all. The stress, the fucking stress, it never stopped. Cathy bit her bottom lip and shook her head, fighting the urge to lay into her car horn and never stop. Then she saw it – and her heart stopped.

It pulled up beside her. The light turned green. It drove past. Previous thoughts obliterated. Cathy ignored the honking from the cars behind her. Fighting back the tears, on the verge of meltdown, she dug deep to bring herself together. Cathy took a deep breath and started driving, not knowing where, just looking for the first opportunity to pull over.

Dispatch: 9-1-1

Caller: Hi ... I ...There's a man in a pickup truck on the road and there's something wrong with him.

Dispatch: Where are you calling from?

Caller: I was stopped at the intersection on Eglinton waiting to turn onto Allen Road but I saw this guy, this thing ... I don't know ... I had to pull over. I had to stop.

Dispatch: Can I get your name, please?

Caller: Cathy.

Dispatch: Cathy, where are you calling from?

Cathy: Yorkdale Mall. The parking lot at Yorkdale Mall.

Dispatch: Was this man driving erratically?

Caller: His face is.... it's swollen ... like the side ... his neck ... looks like ... his mouth is ... I, I don't know ... His face is just ... There's something wrong with him.

Dispatch: Did you get a make on the truck or the truck's license plate number?

Caller: No, no. I just ... this guy's face ... It was, like, it was moving ... this thing on the side.

Dispatch: What color was the truck?

Caller: Black ...or gray. I don't know, I don't know. Black ... I think it was black.

Dispatch: Try to relax. Take a deep breath. Slow it down. I'm not going anywhere. Is everything all right with you?

Caller: Yeah. No. Yeah, I'm fine. It's just ...what ...? I don't know what it was.

Dispatch: So you haven't suffered any kind of trauma? You weren't in a collision or anything?

Caller: Well, no. I mean ... no.

Dispatch: Are you under the influence of any kind of medications, drugs, or alcohol?

Caller: No.

Dispatch: So you're waiting to turn onto Allen Road and that's when you saw this man?

Caller: At the second set of lights before you can turn off Eglinton, where the buses leave the station, I saw it. In the lane beside me.

Dispatch: And he turned onto Allen Road?

Caller: Yes. I lost him at the light. I couldn't drive. I couldn't move.... That man is sick. There's something wrong with him.

Dispatch: Okay, Cathy, I thank you for your call. We're going to find this man and we're going to help him. I need you to do something for me. I need you to stay where you are. I'm sending a police officer over to you right now to make sure you're all right. All other patrolling officers will be notified to look for a gray or black pickup truck that may be driving erratically.

Caller: I'm telling you, there's something wrong with this guy. There's something very wrong. It's bad. This is bad.

Officer Darcy Bourassa sipped a coffee in the Petro-Canada parking lot at Bayview and Sheppard. He was furious about a recent property assessment he'd received from M.P.A.C. Where the fuck did they get their numbers from? No one's buying a semi-detached with a shared driveway for that price. How was that fair market value in an economic downturn? Once again the city he'd sworn to protect was gouging him. After handing out enough traffic tickets to pay for five city daycare centers, a slap in the face is the thanks he gets. It was fucking insulting.

Darcy imagined when he became a cop that he'd joined a brotherhood. He'd be among the upper ranks of society, taken care of, appreciated, respected. But nothing changed. Six years later he was still pulling traffic duty. There was no justice in the world. Corporate executives bankrupt their companies while earning billions in bonuses guaranteed by law, paid for with taxpayer money. How fucked is that! The rich made the rules and everyone else had to eat shit. Cocksuckers! There was no fucking way he should pay that much in property taxes! Now he had to waste more time and money appealing M.P.A.C.'s bullshit assessment. Just another clusterfuck.

He could not work in such an agitated state. He needed relief. He had to clear the pipes. Darcy knew a nearby side street that led to a quiet little enclave between a collection of condominiums. He could safely rub one out there. He already had his subject matter picked out. There was a new receptionist working at his gym. The second he saw her in those skintight Lycra pants he wanted to beat his dick like it owed him money. He wanted to make this one special and considered using hand sanitizer as lubricant. That's when the call came out over the radio. The wank would have to wait.

Darcy was patrolling the 401 East for a black or gray pickup truck. He'd been driving for fifteen minutes when he tagged on to one. The truck wasn't speeding and stayed within its lane but he ran its plate number anyway. It came out clean. Time to get a closer look at the driver. Officer Bourassa changed lanes and pressed the throttle so he could side-up with the black truck.

A fraction of a second was all it took. In a knee-jerk reaction, going 130 M.P.H., Officer Bourassa yanked the wheel away from what he saw inside the truck. His car fishtailed, spinning out across the highway and smashing into the concrete divide. Oncoming traffic didn't have time to stop. Officer Bourassa was killed on impact. The U-Haul driver succumbed to his injuries later in hospital.

The truck has been running on empty for several miles. The engine sputters and conks out. Greg coasts off the highway onto a dirt road. The truck stops at the mouth of the road.

Greg opens the door and collapses onto the ground, gravel and dirt digging into open wounds. He forces himself to his knees, leaning against the truck to help him get back on his feet. He totters forward and lurches down the dirt road.

Swarmed by blankets of mosquitoes, their whining buzz filling his ears, Greg follows the road over winding hills until he reaches the lake. The urge to rush the lake, to drink, is overwhelming, but if he starts he will never stop. He needs shelter from the road. Greg descends into the woods.

He cannot see ten feet in front of him. The night sky is filled with stars but their light cannot penetrate the darkness of the woods. Branches snap back across his face. Jagged rocks, tree stumps, scrape him open as he stumbles. Thorn bushes pierce his skin and burrs cling to his clothes.

His lips are gone, shriveled up and sucked into his face. His mouth is caked with wax. He can feel it forming in his throat. The mass swelling in his head and neck throw him off balance. The excruciating pressure makes him retch. His knees threaten to buckle with every step as he staggers forward blindly. His body shakes and convulses. It screams for water.

Through gnarled tree branches, he sees moonlight reflected off a glass surface. He slides and tumbles down the dirt hill towards it, landing at its edge. Wooden dams held together by mud and stone line the shore. Fallen white birches stand out against the night like a bed of bones. A loud smack cracks across the water -- a warning against his presence -- but the sound falls on deaf ears.

Oblivious. *We are here, far removed. Safe to drink.* Greg rushes the lake, plunging into it. He sucks it in. Salvation.

The cycle continues throughout the night and into the morning. The sun has risen in the sky. The chain cannot be broken. Greg drinks until every molecule of his being is submerged under water. He pisses, and regurgitates, out everything by the base of a nearby tree, always by the tree.

So it went until it stopped. It stopped like this:
Electrolyte imbalance, tissue swelling, irregular heartbeat, fluid enters the lungs, pressure on nerves, pressure on brain, but he can't stop. *You drink, drink, drink the lake.* Water pours from Greg's mouth and nose, soaking into the ground. The tremors begin. Greg's eyes roll back into his head. His body shakes until it stops.

———

Her first and second pre-molars were compacted. Severe swelling of the surrounding periodontal tissue had created an infected abscess. The adult teeth were forcing themselves in but there wasn't any room. The central and lateral incisors had broken through but were horribly twisted from crowding. Her bite alignment was also cause for concern; the anteroposterior discrepancies were severe. He would implement growth modification but was confident the girl would need orthognathic surgery when she was old enough. It would be a costly and painful process: tooth removal, braces, headgear, and jaw surgery. Still, It was better than being permanently ostracized. It gave her a chance. If they did not take action, her teeth and bones would grow into a twisted, chaotic mess. The harsh flaws in her dentofacial structure had already caused the poor girl a great deal of pain and mental trauma. Her health had also been put at risk with the infected abscess. This is why fifty-five-year-old Carl Krenske, working orthodontist for twenty-two years, knew intelligent design was really a matter of opinion.

It was random chaos. Destiny was a bullshit concept. You forged your own path the best you could. Nothing was promised. Life could be exceedingly cruel. The natural order wasn't concerned with what was 'fair' what was 'right'. Carl considered his divorce with his wife, Emily. He appreciated Emily's many endearing qualities but the attraction was gone. He could see her age, an expiration date. He didn't feel like fucking her any more. More to the point, he felt like fucking somebody else. Carl thought Emily might consider the idea of an open relationship if it meant salvaging their marriage but he could not stomach the idea of her being with another man, not while they shared the same bed. Carl was aware of his hypocrisy in the matter but could not change his mind about it.

Carl strayed twice during their marriage and was sick with guilt both times. The guilt was enough to prevent him from being a repeat offender. Despite his actions he held Emily in the highest regards. She was good to him, she loved him. It was far more than he deserved.

It was a cold, hard fact: the spark was gone and he couldn't be bothered with the rest. When he petitioned Emily for the divorce, he emphasized what a hard decision it was for him. He made sure to clarify that it was not her fault. He loved her and always would. She deserved better. Emily took a moment to absorb the news and, with a weary voice, replied, "Bullshit. You want to fuck other women and not feel guilty about it. I'll give you your divorce but don't insult my intelligence."

The divorce was granted. He was free to pursue other women with reckless abandon. He imagined that the second the papers were signed he'd be off to the races, making up for lost time. Then he met Brenda, and within a year they were married.

Carl met Brenda at a wine and cheese event organized for their shared charity, Oceana. Brenda was an unrepentant flirt but not a dumb one; it was good business. That night she chose to flirt with Carl. Her brash confidence was a trait Carl normally loathed in others but there was something seductive about Brenda's performance, that and her incredible body, which she dressed for. Carl wanted to fuck her. He had to. Luckily for him Brenda loved the good life and he had the money to pay for it.

Carl was fifty-two the night they met. Brenda was thirty-eight but told everyone, with the exception of her closest confidants, that she was thirty-two. She worked as a legal secretary but held firmly to the dream of celebrity.

Brenda's blond hair was chemically treated. Her breasts came from a gifted plastic surgeon although it was not immediately apparent. She wanted a look that was perky and full but was adamant the breasts not look plastic. She was thrilled with the results -- her breasts were spectacular -- however she did not rest on her laurels. She had a strict diet regime and worked out daily. Brenda's strong, perfectly toned body was a testament to her devotion. She fought hard to retain her youth and, for the most part, had managed to stave off the aging process.

The only chinks in Brenda's armor were the beginning of crow's feet and subtle laugh lines that could be seen when she was without her makeup. Otherwise her skin was smooth and radiant. She visited her esthetician religiously and received the occasional Botox injection.

Brenda also paid top dollar for her orthodontic work, Carl could vouch for that. His friend and colleague Phil Rosenberg was her orthodontist. It was Phil who introduced them that night. Phil did good work. Brenda's lustrous smile was in perfect alignment.

Her eyes, beautiful ocean blues, possessed a spark of mischief that could instantly trigger Carl's desire. He lusted for her in a way he'd never thought possible at his age. Brenda's endless devotion to physical perfection, the absolute vanity of it all, only added to blood flow.

They'd been married for three years. The first two years were a dream. Carl bought them a beautiful home in Forest Hill, and they adopted a dog named Chief from the S.P.C.A. to share it with them. Carl hired on more staff at work and managed to clear his schedule for a few sun-soaked vacations. Brenda never went without and she made sure he didn't either. Carl was happy in marriage. Good times all around.

By the third year romance had been usurped by apathy and agitation. Brenda seemed distant and bored. She was easily irritated. Carl's mere presence seemed to annoy her at times. Carl asked what was wrong and how he could help. To no avail. With a manic urgency, Brenda refocused her energies into acting. She filled her schedule by seeking out and attending auditions. She took acting workshops, paid to have a new demo reel cut, and had four different sets of headshots taken within a month.

This all started shortly after her forty-first birthday. Carl suggested a vacation to the Galapagos Islands but Brenda wasn't interested. Since their marriage she had neglected her craft. Acting was her passion and it could no longer be ignored. She needed to fully recommit to it.

Carl had no problem supporting Brenda if she wanted to quit her job as a legal secretary and focus on acting. He'd seen her demo reel: minor roles in failed TV pilots, some commercials, volunteer performances in average-to-awful student films. He knew her reverent devotion to acting was merely cover for another celebrity pipe dream. The cold reality would dawn on her one day. Her level of talent could not match her desire. She would not be part of the chosen few worshipped by the masses. She'd be forced to let it go and return to what by any normal set of standards was a privileged life. Until then he'd continue to give his support and encouragement.

Brenda was flashing her beautiful smile again after landing the lead role in a student film for which she'd auditioned. She insisted Carl read the fifteen-page script, heralding its greatness, predicting its genius would knock him on his ass. "Within the Frame" was about a family, struggling to get over the loss of their only child when the father goes on a hunger strike against God.

Carl thought it was garbage. It reeked of self-importance, melodrama of the lowest order. He had to fight the urge to scoff aloud at some of the dialog. Brenda declared the scriptwriter, a twenty-four- year-old aspiring director named Kurt, to be a prodigy. Carl bit his tongue. What audience would grieve for these one-dimensional characters with whom they've spent all of fifteen minutes? He knew he didn't give a shit about them. It was glaringly evident that Brenda's desperation had blinded her better judgment. Brenda's unwavering enthusiasm for Kurt and his movie was grating beyond belief. All Carl could do was smile and nod false encouragement.

One night Brenda asked him to rehearse with her. Carl would play the role of the disturbed husband. Brenda told him to read the script straight without emotion. Carl was thankful. Any attempt at evoking emotion from such vapid dialog would cause an outburst of laughter.

He was perplexed by how much Brenda tortured herself over delivery during the reading. She was not happy with her choices, expressing frustration at her inability to find the character's voice. Carl wanted to scream that it didn't have one. Brenda asked to be alone. Carl was happy to oblige and retired to the living room to pour himself a much needed drink.

The sky was overcast. He could feel the gloom. The travel group of decrepit seniors doddered around him aimlessly with their slack jaws. The dilapidated glass-bottomed boat passed over the remnants of extinguished coral reef, now covered in thousands of spined sea urchins. The seabed was barren. The fish were gone. The further out they traveled, the murkier the water grew, and then it turned black. The ocean was a tomb. The panic rose in Carl as the boat continued further out to sea. He demanded a return to shore but no one was listening. There was no captain aboard, no wheel for Carl to grab ahold of. It was just him and the lobotomized geriatrics.

Carl looked for the shore. It was gone. It was never there. The sudden realization made him sick and he laid down on the cool glass bottom. He could hear the groan of the black water underneath as wizened legs circled around him.

His eyes opened to darkness. He was short of breath and the room kept spinning. Finally his heart rate slowed and he gained his bearings. Carl's side of the bed was damp from sweat. He rolled over and smelled Brenda's hair. The hint of shampoo brought him back. This was home. This was safe.

When Carl saw Kurt for the first time the dislike he'd already been feeling for the scriptwriter immediately turned to hate. Carl and Brenda had met earlier for lunch. Brenda talked about the movie the entire time. After lunch she asked Carl to drive her to the café where she was meeting with Kurt to discuss character motivation.

As they approached the café, Brenda perked up and pointed out the window. "There it is. There's his motorcycle. I think its vintage. What a beautiful bike! Oh, I see him! There he is on the patio."

Carl parked the car in front of the patio to get a good look at Kurt, who was sitting at his table, sipping a coffee between practiced (Carl imagined in front of a mirror) drags of a cigarette. He was handsome in a way that made woman nervous and men angry. High cheekbones, square jaw, full lips, a fashionable layer of stubble. He had thick black hair like a young Elvis.

Kurt had cultivated the look of effortless style. He wore aviator glasses, a threadbare gray T-shirt dusted with specks of paint, dark denim jeans distressed in all the right places, and a pair of rustic motorcycle boots. The tattoos covering his arms brought it all together. It looked like he'd walked into Sailor Jerry's and asked for the works. Except they weren't the muddy, faded-blue, prison tatts Carl saw growing up. You could make out the line work and the colors popped. Kurt's tattoos looked expensive.

Carl wasn't impressed. So many people thought they could buy themselves an identity by covering their bodies in ink. Kurt was just another poser playing it hard, overcompensating, trying to act the part. He had trust fund baby written all over him.

Brenda quickly squeezed Carl's hand, promising to call him later, already waving to Kurt, who took another slow drag of his cigarette and calmly nodded back.

A month had passed since the shooting of Kurt's movie. The film was still in post-production. Brenda had yet to see a single scene but had already declared it the most creatively rewarding experience of her life. Carl could only find solace knowing the whole experience was almost over. Soon they would screen that piece of shit and Kurt would be revealed for the fraud he was. For Carl it couldn't happen too soon. He wanted his wife back.

The afternoon was spent in a seminar on Smart Brackets, which contained a microchip that measured the forces acting on the bracket and, subsequently, the tooth interface. The targeted aim was reducing the duration of orthodontic therapy, expenses, and discomfort. Carl was impressed. It was a far cry from the ancient Greeks using base metals and catgut to provide a better smile. He had been following the new technology with great interest and anticipating the seminar for some time. The day was now upon him, but he felt anxious and distracted by thoughts of the previous weekend.

That Saturday had been their anniversary. He and Brenda went for dinner at an obscenely expensive restaurant. They spent it struggling through one failed conversation after another. The night was going as expected. In recent weeks Brenda would hardly look at Carl, let alone talk to him.

When Brenda declined dessert, Carl asked if she was feeling well. Brenda responded, "I'm just really disappointed by the service." After a silent drive home they brushed their teeth and went to bed. Carl caressed Brenda's body but she offered no reaction. Her complete disinterest caused him to lose his hard-on. Carl questioned if disinterest was even the right word. It bordered on repulsion, like his very touch made her skin crawl. On their anniversary, of all nights. Brenda said she had a headache and was feeling nauseous. Carl didn't accept either defense. She sarcastically apologized for not being able to fuck on demand and rolled onto to her side, away from Carl.

When Carl arrived home from the seminar Brenda wasn't there. Chief was anxious. Carl put on his leash and took him to the dog park. Carl usually derived great pleasure watching Chief socializing with other dogs. Chief was a very expressive dog. It was never more apparent then when he was frolicking about outside and off leash.

It was a hot sunny day. The dog park was busy. Chief was in full play mode but Carl was paying him no mind. Carl was debating what to text Brenda. He wanted to ask where she was but thought it sounded too needy and possessive. He decided to ask instead if she had any ideas for dinner. The writing of the text was interrupted by a cacophony of snarls and barks.

Chief was kicking up dust with a Rhodesian ridgeback under a picnic table. The ridgeback was the aggressor. It snapped at Chief, who was pressed against the inside of a bench. Not enjoying being cornered, Chief lunged at the ridgeback, grabbing its neck in his mouth. The Rhodesian started yelping. The other dog owners gasped in horror.

Carl reached his hand under the bench to grab Chief in a desperate move to separate the dogs. The frenzied ridgeback snapped at Carl's hand, catching it several times. Carl recoiled, shaking his bitten hand. Chief pinned the ridgeback to the ground. Carl flipped the picnic bench over. He grabbed Chief by his back legs and pulled. Chief let go. The Rhodesian sprang back on to its feet, yelping, it ran behind its owner. Chief looked up at Carl, completely unfazed by the experience, smiling and panting with his tongue hanging out.

The owners inspected the damage to their dogs. Both appeared to be unharmed. The two owners briefly discussed the situation. The ridgeback named Molly had been chewing her ball in the shade under the bench, when Chief came by to say hello. Molly, being very possessive of her ball, started in with some warning growls that Chief ignored, and it escalated from there.

Both owners agreed that neither party was at fault and were thankful neither dog was seriously injured. Carl's hand bore the brunt of the altercation. Molly's owner, a hefty older woman with bad eczema, had seen Carl recoil when trying to separate the dogs. She asked if he'd been bitten. Carl held up his hand. The skin on the top was bruised and torn. The woman gasped. Carl assured her he was fine but had better get home to wash it. Meanwhile Chief and Molly were busying themselves sniffing a new group of dogs that entered the park.

Carl put the wine down on the kitchen table. He scrubbed his injured hand under hot water and applied more hydrogen peroxide. He found some antiseptic Band-Aids in the bathroom cupboards and covered the bite marks as best he could. Carl returned to the kitchen to pour himself a glass of wine. He took a generous first sip, then noticed the bloody paw prints covering the floor.

Carl called for Chief, who trotted in sporting a large grin, seemingly oblivious to any pain. Carl knelt down beside him, Chief rolled onto his back, paws in the air, hoping for a stomach scratch. Carl inspected the bloody front paw. There was a nasty gash in it. He saw a piece of brown glass, no doubt from a smashed beer bottle, lodged inside.

He commanded Chief to stay and grabbed tweezers from the bathroom. Carl took hold of Chief's paw, pinched the piece of glass between the tweezers and carefully removed it. Chief didn't so much as flinch. Carl held up the piece of glass, a sizeable shard. Carl dropped it into a tin can, which he then threw back into the recycling bin. He finished cleaning Chief's wound with hydrogen peroxide and dressed it with gauze. Afterwards he made sure to toss Chief a doggie biscuit.

The bloody paw prints were tracked throughout the house. Chief had the habit of quickly inspecting every room whenever they returned from a walk. It gave Carl endless amusement but now he had a mess to clean. Carl saw he'd missed some bloody prints in the bedroom. He had just emptied the mop bucket down the toilet and, not wanting to bother to refill it, he grabbed some Easy-Wipes from the kitchen, used them to wipe the blood from the hardwood floor, and tossed the dirty wipes into the designer trash bin near the bed. The fact that the garbage lining was empty gave him pause.

Two days ago Carl had happened to notice that the lining bag was about one-quarter full with useless receipts, dirty tissues, an empty Otrivin bottle, used papers from the lint roller, and a sock that Chief had ripped up. Now the lining bag was replaced by a new one. Something was amiss. Brenda was a neat freak but wouldn't lift a finger to clean, not when Carl could pay someone else to do it. The cleaning lady worked Monday and Thursday. It was Wednesday. Why had Brenda emptied the trash bin? Carl needed to find that lining bag.

He found it outside, stuffed to the bottom of the city garbage bin, tied off and about one quarter full, just as he remembered it. Carl ripped open the top of the bag and looked inside. There it was: the ugly, undeniable truth.

Carl knew what he was looking for evidence but the shock of actually finding it felt like a kick to the stomach. There at the bottom of the bag was a discarded condom with a full load in it. Carl and Brenda had stopped using condoms their first month together.

Carl dropped the bag back into the garbage bin. The discovery shook him to the core. He'd been poisoned, overwhelmed by a sickening surge of negative emotion. Carl lost his balance and was forced to sit down on the front steps. He wanted to throw up. His hands could not stop shaking.

Sitting in the corner of the pub, staring into his glass of whiskey, Carl seethed with torrents of hate. "She fucked him in our house. She fucked him in our bed. She laid on her back, waited for him to pull a condom on, and fucked him in our bed. The bed I paid ten grand for, the bed she had to have. The bitch. That selfish bitch. I spoiled that fucking bitch. She sucked his cock, then kissed me on the lips, that fucking bitch, that fuckin' whore. The money I spent ... the money I spent on that selfish fucking bitch. That stupid fucking cunt. My lawyer is going to crush you, bitch. You're not getting one red cent from me. You have no idea, no fucking concept, what it takes. I make top dollar because I earned it. I fucking earned it. You'll have to go back to answering telephones for a living. How else are you going to pay me my settlement? Acting the trophy wife, the tit job, the Botox, the yoga ... No, fuck you, Brenda. You're no prize. You peaked long ago. Menopause is right around the corner. Gravity's taking effect, the skin is starting to sag. There's nothing your esthetician or plastic surgeon can do to stop the slide because you won't be able to pay them. You won't have a pot to piss in when I'm done with you. So then what? You're going to run to Kurt? I'd pay money to see your expression when that selfish little prick slams the door in your face. Fucking Kurt. The great pretender. You won't even see it coming. You're too busy staring at your reflection. They are going to have to scrape you off the floor, kid."

The waiter removes another empty glass from Carl's table. Carl receives a text from Brenda asking, "What happened to Chief's paw?" The waiter drops off another whiskey.

After staggering home, Carl checks to see that Chief is in his room. He finds the dog snoring on his giant throw pillow. He walks upstairs, steadying himself on the railing. The bedroom door is open. The light is on. Brenda is in bed reading another script. She does not look up to greet him.

"Where were you? Did you lose your phone?"

Carl says nothing and sits down on the side of the bed with his back to Brenda.

"Did you hear me? Did you get my text?"

"What are you reading?"

"I asked you a question."

"He stepped on some glass. I pulled it out. He's fine. What are you reading?"

"Were you drinking? You smell like alcohol."

"I asked you a question."

"It's the script for Kurt's first feature."

"Did he promise you a part?"

"He just wanted my opinion."

"How is it?"

"Are you drunk?"

"Tell me about this script."

"It's dark, but very funny. He's got such an understanding, such a grasp, of character and subtext. He's not a slave to clichéd plot devices or structure. He's interested in exploring the human condition. As an actor that's so refreshing. I have such respect for that and at such a young age--"

"-Shut the fuck up." Carl rips Kurt's script out of Brenda's hands and tosses it onto the floor.

"What the fuck is wrong with you?" yells Brenda. Carl grabs a fistful of her hair, yanking her head back.

"There's nothing wrong with me, Brenda. You think I'm a fucking idiot. You think I'm fucking stupid." Carl twists Brenda's hair in his fist. Brenda eyes fill with tears.

"You're hurting me --" Panic chokes off her airway. She can barely get the words out. Carl squishes Brenda's face together with his free hand.

"You think you're special because some slapdick, twenty-four-year-old tortured artist stuck his dick in you? You think he'll take you to Hollywood? I've seen your demo reel. Who the fuck are you kidding? You're washed up and there's not a goddamn thing you can do about it." Carl slams Brenda's head against the headboard, keeping a firm grip on her hair.

"Please, Carl. I'll leave. Just let me go, please."

"Why? So you can run to the police, tell them I assaulted you, use it against me in court, take more of my money, buy yourself a new pair of tits? You haven't even said you're sorry."

"I'm sorry."

"What are you sorry for?"

"I'm sorry."

"What are you sorry for?"

"Please, Carl."

Carl yanks Brenda's head back.

"What are you sorry for?"

"Please, Carl."

"What-are-you-sorry-for?"

"I'm sorry I couldn't be faithful to you."

"You couldn't be faithful to me. That's an interesting way to put it."

Brenda begins to hyperventilate. Her cheeks are streaked with tears. Snot runs out her nose onto trembling lips. Carl is disgusted. There is nothing left but hate. He pulls her off the bed by her hair. She screams. He kicks her in the stomach. She gasps for air. Chief is barking downstairs. Carl sits on Brenda's chest, pinning her shoulders down with his knees. He wraps his hands around her throat and presses down, cutting off her airway, forcing her tongue out. Brenda's fingernails dig into Carl's wrist. Every vein in her face pops to the surface. Brenda's face turns from red to purple. Her gag reflex kicks in. She pukes but it has nowhere to escape and enters her lungs. Brenda's blue eyes roll back in her head.

"You fucked him in our bed!" Carl uses all his weight, pouncing down on Brenda's throat with the bottom of his palms, snapping her hyoid bone. Blood spurts from her mouth. The struggle is over.

Carl stares down at the wreckage. Brenda's throat has swollen to obscene proportions. It appears to be swallowing her face, which is marbled in broken blood vessels. Ruptured capillaries have turned the whites of her eyes crimson red. Her mouth hangs open. A frothy mixture of blood and vomit leaks out the sides.

Carl gets off Brenda and falls back against the wall. He leans onto his side and pukes. Pushing against the wall, he stumbles down the hallway into the kitchen. He swills the red wine to rinse the taste of bile from his mouth.

Carl brings the bottle of wine back into the bedroom. He stares at the damage done. His hands tremble. He takes another swig of wine. Kurt's script is strewn across the floor. Carl picks up the cover page. The title "We All Fall Down" is written in bold font. In the bottom corner of the page is a copyright notice with the name and address of Kurt's production company, Media Militia Ltd.

Carl goes to his computer and searches the street address on Goggle maps. The results show that Media Militia Ltd is located on a residential street in East Toronto. Carl is certain this is where Kurt lives.

Carl sits at the edge of the bathtub, soaking wet with the shower on. His fingers and feet are pruned from the steam. He's been sitting there for forty-five minutes, weighing his options. He hadn't planned on killing Brenda but rage erased reason. Now he has to finish what he started. Kurt has to die. For Carl, the idea of rotting away in prison while the little cocksucker who fucked his wife walks the streets with impunity is a fate worse then death. The longer he waits, the more variables enter the equation, closing his window of opportunity. It has to happen now.

He turns the water off and sits naked in the tub shivering, his booze-addled, oxygen-deprived brain sifting through broken fragments of thought, trying to seize ahold of the necessary details to formulate a plan. "Drive to Kurt's and shoot him dead. If Kurt's not home, wait for him. No hesitation. Doesn't matter who's watching. Get him in the crosshairs. Pull the trigger. Then what? Then you start running. Where? The border? What if they get your license plate? The call goes out, they'll be waiting, and don't forget money. You need money. How much? As much as you can get. The bank's closed. What's my withdrawal limit? Fifteen hundred dollars? Three thousand? Five thousand? What else? Credit cards. What's their limit? Take it all out. They can freeze your accounts. So what's that give us? Accounts are frozen tomorrow. What's that give us? Bank card, credit card, total what? Five thousand? You've got close to a million in the bank and all you can get your hands on is five thousand dollars? You idiot. You knew. You fucking knew. Plan for the worse. Make sure the money's available. You were going to buy a safe, fill it with cash, but you waited, the markets crashed. Still, you didn't take the hint, you waited, you procrastinated, now what? Now you're fucked! Five grand in pocket. Not enough, that's not enough. Wait another day. Wait another day. No one's looking for Brenda. You got time. Go to the bank, withdraw everything, then kill him. Then you kill him. You need the money. You need a place to hide. Going to cost you. Money buys time. Money buys freedom. Without money it's over, it's over. Without money, you're fucked. So what now? Right now? Get some sleep, sleep on the couch, wake up. Wake up rested, go to the bank. I can't ... I can't sleep. It's too much. I can't wait. This can't wait."

Carl brushes his teeth and goes back to the bedroom for a change of clothes. This time he avoids looking at Brenda's body. He pulls on jeans, T-shirt, and a hoodie. Standing in the walk-in closet, he unlocks the gun safe and pulls out his Beretta 92FS 9 mm with a 15 round mag. He places the gun into its steel blue traveling case.

Ten years prior Carl's friend Raj Bhanjee introduced him to the Canadian National Recreation Association's handgun club. Raj was a member. The C.N.R.A. had a shooting gallery in the top of Union station. To get to it you had to take a scissor-gated elevator to the sixth floor, then climb a twisting narrow stairwell.

Raj knew that Carl and his first wife, Emily, had been discussing the idea of having children. Raj believed in the common decency of man but stressed the need to protect your family against those who didn't. To lighten the tone of the conversation Raj also mentioned what a great form of stress relief firing off a couple rounds of ammo could be. Carl told him he'd stick with the tried and true method of masturbation.

Carl had never felt a compelling desire to be a parent. He craved job security in a career that paid enough so he could enjoy life outside of the workplace. That was the dream. That was it. With a great deal of struggle and sacrifice he finally achieved his goal, but meeting Emily had complicated things.

Carl was filled with pride in her presence. Emily was a beautiful woman who carried herself with great poise and had a soft-spoken humility he found completely endearing. She also possessed a razor-sharp wit and a healthy dose of ambition that kept things interesting. Carl was honored to share a life with her. When she teased with the idea of children, Carl could only reply, "Sure babe, let's do it."

They were in agreement but would not force the issue. Both were busy with work and hated the idea of sex turning into an assignment. They would keep things simple. Emily would stop using the pill and they'd see what happened.

Months later, after another day spent tightening braces, Carl came home to steak and lobster. Emily had cooked both to perfection. The dinner was a surprise. The quality was not. Emily had chef de cuisine certification and worked as sous-chef at Danos, which was a recent recipient of two Michelin stars. She had an ingrained passion for the culinary arts and possessed a preternatural level of talent, combined with a focused determination that demanded respect. Carl was surprised Emily would even consider taking the requisite time off work to have a baby. When he asked, "Why now?" Emily replied, tongue-in-cheek, "I won't have time when I open my restaurant, and we need to test the kids' menu on someone."

With a strong suspicion that he knew the answer, Carl asked what occasion merited such a dinner. Emily poured their wine glasses and stated, "I can only have one glass and should probably be avoiding shellfish, but they had a such great deal on lobster at Mike's fish market. I couldn't pass it up. "

Emily raised her glass. "Congratulations. Carl, your boys can swim. I'm pregnant."

She was glowing already. Carl felt a rush of bewildered excitement. It was happening: he was going to be a father.

Emily was in her second trimester of pregnancy when she and Carl made a date for the movies to see the film *Seven*. It sounded like standard fare - cops chasing down a serial killer – but they'd both heard good things about it.

It was a rare occasion for Carl to spend money seeing anything in theaters. He hated waiting in line and tried avoiding crowds at all costs. He didn't view movie going as a communal experience. He loathed the many rude distractions. There was always some idiot shaking a bag of popcorn or talking in an annoyingly loud whisper to the person beside them. The crowds at movie theaters had seemed to get worse over time. Now, even after the movie began, people talked at full volume, offering opinions no one had asked for. There was no sense of decorum. The only thing that kept Carl coming back was a firm belief that great films are meant to be seen on the big screen. Carl hoped *Seven* would be one of those films.

They didn't make it past the first twenty minutes.

The tension started before the movie even began. During the coming attractions a large group of teenagers strolled into the theater, loudly laughing and cursing. The group consisted of ten rowdy young men in baggy gangster wear and six scandalously clad girls wearing plenty of makeup. The group was mixed in ethnicity, the individuals ranging in age from sixteen to twenty. Carl knew the type: loud, uneducated, abrasive, and angry. The boys walked with absurd swagger and with scowls on their faces. Not giving a fuck was a point of pride. Their ignorance combined with their fragile egos made them dangerous.

The second the rowdy group entered the theater; Emily squeezed Carl's hand as a signal to remain calm. Emily knew that Carl, when provoked, had a temper that was nearly impossible to control, and being at the movies seemed to be an endless source of provocation. In the past Carl had been engaged in several heated arguments with people because they'd talked during movies. Carl spilled a drink in the laps of one couple for ignoring his request for silence. This resulted in a physical confrontation between Carl and the boyfriend, ending when security separated the two men, escorting Carl outside, with Emily trailing behind.

The last time he was eighty-sixed from a movie theater was when he berated a mother for not removing her crying baby from the movie theater. When security arrived Carl stayed on subject, pointing out the unfathomable rudeness of such a woman, the sheer audacity of her thinking that being a mother entitled her to ruin the movie for everyone else. It took over a year before he and Emily spoke of going to the movies again. They agreed to try it out, with the stipulation that if anything bothered Carl to the point of anger; they would leave before a situation developed.

Emily cringed when the group of teenagers took up the row directly behind them. It began immediately. They heckled the coming attractions and threw popcorn at the screen. The movie hadn't even begun when Emily whispered in Carl's ear, "Let's just leave and go to the next screening. We can grab a coffee or something." Carl ignored her, staring straight ahead at the movie screen.

"Please, Carl. For me. Let's go. I can't handle this."

Carl continued to ignore her. The movie started and the group antics continued. When Morgan Freeman appeared onscreen, one of them yelled, "Hey, that's the nigga from *Driving Mrs. Daisy!*" which got laughs from his entourage but the rest of the theater was silent.

The laughter continued, along with the running commentary. Some people in the side rows exited the theater. Emily prayed they were getting security. One belligerent youth pushed out a loud fart, sending the entire row into hysterics.

Emily begged, "Please, Carl, let's go. This is too much. There's no point. Let's just go. I'm leaving. Carl, I'm leaving."

He ignored her and she left. One obnoxious juvenile heckled, "Where you going, honey? You want me to meet you in the bathroom?" Then he turned his focus to Carl. "Yo, man, she looks pissed. Yo, man, for real, what you say to her? Serious, dog, I think you hurt her feelings and shit."

Carl stared straight ahead, offering no response. Soon the popcorn started to rain down on his head. He felt the noxious brew of fear, adrenaline, and rage.

"Where the fuck is security?" he cursed to himself as the popcorn showered down. It was too much, the disrespect.

Carl walked up the aisle and crouched down, staring at the youths in the next row back. He calmly asked, "Why are you doing this?"

The entire row, girls and guys, laughed like he'd nailed the punch line to the funniest joke they'd ever heard. Then the posturing started. "Sit the fuck down, man. We tryin' to watch the movie."

Carl stood his ground.

"Yo, seriously, you best sit the fuck down man, cause you starting to creep me out."

At the end of the aisle closest to Carl was a pasty, pimply, white boy with a blond pube-stache. He wore a boxed-out ball cap that was several sizes too big, like the rest of his clothing. He looked like a petulant toddler wearing daddy clothes (if daddy had a penchant for T-shirts with giant pictures of Tupac on them).

Pube-stache scowled at Carl and said, "You want to kiss me or something faggot? Your breath stinks. Get the fuck out of my face."

Carl grabbed the beak of Pube-stache's hat and ripped it down over his face. Pandemonium ensued.

Carl swung for the fences but was quickly swarmed. The stomping began and the theater erupted. Shrieks, screams, profane encouragements of violence were hurled by the angry mob. Kicks, knees, and punches overwhelmed Carl. The angry young men had something to prove. The attack was relentless and lasted just under two minutes. For Carl it felt like an eternity.

All he could do was turtle and try to cover his face. His body went numb. Carl heard Emily screaming for help but it sounded muffled and distant. One brutal kick to the solar plexus caused Carl to shit his pants. This was followed by a series of teeth-rattling blows to his head. That's when the lights went out.

The list of injuries was substantial: A broken nose, broken orbital bone, broken jaw, cracked ribs, ruptured ear drum, and class two concussion. The nose required resetting, the orbital bone required reconstructive surgery, the jaw needed to be rewired, the broken ribs and ear drum required time to heal. The physical wounds would mend but the emotional fallout from the subsequent tragedy of Emily's miscarriage, three days after the attack, was irreversible.

As for the perpetrators, the police rounded up most of them shortly after the assault. The rest were arrested in following days. Six from the group were charged with aggravated assault, and two were charged with assault causing bodily harm. Four were old enough to receive adult sentencing; the others were processed through the juvenile system.

Later, Carl could remember every horrible detail of the assault up until the moment he lost consciousness. The disgust and contempt he felt for his attackers consumed him. They had been sentenced for their crime but it was not enough. He was possessed by revenge fantasies. He needed to see fear in their eyes. Carl forced aside these visions of vengeance while at work but always brought them home with him. Emily begged him to see a psychiatrist. Instead, Carl asked Raj to introduce him to his gun club.

Carl passed the Canadian Restricted Firearms Test, consisting of both a written and practical exam, and then submitted an application to the Canadian Firearms Program. After processing applications, the C.F.O after forwarded them to the Chief Firearms Officer, who conducted a background check and then approved or denied the license application.

Carl had no previous convictions, but he was concerned the C.F.O. might deny his application if he became aware that Carl was the victim of a recent assault and believed the application might be Carl's first step towards retaliation. Carl's worries were put to rest when he was granted his request for a possession acquisition license for a restricted firearm.

He bought a Beretta 92FS 9 mm, became a member of the C.N.R.A. handgun club, and made weekly visits to the Union Station shooting gallery. Carl always took a moment to picture his assailants before taking aim and pulling the trigger.

Weeks turned into months, months into years. Carl's physical wounds had long since healed. The memory of the attack was permanently etched in his memory but, gradually, the percentage of time that it occupied his thoughts lessened. At first he couldn't look in a mirror without tracing the outlines of the scars with his fingers: the splits over his brow, the jagged cross on his chin, the ridge on his nose.

Time continued its grinding march. Carl rose with the alarm every morning for another day of staring into people's mouths, seeing work to be done. Eventually the trips to Union Station stopped. Reason replaced rage. Loathing lost to lethargy. The gun stayed in its safe, and Carl traded in his C.N.R.A. membership for a gym pass.

Carl loads the trunk of his Benz GL550 SUV with a suitcase of clothes, camping gear, several bags of non-perishable foods, and the gun, safely stored in its steel blue case. After returning with his dog, Carl puts on his seat belt, lowers his window, and lowers the passenger side windows enough so that Chief will be able to stick out his nose. Carl watches the garage door open, a detached witness to his own unraveling.

Carl drives cautiously, not wanting to get pulled over on a DUI. The breeze from his open window helps him focus. He will not lose his resolve. There will be atonement.

Kurt's place is a semi-detached in the east end of the city. Carl parks several houses down. The street is quiet and sheltered from passing traffic. Carl grabs the gun from the trunk and sits back down in the driver's seat. He removes the gun from its case, inserts a loaded clip, and removes the safety.

Carl holds the gun inside his hoodie pocket as he walks towards Kurt's front door. The blinds are closed but he can see lights on inside the house. He walks up the front steps and knocks on the door.

A young woman answers, speaking through the chain in the door. She's beautiful; a brunette with luminous green eyes, a cute button nose, high cheekbones, and heart-shaped lips. Nothing fake about it, the girl is a natural. Carl's hate for Kurt grows exponentially.

"Hi. Is Kurt in?"

"Who am I speaking with?"

"Tom. I'm an old family friend. You're his girlfriend, right? I'm sorry. I know he told me but I'm horrible with names?"

"Kurt's out. Did he know you were stopping by?"

"It's late, I know. I apologize. I told Kurt I was driving through but I didn't know when I'd get here. I wanted to call but my cell phone is dead and I lost my charger. I was just going to drive through. I probably should have. I'm sorry to bother you."

"Okay. Well, I'll tell him you stopped by."

The young woman wears a look of confused suspicion as she closes the door and turns the deadbolt. Carl backs away and walks down the steps. Returning to the Benz he sees Chief with his paws up on the dashboard, wagging his tail, eagerly awaiting his return. Carl curses. He'd forgotten to bring dog food.

Dawn is breaking. Chief is snoring in the back of the car. Carl yawns. He's feeling nauseous and irritable from the effects of sleep deprivation. His mind is starting to wander down divergent paths. He slaps his cheek to wake himself up. He needs to maintain vigilance.

The stress is mounting. In another hour or so, people will start waking up to get ready for work.

"Where the fuck is he?" Carl wonders, bouncing his knee to stay awake. It suddenly occurs to him that he needs to take a raging piss. He steps outside, stands behind the SUV, closes his eyes, and listens to the steady stream splashing the concrete. With his bladder drained, Carl lets out a sigh of relief and opens his eyes. That's when he sees him.

Kurt swerves drunkenly down the road on his bicycle, an apple red 1975 Schwinn Sting-ray. Carl is sure he's been spotted but Kurt rides up and over the sidewalk and across the front lawn to his house without so much as a second glance at him.

Chief is still snoring. Carl grabs the Beretta he'd returned to the glove box. He steps out of the car, closing the door gently behind him. Kurt takes his bike around to the back of his house. He doesn't close the gate behind him.

Kurt's back is turned while locking his bike to the patio. Carl assumes the power stance, raises the gun, and set his sights between the man's shoulder blades. Kurt pulls a blue tarp off the ground and covers the Sting-ray. Carl cocks the hammer for single action.

"Kurt."

Kurt jumps back with a start, facing Carl. "What are–?"

Carl fires three shots into his chest.

Kurt's chest cavity fills with blood. His punctured lungs fight for air.

Carl stands over him. He fires two more shots into Kurt's stomach and then places a kill shot between the eyes.

Six shots in twenty seconds.

Carl runs back to the car. Chief is wide-awake with his head up and his paws on the dashboard. Carl returns the block on the firing pin and stashes the gun in the car's glove box. He turns the ignition, checks for oncoming traffic, and drives away.

He takes Gerrard Street to River Valley Road, which connects to the Don Valley Parkway. He plans to drive north on the DVP to the 401 and follow the 401 east until he reaches Highway 35, where he will turn north again and head to the Kawartha Lakes region.

Just past the 401's Victoria Park exit, he notices a police cruiser in his rear-view mirror. Carl waits for the cherries to start flashing. He remains calm. A high-speed chase would be frivolous and could only result in innocent casualties. The squad car tails him until it exits at Markham Road. Carl continued east.

Carl waits to pay the till at a gas station in Pickering when he sees two police cars pull into the parking lot. The officers remain in their cars, talking on the radio. He's sure they are running his plates. Keeping his composure Carl walks back to the Benz, coffee in hand. He sits down in the driver's seat, takes a sip of coffee, calmly places it in the cup holder, and turns the key in the ignition, fully expecting the squawk of sirens to follow.

Carl exits the gas station and takes the east ramp back onto the 401. Once again, he's evaded capture. How long can it last? How long before the pieces come together? How will Kurt's girlfriend describe him to the cops? How long will it take to get a positive identification? How long before they find Brenda's body? Do any of Kurt's friends know about Brenda? Does his girlfriend? How can he control the variables? To start with, he needs to call work. He doesn't want to raise any alarms by his absence.

Carl calls work, and leaves a message. "Hi, Sara, this is Carl. I'm not coming in today so cancel my appointments. I'm sick, been up all night coughing. Not to worry. Brenda's taking care of me. If there are any emergencies please direct them to our friend, Mr. Rosenberg. Thanks and take care."

Carl knows it's a stalling tactic at best. He'd made his decision and would suffer the consequences. Carl sips his coffee and scans the radio, trying not to dwell on the fact that he'd forgotten his I-Pod.

An hour later his fatigue can no longer be ignored. He's hit the proverbial wall. A dizzying wave of exhaustion forces him to pull into a highway rest stop near Pontypool. He parks in the far corner of the lot. He lets Chief out to pee and stretch his legs. There isn't a cloud in the sky. It's going to be a scorcher.

The sun blasting his face, forces him awake. The stagnant heat of the truck is like a blanket wrapped around his face. Carl pushes open the door for some fresh air. His ass is numb. His legs have fallen asleep. Carl lifts them out from the truck and pulls himself up by the door. His legs burn from the blood rushing back into them. Chief hops out to pee. He sniffs around the rest area while Carl tries to shake the pins and needles from his legs.

With feeling restored in his haunches Carl starts moving. He digs out the water canteen from the cooler and fills Chief's bowl with water. Carl estimates they're approximately an hour from Sherbourne Lake. As Chief laps up the water, Carl remembers he still needs to buy dog food.

Carl pulls off Highway 35 so he can go to the I.G.A. grocery store in Minden. When entering the store he passes a newspaper stand. With some trepidation he glances at the front page. He knows the paper had gone to press before he fired the first shot but he checks anyway. There is no mention of the double homicide. Carl knows if he turns on a TV to CP24, Brenda and Kurt's shootings will be leading the news cycle. It was perfect fodder for the twenty-four-hour news machine.

Carl buys a bag of dog kibble, butter, sea-salt, a twelve-ounce steak, sweet corn, hot dogs, hot dog buns, and a bag of ice. He plans on cooking the steak and corn over an open fire that evening. The idea makes his mouth water.

Carl feeds Chief in the I.G.A parking lot; the dog pushes his bowl across two empty parking spaces as he tries to lick up every morsel of dog kibble. Carl wonders what will happen to his four-legged companion. He hopes Raj will look after him. Raj scoffed openly at the notion of pets, saying it was asinine to provide for an animal that did not work for its keep. But Carl knows Raj has a soft spot for Chief. It was evident from the way Raj smiled whenever he saw Chief. He always knelt down and scratched Chief behind his ears.

The cashier with the cleft lip tells him there's a C.I.B.C. branch on Main Street. Carl wonders how long it takes the police to obtain a subpoena to access someone's banking records. He knows that every transaction is giving away his location, but he also knows that, in the end, it makes no difference. Without money, he is as good as caught. He can't live out in the bush forever. Life as a fugitive will be short-lived. There is nowhere to hide in a world with security cameras posted on every corner, a world where you can't take a piss without photo id and a credit card deposit. It's a losing proposition either way. For his immediate future cash is key.

The security guard with the unfortunate combination of acne and male-pattern baldness sits on his stool, looking miserable, while Carl makes a maximum withdrawal of fifteen hundred dollars from the automated teller.

After his stop at the bank Carl waits in line at Kawartha to get a milkshake, stuck behind a group of senior citizens dressed for battle against their enemy, the sun, their faces painted white with sunscreen, wearing Tilley hats and ridiculous Blublocker sunglasses. In front of them is a collection of sluggish-looking housewives with giant pear-shaped asses. Their fat children pull at their shirts, anxious to stuff their faces with ice creams named Muskoka Mocha, Sugar Shack Maple, Heavenly Hash, and Death by Chocolate.

He had stopped at the same Kawartha dairy stand with Emily one distant summer past. They'd been returning from a camping trip at Sherbourne Lake. Both felt rejuvenated after a much-needed escape from the city -- beautiful weather, canoeing, and campfire was all it took. When they arrived there were nearly thirty people in the line for ice cream. Carl refused to have any part in it. Emily solemnly conceded that it was best to continue driving to avoid the traffic gridlock. They pushed on without ice cream but an hour later they were stuck in bumper-to-bumper traffic anyway.

Emily attempted to lighten the mood with conversation. Carl ignored her. Emily scanned the radio. Carl turned the volume down. Emily gave up trying, and Carl stared straight ahead. Not a word was shared during the painful crawl back to the city, their weekend escape already forgotten.

Carl ties Chief to the picnic table and sits down with his vanilla milkshake. It's the best he's ever had. His depleted body rejoices from the sudden sugar rush. He savors every sip. Pure satisfaction. Blue skies and sunshine. He'll be buried under metal and concrete soon enough but now, right now, he's going to enjoy his milkshake.

The Frost Center is the Algonquin Highlands municipal office. The young lady working reception has orangutan orange hair and a cooked lobster sunburn. Carl requests a five-day camping permit for Sherborne Lake. The receptionist tells him that all the Sherborne Lake campsites are occupied. She points out the two remaining campsites on a map. The choice is between the Avery Lake and Plastic Lake campsites. The receptionist recommends Plastic Lake. Avery is notorious for leeches.

Carl books the campsite on Plastic Lake (the most uninspired name for a lake he's ever heard). He then signs a waiver and gives a credit card deposit for a sixteen-foot Algonquin Swift Kevlar canoe, which includes a personal floatation device and a boat safety kit. Carl imagines drifting in the middle of a lake with Chief while an army of cops, one speaking through a bullhorn, demand his return to shore.

He ties the canoe to his roof rack and proceeded north for five minutes. He reaches the old logging road, which leads into the campgrounds. At the mouth of the road, tucked off to the shoulder, is a black pick-up truck. It has a three-day removal notice under the windshield. Carl follows the narrow, twisting road. It takes him eight minutes to reach his campsite from the highway.

The campsite overlooks the lake, but it's less then fifteen feet from the road, which means there's zero privacy from oncoming traffic. Carl will be breathing dust clouds every time a car drives by. Plus, the murky ponds in the roadside ditches are horrible breeding grounds for mosquitoes and black flies. He was slapping them off his neck the second he stepped outside.

Carl stands at the edge of the shore and stares out across the lake. A gentle breeze ripples the water. Sunshine reflects through the trees. A red-tailed hawk circles overhead. Carl is unimpressed by the campsite but the lake has potential.

The decision is made. He'll remain parked there but will paddle across the lake to find his own campsite. Grounds policy states visitors can not camp outside designated areas. Carl doesn't care. Let them fine him. Good luck collecting it.

Chief springs into the water as Carl drags the canoe ashore. His newly chosen campsite is high on a flat rock surface, from which the front edge has disintegrated, creating a rocky cliff that slopes into the lake. Obviously other campers disliked the designated area as much as he does, because there's a large stone fire pit waiting for him. This location is a vast improvement. It offers seclusion and a perfect view of the lake. He can look across and see his truck. The surrounding brush is filled with fallen trees, providing plenty of dry wood that Carl can use for a fire.

Carl spots a mossy area on the rock, just the perfect size on which to place his tent for added cushioning. Unless he's prematurely dragged out in shackles, he's found his home for the next five days.

The sun warms his naked back as he establishes the campsite. He sets up the tent, then collects firewood, while Chief charges through the woods after squirrels and chipmunks. The dog is in his element, off leash and loving life. Carl is happy to see it.

Two hours and many bug bites later Carl has collected enough firewood to burn through the evening. It's time to jump in the lake while the sun is still shining.

When collecting firewood he found the perfect swimming spot, no more than fifty feet away from his tent. Smooth rock sloped gradually into the water. As the water reached three feet in depth, the rock broke off into a series of large stone platforms that formed a wide staircase into the water. One could descend, standing at varying depths, until the final and lowest ledge, where the drop was still deep enough to dive from without risking hitting your head on the bottom.

There are tadpoles all along the shoreline. Three frogs bask in pools of water on the rock surface. Their tiny heads poke above the surface, facing the sun, less than a foot from Carl's toes. Chief trots into the water and lowers his nose to sniff the frogs. He springs back with a start when they hop away, into the water. Chief tilts his head with a confused expression, then looks up at Carl, seeking answers.

"What do you think of that, buddy? You're not going to let a couple of frogs scare ya?" Carl chuckles and gives Chief a friendly splash as he wades into the water. The light has shifted to a golden hue, signaling the magic hour before sunset. Carl reaches the final rock ledge. He's up to his waist in water. A school of about forty young perch swim around the rock ledge, then scatter when the black silhouettes of two large bass float by. The bottom of the lake is covered in sediment and submerged logs.

The water is cool but comfortable. Chief nervously paces the shoreline before jumping in after him. Chief enjoys splashing about in shallow water, preferring when his feet can touch bottom. He paddles out to Carl, swims around him, then returns to shore, gets out of the water, and shakes off. Carl encourages the dog to jump back in but he's having none of it.

The water temperature drops the farther Carl swims from shore. It's shocking how quickly the temperature changes as he breaks through another layer of colder water. Carl is fifty-five years old and still gets nervous swimming in a lake. Logic tells him whatever shares these waters is more frightened of him, but he can't help imagining a large jackfish circling his toes, ready to separate them from his body. The imagination in full bloom has a way of defying sound logic, going from the implausible to the supernatural in seconds, from a ravenous jackfish to a cold dead hand grabbing ahold of your ankle and dragging you under. Carl ends his swim and returns to shore.

The sun is setting but still projecting enough heat to warm Carl's skin while he dries out on the rocks. Three animals -- Carl assumes they're either muskrats or beavers -- swim past the shore, disappearing into a nearby bay. Carl feels an ant crawling over his foot, swipes it off, then notices the long lines of ant trails covering the rocky campground. Thankfully they aren't fire ants and he can keep his campsite but he wonders how he'd fail to notice the mass network earlier.

The air is starting to cool. Time for a fire. Time for food. Having plenty of kindling, dry grass, and firewood, it feels like cheating using fire starter but Carl can't argue with the results. He has a roaring fire in minutes. He salts his steak and waits for the stones to get hot. When the water starts boiling he drops the corncobs into the pot and cooks the steak in the frying pan.

The fresh air has a way of working up a man's appetite. The steak is delicious, despite being slightly undercooked in areas. It was hard to get even heat distribution over the open flame. The corn is perfect, sweet and juicy. Carl wishes he had beer to wash it all down with. But he'd thought he had enough stuff to carry and there was hardly any room in the mini-cooler. Still it was no excuse. He could have placed the beer in the lake when he got there and it would have stayed nice and cold. Who knew when the next time he'd get to enjoy an icy beer would be, if ever?

Carl looks at Chief, who, despite having just eaten a mountain of kibble, stares longingly at the remaining steak fat on the plate. Carl tosses it to him. Chief catches and swallows it with one chomp.

Carl washes his dish and cutlery in the lake. A loon call shoots across the lake, giving him chills. It came from someplace distant where he held no dominion, echoes from the afterlife. The loons are apparitions, floating across the lake, then instantly vanishing underneath.

Carl watches the flames spring forth from the stone fire pit. It giveth and taketh away. Everything is dependent on the flame. It means the world. As long as it burns he has a chance. It cooks his food, gives warmth and protection from the dreaded black flies and mosquitoes. Tending to and observing the fire gives Carl reprieve from the dark thoughts that descend upon him with nightfall.

A mosquito fills the darkness of the tent with its whining buzz. Carl hears it hovering over his head. He tries to smack it between his hands but keeps missing. He turns on the flashlight. Instantly the buzzing stops and the mosquito disappears. When he turns the flashlight off, the buzzing recommences.

Carl forms a new strategy, waiting in the darkness hoping to feel the mosquito land on his skin. The buzz grows louder as the mosquito draws closer to his face, but Carl remains patient, waiting until he feels it touch down on his cheek. Carl smacks his face, crushing the mosquito. He wipes the crushed mosquito off his face and onto the tent wall. He got the little bastard. A distant crashing of trees in the woods behind him jolts him from the moment.

Was it deer, moose, beavers at work? Are beavers nocturnal? Carl is sure there are no bears in the area, but his confidence wavers with another loud crash. Chief's ears pin back as he emanates a low growl, his upper lip curling, showing teeth. The dogs hostile reaction to the sound sends Carl's heart racing.

Carl flicks on the flashlight and rummages through his knapsack. When he finds the bear bells, he begins to ring them with fervor. The noise stops. Was it a bear? He's glad he stashed the food safely away from the tent. Chief's growling subsides. Carl takes a breath. He's being paranoid; there's nothing to worry about. Besides, if any bear comes clawing at his tent, he has his 9 mm stashed safely by his side.

His thoughts slowly shift from what lurks in the woods to a life in prison. The most likely outcome for his sudden free fall was permanent lodging in Kingston Penitentiary, Ontario's very own supermax prison. Bye-bye blue sky. Hello to life in a box under rule of lock and key, fed whatever gruel they give you while taxpayers collect the bill.

Carl recalls a riot at Kingston pen during the 1970s. The inmates' dragged "undesirables," including sex offenders and informants, from their cells, tied them up, and tortured them. Two were killed. The "experts" deduced that boredom was a major factor, fermenting a culture of agitation, restlessness, and pent-up rage, common among maximum-security penitentiaries. They dubbed it the "rage complex." Reforms were made, and Carl hopes they strongly discouraged prison rape. It will be hard to write his memoirs while being brutally sodomized (not that anyone was ever gently sodomized).

His gallows humor is a distraction. It denies the truth. You can not feel if you do not accept. There are no ghosts, no hauntings, just the anguish of a guilty conscience. Guilt was cancer for the soul. Carl refuses to feel remorse. If hell is waiting there's no point checking in early.

Carl begins to drift into sleep but the nagging need to piss forces him from his sleeping bag. Chief is fast asleep, his legs and face twitching, reacting to whatever dream world he inhabits. Carl opens the tent and steps outside. He's shocked by the luminosity of the moon and stars. After sunset, the darkness was impenetrable but now the land is cast in an ethereal glow, illuminated by the night sky.

Carl stands barefoot in boxers at the edge of the rock. The rock is radiant white as if placed under a black light. His surroundings feel completely alien to him. He walks to the water's edge and drains his bladder. His blood runs cold when he senses a presence standing in the corner of his peripheral vision. Logic forces his courage and he turns around. There's nothing but shadows.

The morning sun is beating down, heating the tent walls. Chief whines to be let out. Carl unzips the door and the dog shoots outside. Carl's mouth is dry and tastes horrible. He drinks from his canteen. The water is warm. He steps out of the tent and spits out the water onto the ground. Within seconds mosquitoes are biting him. The lake is eerily calm; there's no breeze whatsoever. He can see the Benz, still parked on the other shore.

Carl's shoulders are tender from yesterday's sunburn. The bugs are bad without the breeze. He has to get another fire going to smoke them out. Carl wipes the sleep from his eyes. He wonders: Is this it? Is this all he has left? Waiting it out the woods, getting sunburned and eaten by bugs?

Carl zips up the bug screen and flops back down inside the tent. He has a serious case of morning wood that has yet to subside. A memory of a vacation to Maui comes to mind -- Brenda, splashing around in the waves, her perfect body on display in that baby blue bikini. Smiling back at him with all the love in the world. The memory erased by a horrid snapshot of Brenda as he last saw her, broken, bloated, and purple. Bloodshot eyes. Vomit running down her chin.

Carl forces away the memory. He starts pulling on his dick, choosing to focus instead on his young receptionist, Sara, her tight little ass with the diamond shape between her legs, perfect parking. That's the kind of company he needs. That's who he wants to share his sleeping bag with. Sara, that pretty young thing. To think he could have had that. Why didn't he? Why didn't he let Brenda have her fun while he had his? What did it matter in the end?

Carl imagines Sara's nubile young body prancing around the campsite naked, having fun teasing a dirty old man, a dirty old man that was her boss. Just waiting for him to pounce. He'd pound her ass into the rock and she'd love every second of it. She'd be pulling the pine needles out of her ass cheeks when he was done with her. Carl is ready to bust when he's struck by an epiphany: If his days are numbered, why settle for a simple morning wank when he can pay for the real thing. It's a true moment of clarity.

There's a twenty-four hour massage parlor Carl had frequented on occasion between his divorce with Emily and his subsequent introduction to Brenda. The staff is a rotating cast of young woman from the Eastern bloc. This time he'll pick three girls from the line-up, drop two grand on the table, and tell them he doesn't want to be rushed. He's never been serviced by multiple women. Better late than never. He'll go through every position, every possible scenario, and won't blow his load until he's good and god-damn ready.

When the sexcapades are over, he'll shower off and drive to the beer store. He'll pick up a six-pack of Stella tall boys and grab some ice to keep them frosty in his cooler. With beer secured, he'd drive to Casa del Habano and purchase a box of Cohiba cigars. Then he'll take Chief to the off-leash area in High Park and let him stretch his legs. After that he'll feed Chief and take himself out for a nice dinner -- he's thinking Italian -- complimented by a quality bottle of wine. He'll be sure to leave a nice tip before driving to the lakeshore, toward the city beaches.

He'll take Chief for their final walk along the beach before tying him to a nearby bench. Whoever discovers Chief will find a folded letter taped to his dog tags, with Raj Bhanjee's phone number.

After a tear-choked good-bye to his dear friend, Carl will return to the Benz, untie the canoe from the roof rack, and carry the canoe across the parking lot to the beach. Then he'll go back for the Beretta, beer cooler, and box of Cohibas, place them in the bottom of the canoe, and drag the canoe across the sand toward the water. Once in the water he'll paddle out onto Lake Ontario. When he's far enough from shore, he'll spark the cigar and crack open a tall boy. When the last beer is gone and he's formed his final thoughts, Carl will put the 9 mm to his temple, take a deep breath, and pull the trigger.

Carl checks his watch. It's 9 a.m. Still plenty of time left in the day. He puts on shorts and stepped outside. With a yawn he stretches his arms and greets the sun again. He decides on a morning swim to freshen up. This time around he swims further from shore, feeling more at ease. Once again Chief plunges in after him, huffing and puffing water. Following the same routine, Chief swims out to Carl, circles around him, and immediately heads back to shore.

Carl laughs and floats on his back. Looking up to the bright blue sky he forces himself to remain calm. As a child he hated being forced to float on his back during swimming lessons. He never understood why the others looked so calm. He found it disorienting, the muffled roar in his submerged ears and the strange distortion of sound. It seemed like a miracle, floating on water like that, and the second you stopped believing, you'd go under, which he inevitability did, always getting water up the nose. Today he will overcome; he will find his center. He will not leave the water until he finds that place of tranquility that he so envies in others.

Carl stands on the rock, air-drying in the sun. The water quickly evaporates in the heat of day. He watches another ant crawl over his foot. The swim was invigorating. He is relaxed and ready. It's time for breakfast. Carl pours Chief a bowl of kibble, brews a pot of coffee, and cooks himself some franks and beans.

Chief licks his plate lick clean while Carl collects water to put out the fire. He enjoys the satisfying hiss as steam rises from the smoldering ashes. When the fire is out, he takes down the tent, organizes and packs up the rest of the gear, and makes sure he isn't leaving any belongings or garbage behind. He loads the canoe and is ready to go. But before paddling back across the lake he wants to take Chief hiking for an hour or two so the dog can expend some energy before the drive back. It's the least Carl can do.

Crashing through the brush, Chief rushes on ahead; at times stopping to make sure Carl is following, and then, when Carl eventually catches up, enthusiastically bounds ahead again. The assault from mosquitoes and black flies intensifies the farther they hike into the woods. Insect repellent is no defense. The bugs are maddening but Chief is enjoying himself so Carl decides to soldier on awhile longer.

The terrain isn't getting any easier. The land is uneven and filled with dense brush. Chief has no problem navigating the terrain but Carl needs to take his time. He walks with his arms held up in front to shield himself from branches snapping back and thwacking his face, but despite his best efforts to cover up, the branches get through. It's slow going. The bugs, the brush, and the heat are wearing him down. Carl stops a moment to catch his breath and chart a new course. His shoelaces are covered in burrs.

Carl trudges his way back towards the shoreline hoping for easier travel. A steep decline down a dirt hill leads to the water. The soil is loose and Carl has to check his footing with every step to ensure the ground won't crumble away. He has to put his hands down behind him several times to stay balanced.

When he reaches the bottom Carl enters into a sheltered bay. He's in the shade. The sun has gone around the corner. Chief splashes his way toward a collection of beaver dams in the middle of the cove. Carl makes up his mind to turn around after they reach the dams, a self-imposed finish line. Following the boggy shore he steps over a half submerged tree, snagging the loop of his shoelace on the end of a broken branch. He comes crashing down. A concerned Chief rushes over and licks his face.

Pushing Chief away Carl lifts himself back to his feet. He's soaking wet. He's scraped open his knees, shins, hands, and elbows. He removes the thorn bush embedded in his forearm. He's done enough bushwhacking but isn't ready to surrender. He resumes making his way toward the dams when the sound of a helicopter stops him in his tracks.

Carl ducks into the brush and kneels down. The chopper hovers over a neighboring lake, circling it twice. Are they looking for him? Did the girl at the Frost Center recognize him and report him from a news alert? No, impossible. The chopper would be right on him. With the cops waiting at his truck able to see his tent from the shore.

Is it biologists in the helicopter doing a field study? Maybe it's commercial chopper doing aerial tours of the Highlands.

Carl watches the chopper fly southeast. He loses sight of it eventually, its sound fading into the distance.

The sudden rush gives Carl an instant shit cramp. Toilet paper is back at camp but this can't wait. He drops his pants and holds himself up between two trees, making sure to stick his ass out far enough not to shit into his shorts. It's his first bowel movement since leaving the city. He breathes a sigh of relief, then looks for something with which to clean himself. A few handfuls of leaves and dry grass aren't enough for the job. It will be easier to wash in the lake.

Carl steps out of his shoes and pants, then crab walks down to the water. He wades in up to his knees and crouches down to wash himself. He amuses himself with the thought of a police chopper finding him at that exact moment.

The levity of the moment is broken by Chief's frantic yelping. Carl runs towards the sound, crashing through water, stumbling over rocks and fallen trees. Chief is madly thrashing around between the shore and the woods, furiously shaking his head, dragging it across the ground and pawing at his face.

Now less than fifteen feet away, Carl can see blood covering the ground. Chief leaps into the bush and tears through the woods. Carl screams after him. Running forward at top speed he sinks his foot into something that won't let go.

The forward momentum rips his knee out of its socket, bending his leg the wrong way at a ninety-degree angle. The pain shoots through Carl's spine. At first he can't find the air but then releases a blood-curdling shriek. He wails in agony, while twisting around to free his foot.

The horror of his injury is trumped by his revulsion toward the disgusting mass of yellow wax trapping his foot. A low buzzing sound fills the air. Carl grabs the back of his calf and pulls, desperate to free his foot. The buzzing grows louder. Carl pulls harder, straining every muscle. The noise morphs into a loud drone. Carl sees what is unmistakably a human hand protruding from the vile mound, the wax growing over it.

Panic turns to terror. Through gritted teeth Carl twists and contorts his body, ignoring the destruction of his knee. It's useless. He's stuck. He screams for help.

There's no reply but the ominous drone. Carl twists back onto his stomach, digging his fingers in the ground, trying to claw himself away from the horrible mass. There's no movement, nothing. It appears futile but with sustained effort his foot begins to dislodge. Carl roars and, with one surge of adrenaline, pulls away, freeing himself from the mass.

Rolling onto his back, pushing with one good leg, Carl scrambles away from the carcass before slamming into a tree behind him. He raises his hands. They're covered in a foamy pink slick. Carl turns around. The foam is growing over the ground, spreading over the tree. The hostile drone crescendos in a piercing whine, emanating from above.

Carl looks up, and the swarm rips into him.

Ghosts Are Bullshit

It had been three years since James last saw Marcus Hindle. Three years since he'd given him $20,000 and a simple set of instructions:

"Go out and find something. Take pictures, get footage, bring it back. I don't need receipts. Do what you want with the money, it's yours. Snort it, drink it, shoot it, smoke it. I don't give a fuck. Just don't call me asking for more."

Two years later Marcus called, asking for more - $80,000 more.

"I've found it, James. This is the one. That's the cost of doing business. They don't fuck around. They need to know I'm serious."

James wired him the money.

James trusted Marcus' talent implicitly. His reliability was another matter. He'd tried to establish deadlines and parameters for Marcus in the past but it was a losing battle. Marcus was an odd man with a particular brand of genius. He experienced massive lulls of inactivity, peppered with moments of head-spinning depravity, followed by bouts of hyper-productivity. That's when his talent shone through, generating content that shaped the direction of the magazine, which paved the way for everything else.

A year later, after wiring him $80,000 on the promise of a potential story, James got the call. Marcus was passing through town that night. It was three o'clock in the morning. Both were hungry. They agreed on Chinese.

Marcus never engaged in conversation while eating. He stopped talking the moment food arrived and didn't speak until everyone had finished his meal.

After the waitress clears the table, James orders more beer.

With two cold Tsingtao on the table the conversation begins.

"Was it worth it?"

"For me, yes."

"For you."

"Yes."

"And what did you bring back for me?"

Marcus takes an easy draw from his beer.

"Opportunity."

"For what?"

"To see a ghost."

"That's what you did with the money? You saw a ghost?"

"Yeah."

"Someone you knew?"

"Yes."

"Who?"

"My uncle."

"How?"

"They made it happen."

"Who are they?"

"I can't say but they are willing to show you a ghost, too."

"How 'bout you show me? Show me some pictures, some video, I can look at."

"Cameras aren't allowed. No recording devices. You can't document the process."

"Then I've wasted $80,000, not to mention the twenty grand you started with. That's $100,000. For what? So you can get high and tricked into believing you're speaking with your uncle's ghost."

"So you're not interested?"

"Is it going to cost me another eighty grand?"

"Yes."

"You've got to be kidding. Tell me this is a joke. You're fucking with me."

"I'm not kidding. You will see a ghost."

"But I can't fucking show anybody!"

"Do you need to?"

"Are we really having this fucking conversation? Yeah, I need to. That's the fucking point. I hire you for content. I'm not interested if there's nothing to show from it."

"Nothing to show?" Marcus looks hurt. "You're not interested in seeing a ghost."

"Ghosts don't exist, Marcus. Obviously it's a scam. The only thing I take from this is whatever material I get documenting the process, whatever racket, fuckin' confidence trick, it is they're running. That's where the value is."

"That's not what it is."

"No? So what did your dead uncle tell you?"

"He never spoke but there was communication."

"Okay. What did he communicate to you?"

"That's something I'm still processing."

James shakes his head. He finishes his beer and motions to the waitress for two more.

"I know money is an abstract concept that you don't waste a lot of time worrying about. But eighty grand is no fucking joke to me. And right now I'm taking this as a loss."

Two weeks later James is in the back seat of a limo, getting head from the girl with blue hair and green lipstick. At the after-party, she'd handed him a plastic card with a code containing a free download of her brand new album. She wanted to sign with his record label. James placed her in her early twenties, tattooed from head to toe.

Where'd they find the time? Why the rush? She was covered in what must have been several thousand dollars worth of ink. Did she pay for it? No, it was her parents. He could smell the trust fund. This hot young thing playing the bad girl in New York. Although, in fairness she gave a slobbering good blowjob. Surely she could entice a tattoo artist to waive his fee.

In the middle of this thought, his cellphone rings. The girl stops, gasping for air, wiping her lips. James reaches into his pocket for his phone. James answers the call. It is a woman's voice.

"James Sampson."

"Yes."

James nods for green lipstick to continue and she gets back to work.

"Marcus Hindle gave us your number."

"Why?"

"We understand you're interested in our service."

"I am?"

"We must inform you there's no guarantee on the encounter. We cannot promise the communication you request. There is no contract. There is no refund."

"Well, that sounds legit."

"Do you wish to pay for our service?"

"If this is about that ghost bullshit, then I already have, and Marcus didn't even bring me back a T-shirt."

"Eighty thousand dollars in cash, American currency. You will receive a text after this conversation. When the money is ready, notify with a reply to this text."

"One question. How did you decide on eighty grand as your asking price?"

"Can you pay it?"

"Yes."

"That's what matters."

Two days later James sends the text. The money is ready for pick-up. The responding text gives a time and place for delivery, along with the instruction that James not send a representative. The payment has to be made in person by James and he has to come alone.

The address is in Camden, New Jersey. Once a thriving center for manufacturing and industry, it is now one of the poorest cities in the U.S.A., possessing one of the highest crime rates, a city where three of its mayors were jailed for corruption. Camden's reality stood in stark contrast to its motto- "In a Dream, I Saw a City Invincible."

Upon reading the address James texts back, "Camden? In person and alone? At three in the morning? I don't fucking think so. You want my money, come pick it up."

There's no reply.

On the day of the drop James' morbid curiosity gets the better of him and he fires off another text. "If you still want to do business I will be in Camden tonight."

Again no response.

James calls Marcus to demand some answers, but Marcus isn't picking up the phone. As the day progresses so does James' agitation. He can't let it go. He explains the situation to his friend and former mercenary, Joseph.

Joseph Dumois, of Haitian descent, stands six foot seven and weighs 270 pounds. He sports a shaved head and full beard. Joseph is not an easy target. James has seen him fuck people up when provoked. He'd watched him crater the face of a hostile bouncer with a single punch. When filming in volatile regions of the world, James made sure Joseph was there watching his back.

Joseph scans satellite photos of the address. It's a warehouse in an industrial area of Camden. Joseph hires two colleagues to follow them in separate cars, for insurance.

They leave New York at 1:30 a.m. The drive takes two hours. It's nasty weather, gusting snow, with harsh, cutting winds. Camden is as bleak as James imagined. The city has been abandoned. There are hundreds of derelict, gutted row houses. All the factories, and warehouses are boarded up.

The streets are empty with the exception of a few weary stragglers, limping along with grocery carts of scrap metal covered in frost. Rows of street lights have been turned off. Many are broken, due to corrosion and vandalism. This city, once a model of American innovation and productivity, is now a postcard of industrial decay, perfect for someone's photo-blog.

James watches Joseph survey the area, making mental notes. The old brick warehouse has bars covering its windows. Joseph and his team find three potential escape routes from the building, positioning a car at each of them.

When the clock strikes three, James steps out of the car with a duffle bag holding $80,000 cash. The stench of sewage wafts through the streets from the county's sewage treatment plant. James approaches the main door of the building and presses the buzzer on a rusted intercom. It's dead, either disconnected or without power. James bangs on the front door without a response. He checks his watch, then steps back, looking at Joseph waiting in the car.

"Well, what the fuck now? Am I supposed to start throwing rocks?"

About to get back in the car and drive away, James sees someone biking down the street toward him, a man in a red balaclava and black snowsuit. His headlamp lights the way. A Velcro strap keeps his pant leg from catching in the bike chain.

The man nods to James as he pulls up to the front of the building. He takes a set of keys from his pocket and unlocks the doors. He carries his bike inside, waving for James to follow.

The building is pitch black; any illumination comes from the headlamp. The bike is left inside by the door. They ascend several staircases to the top floor, a giant open space, empty except for a large wooden desk and two chairs by the corner window.

The man reaches into the middle drawer of the desk and grabs a lighter. From a side drawer he takes out pillar candles, which he lights and places along the sides of the table.

"You're breaking out the candles. How romantic."

The man removes his headlamp and balaclava. The damage is immediately apparent. James steadies himself, trying to conceal any reaction. All of the man's distinguishing features have been burned away: hair, eyebrows, nose, ears, lips. One of his eyes shines black. The other is clouded over.

He motions for James to sit down across the desk from him. There's no heat. James can see his own breath. Burn Victim rubs his fingers together, signaling for the money. James puts the duffle bag on the table. Burn victim takes it, placing it by his side on the floor. Then he takes a pen and paper from the top drawer. He slides them across the table. James eyes the form. There's one question written on it: Name the person you seek.

`"What about pets? Does anyone ask to see their pet? Like their dead dog or hamster? Could you conjure up my cat? Can you communicate with the animal spirits? I mean I know we're all animals -- I certainly am. I'm just asking, right?"

Burn Victim leans across the table, picks up the pen, and underlines "person" on the form.

"Is that not a legitimate question? Some people are closer with their pets than their families. From a business standpoint, it makes sense. Why limit yourself? Obviously proceed with caution, but you shouldn't be scared about cornering other markets."

Burn Victim slams his fists down, rattling the desk. James flinches in his chair.

"Jesus, all right, just saying ... I didn't know I had to have a name ready. You guys haven't exactly been forthcoming with the information. You must have one hell of a product because your customer service sucks."

Burn Victim freezes James with a cold stare. James catches himself sinking back in his chair. He antes up, leaning in, locking eyes.

"Look at you. You're straight out of central casting. Those burns aren't real. They're some shitty latex prosthetics. You're supposed to shake me down? Is this an episode of *Scare Tactics?* Where's the hidden camera? You have no idea where I've been, who I've dealt with. You think I'm impressed by this bullshit?"

With the speed of a cobra strike, Burn Victim slaps his hands on either side of James' head, sinking his thumbs into his eye sockets. James howls, begs for him to stop then gets his face slammed against the desk.

Slumped in his chair, James holds his face in his hands, absorbing the pain, collecting himself. The blood drips from his nose between the cracks in his fingers.

Burn Victim knocks on the table. James looks up to see a gun pointed at his head.

James picks up the pen and writes down a name. His blood drips onto the page. When he's done, he slides it back across the desk. Burn Victim blows out the candles.

James feels his way down the darkened staircase. Burn Victim might still be sitting in the dark, or maybe he's right behind him. Exiting the stairwell, James takes a left towards the entrance. When he reaches the front doors he sees the bike is gone.

No one on Joseph's crew saw anyone leave the premise. Baffled, they scour the warehouse but the burn victim is gone.

James tries returning to his duties at work but the distraction proves overwhelming. It has been weeks since the drop-off without any form of communication on how to proceed. He obsesses over it. Had he been scammed that easily? Was his friend in on it? He repeatedly tries contacting Marcus to no avail. He gives Joseph the assignment of tracking down Marcus, also to no avail, at least so far. Retaliation is on his mind. James is convinced he's been cheated. He isn't sure how deeply Marcus is implicated. It pains him deeply to believe Marcus is capable of this kind of betrayal. It seems completely out character. James can't accept it. They must have forced his hand. He needs to know. He has to find Marcus.

The search continues for over a month. Joseph questions all possible contacts about Marcus' whereabouts. The problem is that it's not unusual for Marcus to disappear for months at a time without word of where he's going. His absence didn't raise any alarm with family or friends. They're used to it. You'd hear from him when you'd hear from him. Marcus kept it close to the vest. There is nothing to go on. One friend mentions mumblings about a trip to Fukushima, another says there were ruminations about an Arctic expedition. Joseph follows these leads, searching for travel records, but nothing can be corroborated. It doesn't matter. James will keep Joseph on the case until they find Marcus or his body.

Then, during the tour of a potential investment property, James receives a phone call from a blocked number.

"I hear you're looking for me."

James excuses himself, stepping outside to take the call. "I gave your fucking ghost whisperer eighty grand over a month ago and I haven't heard jack shit since."

"I can't explain their methodology but the experience is real."

"Real. It's real is it? Eighty thousand dollars stuffed in a duffle bag, gone, never to be seen, that's real. How the fuck did I fall for this twice!"

"Is there something you need from me?"

"Are you giving me attitude?"

"No. I'm asking how I can help."

"You can tell me how the fuck this works. What am I waiting for? Explain step by step the entire process. How you first heard about these guys to the moment you're talking to your dead uncle."

"It doesn't matter."

"It doesn't matter? Yes, it fucking well does! Leave nothing out. I'm done with the shroud of secrecy clandestine bullshit. Brass tacks, real talk. How does it work?"

"However it needs to."

"It needs to give me my money back or show me a goddamn ghost!"

"I'm sorry this has been such an ordeal for you."

"Marcus. ...Marcus, now you're pissing me off."

"James, I have to go. Dinner is on the table. We'll speak later."

"Fuck dinner. Fuck dessert. You talk now. Start with their bagman, Freddie fucking Kruger."

The line goes dead.

James hits the heavy bag and swims laps to burn off the toxic amount of anger he's carrying. After a soak in the steam room, he towels off and calls Haley. She's a swimsuit model he'd met on a friend's yacht in Cannes several years ago. During their initial encounter, James had her bent over the stern of the boat. In the middle of the act Haley started puking vodka Red Bulls. James stopped but she insisted he keep going. They met again a year later on a heli-skiing trip where she sucked him off in a snow bank. She'd called him a couple of months ago, telling him she'd moved to New York and they should go for drinks sometime.

When Haley arrives there's no hesitation. He knew. She knew. Good times. When it's over Haley asks if James wants to watch a movie, maybe order some food. James fakes an emergency at work, checking his phone.

"Shit. Fuck. I just got this email. Something fell through on a project we're working on. I've got to recalibrate, damage control, try and salvage this thing. I'm sorry. I don't mean to be rude but we're on a deadline. I've got to make some phone calls."

"What's the project?"

"It's in the early stages. I can't really discuss it just yet. Legalities, disclosure agreements, all that nonsense."

"So I should leave then?"

"Unfortunately, yeah. I've got to deal with this."

After Haley leaves James smokes a joint, orders a pizza, then scrolls through the movie menu looking for something to watch.

His eyes won't open. He can't lift his arms. He can't lift his arms and his eyes won't open. Panic... He flails. Movement cut off by restraints. Pinned down. Head, arms, legs. The primordial "no" screams through his consciousness before he's put back under.

Name the person you seek.

The choice seemed obvious. It would be his father, David Sampson. He'd passed away two years before James founded the magazine, which launched the website, which grew into a media empire. They'd had a massive falling out over James' drug and alcohol abuse. And David had lambasted James when he requested another loan.

"Who the fuck do you think you are, asking me for more money? Acting like you're a fucking rock star? I'm supposed to keep you in the lifestyle?"

He was relentless in his rebuke.

"What's this fucking role you're playing? Tortured artist? I don't think so. You'd have to actually create something instead of talking about it. I've always provided for you, yet here you are, almost thirty years old, asking for more money. Obviously you pissed away the last loan, for which I have yet to be reimbursed, not that I imagined I ever would be. You have zero respect for your mother and I. You don't give a shit. You're too fucking cool to grind it out and earn a living like the rest of us."

After the blowout James sold his car, the car his dad had paid for. He went on a binge that ended with him being beaten, knocked unconscious, and nearly drowning in a mud puddle. After being resuscitated by the paramedics, he surrendered to a rehabilitation clinic.

Less then a week into rehab, James was ready to leave. David asked the counselor to escort James' mother, Linda, who was inconsolable over James's refusal to finish his rehabilitation, to another room. David wanted a moment with his son. Alone in the room together, James avoided his father's gaze, choosing to stare out the window instead.

"I don't get it, James. Is life that cruel? Are you that bored? Do you need that much attention? What is it? They talk about addiction as a disease. Of what? Endless entitlement? Don't you get bored with this bullshit?"

James' reply was stripped of emotion, as though he was reading cue cards.

"I realize how fortunate I am for everything I've been given. My behavior is disgraceful. I apologize. I need to find a way that I can make enough money to destroy myself comfortably."

"You know, James, maybe you should pursue a career in comedy because you're fucking hilarious."

That was the last thing David said to his son. Then he got up and walked away.

The next time James saw his father he was in the critical care unit of Hamilton General Hospital. David was being kept alive by a medical ventilator, after suffering a hemorrhagic stroke from a brain aneurysm. His condition deteriorated rapidly, with no sign of recovery. The decision was made to remove the breathing tube. James sat by his father's side, finding the strength to say goodbye, searching for the words, overwhelmed by the emotion. His mother placed a gentle hand on his back as his body shook, quaking regret, an endless apology.

"James."

From extinction, spinning back towards his name.

"You're safe now."

A voice in the dark.

"I'm going to enter the room and release you from your restraints. I ask that you remain calm so we can continue without complication."

He hears the static. It dawns on James that the omnipresent voice is coming through an intercom.

A door opens. Light floods in from the hallway. James squints, as his eyes adjust. He can sees the blurred outline of the man standing hunched over in the threshold.

"You're still feeling the effects of the anesthetic. Take your time. Don't sit up too fast. Don't try standing until you feel your balance has been restored. There's no rush."

The man shuffles towards him and removes the restraints. James blinks his eyes, trying to regain their focus. "What is this?"

"I'll be in the living room. Join me when you're ready."

The room is sparsely furnished: bare walls, hardwood floors, and the gurney onto which he'd been strapped. James himself is dressed in black: T-shirt, sweatshirt, jogging pants, underwear, socks.

He takes a moment to ensure his legs will hold his weight before walking out of the room. From the hallway he can hear the crackling of a fireplace. In the living room, sitting on a brown leather recliner, writing on a yellow notepad, is a man whom James places in his sixties. He's wearing a navy cardigan over a gray T-shirt, with a pair of faded black jeans. On his feet is a pair of beaded moccasins. The man has a gaunt face and appears malnourished, underweight for his frame. His brown hair is closely cropped with specks of gray that match his stubbled cheeks.

James scans the surroundings. It's an old house with high ceilings. The living room is cleared of clutter except for basic furniture. There's no ornamentation, no pictures or paintings adorning the walls. Snow falls outside the window. Facing a forested area, James sees no evidence of neighbors, nothing to give away their location.

The man puts down his pad of paper, rubbing his temple. He looks up at James. James sees dark circles under gray eyes.

"How are you feeling?"

"You've got me dressed like I'm going to toilet paper the principal's house."

"Yes, it's meant for comfort. All black to eliminate confusion."

"So apparently I've been abducted."

"My apologies."

"Oh, okay. Well, I guess we're good then."

"Please take a seat."

The man motions him to sit down. James' legs feel weak, wobbly. He accepts the offer, dragging his feet over to the burgundy couch. He sighs and sinks into the cushions.

"That's a nice fireplace. I like the mantel."

"Do you have any other questions before we begin? I'll answer what I can."

"Great. Yeah, just a couple, but let's start with something simple. Like, who the fuck are you?"

"Your liaison."

"With what?"

"The deceased."

"So you're the guy. Freddy Kruger is just the bagman."

"When the encounter is over, I welcome you back but I do not offer counsel. My job is done. I am done."

"I have no idea what you're talking about."

"When it's over we bring you home."

"In a body bag?"

"Let's hope not."

"Oh? That's a legitimate concern?"

"There are inherent risks."

"That's reassuring."

"The choice is yours."

"If I say no, can I get my money back?"

"No."

"Of course not. Fuck it. Let's get started."

The upstairs bedroom is empty. Just four walls between floor and ceiling. The windows have bars over them. Sitting across from the man, James studies him as he pours them tea.

"So that's your magic trick. We're going to ingest a psychoactive tea, then classify whatever hallucinations we have as communing with the spirit world."

"You can classify it however you want."

"But we couldn't have the same experience without the tea. Correct?"

"The tea is part of the process."

"Or maybe it's the entire process."

"Fair warning. This could make you nauseous."

"Of course it will. You want to see God bring a barf bag."

"If it forces a purging, don't fight it."

"For fuck's sake. What if I can't stop puking, I stop breathing, I have a heart attack? Who's monitoring the situation? Who calls 9-1-1?"

"No one. The risk of interruption is too great."

"How 'bout the interruption of me dying?"

"It's hard enough navigating without interference from outside projections."

"I like my life. I'm amazed and entirely grateful it's mine. So I'd appreciate some kind of assurance."

The man slides a cup of tea on a saucer across the floor to James. "The choice is yours."

James holds the cup under his nose and cringes.

"Nice. Smells like an old tool shed. Did you filter it through a rusted lawnmower? You go first. Let's see you drink it."

The man takes a slow sip.

"I've got one question before I drink this poison."

"What is that?"

"What's your name?"

"Adolf."

"Seriously?"

"Yes."

"That's the name you go by?"

"Yes."

"Fair enough."

James raises his cup. "Cheers, Adolf."

He takes his first sip and immediately starts gagging.

"Nasty. Fucking awful. Damn ... my God ... That's just wrong. That's fuckin' gutter water, man."

Slow and steady Adolf sips from his cup.

"How are we drinking the same thing? How do you keep a straight face?"

"I don't enjoy it, if that makes you feel better."

With several false starts and near surrenders -- heaving, gagging, coughing -- James finishes his cup of tea. Then Adolf pours him another one.

"No way. No. No fucking way can I drink that."

Adolf doesn't say a word, calmly pouring himself a second cup.

"Oh, fuck you."

Shortly after his second cup, James starts retching. The room spins. The floor won't sit still. He can feel the sickness rise. He falls backwards. He's being smothered, deprived of oxygen, suffocating. James flops onto his side. Reject, eject, project. A torrent of vomit splashes off the floor. It won't stop. He's going to drown.

When James wakens he sees Adolph mopping up the lake of puke that surrounds him. The teapot and cups have been cleared away.

"There's a clean change of clothes for you in the corner. Throw the dirty laundry in the hamper."

James slowly rises from the floor, proceeding with caution; concerned his spirit might break from his body if he sits up too fast. It feels as though he's breathing underwater. Gentle shimmers of light ripple through the room and through James.

James changes into a clean black jogging suit, dropping the soiled version of the same outfit into the hamper. With the floor now clean, Adolph takes the mop and bucket outside the room, then returns for the laundry hamper. James feels the undulations of each breath. The waves.

Adolf sits back down. He is a calming influence. Under his solemn gaze James is ready for confession.

"My father couldn't recall her face without a photograph."

Outside the room labored footsteps climb the stairs.

They stop. They start. The slow ascent.

"Can you lock the door?"

"No."

"I don't want this. I don't want it."

"Why?"

"She hates me."

"You've never met."

"Doesn't matter."

The door creaks open.

She peeks her head inside, scanning the room. She spots James. Her expression changes, eyes going wide, like a deer in the headlights, transfixed. Her head tilts back and forth as she moves towards him. Her skin has the translucence of wet paper. Her green eyes, with heavy bags dark as charcoal. She is sick.

James stands up. "Don't touch me. Don't touch me. I don't want her to touch me."

She stops, keeled over by a violent coughing fit. Her chest heaves for air. The whites of her eyes fill with blood as she reaches out to James.

"Please stop. Stop. Put your hand down. I can't help you. I'm sorry. I can't help you," pleads James.

She staggers forward as James backs away.

"I'm sorry. I'm sorry I brought you here. It was wrong." James circles around the room while she trails after him. "I can't help you. I can't. Stop. Please stop. Put your hands down."

James looks back to Adolf. "What does she want? Get her away from me. Send her away."

Adolf is unresponsive. James watches him fading in and out of the room, the waves rolling over him.

James keeps ten feet of distance between the two of them as she stalks forward. Without warning she strikes out, closing the gap between them in a fraction of a second. With a defensive reflex James kicks his grandmother in the stomach.

She drops, crippled. The betrayal twists her features with contortions of anguish. A stifled wail, everything muted. The volume is sucked out of the room and then it comes screaming back, fury bridled in grief, fracturing the fabric. It is deafening. James' knees buckle as he covers his ears. In exclusion Grandma weeps into a slow dissolve.

Gone.

Adolph has been knocked flat on the floor. His eyes open, his breathing shallow.

"Adolph. You all right, man? Adolph?"

James kneels down beside him. "It's over. Talk to me, man. Say something."

No response.

"Adolf, it's done. It's over. Can you hear me? Nod, or blink your eyes, if you can hear me."

Eyes flicker back. Convulsion.

"Stay with me. Stay with me. We're all right. It's all right."

The tremors continue.

"Adolf, I gotta go. I'm getting help. I'm getting help, okay?"

He hears it before he sees it -- the initial inhale, purgatory drawing air through a straw. From the corner of the room, it rises from the floor.

Automatic retraction. James scrambles, crawls, falls for the door, reaching the edge of a cliff instead. A steep drop. Infinite darkness. Absence welcomes company.

James launches himself towards the opposite corner of the room, tripping over his feet, crashing to the floor.

Lurching forward, the ghoul pauses and percolates. It's garment, a filthy tailcoat melded to scabbed-over flesh. It looks down at Adolph, puzzled.

James rushes in, grabbing Adolph's arm, dragging him away.

"Stay away. Keep the fuck away from us." It's like yelling at a shark -- it hears the noise but doesn't understand the words.

It tracks, from side to side, backing them into the corner.

"Fuck you, monster. Fuck you."

The ghoul starts heaving. Eyes roll back, tear ducts leak, toxic run-off streaking down the face. Choking. The back arches. The jaw disengages and a rotten mass slides out onto the floor, dripping with black bile.

With outstretched arms the ghoul dips its head in a malformed curtsy over the regurgitation. A presentation? A gift?

"What the fuck?"

James looks away. This cannot be.

The strange clicking starts at the back of its throat, builds to a rattle, racing towards demonic amplification. It requires his attention.

James stares back. The ghoul falls quiet, nodding down at the regurgitation, the tumor, the 100-pound biomass, a translucent membrane sliding off it into the black slick.

"That's great. You should be very proud."

The clicking recommences.

"What? What do you want?"

Again it nods down.

"Thank you. Thank you for the gift. It's lovely."

And the clicking starts again.

"What? What? I don't know what you want."

A vacant pause while its mouth hangs open. The ghoul's head slowly twists counter-clockwise, turning upside down, in a full rotation.

James smacks Adolf across the face. "Wake up! Adolf, wake up! Get us the fuck out of here!"

It's of no use. James can hear the death rattle. He closes his eyes, bracing for the evisceration.

When it doesn't arrive, he takes a peek, keeping one eye closed.

The ghoul, now petting the disgorgement, tilts its head, motioning for James to do the same, insisting.

James steps up to the boulder-sized mass. He runs his hand through the black bile and membrane, over the clotted surface.

The ghoul watches, completely enamored by the moment. It emanates a low vibration, a purr. The ghoul is purring.

"That's very nice. Well, thanks for that. Thanks for the introduction."

James wipes the slime off his hands onto his jogging pants.

The clicking starts again.

"Jesus fucking Christ."

James goes back to petting the mass and the clicking recedes into a purr again. And so it goes for what seems like an eternity.

Eventually the ghoul tires of standing and sits down. Soon its rumpled eyelids start drooping. Its long neck sags. Its head jolts back, as if the ghoul is fighting to stay awake. Finally it surrenders, lying down on the floor, drifting off.

As it sinks deeper into sleep, the ghoul fades out, physically disappearing, but its regurgitation remains.

Adolf opens his eyes.

"Adolf, you back? You with me?"

Adolf blinks.

"Can you talk? Talk to me."

Adolf releases a low moan.

"Come on, Adolf, I need some guidance. I'm lost out here."

The moan turns into a spastic wail. Something is very wrong.

Without looking James registers a new presence in the room. He can feel the hate radiating off it. Pink. Raw. Clouded black eyes, buried into massive slabs of ground beef. Nothing sacred, nothing safe. In its wake, failed mercy, bludgeoned babies smashed against the wall, new love shattered by shotgun shells, a gut shot, the next one rips the jaw clean off.

His lips aren't moving but James can hear Adolf's voice. "Eyes down. Be still. If it stops to look, you cease to be."

As it draws near, James' every cell screams.

"No. Fall quiet. Do not acknowledge it. Leave me. Walk away. Ignore it. Walk to the stairs." Communicates Adolf.

James, holding his breath, stands up and walks toward the door. "It sees me."

"Keep to yourself. Keep to yourself," Adolf repeats like a mantra.

"It knows. It knows." P-p-p-p-panic.

"Run!" screams Adolf.

Malicious intent snags James by the forearms. In one violent motion, pushing up, then snapping down, breaking his elbow joints at an inverted ninety degrees. James howls in pain. The methodical dismantling continues. Ground Beef drives its fist into James' shoulder, separating it. Then, with a kick, it shatters James' kneecap, folding his leg like an accordion.

"Enough!" Adolf roars from the ground, gaining control of his motor function, trying to push himself to his feet. Ground Beef smirks. Turning away from James, it lumbers over to Adolf, raising a red granite foot over his head, about to stomp when Adolf wraps his arms around the other leg and bites down, sinking in his teeth.

Adolf foams at the mouth as the poison scores through his flesh. Ground Beef sets down its foot, watching in amusement as Adolf claws at his tongue, vomiting. James feels himself going into shock, the edges blurring, he can't breath, it's as though the oxygen's been sucked out of the room. Ground Beef kicks Adolf across the floor, shattering his ribs.

James gasps and screams, "You fucking coward! All you do is break things! You're too fuckin' dumb to do anything else!"

The Beef makes a slow measured turn. Its smirk widens into a smile. The skin around Adolf's mouth bubbles and froths. He looks at James, his gray eyes flashing blue.

"Drop off," he orders. James understands the command.

With one working leg, James pushes himself across the floor toward the door. He reaches its edge. There's no choice. Ground Beef doesn't take hostages. James stares into the abyss, into the impenetrable darkness. Ground Beef chuckles, daring him.

James falls off, tumbling, in darkness. Broken limbs, spitting pain, the endless drop its own form of hell, diluting consciousness. Did he stop, or is he falling still? Feet first or upside down? No breeze. Stale air. Stationary? He feels an overriding panic, the mind trapped in body, buried in the dark.

Plead. Crumble. Weep. Beg. Surrender.

Fold.

Everyone's is in hazmat suits except for Burn Victim, who stands in the middle of the room; gun in hand, wearing his black snowsuit. He watches while covert medics rush to save Adolf. Third-degree burns cover the lower half of the man's face and neck. The medics begin endotracheal intubation to keep his airway open. Other members of the response team wheel the regurgitation out of the room on a panel cart.

Sensory overload. James has to close his eyes.

"Aloha kaki aka."

"What?"

"Good morning." says the nurse, her broad face smiling down at him.

James's throat is raw, torn by shards of glass, covered in a million lacerations.

"Water."

The nurse returns to his bedside with a bottle of water and a straw. He does not have the use of his arms. They are in casts.

"Where?" asks James, unable to finish the sentence.

"Kona Community Hospital. You're in good care now."

James sips slowly, until the water is gone.

"I'll let the doctor know you're awake."

It was a motorcycle accident. James was driving, winding through the mountains of the big island, when he lost traction coming around a corner. Some local surfers making their way back up the mountain found him unconscious on the side road and called 9-1-1. His Harley Davidson was wrapped around a palm tree.

James wants to leave the hospital as soon as possible. With two broken arms and a broken leg there's mobility issues. He'll require someone to wheel, and drive, him around. Operating from a heightened state of paranoia, needing someone he can trust, James arranges for his mother Linda to fly down.

When Linda first arrives at the hospital, and see James in his broken state, she can't contain her emotions. "What were you doing, racing around on one of those stupid bikes in the rain anyways, you big dummy!"

After James' release from hospital, he has Linda drive him to an outlet mall to purchase a new cellphone, his last one destroyed in the crash. From there it's back to the King Kamehameha hotel, where he was a registered guest, something he'd discovered during questioning for the police report.

His suitcases are waiting for him at reception. The hotel staff remembers seeing him but is confused by his line of questioning. Not satisfied, James tries bribing hotel security to show him the hotel surveillance footage, to prove that he was in fact a guest at the hotel. Hotel management intervenes, denying his request. James relents. He asks if he can retain his room and get another room as well, for his mother.

After receiving the room keys, James has Linda drive him to 69-250

Waikoloa Beach Drive, the location of Big Island Motorcycle, the store from which he'd rented the Harley. The manager, a tattooed Samoan, recognizes him immediately.

"*Howzit, brah?* I saw what happened to our bike. It was *pau.* Insurance gonna write that one off. You lucky to be alive."

James points to the security camera above their heads.

"I'm dealing with a case of identity theft. I need to see your surveillance footage. Someone else rented that bike under my credit card number, it wasn't me."

The manager squints at James. "No act. I was there. You rented the bike."

"Then prove it. Show me the footage."

"Sorry, no can do."

"I'll pay you."

"*Ainokea.* It's videotape *brah*, changed every day."

On the drive back to the hotel Linda demands answers. "Now, what the heck is going on here? What's this about identity theft? You tell me now, if you want me to drive you anywhere else."

"Someone stole my identity."

"You said 'someone else rented that bike'. You rented that bike."

"I wasn't in a motorcycle accident."

"James? The paramedics found you unconscious in the ditch."

"If that's true I was placed there."

"By who?"

"That's what I need to find out."

"Well, how'd you break your arms and legs then?"

"A demon broke them."

"A demon?"

"Yes, an evil tormentor of the supernatural variety."

"Well, now ... That is ... that is ... Well, now ... I think this is the result of head trauma. I think we need to bring you back to the hospital and -- "

"Mom, I'm fine. Drive us back to the hotel."

"Well, obviously you're not fine."

Call history, e-mails, credit card transactions, everything was accounted for. Friends swore they'd spoken with James over the phone regarding his panic attacks, anxiety, burn out, vague references to ongoing personal drama. There was mention of vacation, maybe Hawaii, hoping some island magic would reduce stress levels. They'd covered their tracks from every angle. James can't find a break in the narrative but will not leave Hawaii until he does.

From his balcony James watches the lights on the boats creep across the Pacific. All evening James has been trying to reach Marcus. Each call is greeted with the same automated response: "The person you are attempting to reach is not accepting calls at this time."

James sits in bed, switching between the endless cycles of news and sports highlights. The phone rings. James checks the call display. It's his friend and business partner Qasim.

"Qasim, what's happening?"

"I just got a call from Jim Sheffield. Marcus is dead. Overdose. Jim found him. He had to kick the door down."

Marcus was gone, surrendered to the current. Rare frequencies forever lost.

James is up all night, wrecked.

Just before dawn he calls Linda. He's ready to leave.

They ride the elevator down. Linda wheels James through the quiet lobby. Outside the world is cast in blue. Low tide.

Stoned Wheat Thins

Trent was nineteen years old and unemployed. He lived in a bachelor suite with zero sound insulation, which is unfortunate considering his apartment unit was directly above a crack den.

One particularly rowdy evening, Trent was kept awake by the sound of beer bottles being smashed against the neighboring apartment building. Desperate for sleep, he leaned over his balcony and pleaded for quiet. The bottle smashers immediately threatened him with rape.

The crack den was primarily occupied by a young couple. A chubby blond girl that always had a tangled thong sticking out the back of her pants, and her boyfriend, a young native man with a permanent scowl and a penchant for track suits. When they didn't have their friends over to smoke rock and create general havoc, Trent would hear their conversations digress into vicious screaming matches. Inevitably the boyfriend would smack his girlfriend around and she'd start crying. Then the boyfriend would switch gears.

"Baby, I'm sorry. I hate this shit. It's rough out here, girl. You know I love you. You know that, right? You and me baby. Look at me. Please, baby. You know it ain't like that. I hate myself but I got love for you, girl."

Soon enough Trent would hear them laughing, which would lead to fornicating. The girl's moans seemed to drag on forever and would transform into strange bellows. The seduction was as predictable as it was bizarre. Trent was forced to start wearing earplugs.

The stress derived from hostile neighbors, is compounded by serious financial strain. Low finances meant Trent's cell phone service was been suspended, his fridge was empty, his bank account had gone into overdraft, and his credit card was maxed. Rent was due.

The constant anxiety seemed to be taking a toll on his physical health. He was rail thin with such a horrible case of acne that, before going out, he'd have to check his ghastly reflection in the mirror for white heads that needed popping. He'd recently started taking a prescription medicine to treat his acne but it wasn't helping. In fact his skin looked worse. It was so dry he couldn't yawn without the corners of his mouth cracking. And, as if things weren't grim enough, he'd started losing hair by the fistful.

It was Trent's first winter below the poverty line. His confidence was at an all-time low but he had to keep looking for work. His lack of education and work experience crippled his chances of employment anywhere that paid above minimum wage. And even minimum wage jobs weren't calling him back.

His situation was so dire he'd resorted to stealing food from the grocery store. So as not to look too suspicious, he'd always purchase something while there. But now he was so broke he couldn't afford to pay for the Wonderbread to go with his stolen pack of baloney. Trent started visiting the local food bank. The line-up always stretched around the block. It sometimes took hours to get his bag of groceries.

Trent continued sending out resumes and filling in applications but there were no job offers. His job counsellor, Jason, understanding Trent's desperation, suggested he register with a temporary labor agency. Jason explained to Trent that the agency would send him out as a day laborer to work menial jobs, mostly at warehouses or construction sites. He'd earn an hourly wage from which the agency would take a percentage. Jason was clear that he'd receive meager earnings but at least Trent would be paid in cash at the end of the day. He also mentioned that if he worked hard, Trent might get noticed and then hired on by the company who had hired him as a day laborer.

Trent asked why businesses didn't hire directly in the first place. Jason shrugged. "They just need warm bodies to throw at half of these jobs. They don't want to deal with payroll taxes. It also allows for easy termination without having to pay severance or unemployment."

It seemed like a rigged system to Trent, but he'd been living off a bag of rice for the last week and "cash in hand" was exactly what he needed. Jason warned him that although most labor agency doors opened their doors at 6 a.m., workers usually started lining up at five thirty for top placement on the list. It worked on a first-come, first-served basis.

At 4.45 a.m. Trent put on his steel toes and walked to Labor Ready getting pelted with sleet along the way. Arriving at five thirty he waited in line with eight other people. They were a dejected-looking crew, standing there chain-smoking, waiting for the doors to open.

After being let in and placing his name on the work list, Trent told the receptionist he was new and asked if there would be any paperwork he needed to fill out. The receptionist glared at him, shook her head, and slapped down some information forms.

"Fill these out and give them back, but you won't be working today. You need to take our safety orientation seminar. And testing only takes place on Wednesday starting at ten."

It was Thursday.

The next morning Trent woke up to discover an eviction notice that had been slipped under his door. It stated he had fourteen day to pay the rent owing or he'd be evicted. And the first of the month was fast approaching, to pile on more debt.

Trent spoke with the building managers, a grey-haired couple with an affinity for the Grateful Dead. Trent told them he refused to pay his rent until his downstairs neighbors were evicted. The building managers were aware of the situation, having received numerous complaints from other tenants, but they explained it was proving difficult to serve the couple with an eviction notice. The building's owner did not want to lose the government checks he received from the housing subsidy granted to Trent's disruptive neighbors. Unfortunately, they informed Trent, the situation had no bearing on the realities of his own eviction. They understood his protest but it was out their control. He was still expected to pay his rent.

When Trent moved to Vancouver from Oxbow, Saskatchewan, his father had written him a $4000 check and wished him luck. He father gave clear instructions not to expect more. But Trent had to call his mom to ask for another loan. She relented and agreed to wire him $200 for groceries. "But, Andrew, you know this is a temporary fix. I can't keep wiring you money."

The following Wednesday, Trent and several other miserable souls were forced to sit through a two-hour work place safety video with an open book test at the end. Everyone passed. Now they were eligible to wait for work with everyone else.

Trent's first job was unloading freight trucks in China town. He was repulsed by some of the smells he encountered at the market but tried not to let on. He didn't wish to offend. At the end of the day, with the trucks unloaded, the storeowners rewarded the workers with juice boxes. Trent had never tried lychee juice -- he wasn't sure he liked it -- but he appreciated the gesture.

The next day he was sent to a downtown nightclub that was under construction. Because the elevators were not yet operational his job was to unload pallets of cinderblocks and carry them up two flights of stairs. It was a full days' work, pushing Trent to his physical limits.

His hard work did not go unnoticed. The foreman asked for Trent's phone number, in case they ever needed someone. Because his phone was suspended, Trent gave Jason's work number to the job foreman, explaining his situation.

It felt good to be recognized for his work effort. It would feel even better to never have to wait in line at Labor Ready again, to not have them skimming money off his paychecks. Trent held out hope that his situation was about to improve -- he checked in with Jason every day -- but unfortunately the call from the foreman never came, so he kept dragging himself back to the labor agency.

It's another dreary morning, waiting for the doors to open. The man standing in line beside Trent introduces himself. His name is Agwe. He's recently emigrated from Haiti. He looks at Trent with concern.

"My friend, you are tired?"

"Yes, Agwe, I am tired."

Agwe smiles back. He explains that during his army training, recruits were forced to endure extreme sleep deprivation. That's where he learned to sleep standing up.

Trent laughs. "That's impossible. How do keep your body from buckling when you fall asleep?"

Agwe's smile grows wider. "It's as simple as closing your eyes."

Agwe proceeds to shut his eyes, feigning sleep, until they both break out in laughter.

Inside the building, waiting to be called for work, Trent sits beside a bloated looking native man, with a pockmarked faced and bulbous nose. The smell of alcohol permeates him. The man sips his coffee, imparting wisdom to everyone at the table. "You gotta scrub behind the ears. Cleanliness is next to godliness. Wash your bed sheets every week. Change your socks every day."

As the morning drags on, the lobby fills to capacity, but no one is being sent out to work. The men are getting restless. They start pestering the receptionist about the chances of work. They all get the same answer: "You need to sit down and wait until we call your name."

Around 10 a.m., a lanky man with the complexion of a cadaver strolls into the office, approaching the front desk. The receptionist doesn't bother to look up from her computer. "You didn't show up for work yesterday," she says.

"My daughter was sick. It was real bad. She was throwing up all night. We had to bring her to emergency."

"Don't bullshit me, Neal. You didn't show up for work because it was welfare Wednesday and you wanted to go spend your check. We had you scheduled to work at that site for three days and you blew it."

"That's not fair, Gail! Fuck that. My daughter was sick! She had to stay home from school. There was nothing I could do!"

"You haven't figured out how to use a phone? If you can't make it to the job, you need to call us. You made me look bad. I don't appreciate that."

"I should have called but I was super stressed. That's my daughter, man. Sorry, I was distracted."

"Go away, Neal. I've got work to do."

"C'mon, Gail, I work hard for you guys. You make money off us, don't forget that."

"Well, you won't be working today, and I'm sure we'll survive."

"You're a real cold bitch, you know that?"

"Get out! Get the hell out before I call the cops! No one talks to me like that! I don't deserve that shit."

"Where's Scott? I want to talk to Scott. Let me talk to Scott."

"Oh please, I'm not wasting Scott's time on you. He's busy. Now I'm serious, leave now or I'm calling the cops."

"Don't worry, I'm fucking leaving. Just remember, karma has a way of sorting people out."

"I hope that's not a threat."

"I'm just saying you reap what you sow."

"Well, I'd hate to know what you did. "

"Yeah, fuck you too!"

Neal slams the door behind him. Gail makes her decree. "Everyone needs to clean the wax outta their ears right now, and listen up, because I will not repeat myself! Do not ask me about your chances of work today. If you do, I'm sending you home. You sit there and wait for your name to be called."

Just past noon Agwe is sent on a work call. He shakes Trent's hand and wishes him good luck. An agonizing hour later, Grace yells into the room, "Listen up. I need three workers for this job, one with a car. The work site's at least a forty-five minute drive away, near the airport."

"I got a car! Send me out! I'm ready to go!"

"All right. Lonnie's got a vehicle, so I'll take him and the next two guys on the list."

Lonnie was chomping at the bit all morning to be sent out. Trent had watched him drink a dozen coffees, pacing the room with his dirty high-tops undone, stepping outside every ten minutes to smoke. He did not look to be in good condition.

Lonnie is a wiry little man with bugged-out black eyes, a skeevy mustache that overhung his lip, and mullet of greasy black hair spilling out the back of his Vancouver Grizzlies ball cap. He wears a cheap leather jacket with "Popeye's Weight Supplements" embroidered on the back, which is several sizes too big for him, in contrast with the stonewashed jeans that cling to his legs.

Trent is surprised that Lonnie has a valid driver's license, let alone an insured vehicle. Regardless, being next on the list, and not having a car, he had to accept the drive. Also along for the ride is Bill, a squat man with no neck, large sloped shoulders covered in dandruff, and a matted ginger beard. Trent can't understand how Bill can see through the layer of grime on his glasses.

With a hoodie and a windbreaker Trent is poorly dressed for the weather, which has turned from miserable to downright hostile. On the walk to the car they're hit with gusting winds and ice pellets. Lonnie isn't discouraged and even seems to have some bounce in his step. "Nice to get the fuck out of there, hey, boys? That Gail can be one cranky bitch."

His car is an old Honda Civic covered in rust and riddled with dents. It's missing the passenger-side windshield wiper. Packing tape holds together a smashed headlight. The inside of the car is a garbage pit of fast food wrappers, rotting apple cores, pizza crusts, empty cigarette packs, tattered newspapers, and tangles of scrap electronics. There is a burnt-out crater in the middle of the front passenger seat. Blackened springs jut out from it. In the back of the car is a pile of damp clothes and miscellaneous shoes that reek of mold. Lonnie shifts the clothes onto the scorched front seat so Trent and Bill can cram themselves into the back.

Unfortunately Trent's window has been smashed out, and his seat is soaked from the rain and snow.

"Some fucking junkie asshole was trying to get at my stuff. I gotta get glass from the salvage yard, but I've been busy. Bill, mind lifting your feet for a second?" Lonnie places a phonebook over a hole in the floor through which Trent can see the road.

Because the broken driver's side door won't open, Lonnie climbs through the passenger side door, crawling over the pile of wet clothes to get to the driver's seat. Lonnie fires up a cigarette. "Alright boys, we're off to the races!"

It's a terrifying experience. Lonnie's got the pedal to the floor, weaving all over the road, blatantly cutting people off. As he bombs across lanes without signaling or doing a shoulder check, he has a horrible habit of looking back at Trent and Bill to mutter something unintelligible, his cigarette dangling out of his mouth.

When an elderly Asian woman blocks Lonnie from cutting in to pass her, he explodes into rage, leaning on his horn. "You stupid fucking zipper head! What the fuck are you doing? Open your chinky eyes, you stupid fucking gook bitch!"

The woman ignores him, staring straight ahead. Trent looks to Bill, who stares blankly ahead, chewing his fingernails. Lonnie continues berating the woman. "Don't pretend ya can't hear me, fried rice! Ching chong chow fuckin' China! You got chicken ball, you slant-eyed bitch! Fucking slope!"

The woman appears oblivious to his tirade and eventually turns off the highway. Lonnie continues his tirade. "Goddamn ungrateful immigrants! And our government keeps letting them in while they sell off all our natural resources! It's fucking sickening!"

Huddled over in his seat Trent is whipped with sleet and gravel from the open window. His face is numb, his body frozen to the core.

After what feels like an eternity, Lonnie takes an exit and pulls over to the side of the road to check a wrinkled piece of paper with the directions he'd written down at Labor Ready. "That fucking bitch gave me bad directions. I wrote down exactly what she told me and now we're fucking lost!"

Lonnie passes the paper back for Trent to verify. It's illegible chicken scratch. He hands it back without saying a word. Trent tries warming his face in his frozen hands while Lonnie fires up another cigarette. "Either of you boys got a phone?"

The answer is no.

"Well, that's just fuckin perfect. I think we gotta double back. I'm pretty sure I know where we fucked up."

After thirty more minutes of frozen hell, followed by another wrong exit, Lonnie declares, "She's fucked us, boys! She really fucked us!"

By the time they pull in to a gas station they're over two hours late for the job. Lonnie races inside, telling them to wait while he makes the call to headquarters. Trent is completely despondent, has never felt so hopeless. He contemplates warming up inside the gas station, but it would only be a cruel tease at this point. Then he considers hypothermia as an actual concern.

That's when Lonnie returns, livid from his phone conversation. "That fucking bitch has some nerve! I tell her we're lost and she snaps at me! Starts screaming! The cow accuses me of not listening. She can't accept she gave us the wrong directions! The cunt tells me she's sending another crew to the job. She directed us so far of course we can't make the day. I'm done with this bullshit, boys. No more. There's no respect. And I'll tell ya another thing; if she doesn't pay my gas I'm going to raise hell. I'll tear that fucking place apart."

Lonnie continues raging about the injustice of it all for the duration of the drive back, stopping only once to mention food. "I haven't eaten a goddamn thing all day."

With one hand on the steering wheel, Lonnie reaches into the glove box and pulls out a box of crackers. He crams some crackers in his mouth. Chomping away, he looks back, offering the box to Trent and Bill, pieces of cracker flying out of his mouth towards them as he speaks. "Try these crackers! They're fucking great! They're like a full meal."

Still not facing the road, Lonnie reads the side of the box. "Stoned... wheat... thins... Stoned Wheat Thins. Awesome fuckin' crackers, boys. Have some."

Trent declines. Bill says nothing. He's in another dimension.

"Your loss, these crackers are the real fuckin deal. I've gone days where they're the only thing I eat. No joke. Stoned Wheat Thins. Let me tell ya, it's the only cracker worth spending money on."

When they get close to the Labor Ready, Lonnie offers some form of an apology. "You know, boys. It's not my fault but I'm sorry about this whole mess. It fucking sucks losing a day's work 'cause of someone else's incompetence. They owe us compensation for our time."

Lonnie parks in a loading zone near Labor Ready. Without a word of goodbye, Bill shuffles across the street to the sky-train station. Lonnie sparks a cigarette and spits on the ground. "Strength in numbers. Bill doesn't want his money, fuck him."

Trent shakes his head. "Sorry, man. You're on your own."

As he walks away he can hear Lonnie cursing him under his breath. Trent doesn't care. He doesn't care what anyone thinks of him, not anymore.

In Bloom

LUCILLE SITS UP IN BED AND TURNS OFF THE ALARM. SHE FEELS SICK, exhausted, the craving for sleep overpowering. She wants nothing more then to fall back into her mattress and forget the world, but outstanding bills won't forget her. So she rises, needing to pee, but of course the washroom is occupied by her roommate/landlord, Ashley.

Lucille's first shift is at a breakfast diner where she works as a line cook from 6 a.m. until 3 a.m. Her second shift is at a bar, where she works as a line cook from 6 p.m. until 2 a.m. In between shifts she might run errands. If she has none, she'll likely return to her apartment to draw, play the cello, and take a nap. Today she must transfer, then withdraw, money at the bank for rent. She was a day late with last month's rent and Ashley had a conniption fit. Lucille detests her living arrangement but she required a place on short notice after breaking up with her boyfriend. Ashley's condo was the first she'd found that was readily available.

Ashley owned the condo they shared. It had been compensation in her divorce settlement. Ashley was a real estate agent before she quit her job to focus on selling her handmade jewelry online. Unfortunately there wasn't much demand for her bedazzled butterfly's broaches and pendants. With her husband gone so was the disposable income. Ashley attempted a return to her real estate career, but none of the brokerages were hiring. She decided to transition into the insurance industry and was now taking an online course to become an agent. In the meantime she needed some form of income and so had placed one of her two rooms for rent. Lucille was the lucky applicant.

The first shift is a grind. Breakfast and lunch are busy, and it's hard for Lucille to stay focused. She falls behind, botching several orders. The last two hours of her shift drag on for an eternity.

When her shift at the breakfast diner is over, Lucille goes to the bank and withdraws rent money. Her account balance is cringe inducing. She returns to the condo. Ashley is occupying the bathroom once again, blow-drying her hair, a daily ritual despite the fact that she rarely leaves the condo now.

Lucille closes her bedroom door. She drops some crickets into her chameleon's terrarium and sets the alarm so she can sleep before her evening shift. No drawing, no cello, just sleep. Lucille wakes up five minutes before the alarm. Ashley is microwaving something in the kitchen, and Lucille hands her the rent money on the way out. As usual, Lucille must wait while Ashley counts out the money in front of her. "To ensure there's no confusion."

Halfway through this second shift, Lucille takes her lunch/dinner break. She sits at the end of the bar to eat her grilled chicken sandwich. It's been a quiet evening so far. Across the bar from her are two middle-aged men. One of them reminds her of Paul Newman in *Slap Shot*, a less attractive, less symmetrical version but the blue eyes have that same twinkle. His friend, a black man, reminds her of American blues legend Robert Johnson, just older with looser skin and some creases in his face and across the forehead. The strongest feature of resemblance is the way his upper right eyelid droops.

The two men speak in hushed tones in between the breaks in their laughter. She feels drawn to them, wanting to take part in their conversation. Lucille finishes her break and returns to the kitchen.

After replacing the oil for the deep fryer, Lucille shuts down the kitchen. Changing from her kitchen smocks she returns to the bar. With the exception of a few stragglers the bar has emptied out. Poor man's Paul Newman is still there but Robert Johnson is gone. Scott, the bartender, asks her what she's having. Per usual, "beer" is the answer.

Poor man's Paul Newman tips his drink to Lucille. "Compliments to the chef. You cook a mean burger."

"Glad you enjoyed it."

He gets up from his bar stool and walks toward her, sitting down at a stool around the corner of the bar from her.

"My name's Hank."

"Hello, Hank."

He stares at her, holding a smile that contains just enough mischief to stop it from being creepy.

"Blue eyes, black hair, that's a deadly combination."

Amused by this man, Lucille sips her beer. "Is that a compliment?"

"Of course."

"How do you keep that alabaster skin in this climate?" the man asks.

"Well, the key to a pasty complexion is staying out of the sun. How's your day been?"

"I've got no complaints. You?"

Lucille shrugs her shoulders. "The day's kind of blur together at this point."

Hank gives a solemn nod.

"My name's Lucille."

"Nice to meet you, Lucille."

"Where you from, Hank?"

"The future."

"Oh, really? What's that look like?'

"Seeing as this place is about to close, why don't you join me at my hotel for a few more drinks and I'll tell you all about it?"

"Sounds like a trap."

"My intentions are pure."

"Pure evil?"

"I promise no harm shall come to you."

"What brings you from the future, Hank?"

"Work."

"You're not here to save the world from imminent disaster?"

"Well, there's that too."

Lucille holds up her empty glass, motioning Scott for another beer.

"Hank short for Henry?"

"It is."

"My dog's name was Henry."

Lucille shows Hank her shoulder. It has a portrait tattoo of a bullmastiff's giant head and the name 'Henry' inscribed on a banner underneath.

"Handsome fella."

"The best."

"Let's take a look at the rest of these tattoos. You've got Henry on that shoulder, on this one you've got a chameleon wearing a birthday hat."

"That's Vincent. It's from a photo I took on his birthday."

"You own a chameleon?"

"I do."

"Vincent Van Gogh?"

"Vincent Cassel. The French actor."

"Okay. So what do you feed him?"

"Crickets mostly."

"How long have you had him?"

"Six years."

"Is that old for a chameleon?"

"Males rarely live past eight years."

"A fellow senior citizen."

"You don't look that old."

Hank laughs. "Why, thank you, Lucille."

"The gray hair is distinguished."

"That's what I keep telling everyone."

"How old are you, if you don't mind me asking?"

"Fifty-two. So you've got "MOM" written under the shark fin peeking outta the water on your bicep."

"*Jaws* was one her favorite movies. Mine too."

"A classic."

"I'll drink to that."

"What have you got on those forearms?"

Lucille shows the inside of her forearms. "On this arm, the creature from the Black Lagoon."

"I like the black and grays. Some impressive shading. Now, what's this ghoul on your other arm?"

"Bernie Wrightston's Frankenstein."

"Wow, the detail is incredible."

"Wrightston's an legendary illustrator. Chris, the guy who's done most of my tattoos, did an amazing job replicating the image."

"Very nice."

"Thank you."

After Lucille's second beer it's time to leave. Scott is closing the bar. She accepts Hank's invitation to share a joint with him outside.

"Is this weed from the future?"

"If you want it to be."

Lucille takes a toke. Hank waits for her to stop coughing.

"So what do you say? Want to share some beers with me at my hotel room? It's got a balcony we can drink them on."

"I have to work in the morning."

"How early?"

"Six-thirty."

"Damn."

"Yeah."

"Where?"

"Breakfast diner."

"Quit."

"I need the money."

"No, you don't."

"Yeah, well my account balance says otherwise."

Hank hands her back the joint.

"Understood, I just … It's been a pleasure making your acquaintance, and I was hoping to keep it going."

"It's been nice to meet you too but I need to get home."

"Hey, I had to try."

Lucille exhales the smoke through her nose and flicks the joint roach onto the ground.

"There's a pullout couch you can sleep on. Or I'll sleep on it and you can have the bed."

"Sounds like you're still trying."

Lucille sighs, shaking her head.

"Fuck it. Let's go."

"That-a-girl. High five."

Lucille rolls her eyes and slaps his raised hand.

After a quick stop at the gas station for beer, Lucille drives them to the hotel. Hank puts the beers in the fridge.

"What do you think of the room?"

"Very nice. A lot bigger then the room I live in."

"Roommates?"

"Unfortunately. What exactly do you do for a living?"

"Jack of all trades, master of none."

"Seriously."

"It's an oxymoron but I work in intelligence."

"What? Like a spy? You're a spook?"

"I don't have a license to kill. It's nothing sexy. Mostly data collection."

"For who?"

"A branch of the military."

"Specifically?"

"You wouldn't recognize the department."

"It's like an area 51 type deal?"

"You know it."

Hanks hands her a beer and holds his ground.

"So..."

"So..."

They inch closer, navigating the awkwardness, trying to read the other's expression for confirmation before committing to the kiss.

And it works. The connection is there. Before things get too heated, Lucille pulls back.

"Do you mind if I have a shower? I'm gross. I've been sweating in the kitchen."

"Be my guest."

"Don't go anywhere."

"Nowhere I'd rather be."

After the shower Lucille steps out of the bathroom, a towel wrapped around her waist. Hank is kicked back on the bed, still fully clothed, watching sports highlights. He turns to her and nods in appreciation.

"Hi."

Hank turns off the TV, takes a sip of beer, puts it down, and stands up to meet Lucille at the edge of the bed.

"Hi."

The towel drops.

Satisfaction all around. The two lie in bed, at ease, content. Ready to drift off, Lucille remembers to set her alarm. It's 4:00 a.m. She can get two hours sleep before she must leave for work. Lucille groans, anticipating the sleep-deprived pain of her fast-approaching work shift.

"You all right?"

"Yeah, just setting my alarm for work."

"Forget it. Call in sick."

"They'll drag in the other cook. I can't do that to him on his day off."

Hank gets out of bed, pulls on his boxer shorts, and takes a sheet of paper from the desk drawer, then sits back down beside Lucille.

"Here's a list of sports teams playing today and the results of each game. I memorized them, then wrote them down when I got here. You can copy them but don't get greedy. You can't run the board, just make a couple of picks. You don't want to alert the wrong people. I know a bookmaker or you can go online. I'll front you some money to place the bets if you need it."

"These games haven't happened yet?"

"No."

"So you can predict the future?"

"No, I'm from the future. I told you this."

"I'm sorry, silly me, I thought you were joking."

"I'm just fucking with you. Well, I'm serious about the time-travel part but I understand your confusion."

"What the fuck?"

"The point is you get to sleep in guilt-free because you're going to give a share of your winnings to the cook who's replacing you today as compensation for the inconvenience."

"Did we just take a turn into crazy town?"

Hank gets up and grabs two beers, offering one to Lucille, who declines.

"Okay, I'm going to break it down for you, start to finish. Let me get through it, and then you can ask questions."

"Yeah, so I'm starting to get nervous about this."

"Don't be. You're fine. Right here, right now, you're safe."

"Good to know."

"There's a lot of information to convey and I'm not sure the best way to present it so I'm just going to start. When you wake up tomorrow, massive portions of the Gulf Coast are going to be covered in a red algae bloom. People think it's another red tide but this is different. In a week's time that bloom turns white and releases its spores into the air. You can see it, like a fine haze, as the spores travel over 200 miles inland. They germinate in anything with a pair of lungs.

"The first symptom is lethargy, as it begins stealing the body's nutrients. The second is muscle ache, stiffness, cramping. Black streaks appear under the skin, spreading out from the spinal column. Soon after the streaks appear the hosts can no longer lie down. They can't rest their weight on the spurs that have grown along their vertebrae. The pain is excruciating, so they're forced to stand. Soon after they "lock up." The parasite has completely fused with the vertebrae.

"As the parasite branches out, each host's arms are forced upwards, stopping just above their shoulders, like the host is nailed to an internal crucifix. If knocked over, the lungs are punctured, which kills the host. Remain standing, the host withers and dies, left to rot on the branch. At this stage its informal designation is "totem pole."

"Eventually the branch starts breaking through skin, consuming the host completely. What's left is a gnarled black tree covered in toxic thorns. That tree grows magenta-colored buds, which release more spores.

"Soon after its appearance on the Gulf coast the blooms start appearing all along the world's coastlines. Mercy squads kill the infected, "landscapers" come around, collecting and incinerating the bodies. The economic implosion is immediate. Paper currency loses all value almost overnight. The death toll is catastrophic. The surviving populace is pushed far inland, towards northern climates where the bloom can't take root and dies out under cold temperatures."

"You are fucking with me, right?"

"The first time I saw it with my own eyes was when we were sent back to work inside a contamination zone. This was in the first month. People hadn't grasped the full scope of the infection. It's complete pandemonium, chaos on the streets. I see this woman through my gas mask. I watch her "lock up" right then and there on the sidewalk. She starts gasping for air. Her sister's screaming for help. The woman can't breath. She's experiencing angioedema, her throat's swelling shut. This can happen during "lock up." Epinephrine doesn't work. All you can do is intubate. In acute cases a tracheotomy is required. But there's no point. It's better to asphyxiate on the spot then hang on the rack."

"Okay then, okay ... Well, that's a story. So, you've described this ... this horrific extinction event. Now do you care to enlighten me on the whole time travel business? How that works?"

"The gentlemen you saw me conversing with at the bar..."

"The black guy?"

"Dezmond. We're both Nomads."

"Nomads? Is that an acronym?"

"No, just our designation as time travellers."

"Why not Travel Agents?"

"It wasn't in the suggestion box."

"Do you work with Dezmond or is he just another Nomad?"

"We're co-workers. Protocol states we have a partner during each transport. Partners are changed each shift. They say it's for safety but I think it's to keep us honest, prevent us from going off-script."

"How long have you been a nomad?"

"The advent of time travel coincides closely with the initial bloom, a matter of weeks. Obviously you can't travel past the machine's existence."

"Obviously."

"Regulation dictates you can't travel past your initial transport. You can't cross paths with the old self. Dispatch staggers the dates."

"Who decides these things?"

"The machine itself is a mechanism of military industry. There's a council that makes the decisions, but I only communicate with dispatch."

"How does it work?"

"The council or dispatch?"

"The machine."

"That's a fucking great question. But that information's not available to me. A friend of mine, Ed Orlik, who works dispatch, told me he talked with an operator over drinks once and picked his brain about the machine. He claims high-powered magnets integrated with a chemical processing that create a massive electrical discharge; channeled through one monolithic microchip, power it. Which makes perfect sense."

"Does it?"

"I'm joking. However it works, I'm sure it's beyond my grasp."

"How long did it take to build?"

"Years, decades, centuries. I don't know how long they were working on that thing before they brought us in. But the machine itself is several miles wide and resides in an underground bunker in the desert. Like you said, it's area 51-type shit."

Hank finishes his beer, grabbing another.

"How does one become a time traveller?"

"You're selected. I'm from the first class. I was brought into the initial testing program right out of the army. I was Private First Class at the time. I had no idea what I was testing for. We were subjected to grueling physical and psychological trials but were compensated well above our pay grade, so I went with it without asking too many questions. Five years into the program I did my first launch. I didn't know what the fuck it was. Strapped into the machine, I was told I was testing a new fight simulator, then they shot me out. Sent me back a full ten minutes. Thankfully I managed to make it through the other side without scattering."

"What's 'scattering'?"

"Your body makes the transfer but the mind doesn't. You're cooked. They have to put you down."

"How? How are you cooked?"

"Your mind doesn't reintegrate so you're lost, completely fucking scattered, complete loss of motor function and self-awareness. You're cracked, you're done, there's no coming back."

"Jesus..."

"Like I said, we're well-compensated, danger pay, but to spend on what? We live on base and don't have access to the gated communities. Those are your options. It's misery on the outside."

Lucille leans out of the bed, picks her shirt off the floor, and slips it on.

"Why do some make it through transport and other's don't?"

"I don't know, just my constitution, I guess. It's not fun. Traveling destroys you. And it's getting worse. It takes me over a week to recover now. I can't leave the tank for three days. I'm fucking sick of time travel, in every sense of the word."

"What's the tank?"

"This sealed pod, a flotation tank style hospital bed. They administer an IV, give you oxygen, monitor your vital signs."

"So what's your mission here?"

"Data collection. Dezmond and I have been chartering a boat these last two weeks, diving, taking water, tissue, and mineral samples. We bring them back and hope they find something. It won't change my timeline, but it could save yours."

"What if you stayed, if you didn't go back?"

"They'd send the Shepherds after me."

"What do they do?"

"Turn me too dust. Erase me from any timeline I might exist in. If you stray from protocol the council sends them after you. Very strict. They don't fuck around. We're supposed to limit our interference to an absolute minimum."

"Butterfly effect. Everyone knows that. So how do we, this, stand in that regard?"

"Oh, I broke code. Smashed it to smithereens. We're supposed to check back in with the greeters yesterday, but Dez and I agreed we weren't going back. They had enough samples. We weren't finding anything new. We've made this trip many times and this will be our last stand. "

"So they're going to send the Shepherds after you?"

"I'm sure they already have."

"And might they kill me for being with you?"

"Probably, if they found us together."

"That's reassuring."

"They won't find us."

"How can you say that? What if you've been outfitted with a tracking device?"

"I'm sure I have."

"So they could be kicking down the door any minute now."

"Doubtful. Even Shepherds needs recovery after transport, at least a night's stay in the tank. Then there's the travel time getting here. I've got at least a day's grace."

"What's your plan after that?"

"Eat, drink, party till the wheels come off or the Shepherds find me, whichever happens first. "

"And what should I do? Pack my bags? Buy a gasmask?"

"That's a good start. When you see that bloom, start driving. Head north. Go inland. Fill your car with non-perishables. Get some serious distance between you and the coastline. When people start showing symptoms the Gulf States are placed under quarantine. Soon enough, as it spreads, martial law is declared across the map. There's check stops established at every border. They see your Florida license plate and you'll be detained until they can prove you're not infected."

"Did you purposefully withhold this information until after we had sex?"

"I though it might kill the mood."

"You thought right. So had I decided to head home after work, would you have let me leave without a warning?"

"Would you have believed me?"

"What makes you think I believe you now?"

"Do you?"

"Why didn't you tell Scott?"

"Who?"

"The bartender."

"I didn't want to ruin my shot at you."

"I'm fucking serious. Why aren't you out screaming in the streets about this?"

"How many people do you think will listen? Not everyone heeds hurricane warnings."

"A little different then being horrifically mangled by a tree parasite that eats you from the inside out."

"You can't start a stampede. It has to be a controlled mobilization. The logistics of this kind of mass exodus are beyond our capabilities. The resources aren't there."

"So everyone can 'rot on the branch,' as you described it."

"It is what it is."

"It is what it is. So you're either full of shit or ... Yeah, what the fuck? This is ... Why am I even entertaining the thought that this is real?"

"Lucille, it's real."

"I asked some hypotheticals, played along, but I don't buy it. What's your angle on this? What is this? What's the con?"

Hank holds her gaze. "There is none."

Lucille sees the tired resignation in his face. She gets out of bed and starts pulling on the rest of her clothing. "I'm sorry, this is too strange."

"Then forget it. Don't leave. Let's talk about anything else."

"Can we? Like what? Our favorite movies?"

"Sure, you go first."

Lucille latches her belt.

"Stay the until morning. Have breakfast with me."

"Enough. Enough. It's past the point of return. You tell me you're joking, I'm leaving. You stick with your story, I'm leaving. Either way I'm leaving."

All Hank can do is smile. "You're fucking beautiful. A goddamn gem."

"And you are fucking crazy until proven otherwise."

Lucille leans over to put her shoes on, then stands up to leave.

"Goodbye, Hank."

"Goodbye, Lucille."

She gets an hour's sleep in her condo before the alarm goes off. She's in need of a shower but, once again, Ashley is occupying the washroom. Lucille loses her patience, pounding on the door.

"Clear out. I have to get ready for work."

The door opens. "Excuse me. We share this washroom."

"Yes, unfortunately we do. But I need to get to work, you don't. Once more, I need to get to work at the same time, as on every other day. You know that yet you're always using the washroom when I need it."

"So I should wait to start my day for you?"

"You can work around me."

"Why should I? This is my condo."

"Ashley, you're taking an online course to become an insurance agent. That's what you've got going on. Can you give me a fucking thirty-minute window to use the washroom and get to work in the morning?"

"You don't talk to me like that. I've been more than fair to you."

"What are you talking about?"

"Your being late with rent."

"One time!"

"Don't raise your voice at me."

"Whatever. How long are you going to be? I need to use the shower."

"Another twenty minutes, which is perfectly reasonable. I planned ahead. Early bird gets the --"

"Oh, go fuck yourself. You got this month's rent and you can take my one-month notice with it."

"Eggs and bacon all day long motherfuckers," Lucille mumbles to herself as she powers through the first two hours of the morning shift. Once the lunch rush starts, her adrenaline has worn off, and she hits the wall. Caffeine is powerless at this point and she goes Zen, focusing on one order at a time. She will not be rushed. A clubhouse here, a beef dip there, and soon enough, she's reached the end of her shift.

Lucille hangs up her apron, changes out of her smocks, washes her face, and steps out into the sunlight. She calls Hector, the alternate cook at the bar. He agrees to switch shifts with her. With the rest of her day clear, she must decide what to do with it. Lucille can't go back to her apartment, not now, Ashley will be there. She's always there.

Lucille drives down to the beach. She lies under a gumbo tree in the park and closes her eyes. Hearing the birds, the breeze, the ocean, her mind drifts to Hank. It's all at a distance, too abstract. Exhausted, she can't begin to process it. Forget yesterday. Tomorrow can wait.

Lucille wakens three hours later feeling refreshed; as good as she's felt in weeks. Now what? Hank. She wants to see him again. Needs to know. Time traveller or con man? It has to be the latter. Has to be. But she can't understand the grift. He never asked for money. He didn't try to recruit her to a cause. Just gave her a warning of a future of which she wanted no part.

Lucille takes the elevator to the third floor and walks down the hallway to room 317. The door is open. The cleaning staff is changing the bed sheets. Hank has checked out.

Lucille sits down at a local bar to watch the game. She places her bet online using her cellphone, charging her limit of one hundred dollars to the credit card. The game she picks is the only one she can remember, the one that stood out from Hank's score card, a basketball game: Toronto ninety-eight, Miami ninety-four. The line was six point favored to the Toronto. Best-case scenario is Toronto wins but the scores don't match.

Lucille has never been so engaged in a sports game. With a wager placed, the game is suddenly riveting entertainment. How could it not be?

The fate of the world was riding on the result. She decides, barring the arrival of the death bloom, that she'll place more bets in the future.

Several beers in with two minutes left the score is ninety to ninety-four for Miami. On a lay-up, Toronto makes it ninety-two to ninety-four. Miami bricks their next possession. Toronto follows with a three pointer. Ninety-five to ninety-four. Miami's shot is blocked on the ensuing play. Toronto takes it up court and hits another three. Miami has two more shots. One clanks off the rim, one rolls out. Final score is Toronto ninety-eight, Miami ninety-four. Lucille wins while her heart sinks.

Denial. Fuck it. There's no way. There is no way is what Lucille tells herself. It's a fluke, a mind-boggling coincidence. There's not a chance. Seriously, what are the fucking chances? This is a dream. It must be a dream. How? How is this happening?

Lucille is too drunk to drive. She leaves her car in the parking lot and takes a taxi home, making it pull over once so she can throw up.

Lucille stumbles into her apartment. There's a letter taped to her bedroom door from Ashley. She tosses it on the ground and collapses onto her bed.

The phone is ringing. It's work. It's daylight outside her window. Lucille turns the ringer off and gets up for a desperately needed glass of water. She takes two Advil and goes back to bed.

Close to noon Lucille takes the bus to the parking lot where she'd left her car the previous night. Mercifully it hasn't been towed. Her next mission is food. Feeling light-headed and vaguely nauseous, she needs to eat.

When she's halfway through her omelet, a sunburned man in a captain's hat, with a bushy mustache and a beer belly, strolls into the diner. He takes his sunglasses off and sits at the booth directly behind Lucille. After placing his order, his phone rings. He answers with a boisterous voice.

"Jim, boy, how the heck are ya? You bet I was! Well, let me tell y'all, I was out on the water this morning, I ain't ever seen nothing like it. Goes as far as the eye can see. Appeared overnight. The shoreline is covered. Blood red. Some Biblical-type shit here. Worse I seen. Them poor manatee are fucked."

Lucille can't finish her breakfast. She pushes her plate away and finishes her coffee. She needs to get home and start packing.

CPSIA information can be obtained at www.ICGtesting.com
Printed in the USA
BVOW04s1624231113

337107BV00007B/95/P